Where

Evil

Hides

Dean L. Hovey

Where
Evil
Hides

j-Press Publishing
4796 N. 126th St.
White Bear Lake,
MN 55110

j-Press Publishing
4796 N. 126th St.
White Bear Lake, MN 55110
Phone: 1-800-407-1723

Visit the j-Press website at http://www.jpresspublishing.com

Printed in the United States of America.
First printing
10 9 8 7 6 5 4 3 2 1

Library of Congress Card Number 00-103250

ISBN 0-9660111-8-X

This book is dedicated to George and Lorraine.
George
finds someone to talk to wherever he goes.
Lorraine
makes the world's best homemade bread
and caramel rolls.

Acknowledgements

No book is written without support and contributions from family, a group of dedicated friends, and numerous associates. Hal challenged me to make a New Year's resolution and follow through on it. Because of that challenge, I used my evenings and weekends to tell a story that was whirling in my brain. Julie and the kids put up with my endless hours at the keyboard. My editor, Sid Jackson, helped polish this "plot with potential" into a publishable work. Dennis Arnold made sure the "police stuff" was right. Mark Gjertson, from M&S Locksmith, explained how to pick a lock. Jim Hansen helped me deal with the computer challenges. Lynn, Julie, Brian, Mike, George, Lorraine, Natalie, Bill, Deb, Paul, Laurie, Heather, and Frannie all read manuscripts, made suggestions, and gave me encouragement to go forward. Most important of all, Julie continues to put up with me despite the fact that she'd prefer I write romances.

Where Evil Hides

Prologue

Timothy Ross Cooper screamed as the empty cement mixer whirled him around. He tried to focus on the hole, but his head kept banging on the sides. Timmy could clearly hear his stepfather's voice taunting him.

"Crybaby. I bet you'll run and tell your mommy." The man laughed wickedly. "She won't care. She hates her ugly little boy."

Timmy cried out more loudly as the spinning and laughter continued. His disorientation and fear grew until he felt his bladder release. Then he woke up.

He was sobbing in his own bed, the morning sun glowing through the window shade. His sister was peering at him through sleepy eyes from her bed across the room.

Suddenly the sound of footsteps in the hallway drove him to pull the covers over his head. He jammed his hands into the warm, wet crotch of his undershorts as the bedroom door flew open. As the footsteps approached the bed he curled into a fetal position, pulling his knees to his chest, his fingers clutching his penis through the sodden underwear.

"What's the ruckus?" The covers flew off Timmy's body, the overhead light momentarily blinding him. "You haven't pissed the bed again, have you?" His mother jammed her hand between his legs and let out a snort of disgust. The smell of stale beer punctuated her morning breath and last night's cigarette smoke hung in her hair.

SMACK! The sound of her open palm hitting Timmy's wet buttocks resounded through the bedroom. "Get your filthy butt down to the bathroom and clean yourself up."

The pain of the spanking was insignificant compared to the embarrassment of the wet pants. Timmy scrambled out of the bed, fending off another blow with his left arm. He covered his crotch with his right hand as he rushed past his sister's bed. Mary rose Cooper had pulled the covers up to her eyes but he could see the crinkles of a grin in them. He stuck out his tongue. His sister lowered the covers so he could see her full smile. Timmy hated his sister. She got all the good attention, he got all the whacks. He wet beds; she was perfect.

His stepfather's voice boomed from the second bedroom of the small bungalow as Timmy skittered into the bathroom. "Rosemary, what did the little brat do this time? Wet the bed again?"

His mother's voice followed Timmy down the hallway. "Yeah. The little shit did it again."

Timmy slipped into the bathroom, slammed the door, and pulled the chain to turn on the light. He pushed off the wet undershorts and threw them into the bathtub. With tears of shame streaming down his face he took a washcloth off the towel rack and ran cold water on it before rubbing it over his damp skin. He wanted to scrub off the shame.

His stepfather's voice rang down the hallway, "Don't slam the damned door! Rosemary, you want me to tan his bottom?"

Timmy froze. His stepfather was a construction worker and his hands were like stone. He had threatened to throw Timmy in a cement mixer when he'd mixed mortar for the blocks he was laying in the basement.

His mother's raspy voice swept down the hall from the other direction. "No, I got the sheets off the bed. I'll take care of it myself."

Timmy swiftly threw the washcloth into the tub and

searched for something to cover himself. He pulled a tattered towel off the rack and wrapped it around his waist as his mother charged into the bathroom.

"You little shit. Why can't you learn to hold it until morning?" She threw the threadbare sheets into the tub and ran water on top of them before turning back to Timmy. Her face was hardened from years of physical labor, smoking and hard drinking. She wore a flannel shirt as a nightgown and her pendulous breasts swung freely under the fabric as she gestured with her arms. "Then you slam the damned door and piss off the rest of the house. I should have dropped you on your head in the hospital and pretended I only had the girl." She pulled the big hairbrush from the medicine chest, then grabbed Timmy as he tried to wedge himself into the gap between the toilet and the bathtub.

Timmy's wailing was punctuated by the sound of the flat side of the hairbrush slapping his wet buttocks. After the beating, Timmy wrapped himself in the towel again and ran back to his bare mattress. Without looking at his sister, he pulled the blanket over his head, curled into a fetal position and sobbed until sleep finally brought relief from his fear and loathing.

DAY

ONE

SUNDAY

Chapter 1

The midsummer sun sets at nine o-clock in Minnesota, with twilight brightening the horizon for another thirty minutes. At the Pine Brook Inn, long before nightfall, the early evening crowd of farmers and their wives was changing over to a younger crowd of laborers, store clerks, mechanics, truckers and a couple of hard-core drinkers. They mingled with a few white-collar workers who were also trying to escape the oppressive July heat and humidity. By total nightfall, the Inn was nearly full, a blue haze of cigarette smoke hanging heavily in the air. From the jukebox, Shania Twain's "Any Man of Mine" competed with the dancing feet, the laughter of the patrons, and the low rumble of the ancient air conditioning system,

The Pine Brook Inn was one of those older structures that over the years had settled into its surroundings, much like the town of Pine Brook itself. Its wooden bar ran practically the length of the building. Occupying the stools along the bar were several young men watching the dancers. Occasionally one of the men from the bar would build up enough courage to saunter over to a table of women and ask one them to dance. Sometimes the question was met with an affirmative answer. Other times it was met with a quick rebuff and a round of giggles.

Terri Berg was sitting at a table in the back half of the room with three men. At thirty-something, Terri and her companions were a decade past the average age of the other patrons.

With every slow song a different companion would ask her to dance. When they returned from their trip to the floor there was another round of Grain Belt beers sitting on the scarred oak table. Everyone had lost count of the rounds. The waitresses made sure to remove the "dead soldiers" as soon as they were drained, to make counting difficult.

Terri floated back to the table, her long blonde hair flowing over her shoulders, fully aware that half the eyes along the bar were on her as she crossed the floor. Her denim shorts were cut so short that she wore thong panties that wouldn't show in the back. As she sat down, the men at her table watched her unrestrained cleavage shift against the white T-shirt that advertised the local country radio station. Jamie Arvidson, her partner for the last dance, sat down next to her.

"You boys are out to get me drunk," giggled Terri pouring the remnants of her previous beer into her Pilsner glass, while Rose, the waitress, set another round of bottles in front of the four friends.

Bill Patterson smirked at Russ Lemke and Jamie. "As if we haven't been trying to do that for the whole year."

Terri leaned over and threw an arm around Bill's shoulders as she planted a big kiss on his cheek. "For all the good it will do you." She said. "I'd bet a month's pay that you ain't been in a woman's pants since high school."

Bill, a 250-pound farmer, had never been married and still lived with his mother. He turned bright red and sputtered as the others laughed. Jamie slapped the table. "Hell, Bill's probably still a virgin!" The others roared.

Terri caught her breath and patted the denim covering Bill's ample thigh. "Now you guys quit picking on Bill." She slid her chair closer to him. "He's the one man I can count on when something breaks. Every time I need help fixing something the rest of you disappear like April snow." She gave Bill another peck on the cheek, while pressing a breast against his arm. His ego swelled while the rest were temporarily quieted.

"C'mon Terri," Bill said, rising from his chair. "Let's dance." He grabbed her by the hand and they trotted off to the dance floor as Patsy Cline's soulful voice belted out "Crazy."

No one noticed Joey Berg stagger through the front door at half past midnight. Like an apparition cloaked in cigarette smoke haze, he stood at the end of the bar surveying the crowd. His shirt was plastered to his chest and his blonde hair was matted to his head by sweat. The crowd had thinned since the peak of the evening. Several tables of couples had departed to take their babysitters home, and one table of single women had broken up and left with various partners. The second table of women had melded with a table of couples.

Joey spotted the table in the far corner with Terri, Bill, Jamie and Russ. He staggered across the room, caroming off one of the couples dancing. The ensuing commotion brought everyone's attention to him as he shared epithets with the dancers.

"Oh shit, Joey's here." Terri slurred the words. She set her beer glass on the table and stood up to meet him. Jamie grabbed her and pulled her down, trying to head off the impending confrontation.

"What in hell do you want, Joey?" Terri asked angrily as she struggled to free herself from Jamie's grasp.

Joey's messy blonde hair and wrinkled plaid shirt made it look like he'd been sleeping in the back seat of his car. "I just came by to see what my wife was doing on her Saturday night out. I stopped at the house and you were gone. I figured you'd be getting sloshed here. Just like the old days, ain't it Terri?"

"You come to give me some more bruises? The last ones have all faded." said Terri bitterly. Suddenly, her mind caught up to what Joey had said. "What were you doing at the house? The judge says you have to stay away from me and the house. I can call the sheriff and have you arrested."

Terri stood up, but Jamie jumped up and cut off her advance. "It's okay, Terri. He's drunk. Sit down." He motioned to the heavyset bartender, Harvey, who gave a knowing nod and patted the knob of the baseball bat that rested on the counter behind the bar.

Terri plunked herself back into the chair, a pout crossing her pretty face. "You ain't worth a fight Joey Berg. We did enough of that before the divorce, and I'm not gonna waste my breath on you."

Joey's face twisted into a sneer. "You slut. You gonna bed all these guys tonight? Or are you gonna ration them out over a couple of days?" His focus changed from Terri to Jamie. "You know, she's no good after she's been drinking. She always passes out before she gets her clothes off. Course that way she can't...YEOW!!" Joey screamed out in pain as Bill's heel crushed Joey's toes. The pain caused Joey to hop on one foot until he lost his balance and fell down.

Bill leaned close to Joey's face and said. "Get outta here before someone really hurts you."

The waitress, Rose, who was a good foot shorter than Joey but at least 40 pounds heavier, laid a hand on his shoulder as he tried to stand up. Barb, the other waitress was at her side.

"You broke my toes, Bill. I'll get you for that." As Joey tried to get up, he reached back, scraping Rose's neck with his fingernails. A loud clang rang out and Rose held the large serving tray high, ready for another blow. Joey rolled onto the dance floor holding his head and swearing.

"That's enough Joey. Get outta here and get some sleep," Rose said, with a voice that meant business. She stood with one hand on her hip, the other hand firmly gripping the tray. Harvey was halfway across the floor with the baseball bat. At some point the jukebox had stopped playing and the room was silent except for the commotion at Terri Berg's table.

"Okay! I'm going." Joey picked himself up from the floor and took a step towards the door. He paused at the edge of the dance floor and pointed at Jamie. "You better watch your backside. I don't take kindly to you messing with my wife."

Terri watched Joey disappear out the door in the eerie silence. "I don't feel much like partying anymore," she said, getting up. "I think I'll go home."

Jamie stood up next to her and put a hand on her arm. "I don't think you should drive. I'll drive you home. We can come back to get your car tomorrow."

Terri nodded. "I guess. Let me pee first."

Terri disappeared into the restroom. When she came out, Barb, the other waitress, was dabbing at the scratches on Rose's neck with a damp towel. Terri stopped for a second. "I'm sorry Rose. He's a jerk."

"It's okay, Honey. I'm tougher than you'd guess." Rose pulled a few loose strands of hair back from Terri's face and touched her cheek. "But thanks for the thought anyway."

Terri shook her head. "I'm okay now."

Barb looked up at Terri. Her words came out slowly. "I got one at home just like your ex. They get crazy sometimes, especially when they drink. But they're always sorry the next day when they sober up."

Jamie walked up beside Terri and gave her a hug. "You ready to go?"

Terri nodded leaning into him. "Sure."

On the drive home in Jamie's pickup truck, Terri started to shiver in the cool dampness of the July night. They had driven nearly ten miles and were still only halfway to Terri's farm in Henriette when they hit a bank of fog and had to slow down. She leaned against Jamie and pulled his arm over her shoulders for warmth. "I don't want to be alone tonight."

"I'd kinda hoped you'd feel that way," Jamie said, pulling her tighter to his side.

Terri slid her hand across his chest and undid a button on his shirt. She ran her fingers through the thick hair on his chest. Jamie smiled, his desire for her rising.

The drive to Terri's took them west on highway 23 for three more miles. Jamie drove on the narrowing gravel roads south of highway 23, through the tiny town of Henriette, finally pulling into a gravel driveway. The car headlights lit the small farmstead which consisted of a small house, a granary and a dilapidated barn. The barn was nothing more than a heap of rubble that had fallen down in a windstorm after decades of neglect and rot. The yard was empty and dark. Jamie left the headlights on while Terri fumbled with her keys to unlock the door.

They embraced in the entryway for a few seconds before Terri pushed him back. "You go crawl into bed. I've got a few things to do in the bathroom."

Jamie's clothes fell randomly as he moved through the living room and into the bedroom. He threw off the hand-made quilt and slipped into the crisp sheets that had the fresh smell of having been dried on the clothesline in the sun. Although the outside temperature had dropped into the 60s after sunset, the house held the 90-degree heat of the day. He pulled a sheet over his naked body and lay in the dark, waiting.

Terri scampered through the living room and into the bedroom. Her figure flashed through the door, and in a second she was under the sheet. Their sweaty bodies pressed against each other with urgency as their tongues probed each other's mouths.

After their passions were spent, they each nodded off into alcohol-induced stupors.

Chapter 2

Pine County sheriff's deputy, Sandy Maki, was four hours into his twelve-hour Sunday shift when the dispatcher directed him to render assistance to an address on County Road 114, near Henriette. The address was given as a fire number and he had to pull off the road to check a fire department map to locate the address. The nature of the assistance had not been specified, but he'd been requested to meet a Mrs. Violet Almquist at the location. The request wasn't urgent, so he did not turn on lights or siren as he turned the squad around and headed west, traveling at the speed limit.

The sun had burned off the heavy morning dew so the squad car left a trail of dust as Sandy traveled the gravelled back roads across the southern edge of Pine County. The temperature had fallen to 57 degrees overnight, but both the temperature and the humidity were on the rise as the sun climbed in the east. Sandy resisted turning on the air conditioning in the squad car until the temperature got over 80. He hated the stuffy feel of air conditioning. The temperature was quickly approaching 80 degrees when he pulled into the driveway of an old farmhouse.

The word "poor" came to Sandy's mind as he drove the long driveway. The corn along the driveway was almost two feet high, but the lack of any farm equipment in the farmyard meant that the surrounding acres were either leased out or had been sold. The heap of rubble that had been a barn, and the granary building with a five degree lean, said that no one had attempted upkeep for decades. The yard and the house were in slightly better shape.

Sandy parked behind the two vehicles already near the front door. One was a Ford pickup with a flat tire, the other was an aging Olds from the late 70s. Rust had eaten through the metal over the wheel wells of the Olds and the white paint was stained with rust around the several holes on the fenders and doors. Sandy announced his arrival to the dispatcher. As he turned off the ignition, a woman he judged to be in her late 60s came around the corner of the house. Her hair was wrapped in a red bandana and an old, flowered housecoat covered her considerable bulk.

"Are you Mrs. Almquist?" the deputy asked as he closed the door on the squad car and walked to meet the woman.

The woman shuffled up to him and squinted to see his face. "Aren't you awfully young to be the sheriff?" Violet Almquist pulled the housecoat tighter around her middle and retied the sash. Her feet were in satin slippers with the toes worn through. They were wet with dew. Her face, even without the obvious concern that crossed it now, was as creased and weathered as old leather.

Sandy smiled. "Ma'am, I'm not the sheriff. I'm a deputy."

Violet Almquist sized him up. Sandy was twenty-three and still had the lean look of a young man. "You still look pretty young. Isn't there someone older I can talk to?"

Sandy Maki shook his head. His baby face always made him look three or four years younger than he was. "Sorry, ma'am. I'm the only deputy on this side of Pine County this morning. Why don't you tell me what the problem is and we'll see if I'm up to handling it."

Violet shook her head, showing her obvious disappointment. "I called because my granddaughter didn't show up for work this morning. The restaurant called me and asked if I knew where she was. I thought maybe she overslept, but no one answered the phone. So I came over to check on her. It's not like her to miss work."

Sandy pulled a notebook from his pocket. "What's your granddaughter's name?"

"Terri Berg. She works at the Sportsman's Cafe in Mora."

Sandy made notes. "Your full name is…?"

"Violet Almquist. I live up in Pine City." She squinted at Sandy, obviously in a hurry to get things moving.

"I assume that one of these vehicles is yours? Is the other your granddaughter's?"

Violet shook her head. "She drives a little blue car of some kind. That pickup looks like her ex-husband's truck."

A small flare went off in Sandy's mind. He remembered something about a divorce and some calls about Joey Berg violating a restraining order. "Have they been divorced long?"

Violet crossed her arms and shook her head. "They just got the papers last week."

Sandy put away his notebook as they walked toward the door that faced the driveway. "Do you have a key?"

Again, Violet shook her head. "Terri changed the locks when Joey moved out. She never got a new key made for me. I was trying the back door when you came. They're both locked." The old woman sighed. "Maybe she's not here, you know? With her car gone and everything."

They walked through the thin grass of the lawn. It hadn't been mowed in quite a while and the grass had turned brown with the heat and lack of rain. The few green patches were made up of dandelions and crabgrass. Sandy wiped the dust from a spot in the glass and looked through the window of the door. Inside was a small entry room cluttered with jackets, shoes and assorted boxes. He knocked hard and listened for a response. There was none. The knob turned when he twisted it, but a deadbolt kept the door from opening when he pushed.

He peeked through the kitchen window and could make out dishes in the sink and a shirt hanging over the back of a chair. The paint on the windowsill flaked away under his fingers. The wood hadn't seen fresh paint in a long time.

"What's the layout of the house?" he asked as he walked around the east side of the house with Violet Almquist close behind.

"Terri's bedroom is on this side. There's another bedroom in the back, with the bathroom. The living room's on the other side."

A plastic window shade was drawn inside the bedroom window. Trying to peek around the edges, Sandy was unable to make out anything inside. He tried to lift the sash, but the latch was either engaged or the wood was so swollen it wouldn't budge. He brushed the dust and crumbling chips of paint from his fingers.

Violet Almquist watched quietly. "Pretty dry lately. I been afraid to smoke outside." She jammed her hands into the pockets of her housecoat and fumbled with a pack of Pall Mall cigarettes, then thought better of it. Sandy started around to the west-side of the house, as Violet struggled to keep up.

The shades were up in the back bedroom, but it was empty except for an assortment of boxes stacked around a single bed and a dresser. There was a rear entry door but its lock was secure. The thin gauze-like curtains obscured the view of the dark entry room behind it.

The sun was reflecting off the lower part of the living room windows. Sandy shielded his eyes and looked through the window. Violet was right beside him, her eyes shielded with a hand.

"I looked before, but I forgot my glasses at home. Can you see anything?" She asked.

At first it looked like a normal living room. It was a little messy, with clothing scattered over a rocking chair and the couch. Then something caught his eye. There appeared to be a knee propped up close to the window. He couldn't make it out clearly through the glare.

Sensing a change in Sandy's casual inspection, Violet Almquist pressed herself close to the deputy to look through the window beside him. "Do you see something?"

Sandy shifted to a different pane and looked into the kitchen and bedroom. There appeared to be a lump on the bed. As he shifted again a glint of light reflected off something shiny on the bed. Maybe a watch?

He shifted once again and the flash caught his eye again. He concentrated and could make out a dark piece of pipe at an angle on top of the bedding. The barrel of a gun? "Oh Lord," he said to himself.

Violet pulled back and grabbed him by the arm. "What did you say?"

"Let's go back to the front door." Sandy moved quickly and Violet had to hold her housecoat together as she tried to keep up.

He stared briefly at the door. The old knob and lock were the kind that used a skeleton key that inserted under the knob. Mounted above that was a new deadbolt that provided a greater degree of security. Sandy guessed that the new lock had been added after the divorce.

"Ma'am, I'm going to try to break open the door." The new deadbolt in the door would take a great deal of force to break it. Without waiting for Violet's refusal he swung his hip against the wood near the doorknob. Surprisingly, the door's frame gave a loud crack and loosened. A second thump, and the 80-year-old pine in the doorjamb splintered. A rush of warm air hit his nose, filled with the metallic-sweet smell of blood and the stench of death.

Sandy quickly retreated and put his hand on Violet's shoulder. Her face was filled with apprehension and an unasked question was on her lips. He turned her toward the cars. "Please wait in your car, Mrs. Almquist."

She started to protest, and he interrupted her. "Please...I suspect that this may be a crime scene. I don't want you to come in."

Her face turned white and she gave a weak nod. She thought again about protesting, but then resigned herself. "Yes, I think I'll have a smoke in the car." Tears formed in the corners of her eyes as a further awareness crept over her.

Violet had almost reached her car when she suddenly wobbled and collapsed. Sandy rushed to her side and checked her breathing. Satisfied that she was in no immediate danger he pulled the portable radio from his belt. "Dispatch. 611."

"Go, 611."

"I need an ambulance at my ten-twenty. Requester has a medical emergency. Send the duty sergeant, then give Dan Williams and the sheriff a call."

"Ten-four, 611." The call for the duty sergeant and Dan Williams indicated there was a major crime involved. Dan Williams was Pine County's chief investigator. The dispatcher initiated the calls after directing the Pine City ambulance crew and rescue squad to go to the scene.

Sandy pulled a blanket from the trunk of the squad and covered the woman, who showed no signs of regaining consciousness, then walked to the house. From the entryway, he eased around the corner into the kitchen, being careful not to touch anything. He rested one hand on the butt of his gun out of habit, but expected to find little to threaten him.

"Hello?" he called. There was no response. He eased further into the living room and froze. The naked, bloody female he saw next to the window bore little resemblance to anything human. The face and torso were bruised almost black, and her hands and ankles were under her body in a painful position that gave him the impression that they might be tied together. There was no sign of breathing and the blood pooled on the floor around the body had been there so long it had turned dark and had hardened around the edges.

Sandy turned quickly to the bedroom, expecting to see a murder weapon lying on the rumpled bed. Instead, he confronted a nearly decapitated body lying next to the gun he had seen through the window. The wall over the bed was splattered with blood and tissue. The neck ended in a blackened stump, the remnants of the head hanging by threads of flesh with the face completely obliterated.

Sandy ran out the door and retched for several minutes. When he regained his composure he wiped his mouth on a handkerchief, and reached for the radio again.

"Dispatch, this is 611. Send the coroner to my location, too."

Chapter 3

Dan Williams was reading the sports section of the Sunday *Minneapolis Star Tribune* when the phone rang. His dog followed him across the kitchen and he patted her head as he picked up the phone. "Hello."

"Dan, this is dispatch. Sandy Maki called for the duty sergeant, an ambulance, and the coroner. He responded to a call down by the town of Henriette. He asked for you too."

Williams put down the paper and looked at the clock. It was 10:34 a.m. "What was the original call?"

"A Mrs. Violet Almquist called and wanted a deputy to meet her at her granddaughter's house. The granddaughter is Terri Berg." Dan closed his eyes for a second. Berg was a name with a history. He quickly reflected on the acrimonious divorce between Terri and Joey Berg, and the restraining order that had been intended to keep Terri safe by keeping her ex-husband away from her.

Dan ran through options in his mind. "Don't call the coroner. I want Tony Oresek, the medical examiner from Duluth."

The female dispatcher made a burbling sound. "Ah, sorry, but the coroner is already on the way. Doc Peterson was in the emergency room when I called for the ambulance."

Dan hit his fist on the table, making the dog jump. "Shit! Call the M.E., too. I'll try to hold Doc Peterson at bay." He threw the newspaper onto a pile of newspapers next to his wife as he walked to the bedroom.

Sally Williams, who also had been startled by his outburst, calmly asked "What's up?"

"Sandy Maki called for an ambulance and the coroner at a house by Henriette," Dan answered from the bedroom.

Sally sat up and talked to the empty hallway. "Not an accident? Something suspicious?"

"I saw a restraining order come through attached to a divorce decree." He said as he rummaged around, putting on shoes, shoving the badge holder into his shirt pocket and attaching his holster to his belt. "The husband was prohibited from coming within one mile of the wife's residence."

He walked out of the bedroom and headed for the kitchen door. "Maki called from Terri Berg's house."

"Oh, dear," said Sally, anxiously, "I've heard about some of their problems."

Dan stood by the door and thumbed two Tums off a roll. He popped them into his mouth and put the rest of the roll back into his pocket. "Terri Berg's had her share of bruises."

Dan turned to leave, but Sally's voice stopped him. "You didn't go through as many Tums before the sheriff asked you to be the chief investigator," she said.

The truth in her words was obvious. He had suffered through a dozen medical tests since accepting the job. The results suggested stress as the cause of everything from his heartburn to a case of hives.

"I took the job, so I have to do it."

Sally shook her head. "No, you don't have to do it. You could go back to being a road deputy again. You loved that, even with the midnight shifts and overtime."

The truth was that he couldn't go back. His pride wouldn't let him. He had wrestled with the possibility of going back into a squad since the first day he accepted the undersheriff job. John Sepanen, the sheriff, had needed to rid himself of a political hack that was destroying the credibility of the department.

Dan was the natural replacement. Dan had cracked a major crime and the Pine County public had rallied around him as a symbol of good police work and integrity.

"I can't go back. Four years of undersheriff's pay on my retirement slate will add a couple hundred dollars a month to my pension. I'll stick it out until the next election and then I'll file my papers with the pension board."

Sally shook her head. "We don't need the money that bad."

Dan was out the door before she finished the sentence. He had probably heard her. But even if he hadn't, he knew how she felt. They'd been over it all before—the last time as she was dabbing Calamine lotion on the hives on his back.

When Dan arrived at the Berg farm there were nearly a dozen people milling around the yard. An ambulance was nearest the crowd, with two county squad cars and the coroner's black Suburban nearby. The call for an ambulance had initiated an automatic call to the Pine Brook emergency squad, as well. Most of the firefighters were gathered around two paramedics who were leaning on the open door of a rusting Oldsmobile, talking to someone inside.

Sandy Maki was standing next to the front steps, conferring with two other deputies and a man in green hospital scrubs. The older deputy was wearing sergeant's stripes. He nodded to Dan as he approached.

Sergeant Floyd Swenson was a thirty-year veteran of the Pine County sheriff's department. He was always partnered with the new deputies when they joined the department. Floyd had the patience of Job and experience that would rival that of any active officer in the state of Minnesota.

His newest charge, Pam Ryan, stood next to Floyd Swenson. She was fresh out of the Minnesota State Patrol Academy and had been riding with Floyd for a month while she learned the routines of being a Pine County "road deputy." She was barely twenty-two, and just starting her first law enforcement job. She was cute, rather than pretty, petite, and terribly naïve, having lived in a small farm town in southern Minnesota all her life.

Dan nodded to the group of deputies, but directed his attention to Sandy Maki, who had taken the original call. "What've we got, Sandy?" Dan Williams asked as he approached the group.

Sandy nodded toward the cluster of people in the yard. "Mrs. Almquist collapsed. She's the one who called us. She's Terri Berg's grandmother." He turned towards the house. "We've got two dead inside. A man and a woman. The woman is probably Terri Berg. We have no idea who the man is. He doesn't have a wallet or any ID in his clothing."

Dan glanced at the house then looked back to the deputies. He noticed that Pam Ryan was quite pale.

"Pretty bad?" Dan asked. Pam looked away.

Sandy Maki shook his head in disgust. "Worse than the one down at the Sturgeon Lake trailer park last year. The blood there was all in the tub. Here, it's everywhere."

"The coroner's inside?" Dan asked, nodding toward the house.

They all nodded. The man in green surgical scrubs stepped forward. "I suppose I'd better give him a hand." The man's nameplate said his name was Ken, from the pathology department at the hospital.

Dan shook his head as he stepped up to the door. "I wish he would just leave things alone until the medical examiner gets here. I'm afraid that he's going to screw things up again."

Ray "Doc" Peterson, the county coroner, was hunched over a woman's body lying on the living room floor. He was kneeling in a pool of blood, and probing a wound with his finger. When he pulled it back the latex glove was covered with a thin film of blood. He held it up and examined it intently.

Dan stared at Terri Berg's once pretty face. It was bruised, swollen, and frozen in a grimace of pain. Her unseeing eyes stared at the ceiling. Bruises covered her breasts and upper torso. Terri's feet were pulled up near her buttocks, her hands apparently behind her back. Her knees were splayed like a frog on a dissection

The sun was streaming through the living room windows, shining directly on the body, leaving the rest of the room in a subdued shadow. A table had been overturned and a lamp shattered on the floor next to the portable television stand. The center of the hardwood flooring was covered by a worn rug that was soaking up the almost-black pool of blood that surrounded the body. Most of the furniture looked like items that the Salvation Army would have refused.

Doc Peterson studied his finger for a second, then inserted it into a different wound on the torso. "Classic murder-suicide. Brutal attack. These gunshot wounds were inflicted postmortem." Peterson hesitated, looked up at Dan Williams, then added, "That means after death."

Williams rolled his eyes, amazed by the coroner's arrogance. "Doc, I've called the medical examiner to conduct the investigation. I'd appreciate it if you'd leave the corpse alone until we've had a chance to collect the evidence."

Doc Peterson ignored the request. He rolled the stiff corpse slightly, exposing the dark area on the back caused by the pooling of blood in the tissues after death. The hands were bound under the body with an electrical cord that ran to the ankles. The cord had been tied so tightly that the woman's hands and feet were swollen and discolored.

Speaking to no one in particular as he leaned down to inspect the victim's back, the coroner said, "Huge exit wounds with no associated bleeding. Just senseless violence." Peterson shook his head. Rigor mortis had caused the body to be so unyielding that the coroner had to lift rather hard to roll it to the side. When he let go it fell back with a thud.

Dan moved to the coroner's feet, stopping at the edge of the blood pool. "Doc, I want you to leave the body alone. Don't touch it again. You're disturbing a crime scene that needs to be investigated by trained professionals." Dan spoke as if he were addressing a child.

The coroner struggled to his feet, then pushed the long strands of his graying hair back onto his head with his forearm. He took care not to touch his face with the bloody gloves. His face was sweaty, and sweat stained the armpits of his green surgical scrubs. Blood stained the scrubs where they stretched over his ample belly and at the knees where he'd been kneeling in the pool of coagulated blood.

The coroner went on as if Dan hadn't spoken. He gestured toward the bedroom with his elbow as he tugged at the cuff of a latex glove. "The guy in the bedroom must have really been wound up. Raped her, then beat her to death. Then, he shot her after she was dead. Real sweet fella." The doctor pulled off his latex gloves with a snapping sound, and dropped them on the floor. "Then he felt so bad that he blew his own brains all over the walls." Doctor Peterson blew out a deep breath. "It doesn't take much of a trained investigator to figure that out."

Doc Peterson led Dan into the bedroom and stopped at the foot of the bed. Lying on the bed was a nude male body. The feet were covered by a sheet, and between the knees lay a Remington 742 semi-automatic rifle. At the top of the torso was a bloody stump. The walls and the head of the bed were splattered with human tissue of assorted colors and textures, predominantly red. A single spent cartridge lay on the bed to the right of the body. The odor in the bedroom was different from the living room. Here it was metallic, sickly sweet, mixed with urine and feces. The sheet had apparently been pulled back because everything in the room was splattered except for the man's body from the armpits down, and the corresponding area on the underside of the sheet.

Dan pinched the bridge of his nose. "Did you pull the

sheet back, Doc?"

Peterson stopped talking for a second and stared at Dan, incredulous, before speaking again. "How in hell else was I going to check the body temperature?" His voice had an edge like a parent speaking to a child who had asked too many questions.

Dan let out a deep sigh. "He died after the woman?"

The doctor's eyes narrowed. "I've rarely seen a dead man rape a woman."

"You did check the woman's body temperature, too?"

The doctor went on as though there hadn't been a question. "Been dead about twelve hours, judging from the lividity and body temperature." The coroner left the bedroom, went through the living room and looked at the group of deputies standing near the kitchen door. "Kenny, go get the gurney and a couple of body bags. Maybe one of the brown shirts will help you." The coroner loved to call the deputies "brown shirts." It was a less-than-veiled reference to his well-known view that the deputies were little more than Nazi storm troopers.

"Wait a second, Ken," Williams said, putting his hand on the young man's shoulders. "The bodies aren't leaving with you. They'll go with the ME to Duluth when he's through with his investigation here."

Peterson spun around and stuck a finger into Williams' face. "That's a waste of the taxpayer's money! This is a simple murder-suicide. Nothing to it. She was beaten to death. He blew his brains out. End of story."

The coroner pointed at Terri Berg's body as he spoke. "The ME charges what? Twenty five hundred a body. You're flushing five grand of tax dollars down the toilet, Williams. As a Pine County taxpayer, I object. As the coroner, I overrule you. Get the gurney, Ken."

Tires crunched in the driveway as an unmarked, brown sedan pulled off the driveway and onto the grass. The argument stopped as John Sepanen, the Pine County sheriff, got out of his

car. Doc Peterson threw a disgusted look at Williams and quickly waddled out to the sheriff's side. In the bright sunlight, all of
the coroner's seventy-plus years showed. He limped as he
walked and puffed as he tried to walk and speak. His complexion was gray with blotches of red caused by his anger.

The doctor fell in step with the sheriff, continuing his
protests. "Look, John. We've got a simple murder-suicide and
that shit-for-brains Williams wants to waste five grand having
the ME drive fifty-five miles from Duluth to pick up a couple
of bodies for simple autopsies." Peterson stumbled as he tried
to keep up with the sheriff, who was walking toward the
deputies gathered outside the house.

They stopped a few feet short of the group and the sheriff turned to the coroner. His bass voice was unexpectedly deep
for his short stature. "Ray, are you afraid you're not going to get
your five hundred dollars per body for an autopsy? I'm sure
you'll be able to make the mortgage on your lake house either
way. But let me talk to Dan."

The sheriff grabbed Dan Williams by the arm and took
him aside while the coroner fumed at the deputies and then
stomped into the house. "What's up, Dan?"

Dan kept his voice low. "Someone beat Terri Berg to
death and then pumped a few shots into her dead body. There's
a male body on the bed with its brains splattered on the wall.
We haven't identified him as yet."

The sheriff was ten inches shorter than Williams but carried an air of authority that matched his deep voice. Reaching
into his breast pocket he pulled out a cigar, carefully unwrapped
it and rolled the cigar between his fingers. "You must think this
is more than the murder-suicide Doc Peterson thinks it is." The
sheriff struck a wooden match on the seat of his jeans and
sucked on the cigar while he waited for a reply.

Dan stared out over the field of corn as he spoke. "I
don't know that it's more than Peterson says. I do know that if
we let him haul the bodies away before we even take pictures

we'll never know otherwise."

The sheriff bobbed his head and blew a stream of smoke that drifted toward the house in the light breeze. A trickle of sweat formed at his hairline and ran down his temple. "I'll stand behind you, but I hope to God that the ME finds something that Ray would've missed. Otherwise, you and I will have a lot of explaining to do at the next county board meeting." The sheriff let the words sink in for a moment to see if Dan would balk.

Dan stared at an apple tree on the edge of the yard that looked like it had been struck by lightening. One half was dead, the other half was growing small green apples. It reminded him of how he felt about his job. He loved the half that was investigations. The half that was political bullshit, like dealing with the coroner and the county board, made him feel dead inside.

Dan finally snapped back from the daydream and answered, "Doc Peterson didn't even check the female body's temperature. He has the murder-suicide scenario so fixed in his mind that he won't bother to collect all the evidence."

The sheriff nodded agreement. "Any idea who the male victim might be?"

Dan nodded toward the pickup. "I can't say for sure, but I'll bet money that truck belongs to Joey Berg, the ex-husband. Terri Berg had a restraining order against him. While they were married he beat the hell out of her regularly. We'd get a call to pull them apart once a month."

The sheriff grimaced. "Hell of a lot of good the restraining order did her."

Dan nodded agreement. "You want to take a look inside the house?"

The sheriff took a long drag on the cigar and blew the smoke out before answering. "Pretty bad?" Dan nodded. "Well, let me take a quick look and then get out of here. I think it's better if the young deputies don't see the sheriff tossing his breakfast all over the lawn." The sheriff touched the butt of his cigar to his brow in a salute and headed for the house.

* * *

Dan returned to the deputies as the sheriff walked back to his car. "Pam, you and Floyd take pictures. Floyd can show you the ropes."

Pam Ryan walked inside with Dan, as the sergeant headed for the car to get the camera. "Um, Deputy Williams, could we cover her up? I know it's a crime scene, but it's kinda...indecent, leaving her spread-eagle like that." Pam pointed to the woman's body on the floor.

"Sure," Dan said, "after we get some pictures and check for prints. We don't want to compromise any evidence."

Pam opened her mouth to make a comment, but was cut short by the coroner who emerged from the bedroom with his black bag. "The big man here has to leave her naked until his buddies from Duluth can check her out. Then he'll have to take some pornographic pictures for the deputies to pass around the coffee pot."

Blood rushed to Dan's face. He looked at Pam and nodded toward the door. She and Sandy Maki quickly exited the house, leaving only Dan Williams and the coroner and Kenny. Dan walked up to the coroner until they stood toe to toe. He towered over the coroner by nearly six inches. Although they weighed nearly the same, Dan was still built like the fullback he had once been in high school. Doc Peterson's chest had shifted to his waist.

Williams pushed a finger into the doctor's chest hard enough to leave a bruise. "Listen, you back country Jackass. I've had all I can take of your arrogant crap. You can stand around quietly and offer your opinions to the ME or you can pack up your little black bag and get the hell out of here. Either way, you are officially relieved of the case."

Doc Peterson was crumpling a new pair of latex gloves in his hand while trying to get out a word of protest. He threw the gloves angrily on the floor. "I am a medical professional and

I will not be addressed in this manner!"

Doc Peterson stomped through the kitchen then turned as he stood in the door. The sunlight in the yard gave the impression of a halo behind him. "I have friends on the county board," he said, indignantly. "This isn't over." He exited the door and marched across the yard to the Suburban. Kenny quickly stubbed out a cigarette and jogged hurriedly after the coroner to the vehicle. The Suburban sped out of the driveway spitting gravel and raising dust.

When Floyd Swenson and Pam Ryan came back in, Dan was staring out the kitchen windows watching the billowing dust the Suburban had left in its wake. "You all right, Dan?" Floyd asked.

Dan came back from his thoughts. "I'm fine. Why don't you take some pictures, Floyd? Pam, take a look around and make drawings of how things are arranged. Watch what Floyd's doing with the camera. He's an expert."

When Dan walked back out to the yard he noticed Violet Almquist sitting in the front seat of the Olds staring ahead without seeing. The ambulance crew was gathering up their gear and the rescue crews were climbing back into their trucks. Sandy Maki was standing next to his squad car with the radio mike in his hand.

"Ten-four." He leaned in and hung the radio mike back on the bracket.

"Dan, I ran the plates on the truck. It belongs to Joey Berg," Sandy said.

Dan stopped and gave a feeble nod. "I would've been surprised if it belonged to anyone else. Did you find any ID in the truck?"

Sandy shook his head. "Didn't check yet. I was waiting for the coroner to do his thing first. By the way, what did you say to him? He looked like someone had stepped on his tail when he left."

Dan shrugged. "I gave him an honest appraisal of his

skills. He didn't agree." Sandy chuckled.

They walked together to Joey Berg's pickup truck and pulled the dirver's door open. The floor was littered with beer cans and a patina of dust coated the dashboard and the instrument panel. Mud caked the floor and pedals.

Sandy noted, "No keys in the ignition. The front door was locked when I broke it open. Not the new deadbolt, but the lock in the old lock set. Someone must have locked it from the inside and pulled out the key. I checked and it wasn't in the lock or on the floor."

Dan shrugged. "Maybe Terri left the door unlocked and left the key on the inside of the door. When the killer entered he locked the door and removed the key to keep her from escaping. Check around inside the house and in the man's pockets to see if you can find it after Pam and Floyd finish with the pictures."

Dan pushed the button to lock the pickup door. He closed the door and looked at the flat tire. "Have the garage in Pine City tow this to the impound lot." He walked behind the truck and knelt down, running his fingers over the side wall of the flat tire. "The tire was flat when the truck was driven in here. The rubber is chewed up pretty badly. I suppose that maybe the guy in the bed knew that he wasn't going to leave and didn't care that he was ruining the tire."

Dan stood up and surveyed the gravel driveway. The tracks of nearly a dozen emergency vehicles criss-crossed each other making a mosaic in the dust. "Too bad we can't tell if there were any other vehicles here recently."

Sandy pulled off his cap and mopped his brow on his forearm. He asked, "What makes you think that there might have been another vehicle here last night?"

Dan shrugged. "Instinct. Something just doesn't feel right about this whole scene. It seems too contrived." He surveyed the tracks again and then walked back to the house.

When Dan came back inside, Floyd had finished a roll

of film in the living room and had moved to the bedroom, where he was reloading the camera. Pam stood leaning against the door frame holding a pad of paper and pencil.

"You find anything interesting?" Dan asked.

Pam's face looked stressed, but took on an air of accomplishment. She flipped the pages of her notebook back a few sheets to a drawing of the bathroom. "There's a diaphragm case on the bathroom sink. I know that means she was planning to have intercourse. But I can't explain this." She pointed to a foil condom wrapper on the floor. The foil envelope was black with white printing that extolled the virtues of its "new and improved ribbed design." The brand name was Black Ecstasy. "It's here on the floor near the bedroom door. Why both a diaphragm and a condom?"

Sandy shrugged. "Double protection. A diaphragm doesn't protect you from AIDS."

Pam shook her head. "The condom's not here. At least I can't find it. I think that the killer didn't care that she had a diaphragm. I think he was smart enough to know he didn't want to leave any DNA evidence."

Sandy shook his head. "I think you're being overly dramatic. Doc Peterson says it's a murder-suicide. The guy probably used the condom and threw the wrapper on the floor. We'll probably find the condom buried somewhere in the sheets after we remove the bodies."

Pam wrinkled her nose. "Yuck! You don't throw a used condom in the bed."

Muffled conversation from the kitchen interrupted their discussion. Two of the men from the ambulance crew were peeking into the living room at Terri Berg's body.

Dan shooed them out. "Hey guys, this is a crime scene. I need you to clear out."

One of the men stood with his mouth gaping as he stared at Terri Berg's body. He found his tongue for a second. "Is...is that...Terri?" he asked, anxiously.

Dan put a hand on the man's shoulder, turned him around, and eased him toward the door. "We can't identify any of the victims until we notify next of kin."

The man looked up at him. "There's more than one? Is it Jamie? He took Terri home from the bar last night."

Dan froze, holding the man's shoulder. "Jamie who?"

The fireman took a deep swallow. "Jamie Arvidson. He's been...ah...with Terri a lot lately."

Dan looked out the door to make sure that none of the other crewmen had heard them speaking. "You saw them together last night?"

The crewman nodded. "They left together right after Joey Berg got thrown out of the Pine Brook Inn."

Dan continued to push the man out the door and down the steps. "We can't tell right now. But thanks for the help."

"Umm...I could probably identify him for you if you want.," the man volunteered hesitantly.

"No, thanks. We've got it under control."

The man looked disappointed and relieved at the same time. "Okay." Then he stopped. "Oh, yeah. I came in to tell you that one of our guys is going to drive Mrs. Almquist home now. We're clearing out, too."

"Thanks for your help," Dan said as he closed the door.

Chapter 4

As the medical personnel followed Violet Almquist's car down the driveway, a gray Suburban, with the St. Louis County insignia on its doors waited on the road for the driveway to clear, then slowly drove to the house. Two men emerged, one in a sportcoat and slacks, the other wearing a white lab coat over a pair of jeans. The medical examiner, in the sportcoat, was nearly six foot six, and walked like a stork, taking huge strides across the grass. His assistant, Eddie, trailed behind with the measured strides of a former soldier, carrying a nylon flight bag in one hand.

Dan watched them cross the yard, then stepped forward to greet Tony Oresek, the St. Louis County medical examiner, at the farm house door. "Tony, glad you could make it so quick."

The medical examiner's huge hand engulfed Dan's hand. A broad smile spread over his sallow face. "My favorite thing to do on a Sunday morning." He paused a second. "It is Sunday, isn't it? I lose track working every day of the week."

Eddie caught up and also offered his hand. "Hi, Dan."

"Eddie, I haven't seen you in a year. You still dating the veterinarian from Woodbury?"

Eddie smiled. "Dating is a little strong. We're still seeing each other when she gets a weekend off. But long distance romance is tough and we both work pretty irregular hours."

Tony Oresek wasn't into small talk. He was looking

over Dan's shoulder. "What've we got?"

Dan led them into the living room and introduced Floyd, Pam and Sandy. "Female victim with visible bruising and ligatures on her ankles and wrists. The coroner says that there are multiple gunshot wounds that were inflicted postmortem. The male in the bedroom has massive head trauma that the coroner says was self inflicted." As Dan spoke, Oresek scanned the grisly living room scene.

Eddie was busily donning latex gloves and pulling instruments from the nylon bag. "Are you through taking pictures in here?" he asked Floyd.

Floyd held the camera up. "Yup. I got a roll shot in the living room and a roll in the bedroom."

Eddie approached the female body and deftly inserted a thermometer into one of the abdominal wounds. He ran his gloved fingers over her torso. "Lots of bruising. Looks like she took a hell of a beating before she died. I assume the arms are tied behind the back. They're sure at an uncomfortable angle." He ran his fingers over marks on the victim's right breast. "Nasty character. The bite marks here broke the skin."

Oresek knelt down as Eddie rolled the body over. He looked at Terri's hands. "They're tied with a piece of electrical cord. The swelling indicates that they were tight enough to cut off circulation and were put on while she was still alive." Eddie set the body back down.

Eddie quickly surveyed the exterior of the body and picked at a few spots on the floor with a pair of forceps. He put what he recovered into a tiny plastic bag that he labeled and dropped back into the flight bag. He took a tiny metal spatula and collected some vaginal samples. Eddie held the spatula out for Oresek to examine.

"Evidence of recent sexual activity," Oresek said more or less to himself. He pulled the thermometer from the wound and read the mercury. "Twenty-five degrees centigrade."

Oresek reached to touch a bullet hole in the torso when

he hesitated. "Vicious postmortem attack. Whoever did this wasn't happy that she was just dead. He apparently wanted to disfigure her."

Pam Ryan had been watching the examination with Floyd and Sandy. A gurgle rose from her throat. Everyone looked at her and she quickly turned red. "Sorry."

Ignoring the interruption, Eddie rolled Terri's body over again and whistled softly. "Big bore rifle. Nasty exit wounds." He looked around the floor and spied several spent rifle cartridges. "But I concur with the coroner, postmortem wounds. No bleeding associated with them."

He nodded at the two pairs of latex gloves on the floor near the body. "Were they here too? You can get some prints off the inside of them."

Floyd Swenson spoke up. "No, the coroner threw them there when Dan told him to buzz off before he screwed up another investigation."

Eddie gave Dan a knowing smile. He got up and walked to the bedroom, while shaking down the mercury in the thermometer. He stood surveying the male body for a second, shrugged and inserted the thermometer into an open blood vessel in the stump of what had been the man's neck.

The ME stood next to Dan, watching the technician work. "Why does Eddie bring you along, Tony? Looks like he's got it under control," Dan said with a straight face.

"I have to sign the death certificates." Oresek answered, smiling.

Eddie sampled particles from the headboard and the wall. He picked up a piece of tissue from the floor and turned it in his hand. "Nose," he said, matter of factly. He dropped it in the bag and scribbled on the label.

"How could a single rifle shot do so much damage?" Dan asked, watching with clinical detachment.

"Must've hit the mandible and the bullet mushroomed. The concussion blew the whole top of his head away." The medical examiner spoke with the detachment of a gardener describing an infestation of aphids.

Eddie pulled the thermometer out and read the mercury. "Twenty three Celsius." He looked up at the deputies and ME "He died first. This is a double murder."

Pam Ryan started to say something, but Floyd put his finger to his lips. She stopped and watched.

The medical examiner knelt down at the foot of the bed. He shifted his position around the bed clockwise, then counter-clockwise, bobbing up and down, eyeing the head of the bed from different angles and heights. He stopped at a point near the corner post.

"The shot came from here," Oresek said, pointing toward the head of the bed as he bent slightly. "If you look at the deposition of material on the head of the bed and the wall, the debris centers on the headboard directly across from here. It appears that the shot may have come from somewhat higher than the head. It'd be pretty tough to hold a rifle up that high to shoot yourself in the head. Much easier to support the butt on the bed and pull the trigger."

Oresek looked at the foot of the bed and pointed at the man's feet. They were still covered by the sheet. "Oh hell, look at that. Unless this guy was an Orangutan he couldn't reach the trigger with his hand while holding the muzzle against his jaw. He would have had to pull the trigger with a toe. If you look at the way he's lying, he would have had to tuck his feet under the sheet after he was dead."

Oresek moved to the side of the bed and leaned across the body to look at the muzzle of the rifle. "No tissue residue on the muzzle either. You get some blow-back onto the surface of the barrel if the muzzle is within half a foot of the head when the gun discharges. If the gun is within an inch or less of the head when it goes off, the gases cool in the barrel sucking tissue inside, but there's nothing on this gun or in the barrel at all."

Oresek pulled his huge frame back up and addressed his assistant. "I'll bet you money that the killer sneaked in and shot the man while he was sleeping. We'll have to check the woman's hair to see if there's tissue fragments and nitrate residue from his head wound."

He walked back next to Dan. "They were probably sleeping when the killer sneaked in. He shot the man, and the woman woke up. Then he bound and raped her."

Pam Ryan had been watching quietly. At the mention of the rape she focused again upon the crime scene. "Dr. Oresek, there's a diaphragm case in the bathroom, and a condom wrapper on the living room floor. What do you make of that?"

Oresek addressed himself to Eddie first. "Remind me about the diaphragm when we PM her." He turned to Ryan. "That's easy. She had planned to have sex with the man in the bed, and judging from the vaginal sample, accomplished that. Then she was sexually assaulted by the attacker. If the attacker was sophisticated enough to be concerned about his DNA evidence, he used the condom to capture his semen and remove it from the scene. The other scenario is that John Doe here," he gestured toward the bed, "was concerned about sexually transmitted diseases and decided to use some protection. If that's the case, you should find the condom lying in the waste basket or somewhere around the bed."

Pam started for the wastebasket when Dan grabbed her arm. "Wait until we dust for prints before you touch anything." She nodded in recognition. "Be sure to dust the condom wrapper, too," Dan said to Floyd. "That smooth surface is perfect for leaving prints."

Oresek was helping Eddie load the few instruments that they'd used into the flight bag. "We'll check for two blood types in the vaginal samples, too. Some of these rapists are really weird. They shoot their wads before they get erect and the condom slips off. Or, they're in such a hurry that they pull it off too soon and spill a sample for us. In either case we will probably be able to pull a few of the rapist's hairs from the woman's pubic hair. He may have left a few other hairs on her body too. If we get enough hair we may be able to test his DNA. We'll bag her hands and check under her fingernails to see if she put up a fight and scratched him. That would be another chance at samples for DNA matching."

Dan turned to Floyd Swenson again and was about to speak when Swenson beat him to the punch. "I've got pictures already. Pam and I'll get the evidence kit and start collecting prints. Sandy could go over to the Pine Brook Inn and get the story on the party last night." Dan looked at Sandy. He nodded and headed for the door.

Dan had been mulling the accumulating facts over. The information about Jamie Arvidson being the last to leave with Terri stuck in his mind. Was the male body Arvidson? Had Joey Berg followed them home and shot them both in a fit of jealousy? Or had he decided to not only kill Terri but himself as well?

"I'll go over to Joey Berg's place and check around a little," said Dan. "It's his pickup outside, so I'm assuming this is Joey." He nodded to the male body. "When do you think that you'll do the postmortem, Tony?"

Oresek and Eddie unfolded a body bag and worked the male body to the edge of the bed before slipping it over the feet and then up the torso. "Probably tomorrow afternoon. This is the hottest thing that we've got going right now."

Eddie chimed in as he zipped the body bag. "We've got that floater from St. Louis Bay."

Oresek shrugged. "We'll get him Tuesday morning. Nobody is pressuring us over him."

Dan turned to Floyd. "Can you get free for the autopsy?"

Floyd nodded. "Pam and I will be there."

Pam Ryan paled as she realized that she was going to have to watch Terri Berg's autopsy. "Is it really necessary that we watch? I mean, like, it can happen without us, can't it?"

She continued to look back and forth at the faces, expecting to see a smile, but none was forthcoming. "Is this some sort of rookie initiation thing?"

Eddie threw the nylon flight bag onto the bed next to the body. It landed with a thud, bringing all eyes to him. "Real cops watch their autopsies. Fake ones request a fax of the report." He made the comment to no one in particular, then he looked squarely at Pam. "You want to be a real cop when you grow up?"

Chapter 5

It was early Sunday afternoon when Dan Williams pulled his unmarked squad in front of Joey Berg's trailer a few miles East of the town of Rock Creek. Dan surveyed the lot the trailer sat on. A few acres of poplar trees had sprouted in what was apparently a long abandoned farm pasture, surrounded by high grass that had never seen a lawnmower. A rusting barbed-wire fence defined the front edge of the property. A gap in the fence defined the driveway to the trailer. A hundred yards behind the trailer Dan could see a new barbed wire fence that probably separated this lot from the rest of the farm pasture.

Dan saw a trail leading through the brown grass from the gravel driveway to the trailer's front door. The grass was stunted from the withering heat of the previous few weeks. Streaks of brown stained the white exterior of the aluminum trailer skin where steel screws had been used to attach the windows to the siding. No drapes covered the windows. What appeared to be a beach towel covered the window at the furthest end of the trailer. It was probably the bedroom. He deduced that a man lived here alone.

Dan walked up to the front door and climbed the rough-sawn pine steps. The handrail had fallen off at some time and lay in the grass alongside the steps. He didn't expect anyone to answer the door when he knocked, and he wasn't disappointed.

After a few additional knocks, he opened the screen door, and tried the knob. It turned in his hand and the inside

door pushed open easily. He was greeted with the scent of fried
bacon and old garbage in the eighty-degree air. No air conditioner here. Inside the trailer he looked at a living room covered
with car parts, girlie magazines and dirty clothes. Every piece
of furniture had something laying on it. The only decorations on
the walls were centerfolds torn from the magazines, hung with
strips of masking tape.

The kitchen opened to the living room, and Dan could
see cardboard food containers piled on the countertop and overflowing a wastebasket. The resident or residents apparently
favored Chinese take-out. The table was cluttered with
unopened mail, dirty drinking glasses, Coke cans, beer cans,
foil and plastic utensils, a challenge for any maid. Dan flipped
through the envelopes on the table. All were addressed to either
Joey Berg or Occupant. A dark shiny tube caught his eye and he
walked to the furthest corner of the living room. A deer rifle
leaned against a wall in the corner behind the couch.

Dan carefully lifted it out without touching any of the
metal or flat wood surfaces. It was a semi-automatic Remington
that was pitted with rust in a few spots. He took out a handkerchief and released the empty clip, which fell to the floor. When
he pulled back the bolt, a single live rifle shell flew out and skittered across the magazines that littered the homemade end
table. The smell of freshly burned gunpowder drifted to his
nose. Had Joey been doing some out of season deer poaching,
or had he disposed of a skunk in his yard?

Dan carefully leaned the gun against the entry door
frame and continued his exploration of the trailer. He walked
down the hallway, past a bathroom cluttered with dirty towels.
The smell that rose from the towels was a mixture of sweat,
mold and mildew that reminded him of the boy's locker room
in high school.

The only bedroom was at the end of the hallway. He
peered around the corner and pulled back quietly. On top of a
heap of bedding was a naked male body lying on its side, fac-

ing the wall. His back and legs were covered with a thick pelt of blonde hair. Dan watched for a moment to see if the body was alive or dead. The body gave a sudden snort, followed by a deep breath and a rattling snore.

"Joey?" said Dan. There was no response. He walked up and tugged on one foot. "Joey Berg?"

There was a spasm and the man sat upright, staring at Dan in shock. "What?"

Dan was surprised, too, when he saw who it was.

Joey Berg sat on the bed for a second, trying to get his eyes to focus. Recognition swept over him as he struggled to figure out where he was and why he was staring at Pine County's chief investigator. They'd met after one of the drunken domestic fights while Joey and Terri were still married.

Joey struggled to find the meaning of Dan's presence. "Listen man, I wasn't anywhere near Terri's house last night. I saw her at the Inn, and that was it." He suddenly realized that he was naked. He leaned off the edge of the bed and pulled on a pair of dirty undershorts he grabbed from the floor.

"Get dressed, Joey" said Dan "We need to talk about a few things."

"Like what?" After sliding into the shorts, Joey reached down and retrieved a pair of crumpled jeans from the floor. He stood as he put them on. The jeans hung loosely around his waist, like he'd lost five or ten pounds since he'd bought them. He searched the area for a shirt, smelling the armpits of two before settling on a black T-shirt with a Jack Daniels label emblazoned on the front.

Dan watched and wondered what it would be like if he ever lost his wife, Sally. Certainly, he wouldn't sink this far. "I'd like to know where you were after you left the Pine Brook Inn last night."

Joey stared at Dan with a blank expression. "I can't remember. I guess I was here."

Dan looked at the blank expression on Joey's face and

wondered if he was a good enough actor to be this convincing. Probably not. "You're not sure?"

Joey stood with his mouth open staring at Dan, but no words came out for a few seconds. "Yeah, I was here. Why?" He got a cocky look on his face like he felt he had the upper hand.

Dan suppressed a grin. "What time did you get here?"

The cocky expression melted away. "I didn't check my watch. I just went to bed."

"No television?"

Joey laughed. "Terri got it in the divorce."

"You drive home, or did someone drop you off?" Dan knew Joey didn't have a clue.

Joey hesitated a second too long before replying. "Hey, what's up, anyway?" He walked to the window and pulled back the beach towel that served as his window covering. Immediately, he spun around and pointed a finger at Dan. "Somebody stole my truck. So that's it. I suppose someone used it in a hold up, or had a hit and run."

Dan stared at him passively. "Did you drive it home last night, or did someone drop you off?"

Joey ran his fingers through his hair like a comb and stared at the floor." Ouch! I got a lump on my head." Joey felt his way around his head and gingerly touched the spot again. He grimaced as he considered the knot. "I sure don't remember banging my head." He looked back at Dan and then remembered that he'd been asked a question. "I drove myself...I think." He stepped over a pile of clothing and sat on the edge of the bed.

"Did you go anywhere after you left the Inn?"

Joey stared at Dan. "C'mon, man. My truck's gone and you're asking me all kinds of stupid questions. What's up? Am I under arrest or something?" Joey continued to rub his head when, suddenly, he thought he understood. "Oh yeah! The wait-ress at the Inn cracked me with a tray." He gave Dan an inquisitive look. "Can I press charges?"

Dan let the question slip by. "Do you own a deer rifle, Joey?" Dan looked around the room like he was trying to see it among the piles of clothing. The piles mostly consisted of T-shirts that advertised alcohol or tobacco products, and blue jeans that looked like they hadn't been near a washing machine in a decade. Interspersed with them were a few white socks and a couple of pairs of underwear.

Joey was oblivious to the visual search. "Yeah, I own a deer rifle. It's about the only thing Terri didn't get in the divorce settlement."

"Where is it?"

Joey pointed at the closet door. "In there."

Dan walked to the closet door and pointed. "Is it there now?"

Joey shrugged. "Sure. But I thought my truck was in the driveway too." His voice was almost a whine.

Joey got up and walked to the closet while Dan watched. Dan slid his hand to the small of his back and put it on the butt of his gun as Joey went into the tiny closet. The closet looked like a bomb had gone off inside, with empty clothes hangars hanging off the closet rod and a mixture of clothing and cardboard boxes piled randomly on the floor. Joey waded through the boxes and piles of winter clothing until he pulled out a folded vinyl gun case.

He held it out for Dan to see. "It's gone. What in hell is going on?" He threw the gun case on top of the piles in the closet and began rummaging deeper in the closet. As he backed out, he stumbled on a box and cursed as he fell to the floor. Joey tried to get up but gave up and decided to crawl out instead. "It's not here."

Dan backed away from the closet door and let Joey get up. "What kind of rifle was it?"

"An ought-six Remington." Joey sat on the bed again, his head in his hands. "My uncle gave it to me." Dan said nothing, waiting for the silence to force Joey into saying more.

After a few seconds Joey got up from the bed and led Dan down the narrow hallway. When they got to the living room Joey stopped and stared at the rifle. "Hey! Here it is. What's it doing here?"

Joey reached for it, and Dan touched his shoulder. "Don't," he warned. "I set it there. It was behind the couch."

Joey's face showed his utter confusion. "I don't leave it behind the couch. Who put it there?"

Dan shrugged. "Have you loaned it to anyone?"

Joey shook his head, "No."

Dan asked, "Have you shot it recently?"

Joey shook his head again. "I sighted it in last fall, before deer season. But I didn't even see a deer to shoot at. I guess I haven't shot it in almost a year now."

Dan added, "You know that since your domestic assault conviction you can't possess a firearm anymore."

Joey's answer was a grimace.

"Do you know Jamie Arvidson?" Dan asked.

"Sure. He used to be one of my best friends." Joey started toward the kitchen area. "I gotta have some coffee," he said. "Head's killing me."

Dan watched as Joey started searching through the cupboards, slamming doors as he went and muttering to himself. He finally located a jar of instant coffee and an acceptable cup on the countertop. He rinsed the cup and refilled it with water. Then he popped it into the microwave, punching three minutes into the timer.

"How well did you know Jamie? Dan asked.

"Jamie started to date Terri as soon as we separated. That pissed me off real bad, 'cause I wanted to get back together...at first."

Joey stared out the window for a few seconds. Dan looked closely at him. He looked like a scarecrow, his clothes draping on his frame. His eyes were badly bloodshot, and looked like road maps in hill country—little red highways going every direction.

When the microwave beeped, Joey jumped, then walked over and pulled out the cup. He found a spoon and wiped it on his pants before measuring out the dark crystals and stirring them into the water. He took a deep drink of the brew and stopped, staring at Dan over the rim of the cup. "Oh, did you want a cup, too?"

Dan looked at the piles of dirty dishes and shook his head. "No coffee, thanks. Have you still got a key for Terri's house?"

Joey shrugged. "She got the locks changed. Put a dead-bolt on the door. I might still have the skeleton key for the old lock on the key ring. I don't really know."

Dan nodded toward a ring of keys laying on the counter, with a big catch on the end. The catch was designed to hook on a belt loop. "Those yours?"

Joey felt his empty pocket, then walked over to the edge of the counter. He picked up the key ring and looked at the keys briefly. Then he set them back down. "Yeah. These are mine."

Dan asked, "Is that big skeleton key for the lock on Terri's door?"

Joey caught the meaning of the question and paused to consider his answer. "Well, yeah. But she put a new deadbolt on the door and I can't get in no more. Even with that key." Joey drained the coffee from his cup and set in on the counter. "What's up? I've told you lots and you haven't told me diddly squat."

"There was a crime at your ex-wife's house last night..."

"And you think that I broke in? Okay, that's why you asked me about the key. Listen, I didn't break in, and I didn't take nothin'." Joey stared out the window. "Jesus, am I the only bad guy in the county?"

"Terri's dead," Dan said, watching carefully to see if Joey's reaction to the news was immediate and appropriate.

Joey was visibly shaken. He opened his mouth to say something, then closed it.

"She was shot," Dan continued. "The spent shells were thirty ought six."

Joey looked for an empty chair, then scooped a pile of unopened mail onto the floor before plopping down in one.

"Terri's dead? Shot?" He stared at Dan. "I can't..." Joey shook his head, his eyes glistening tears. His shoulders slumped forward.

"I need to take you down to the justice center, Joey. I need you to answer some more questions there." Dan clipped on the handcuffs and read the Miranda card to him. After the Miranda warning, Dan asked permission to search the trailer. and to take the rifle as potential evidence.

Chapter 6

Sandy Maki drove past the town of Pine Brook and pulled into the parking lot of the Pine Brook Inn. There were no cars in the main parking lot. Sandy parked near the side entrance, next to a white Buick. There was a blue Pinto tucked in a spot near the dumpster in the furthest corner of the lot. He called the Pinto's license number to dispatch and waited. Dispatch quickly confirmed his suspicions that the Pinto belonged to Terri Berg. He requested that it be towed to the impound lot.

He locked his squad car and entered the unlocked side door of the inn. He stopped inside the door, waiting for his eyes to adjust to the dim light. Cool air blew through the air conditioning vent over his head and filled his nostrils with the smell of cigarette smoke and stale beer. As his eyes adjusted he caught sight of a man and a woman sitting at the bar holding coffee cups. The Pine Brook Inn wasn't one of his regular haunts, but, being a single guy, he'd spent a few evenings bending an elbow at the bar.

"C'mon in, Sandy. Have a cup of coffee?" Harvey Ostberg, the owner, pulled his huge body up from the bar stool. He went behind the bar and retrieved a cup from the rack by the sink and the carafe from the coffee machine.

The Pine Brook Inn was close to seventy years old and had survived I-35 bypassing the town of Pine Brook on its path from the Twin Cities to Duluth. The walls, once white, had yellowed with decades of cigarette smoke. The primary decorations were lighted beer signs that looked out of place on a quiet Sunday afternoon. The floor's oak planks were scarred by thousands of feet, sliding chairs and the slop of winter storms. The largest improvement had been the addition of Formica to the table tops in the 1960s.

Sandy grabbed a bar stool next to the woman. He'd never seen her before but assumed she was Harvey's wife. "Hi. I'm Sandy Maki." He offered her a hand.

The tiny woman took it gingerly and gave a feeble shake. Her grasp was gentle. "I'm Harvey's wife, Elaine." She was a tiny woman. With her frosted hair and her fair complexion she looked like a ghost in the dim light of the bar. Harvey and Elaine seemed like the definition of the odd couple, both in size and demeanor.

Harvey filled the cup and pushed it across the bar. Sandy nodded his thanks and took a sip of the coffee. It was nearly thick enough to stand up a spoon. He set the cup down and looked at Elaine. "I don't think I've seen you around here before."

She shook her head. "I'm not over here very much. Harvey's got the personality and runs the Inn. I take care of the house."

Harvey came back and hoisted his 250 pound girth onto a bar stool with a grunt. Sandy guessed that fifty pounds had to reside in the gut that hung over his belt alone. "Elaine keeps everything else together so that I can sit here twelve hours a day. But you didn't come for coffee, or a discussion of floor mopping. What's up, Sandy?"

Sandy swirled the coffee. "I heard that Terri Berg was here last night. Did you notice her?"

Harvey smiled. "It's hard to miss Terri. She's the belle of the ball whenever she holds court here."

"Holds court?"

Harvey's gaze drifted to the ceiling, like he was dreaming. "She always has a group of men hanging around her. She dresses...very provocatively, and drinks like a fish. Every guy in the place has eyes for her, and she knows it. Actually, she makes the most of it."

"She sleeps around?" Sandy asked.

Harvey shook his head. "I think that she's been thick with Jamie Arvidson lately. Before that I heard a few guys complaining that she was just a flirt."

Sandy gave a knowing nod. "Anything special happen last night?"

Harvey turned sour. "Joey Berg showed up. It interrupted things down for a while. He left and Terri cleared out sometime after that."

Sandy pulled out a notebook and scribbled some notes. "Do you remember what time that was?"

Harvey rubbed his hand across his meaty face, pushing his bulbous blue streaked nose around like it was made of rubber. "Must have been about midnight. We were pretty busy and I didn't check the clock. I'm sure she hung around a while longer. But I'm not sure just when she left." He turned back to Sandy. "If it's important, Rosie was waiting on her table. She might remember better."

"What's Rosie's last name?"

Harvey cocked his head as he thought. "Ah, actually, her name is Rose. Rose Mahoney."

"When's Rose scheduled to work again, Harv?"

"Monday. She works every night, except Sundays, when we're closed. She'll be on at six, just like clockwork. Barb Dupre, our other waitress, was also working last night. But she didn't come in on time. Barb didn't have Terri's table."

Sandy smiled at the commentary on the personnel. "Did you notice who Terri left with?"

Again a big smile. "I didn't see them leave. But she was thick with Jamie Arvidson all night. I'd bet money..." Harvey suddenly grew somber. "Why don't you ask Terri? She lives down past Henriette."

Sandy closed the little notebook. "Terri's dead."

Harvey closed his eyes and looked like he'd been struck by lightening. Elaine, with a look of horror, spoke up. "Car accident?" As the owners of a bar they dreaded lawsuits related to alcohol consumption. Losing customers in drunken accidents was bad business.

Sandy shook his head. "Looks like murder."

Elaine covered her mouth with her hand. Harvey found his voice first. "My God! Do you know who did it?"

Sandy shook his head. "We don't even know who the man was who was with her. He was killed too. Rose may have been one of the last persons to see them alive. Can you give me her address?"

Harvey shook his head. "She ain't gonna be happy to see you. She likes her privacy. But she lives in the Frank House, in Rush City. You know it, the old hotel right on the downtown corner."

Sandy made notes. He knew the Frank House. His own small apartment was in a building just outside of downtown. "How about Barb Dupre? Where's she live?"

Elaine looked nervously at Harvey, but didn't say anything. Harvey thought hard. "I think she lives with a guy in Pine City. In an apartment. But I don't think she'd like to talk to you, either. The boyfriend is a little possessive."

Sandy folded the notebook shut and put it in his pocket. "Do you know the boyfriend's name?"

Elaine fidgeted nervously, while Harvey answered. "All she's ever called him is Butch."

"What kind of car does Barb drive?"

Harvey looked at his wife before answering. She gave him a head-shake that indicated he was on thin ice. He answered anyway. "Red Camaro. It fits her personality."

Sandy watched Elaine's body language. She was obviously uncomfortable with the topic of Barb. He needed to know why. "What do you think about Barb, Elaine?"

Her face flushed as she swirled the grounds in the coffee cup. "She's a whore," Elaine answered quietly, without looking up from the cup.

Sandy waited for more. Elaine got uneasy with the silence. "Those weird tattoos. She does them herself. On her nights off she dances naked at a club somewhere." Elaine paused and sipped her coffee. "She's trash, that's all."

Harvey sat quietly through Elaine's comments. When she finished, Sandy looked at Harvey and he just shrugged as a response. "She brings in business."

"Well, thanks." Sandy drained the coffee and bid them good-bye.

Sandy Maki drove south to Rush City to talk to Rose Mahoney. He pulled into the parking lot on the south side of the Frank House. The old brick building showed all hundred years of its age. The red bricks had darkened to rust with age and the mortar was chipping away leaving grit on the sidewalk. He walked through the empty dining room to the front desk and rang the bell on the counter. The lobby was almost as grand as the day it had been built. The walnut check-in counter was polished to a magnificent shine and the antique chairs scattered throughout the lobby fit nicely with the dark paneling on the walls. A carved table under the stairs supported a bright bouquet of daisies arranged in a huge porcelain vase.

A chunky woman in her middle fifties stuck her head around the door jamb. She was leaning back in a chair and had a rim of crumbs around her mouth. At the sight of Sandy, or his uniform, she almost tipped over. He heard the chair scraping and dishes clinking.

She reappeared at the door, her mouth free of crumbs, with a napkin in her hand. "I'm terribly sorry officer. I thought you were one of the housekeepers. What can I do for you?" She had a checkered dress that didn't hide her well-fed frame. Her once dark hair was now salt-and-pepper.

"I'd like to know what room Rose..." he popped open his notebook, "...Rose Mahoney is in."

She didn't need to look up the number. "Number 11, upstairs. Is she in trouble? We don't want trouble." She spread her hands on the counter and spoke earnestly.

Sandy smiled. "Not at all. She saw some people at work last night and I need her help."

The woman visibly relaxed. "I believe she's in her room now. She spends most of the day up there on Sundays." She leaned over the counter as if to whisper a secret, and Sandy leaned toward her. "She *reads*."

Sandy restrained a grin. "I'll just go up and knock."

"Wait a second." The woman eyed him carefully. "Why don't I recognize you? I know all the Chisago County deputies."

Rush City was just south of the Pine-Chisago County line. Sandy smiled and pointed to his badge. "I'm from Pine County. We had a problem up at the Pine Brook Inn, where Rose works."

The woman nodded approval. "Go ahead."

The sculpted green carpeting on the hallway floor blended nicely with the dark stained woodwork. Halfway down the hall there was another antique table with fresh daisies in a porcelain vase. Room eleven was near the end of the hall, on the third floor. There was the sound of a television or radio coming from inside. Sandy knocked firmly to overcome the loud noise inside. There were shuffling sounds, and the radio stopped.

The lock on the door rattled, and the door opened a crack, exposing the left half of a round face at armpit height to Sandy's six-foot frame. The hair over the exposed eye was jet black and cut rather short. The bangs over her forehead weren't quite even. Sandy guessed that the occupant may have cut it herself.

"Rose Mahoney?" Sandy thought that she looked familiar, but it was hard to tell seeing only half a face in the dim hallway light. "I'm deputy Maki. I'm conducting an investigation."

The eye blinked at him for a second. Then a throaty voice croaked at him. "So what's that to me?"

Despite his irritation, Sandy tried to retain his professional decorum. "We need to know about some things that happened at the Pine Brook Inn last night. Could I come in to ask you some questions?"

Rose looked away from Sandy, over her shoulder, then back at Sandy. "Hang on a second. I gotta get something on. Okay?" The door closed without Sandy responding and he heard things clattering around as she obviously did some quick picking up. He thought that she'd had been dressed, but it was hard to tell through the crack in the door.

The door opened and there stood Rose. Sandy recognized her immediately, mostly because she was one of the least attractive women he'd ever seen. Her brow hung out far over the deep-set eyes and the angular jaw protruded despite the fleshy face. A hint of a mustache was partially obscured with makeup. Her blouse was pulled tight over her large girth, and gapped between the buttons exposing bulging layers of skin. It had obviously been purchased when she'd weighed quite a bit less.

She didn't look him in the eye when she opened the door but just gave him an order. "C'mon, if you gotta." She stepped back and let him pass.

The room was small, with a single bed, a chest of drawers, an old corrugated wardrobe, and an overstuffed chair. Across from the chair was an old television on a tubular metal stand. Sandy walked in and she gestured him to the chair. When he sat down it engulfed him, and he wondered how she ever got out of it with her stubby, fat legs. It was still warm, and there was a book sitting on a small table. The book was face down, apparently marking the page where she'd quit reading. Sandy didn't recognize the title or the author, A. A. Fair. It was a dog-eared paperback with a picture of a bloody hand clutching jewels on the cover.

"Rose, tell me about Terri Berg and the group she was with last night."

Rose appeared to be jolted for a second. "Why?" She screwed up her face, making it even uglier than it was naturally. "Just 'cause I hit her ex-husband with a tray? Am I in trouble over that? He was gonna beat on Terri."

Sandy pulled out his notebook. "I don't think so. Some other things happened after she left the bar. I think they may be related to what went on there last night."

Sandy's explanation seemed to assure Rose that she wasn't the one in trouble. "Terri was there with a couple of guys...three guys," she said, shrugging. "She had on those really short shorts, and a tight T-shirt without a bra. They danced and drank and didn't leave a tip when they left."

Sandy suppressed a smile. "Who were the men?"

Rose rolled back her head to think, exposing a nasty rash on her neck and a couple of scratches on the left side of her face, under her ear. There were a few dark whiskers growing in the folds of her neck and chin. Sandy thought that if he knew Rose well, he'd suggest electrolysis.

"There was Jamie Arvidson, Bill Patterson..." She spoke while staring at the ceiling, apparently visualizing the faces. "...and Russ Lemke. That's all. Oh, except for Joey, her ex. He showed up for a couple minutes." Her hand went to the scratches on her neck.

Sandy scribbled the names in the notebook. "I heard that you helped throw Joey out."

Rose bobbed her head. "He's an ass. He scratched me when he fell down. I conked him good with the tray though," she said, with a wink.

"I take it Joey had been drinking?"

Rose gave him a disgusted expression. "He was falling-down drunk. I'm sure Harvey wouldn't even have served him. Anyway, he left right after the commotion."

"What time was that?" Sandy scribbled notes in a small notebook.

"Oh, I dunno. Maybe about ten, eleven. No, closer to twelve. Maybe even later."

"Did Terri leave then, too?"

Rose thought for a moment. "Yeah, pretty soon after that."

"Did she leave alone?"

Rose shook her head. "She never leaves alone. She always goes home with somebody. She's not too particular either. I think she even went home with the guy from the rendering service one night. And he smells." Rose pinched her nose to add emphasis.

"Did you see who Terri left with last night?"

Rose thought for a second. "I think she walked out with Bill and Jamie."

Sandy perked up at the prospect of another suspect. "Do you know if the three of them went in the same car?"

"Don't know. I didn't go out to the parking lot until after they were gone."

Sandy folded up the notebook. "Did they all seem to be having a good time? No arguments or anything?"

"Oh, no. They were drinking and laughing, and dancing. Terri was rubbing her tits against all of them. Well, maybe except for Bill. He's kinda fat and they were giving him a little bad time, if you know what I mean. Nothing bad, just friendly kidding. But he got upset a little bit and kinda pouted for a while. You know, us chubby folks are sensitive about it and some don't take joking too well." Rose patted the folds of her stomach.

"Was Bill still pouting when they left?"

"Oh, I don't think so. But I didn't pay that much attention to them. They don't tip that well." Rose's demeanor suddenly changed from reflective to concerned. "Say, why are you asking all these questions anyway? Something happen between Terri and them?"

Sandy put the notebook in his pocket. "Terri was murdered last night. We found her body this morning, with one other person that we haven't identified."

Rose took a deep breath, her eyes wide with surprise and horror as she covered her mouth. "My God! Killed?"

Sandy nodded and got up from the chair, after a slight struggle with the cushioned arms. "Thanks for your time miss Mahoney. I think this will clear some things up."

Rose ushered him to the door. "If I can help, let me know. But I don't really know any more. You might ask Barb, the other waitress, if she saw who Terri left with. She might have been in the parking lot then. She snuck out a little early…like usual."

Sandy nodded, smiling inwardly at the jibe. "Do you know where Barb lives?"

Rose shrugged. "In Pine City, I think."

"Do you know exactly where?"

"Naw. She lives with some Neanderthal called Butch. And, no, I don't know his last name. But, if you find her red Camaro, you'll find Barb."

"I heard that she moonlights as a nude dancer," Sandy said.

A slight smirk cracked Rose's lips. "I heard that, too, but I think that it's more like she does a few bachelor parties rather than anything regular. Butch wouldn't put up with it. But she says he gets off on other men ogling her. She has a little tattoo on her crotch that says, 'Property of Butch.' She showed it to me once. Keeps it shaved, so all the men can read it."

Sandy gave her a "you're kidding" look, but all he said was, "Well, thanks again for your help, miss Mahoney. We may be wanting to talk to you again here, soon."

"Sure, officer, anytime," said Rose, as she watched Sandy leave down the hall.

Chapter 7

Floyd Swenson and Pam Ryan spent the rest of Sunday afternoon going over Terri Berg's house room by room, and inch by inch. They collected fingerprints from every flat surface and picked up fibers and pieces of lint from where the bodies had been removed. It seemed like a never-ending task as they sifted through the dust on the floor, on the windowsills and under the furniture. Terri Berg's passion was obviously something other than housekeeping.

They picked up hairs and pieces of lint everywhere, and then logged them. Each piece was placed in an envelope which was marked, sealed and put into a larger evidence bag. As they went through the kitchen, Pam stretched. Floyd looked up for a second and thought how well a bulletproof vest obscured a woman's figure. The uniform shirts didn't have darts, and the vest made her look like she had a board jammed under her shirt.

Pam twisted to get her back loosened up. "Can we grab a bite to eat after this? I could use a burger."

Floyd got up from the floor with a sample of dirt and dropped it into a bag. "You must be getting toughened up."

She gave him a quizzical look.

"It took me a day or two after my first bloody accident scene before I was ready to eat meat. I ate a lot of peanut butter sandwiches." Floyd climbed up from his knees, brushing the dust from his uniform pants. A few hours of crawling around on his fifty-four-year old knees reminded him that he could look forward to collecting a full pension in another year.

Pam smiled and loaded up the evidence kit. "Really? You weren't able to leave it behind when you went home?"

Floyd shook his head. "It was terrible. I had nightmares and second thoughts about what I could have done differently. My guts were on fire all the time. I almost quit the first year."

She stopped and stared at the veteran sergeant. She thought of him as strong and tough. He was also the unofficial department philosopher, confessor, and trainer. Every new deputy spent a month with Floyd before they went out on their own. He was well liked and respected. This was a side of him she hadn't seen.

"How'd you get over it, Floyd?"

Floyd shook his head. "In some respects I never did get over it. But what helped was talking it over with someone. I can't talk about it at home. It freaks my wife out. I still need to talk about it sometimes, though. We all do. We all find our own outlet and let it go."

Pam slung the kit's strap over her shoulder. "It's okay, Floyd. I'm dealing with it. By the way, someone upped their cookies on the back step. Did you see that?"

"Yeah. Sandy did that, I'm sure."

Pam gave him a funny look. "Sandy did what?"

Floyd nodded toward the house. "He let it out all over the back steps."

Pam let out a chirping laugh. "Bull. That was from one of the paramedics."

'Nope. It was Sandy."

"I can't believe it. He's been around for what, two, three years? And he still tosses his cookies when he sees blood?"

"Ask him. He's not embarrassed about it. It's how he lets it out. We've all got to deal with this stuff some way."

Floyd picked up the rifle from the kitchen table where they had placed it after lifting the fingerprints. He took a paper

towel from the counter top and wiped the residual black fingerprint dusting powder from the surface. He pulled the bolt one
more time to double-check that there wasn't a live shell in the
action. When he turned the rifle over he paused.

"This isn't the murder weapon," he said.

Pam looked at him with surprise and asked. "Why do
you say that? It has to be the murder weapon. I mean it's here
and there are spent shell casings all over the place."

Floyd held the gun out so she could see the marks
stamped on the barrel. "This is a .308 Winchester. The shell casings are 30-06. They won't fit in this gun."

"What do you make of it?"

Floyd studied the gun for a moment, then the crime
scene once more as he tried to come up with an answer. "Don't
know. Someone is pretty dumb to think we wouldn't know this
is not the murder weapon...unless they're just playing a delay-
ing game."

They walked out and put the gun and evidence kits into
the trunk of the squad. Floyd slammed the trunk, then they
walked back and checked the locks on the door before stringing
crime scene tape across the threshold. They walked back to the
squad and Pam climbed behind the wheel.

"Got a little game going here, you think?" she asked,
looking at Floyd.

Floyd nodded. "Looks like it. We'll see."

Dan Williams drove back to Pine City and booked Joey
Berg into the Pine County jail. "Frank Kelso, the jailer, had
taken Joey's picture, fingerprinted him, and inventoried his
belongings before taking his shoelaces and belt while Dan had
started the paperwork. Then Joey, Dan, and the jailer walked
down the narrow hallway between the twenty cells, their heels
clicking on the cement floor. As the jailer rattled keys, Joey
gave Dan a very sad look.

"How long am I going to be in?"

Dan shrugged. "I've got to process some more paper-work and then I'll get someone to interview you. If we all agree that your alibi is sound, we may let you out in a couple of hours. If you jerk us around, we'll keep you here until Monday when we can get one of the county attorneys to draw up some charges. Then we can get you in front of a judge and hold you until they arraign you."

"Aw, shit. I didn't do nothing." Frank guided Joey into the small cell with a single bed, a stainless steel toilet, and a stainless steel wash basin. The jailer unlocked the handcuffs and Joey rubbed his wrists. Joey looked at Dan through the bars, a hint of tears in his eyes.

"C'mon man. I just got divorced and I'm trying to get a life again. Give me a break. I didn't kill her." His voice cracked. "I still loved her."

"We'll try and finish this up as soon as possible, Joey," Dan said. " If you had nothing to do with the murder, you've got nothing to worry about."

Dan walked back to his office. He decided to let Joey sweat in the cell for a couple of hours before questioning him further. His inclination was to accept Joey's alibi, but there was a lot of circumstantial evidence against him and he had a motive.

John Sepanen, the sheriff, caught him halfway down the hall. "I had a call from WCCO television a couple minutes ago. They're sending up a truck from the Twin Cities with a news crew. Is there anything substantive that I can tell them about the murders or the investigation?"

Dan shook his head. "We don't even have positive iden-tification of the bodies yet."

The sheriff nodded as he made mental notes. Then he changed the subject. "Dan, what'd you do to Doc Peterson after I left?"

Dan frowned. "Why?"

"Doc called two of the county commissioners, raving about bringing you up on age harassment charges." The sheriff paused for effect. "So, what's the other side of the story?"

Dan walked with Sepanen into the sheriff's corner office and closed the door. The sheriff's office was unique, with windows on two walls and heavy wood furniture. All the other offices had gray industrial steel furniture. Sepanen walked to his desk and pulled a cigar from a wooden box. He peeled the wrapper and lit it with a wooden match while Dan spoke.

"Doc Peterson got all pissed and laid a line of crap on me about wasting county money, and that no one cared about a stupid murder-suicide anyway."

The sheriff shook the match to put it out and threw it into a giant glass ashtray. "I know that part. What did the Medical Examiner have to say?"

"Oresek says its a double homicide. We collected a bunch of evidence and are starting our investigation. If we'd accepted the coroner's bullshit there'd be a murderer running around free with no one looking for him."

The sheriff listened and nodded at the appropriate times while puffing his cigar. He finally ended up shaking his head. "Doc's in over his head, isn't he?"

Dan nodded his head. "He should resign. Or the board should fire him. His ego's too big and his capabilities are too limited. He's dangerous. If I hadn't stopped him he could have jeopardized our murder investigation before we even got started."

The sheriff got up and opened the door, indicating that the conversation was over. "I'll make a couple of calls and see if someone can convince him to simmer down. But I'm afraid that you're right about his ego. He's convinced that he's the best thing that ever came to this county and he's not going to let it go without a lot of weeping and gnashing of teeth."

Dan stopped at the door just as the sheriff was about to shut it. "John, I've got Joey Berg under arrest for the murder."

Dan ran his hand over his face. "But I don't think Joey did it."

Sepanen was looking at Dan, waiting

"I rousted him from bed and he didn't have a clue that anything had happened to Terri. I just don't think he's that polished to put on the show of ignorance that he gave me this morning."

"So why are you still holding him now? asked Sepanen.

"Well, there is something fishy going on here. I seized Joey's deer rifle. He didn't know that it was stashed in the corner of his living room, and it has been fired very recently. He swears that he drove himself home from the Pine Brook Inn last night, but there is no vehicle at his trailer and his pickup is at Terri Berg's house. Joey still has a key to Terri's door that was locked, too. There is a lot of circumstantial evidence pointing to Joey. He's either a better liar than I'm giving him credit for, or someone has done a great job of setting him up as the fall guy."

Sepanen considered the circumstantial evidence. "You think he's on the level?"

Dan rocked back on his heels. "Well, like I said, he's either innocent, or one hell of a liar. He seemed genuinely surprised when I told him that Terri was dead. I think that he's just coming to grips with that now."

The sheriff picked a piece of tobacco off his lower lip and flicked it onto the floor. "If it wasn't him, who did it?"

Dan shrugged. "Our next likeliest suspect would be the guy who took Terri home last night, and that seems to be Jamie Arvidson. But my suspicion is that Jamie Arvidson is the dead guy, even though we don't have anything to positively identify him yet."

"Alright, Dan," said the sheriff, taking a long draw on the cigar. "Keep on it and keep me posted."

"By the way, Sheriff," said Dan, pausing at the door "the courthouse is a smoke-free facility."

The sheriff just stared at him for a moment, then, under his breath he muttered, "Smartass."

Chapter 8

Dan Williams was finishing his report and thinking about going back to question Joey Berg further when Sandy Maki walked in and dropped into a chair. The expression on his face made it apparent that he hadn't made a breakthrough.

"What's up?"

Sandy slid further down in the chair and stared at the ceiling. "The Ostbergs, at the Pine Brook Inn, said that Joey Berg showed up late and raised some hell. Then he left. Terri hung around for sometime after, but we have some conflicting stories on just how long. Anyway, however long she stayed, she then apparently left with Jamie Arvidson. Rose Mahoney, the waitress from the Pine Brook Inn, says that Terri had been sleeping around. She and the owner both say that Terri and Jamie Arvidson left together sometime after Joey left. I think that we'd better roust Jamie Arvidson and get his story. Maybe Joey showed up at the farm while Jamie was still around and got the worst of it."

Dan shook his head. "Joey Berg's in a cell in back."

Sandy sat up like a shot. "No shit? He's alive? Then who's the guy in the bed?"

"My suspicion is that it's Jamie Arvidson," said Dan.

"Umm...well, that would fit," said Sandy. "Terri Berg was seen leaving with Arvidson. and her car is still setting in the Pine Brook Inn parking lot. Has Joey confessed?"

"No. His alibi is that he was supposedly passed out most of the night in his trailer. He *was* passed out when I got there and he doesn't remember a thing about most of the evening."

"You sweat him good on his alibi?"

"Not yet, I was just going to try him again, but I don't expect much. He didn't know that Terri was dead. I'm pretty sure of it."

"If he was drunk he could just not remember anything," said Sandy.

"It's possible," said Dan. "I'm not ruling him out just yet. I've got Joey's gun, and it's been fired recently, too."

"Holy shit! That would settle it. You put it in for ballistics?"

"Sure. But even if the ballistics match, all it proves is that the gun did the killing—not who used it. I got a gut feeling on this one."

Sandy's forehead furrowed in thought. He didn't like directly confronting his boss. But Sandy knew that one of the great limitations of an investigator was to make up his mind too early. A closed mind kills an investigation until someone new takes it over and looks at the facts with another set of eyes. "Everything does point to Joey" he ventured. "Except for his truck. His truck had a flat tire. It would have been very difficult to drive on it. How'd he get back to his place—Arvidson's truck? Was it at Joey's place?"

"There was no other vehicle at Joey's," said Dan.

"Well, then, if Joey did it, how would he get back? He could have hitched back, I suppose."

"That's possible. We'll check that out, too. But I don't think he did it, Sandy. He was there, in the trailer, all the time. He didn't need to get back."

"Then how did Joey's truck get to Terri Berg's place?"

"Somebody drove it there, of course."

"And just who might that be?" asked Sandy, with just a hint of exasperation.

"The killer, of course," Dan said, with a grin.

"Jesus, God!" said Sandy. "You mean somebody is trying to set Joey up for this? Just happened to drop by Joey's trailer, picked up Joey's gun and his pickup while he was passed out, drove it to the Berg place, committed the murder, and then left the truck there? Why would he do that?"

"Remember, the truck had a flat tire."

"He drove Arvidson's truck back, then?"

"Could have." Dan smiled appreciatively at the way Sandy sifted these possibilities through his head.

"What did the killer do with Arvidson's truck, then?"

"That's what we're gonna have to find out."

Sandy got up from the chair. "I gotta find Barb Dupre, the other waitress from the Pine Brook Inn. Everyone says that she lives here in town somewhere with a bruiser they just call Butch. She drives a red Camaro and has a tattoo that says "Property of Butch" on her crotch."

Dan grimaced. "A tattoo on her crotch? C'mon."

"That's what the other waitress, Rose, says. She claims to have seen it. I guess Barb does some exotic dancing and keeps it shaved so that all the men can see it. I hear Butch likes to watch."

Dan shook his head. "Just when you think that you've heard it all." He froze for a second. "Say...there's a red Camaro that's usually parked down at the new apartments, on the south end of town. It's there most days. Check it out. But I don't want a report that you personally inspected the tattoo."

Sandy gave him a shrug. "I'm single. Why not?"

Dan pointed to the door.

Joey Berg looked up when Dan walked up to the cell with Frank, the jailer. Frank picked a key and turned it in the lock.

"C'mon out, Joey. Let's talk some more."

Joey didn't move from the edge of the bed. He stared at the floor again. "I been thinking." He looked up at Dan. "The county's got to pay for a lawyer if I can't afford one, right?"

"You think you need a lawyer, Joey?"

The question was leading, and caught Joey off guard. "I...I don't know. I didn't do nothing. At least I can't remember."

"I'll get you one if you need one."

"Does that mean that I'm free to go?"

Dan looked at him. "Maybe. After a couple of questions. Have you had anything to eat yet?"

Joey shook his head. "Not for a couple of days. But I'm not sure my stomach would take food yet."

Dan nodded to the jailer, who quietly left. "C'mon, Joey. Frank's going to pick up something for you. Let's talk while we wait for your lunch."

While they sat in an interview room, with a tape recorder rolling, Joey reiterated the story about the encounter at the Pine Brook Inn and his going home, in his own truck. Frank delivered a tray with sandwiches wrapped in plastic. When they were done, Dan asked Archie, another one of the jailers, to give Joey a ride back to his trailer.

Joey stopped at the door. "Can I move back into the house? And when can I get my truck back?"

"Probably in a day or two. We've got to make sure that we've got all the evidence collected. You can't go back in the house for a while, though. It's sealed up as a crime scene."

Joey nodded. "Can I go now?"

"Yeah, but stay around town. If you decide to go to the Twin Cities, give me a call."

"I can't call. No phone." He gave Dan a doleful look. "Terri got everything in the divorce settlement."

Dan tapped a pencil on the table top. The revelation about the divorce settlement was a strong motive.

Chapter 9

S andy Maki cruised through the parking lot of the apartment building. It was half full on this late Sunday afternoon, and the red Camaro stood out like a ruby in a sea of diamonds. The vanity plate read, "PARTYGRL."

"How appropriate," thought Sandy. He called in the license plate. While he waited, he studied the brick three-story building. It was about five years old, making it one of the new structures in a town that hadn't grown too much.

The dispatcher confirmed the owner of the Camaro to be Barbara Dupre. The address matched the apartment complex and listed apartment number 7.

Sandy stopped briefly at the mailboxes in the lobby. The tag on number 7 had "Dupre/Mattson" written carelessly in blue pen. Sandy climbed the first flight of stairs and found a "7" at the first door on the right. He remembered a balcony that looked over the parking lot, and, as always, wondered what kind of reception he was about to receive.

He knocked hard and waited. When there wasn't a response after fifteen seconds, he pounded again. There was no sound from inside. A third try yielded a grunt, "What?" The male voice came from deep inside the apartment.

"Open up. Sheriff's department."

The door behind him cracked open. Sandy spun, reaching for the butt of his gun, only to see a weathered female face peeking around the edge of the door. Her hair was as white as the paint on the door. The door had a brass "8" nailed on it.

"They sleep late, officer. Barb works at a bar and sometimes she doesn't get in until three or four in the morning."

"Thanks ma'am. I think they're awake now."

The door to #7 opened viciously against the chain. It slammed shut again, then flew open wide. At the same time, the door to #8 closed just as quickly. The male face that greeted Sandy was a vision of the devil, with black hair, tousled and tied in a ponytail secured by a rubber band. The eyes were a piercing dark violet, and a black goatee pointed down to a massive chest forested with black, curly hair. His only clothing was a pair of boxer shorts.

"What the fuck do you want, man?"

"I need to talk with Barbara Dupre." Sandy peered over the man's shoulder into a living room cluttered with clothing and eating utensils.

"Go away. She's sleeping." The man was shorter than Sandy's six feet, but probably had forty pounds of additional muscle on his compact frame. His muscles were so well defined that Sandy immediately thought he was a body builder. The man tried to push the door shut, but Sandy jammed a foot between the door and door frame. Sandy hit the door with his shoulder, knocking the man back and throwing the door open.

The resident reeled back and then moved back toward the door with purpose. "Hey, man! You got a search warrant? If not, you're trespassing." The man suddenly dropped a shoulder and took a step at Sandy. In an almost automatic reaction, Sandy dropped aside, like a bullfighter, and pushed the man into the back of the door.

As the door slammed shut an apparition appeared at the bedroom door. She was pulling a short white silky robe closed over her naked body, the fabric so sheer that the outline of her breasts and nipples showed through. Sandy stared for an instant, then caught himself, but the woman seemed unfazed by his stare. She walked to a chair, threw some clothing to one side, and sat down, exposing her bare buttocks in the process.

The blow caught Sandy behind the left knee, and he crumpled. Sandy's momentary distraction had been just enough for Butch to regain his wits. He pounced on Sandy with the ferocity of a cornered raccoon, gouging eyes and kneeing for solid contact with Sandy's groin. Butch was an old bar fighter, and he knew no rules.

Sandy managed a short punch to the ribs that slowed Butch for a second. When he felt the momentum of a counter-punch coming, Sandy rolled and let the man's weight roll past him. Suddenly, Sandy was on top. He plunged two fingers into the man's throat while he reached for his aluminum 5-cell flash-light with his other hand. Butch was grabbing at the hand on his throat as the flashlight crashed into his head just above the right ear. Butch's eyes rolled back for an instant as his grip on Sandy's hand relaxed.

Adrenaline rushed through Sandy's body as he raised the flashlight for another blow, but reason swept over him before he made the swing and the flashlight dropped to the floor. He grabbed the man's right hand and pulled it down as the pupils of Butch's eyes rolled back into view. Sandy quickly rolled Butch onto his stomach, while pulling his arm firmly into a hammer lock. Butch gasped as Sandy clipped one end of the handcuffs to the muscular wrist. He realized that Butch's other hand had found the flashlight. Sandy grabbed the cuffed hand with both his hands and gave a tremendous push. Butch groaned in pain as the tendons in his shoulder and elbow ripped with an audible Pop, pop, pop. Butch let go of the flashlight.

Sandy grabbed the other hand and pulled it behind Butch's back, securing it with the second half of the handcuffs. Sandy let out a deep sigh, then suddenly remembered Barb. He looked up, expecting her to be gathering a gun or other imple-ment to strike him. Instead, she sat on the edge of the chair, with an expression of sheer amusement on her face.

Her voice was a hoarse whisper. "Why didn't you kill

him? I mean, like, it would have been justified." Her voice had a smoker's rasp and the words came slowly. She pointed a finger at Butch's prostrate figure on the floor. Sandy realized the finger was tattooed with a snake that ran from the tip to the wrist. When she extended the other fingers, he saw that each had its' own tattoo, a snake, a spear, an arrow, another snake and some type of phallic symbol.

Sandy pulled himself up and took inventory. His legs were shaky, and his shirt was badly torn. He wiped a hand across his face and came away with blood. He quickly identified a scratch along the right side of his nose. His thighs ached, but luckily Butch's knees hadn't struck home to his groin. Sandy bent down and picked up the flashlight, returning it to the loop on his belt.

"Hang on a second," the woman said, getting up from the chair and swaying into the kitchen. She returned with a washcloth and handed it to Sandy. "Ice Cubes. Sit down. Put 'em on your nose." Her voice was slow and metered.

Butch was squirming on the floor, trying to pull his knees under him. Sandy looked around for a place to sit down and decided on the spot where the woman had been sitting. He plopped down like there was no strength left in his legs.

Unable to get his knees under his body, Butch squirmed onto his side to get a look at Sandy. "You're a dead man, fucker. No one gets away with that shit in my house."

Butch pushed away from a steamer trunk that was being used as a coffee table, and tried to get up on his knees. Sandy planted a heel between Butch's shoulder blades and pushed. "Down boy."

Sandy looked at the woman. She was leaning against the door frame, her robe opened enough to expose the canyon between her silicone-enhanced breasts. Her face was hard, like she'd had a rough life. Sandy guessed her to be about twenty five.

"You wanted to see me?" The woman's voice was thick,

and the words came slowly, as if she was mildly retarded.

"Yeah. Did you see Terri Berg at the Pine Brook Inn last night?"

Barb's face turned to a pout. "Oh, that bumpkin. She was there with her usuals. Why? What has Terri done?" Again the words came slowly, like she was thinking about each one before speaking.

Sandy ignored the question. "Did you see her leave?"

Barb cocked her head to one side and thought. "I guess."

"Was she alone?"

Barb shook her head. The bleached platinum hair swung from side to side. Sandy thought that her hair was too light for her dark brown eyebrows and complexion and he wondered what her real hair color might be. Butch stirred on the floor again and Sandy again planted his foot on the man's back.

"Do you know the man she was with?"

"Yeah...at least I think so. She'd been hanging on a guy she called Jamie all night. When I went out to dump the garbage he had her pressed against the side of his pickup. Looked like he was licking her tonsils." She gave him a big smile with the attempted humor.

"Was she resisting?"

Barb laughed. "Jamming your hand down a guy's pants isn't resistance. I'd say it was more like encouragement."

"What kind of pickup did he have?"

She shrugged. "I'm not into trucks."

"Color?"

"Orange-like, maybe...or reddish."

"Were they still in the lot when you left?"

She thought hard. "I think so. They might have got into the truck. But it was still there."

"What time was that?"

The question made the woman obviously uncomfort-able. "A little before midnight. I got off early. Has Terry disappeard or something?"

Sandy ignored the question once more, noticing her discomfort.He thought of the other waitress's comments about Barb sneaking out early. "Do you know Joey Berg?"

She gave a snort. "Sure. Worthless as tits on a boar." Again, the big smile lit her face.

"Why'd you say that?"

"He's got no guts. He came around earlier to take her home and left with his tail between his legs. Any real man woulda beat the shit outta her...or the other guys. Joey left after Rosie hit him with a tray. Some man he is," she said, contemptuously.

"Was Joey around when you left?"

"I don't think so. There were a couple of cars in the lot when I left. Not his truck, though." She shook her head emphatically.

"I take it Terri was a regular at the Inn?"

The woman nodded. "Most weekend nights."

"I heard that she slept around. You got any names?" Sandy made notes in his notebook.

Barb Dupre shook her head again. "She hung around with the same group of older guys. I think that she and the Jamie guy were serious. The rest just seemed like friends."

Sandy got up and handed her the washcloth. She reached out for it and the robe slid open even wider, exposing cleavage to her navel. It didn't seem to bother her at all. He looked away.

Sandy looked down at Butch who had been watching the questioning with a malevolent glare. Sandy reached down and put a hand under Butch's biceps. "C'mon big boy. We're leaving now."

Butch rolled against Sandy's hand and stiffened his legs. "Bullshit. You gotta let me go, cop. Unlock the bracelets."

Sandy reached down and grabbed a wrist, lifting and putting pressure on the injured shoulder. "Last time I checked, assaulting an officer was a felony. You and I are going to visit the county jail. Monday, you can talk to a judge about it."

Butch pulled his knees up and struggled to get upright with his hands cuffed behind his back. He stood, pulling one leg up at a time. The boxer shorts that he'd been wearing had slipped around his hips. Sandy hiked up one side.

He looked at Barb. "Can you find him a shirt and pair of pants?"

She disappeared into the bedroom and came back with a pair of jeans and dirty T-shirt. She held them out to Sandy. "You haven't said what this is all about," she said.

"Can you help him get them on?" She shrugged and scrunched up the pants legs. On her knees, she pulled on one leg, then the other, as Sandy steadied Butch, and read him his rights. Barb took this all in with a perplexed look.

"What's this about? Has Butch done something offi- cer?" she asked, looking up at him from her position on the floor, a pout on her lips.

"We don't know, yet, maam. I'm taking him in and booking him. You can see about bailing him out tomorrow, at the courthouse." Sandy took the T-shirt and jammed it under Butch's arm.

Barb got up and shrugged. She pulled the edges of the robe together, and tugged at the hem. Butch glared at her. "You'd better bail me out."

She looked away and Sandy noticed the points of a star- burst tattoo reaching up the back of her neck from under the robe. "We'll see," she said, in a low voice.

Sandy gave Butch a push toward the door, and pulled on the knob. Butch was livid over Barb's lack of response. "Listen, bitch. You don't bail me tomorrow, you better be a hundred miles from here when I get out."

Sandy pushed Butch hard through the doorway and stopped at the top of the stairs. He stuck his head back in the door and stared at the woman's suddenly hollow face. "You gonna be okay? Can I get you some help?"

Barb crossed her arms, which effectively pushed her breasts out further and lifted the short robe almost above her crotch. Sandy strained not to look for the reported tattoo. She came to the door and leaned her head against the door frame. A whisper came from her lips, and Sandy leaned close to hear.

"He's a bastard. He deserves whatever he gets. Keep him locked up." She lifted her left arm and pulled up the short sleeve of the robe. In her armpit were a number of white circular scars and a single black circle with a bloody center. "He likes to use cigarette burns. Never where they show." She nodded toward Butch and shivered as she rolled down the sleeve. She closed the door silently and leaned against it, her eyes closed.

Outside the door, Sandy expelled his breath slowly as he eyed Butch with venom. Pushing him forward to the head of the stairs, he placed his hand in the small of Butch's back and pushed. There was a loud clatter as Butch fell down the steps.

Stephanie Olsen was on duty as jailer when Sandy delivered Butch. She looked Butch over carefully, and then looked at Sandy. Butch's nose was pushed to one side and a trickle of blood had dried on his upper lip. Bruises marked his bare shoulders and arms. The scrape on Sandy's nose had started to bruise, and his badge hung on a torn piece of uniform shirt. Stephanie gave Sandy a knowing look.

Stephanie pulled out a booking form. "Name?"

Butch pressed himself toward the jailer. "Hey, you. I want a lawyer. This guy beat the shit outta me with my hands cuffed."

Stephanie smirked. "Looks like you got a couple of licks in, too." She stared for a second at the Harley tattoo on Butch's upper arm. It was old and faded. An amateur job at best.

Butch shook his head. "Fucking cops. All the same fraternity. Let's get it over with...Alexander Hamilton."

Stephanie started to write, then paused. "He's on a ten dollar bill. Want to try another?"

Butch shook his head. The jailer looked at Sandy.

"His girlfriend just called him Butch,and the mailbox says Mattson" Sandy contributed.

"Listen, Butch," said Stephanie, "I assume that you don't want to give me your real name because you got a record as long as my arm." Butch tried to hide a grin from the jailer. "But you're gonna sit here until I get your real name. Either you give it to me, or we run your prints and you sit until I get an I.D. What's it gonna be?"

Butch gave the jailer a mocking look. "What? My momma named me after a president. Why do I have to put up with your shit? Just write the name down."

Stephanie looked down and wrote, "John Doe." She looked at Sandy. "What's the charge?"

"Assaulting an officer and domestic assault."

Butch sneered. "Give it up, cop. She ain't ever gonna testify against me."

Sandy slapped Butch's bare shoulder and then pinched the pressure point at the intersection of his neck and shoulder. Butch grimaced, but refused to cry out. "Well, tough guy, I happened to see the burns under her arm, and in this state I can testify. She doesn't have to. It's the shits, isn't it?"

Sandy released the grip and Butch rolled his head to loosen the muscles that had begun to cramp. "Fucker. You're gonna be sorry." The oath came through Butch's teeth like venom.

The jailer got up and nodded to a door behind her. "C'mon," she said, and led Butch through the door. Inside the room she pulled out a stamp pad and a fingerprint card. Sandy pushed Butch against the counter and released the cuffs from one hand while he pinned the other arm behind the man's back. Butch's eyes rolled in pain as the torn shoulder and elbow were torqued. The jailer quickly rolled each finger on the pad, and then on the card.

Sandy pulled the first hand back and released the other. The jailer repeated the procedure. Just as quickly, Sandy had the sore arm locked behind Butch's back and the handcuffs reattached. They walked down the narrow corridor of cells. The jailer picked a key and unlocked an empty cell. Butch was pushed in and the door slammed behind him with a clang. Butch backed up to the door so Sandy could release the cuffs through a narrow opening, then Butch stood rubbing the injured shoulder.

Stephanie and Sandy walked back up the corridor. At the end the jailer pulled out a key ring and opened the door. She stood on the other side for a second and looked at Sandy. "You better go to the emergency room and have someone look at your nose."

"It's just a scratch. No big deal."

"I'd have a hepatitis test and AIDS test done, and then ask the judge for a court order to have him tested too," said Stephanie, pointing a thumb at the door they'd just passed through.

Sandy tried to laugh it off, but a look of concern showed in his eyes. "Maybe you're right, Steph. I'll go see Dan first. Run those prints quick. I'd like to know who he really is."

Dan was talking on the phone when Sandy knocked on the door frame. He waved Sandy to a chair. As the conversation went on, Sandy surveyed the chief investigator's office. There were only two visitor's chairs and both looked like they had been survivors from World War II. The gray paint was chipped and scratched, and the vinyl was worn through on the corners. What could be seen of the desk matched the chairs. Rumor was that the sheriff had offered Dan the job before the old undersheriff resigned. They pulled this furniture out of storage and Dan had never intended to spend enough time in the office to both-er moving to the larger office to which he was entitled.

It was also apparent that Dan was not into filing paper-work. Every flat surface was occupied by a stack of papers. In preparation for several cases, the clerk of court had to come to Dan's office and dig through piles to find the sheriff's depart-ment's official file on a pending case. Dan didn't appear to care. Sandy had overheard Dan's part of a conversation between Dan and the clerk: "You don't solve crimes with your butt in a chair." Dan Williams had lived up to that credo.

Dan finished the phone conversation. "Yeah, right. We want to find the pervert that killed a couple and shot the woman after she was dead. One of our deputies found a condom wrap-per on the floor, but no used condom. See if you can find any rapists with that type of criminal history. Maybe someone that's been getting increasingly violent."

Dan listened for a few seconds, nodding at times. "Right. We'll look locally, too. Thanks."

Dan hung up and looked at Sandy. "What in hell hap-pened to you?"

"The second waitress's boyfriend didn't want me to talk to her. I had to persuade him a little."

Dan pushed back from the desk and crossed his legs. "He look worse?"

Sandy shook his head. "He actually looked pretty good until he fell down the stairs."

Dan grimaced. "An accident, I assume."

"Mostly. Feet got tangled. Had the cuffs on and didn't have a chance to catch himself before his face hit the steps."

Dan got up and closed the door. Sandy sank in his chair, knowing what was coming. When Dan sat down he leaned far over the desk and spoke in a very soft voice. "Sandy, you've been around long enough to know that we can't do shit like that. We gotta bring'em in and turn'em over to the courts." Dan leaned back. "Understood?"

Sandy nodded. "Yeah, I know. He's an abuser. Couldn't help myself. This guy looks like a biker and he wouldn't give his name to the jailer when I booked him. I suspect that he's either got some outstanding warrants that he thinks we won't find, or he's in violation of his parole. He's got a homemade Harley Davidson tattoo on one arm that looks like something that was done in a jailhouse somewhere."

Dan pondered that revelation and said, "Do you think that he has something to do with the murders?"

Sandy shrugged. "He looks tough enough. But I don't see what he'd have for a motive unless Terri Berg and her buddies were into drugs. As far as I could see it looked like Terri could barely afford beer unless someone else was buying."

Sandy was about to speak when there was a quick knock and the door opened. The sheriff stuck his head around the corner. Sandy and Dan both stared. It was unheard of to see the sheriff in the office on a Sunday afternoon. Something big was up. "Sorry to interrupt, Sandy. Dan and I have to talk." He added emphatically, "Right now."

Sandy was glad to escape any further ass-chewing and hurried out the door. His parting words were, "I'm going to the emergency room for a blood test. Can you have Floyd and Pam check Jamie Arvidson, Bill Patterson, and Russ Lemke? They were the other people with Terri Berg at the Pine Brook Inn last night."

"Sure. Get a good checkup." Dan scribbled a note on a yellow legal pad.

As soon as Sandy had cleared the door, the sheriff had it closed. He sat down in one of the chairs and motioned for Dan to sit. "The shit hit the fan over Doc Peterson. He's been on the horn to every county board member and to the president of the state medical association. I've had three calls asking for information and two asking...demanding...your resignation."

"And..."

"So far, I've been able to keep the wolves at bay. I've

danced every diplomatic dance I know. The board is having a hearing next week, Thursday. They want to know what happened at Berg's and why you should be kept on."

Dan's face turned to flame. "Why I should be kept on? Why Peterson shouldn't be tarred and feathered is more like it." Dan got up from his chair and started to pace. "Hell, he should have his license to practice medicine pulled. What an ass. He's covering his butt by throwing mud at me. Shit!"

"Take it easy, Dan. It'll probably blow over. We'll smooth Doc's ruffled feathers. But, you've got to get in front of the board and make nice. Be professional and maybe admit you were wrong."

Dan slammed his fist against the desktop. "Damn it, John. I wasn't wrong. I can bring in the ME and a dozen law enforcement people to say I was exactly right. Doc Peterson was wrong, and he almost screwed up a murder investigation. I want him called on the carpet." Dan set his palms flat on the desktop. "He needs to be burned. If you can't see that, I'm the wrong man to have on the team."

Sepanen put up his hands. "Take it easy, Dan. He's been the coronor for a long time. We can get through this with very little blood on anybody's hands. Just play along with me. Let's go to the hearing and see how it flows. Okay?"

"I want to have Oresek there. He's the one who knows how badly Peterson screwed up. If we end up in a pissing match, I want someone to back me up. Agreed?"

Sepanen ran a hand through his salt and pepper hair. "Okay, but, only as a reserve. I don't want to go in with guns blazing."

The sheriff got up and opened the door. He hesitated for a second as he made an obvious scan of the piles. "You'd better get these cleaned up. It looks like hell in here." Sepanen slipped out the door.

To the sheriff's back Dan yelled, "When you stop smoking, I'll clean up my files.

* * *

Floyd Swenson was watching Pam write a speeding ticket when Dan called on the radio requesting a phone call. Pam looked all business as she leaned toward the driver's window and watched the young man sign the ticket. When she returned to the car he punched Dan's office number into the cellular phone.

"What's up?"

"Sandy got banged up a little. I need you two to interview Jamie Arvidson and Bill Patterson. I'll talk to Russ Lemke. They were with Terri Berg last night." Dan read off the Arvidson and Patterson addresses to Floyd.

Pine County was over two hundred square miles of farms and small towns. The Pattersons and Arvidsons lived at the opposite corners of the county. It would take the rest of the shift just to travel to the two houses.

Floyd finished writing. "I've got the addresses. You said that Sandy got banged up. Was he in a car accident?"

Dan sighed. "No. He got into a fight with the Pine Brook Inn waitress's boyfriend when he went to interview her."

"Was he hurt badly?' Floyd's voice sounded concerned.

"Just some scrapes and a torn uniform shirt. He'll be fine."

Floyd punched the "Clear" button and set the handset down. "We gotta question some suspects," Floyd told Pam. He wrote the names on a message slip. "Drive out toward Munch township. Bill Patterson lives on a farm out there with his mother. We're going to talk with the last people that saw Terri Berg alive.

Chapter 10

B ill Patterson lived with his mother on a farm southeast of Pine City. Floyd had bowled with Bill, and had been to the house a few times. As Pam Ryan drove down the gravel back-roads, they passed fields with corn that was higher than the hood of the squad car and a few pastures with cattle that looked up as the car went by. A black angus cow was mooing at her calf who had slipped under the electric fence. Pam stopped the car and shooed the calf out of the ditch and back to its mother while Floyd held the fence up with a piece of wood.

Floyd recognized the weathered, green siding on Patterson's two-story house and told Pam where to turn into the half-mile long driveway. The first crop of hay was just ready for cutting on either side of the narrow, rutted driveway. Three blue Harvestore silos were an indicator that Bill Patterson was a prosperous farmer. The silos provided silage for his hundred guernsey cattle.

A large garage door was open on the metal-sided garage, and Bill Patterson was wiping his hands on a greasy rag as the squad car pulled to a stop. He stepped away from an antique Ford tractor and gave a small wave to Floyd. Floyd waved in return.

"Hi, Bill. How's life?"

Bill looked at his hands. Despite the wipe, they were still black. He didn't offer a hand for a shake. "Pretty good. What's the law doing in this part of the country?"

Floyd walked up to the garage and looked at the old Ford tractor. The fuel pump was in pieces on top of an overturned five-gallon bucket. "Just checking on a few things, Bill. How are things?"

Pam Ryan watched the exchange with consternation. This was about as far away from textbook questioning as it could get. She wondered if this was typical. If it was, she hadn't been properly prepared by her law enforcement classes.

"I hear you were out at the Pine Brook Inn last night." Floyd pulled out a little Swiss Army knife and removed the plastic toothpick. He inserted it between the back teeth on the left side of his mouth. He worked it around, waiting for Bill's response.

"Yeah. Had a few beers with the guys. Why you asking?"

Floyd pulled the toothpick out of his mouth and inspected the tip before slipping it back into the red handle of the knife. "Terri Berg with the guys, too?"

Bill's face grew into a wide smile. "Sure was." It was obvious that he was proud to be considered one of her companions. He jammed the rag into the back pocket of his dirty overalls and wiped his hands across his broad belly, leaving gray streaks across the blue denim fabric.

"What time did Terri leave?"

Bill's eyes lit up. "Oh, I get it. This is about Joey, isn't it?" When he didn't get a response from Floyd he went on. "Rose cracked him on the head, but he had it coming. He was mouthing off real bad. He deserved all he got. Is Joey suing?"

Floyd shook his head. "Not that I know of. What time did Terri leave?"

Bill shrugged. "About midnight. Before they closed up. We all left together."

"Who was in the group that left with you?"

Bill hesitated and then counted off the party on his fingers. "Well, it was me, and Terri, and Jamie, and Russ."

"Anyone else?"

Bill took a deep breath and thought hard. "There was a few other folks around. The blonde waitress, Barb, was there. One or two couples at the next tables, maybe, but I didn't know them." He shrugged. "That's about all. Why?"

The house door slammed and a woman who looked to be in her sixties walked across the yard to where they were standing. She was almost as large as Bill, and had the same round facial features. They all watched her approach.

Before she got to the group, Floyd spoke in a low voice. "We found Terri dead this morning."

Bill Patterson's face blanched almost white. He stared at Floyd for a moment, trying to comprehend. "Terri? Dead? How? But...?"

Floyd shrugged, not yet wanting to reveal that Teri had been murdered. "Don't know yet. We're trying to follow up on a number of leads."

The woman stopped next to Pam. "Hi, Floyd," she said. "I've got coffee on. Why don't you come on in?" Mrs. Patterson saw the streaks of tears cutting Bill's fleshy face. "Oh dear, what's the matter, Billy?"

Pam reached out, took the old woman by the elbow, and turned her toward the house. "My name is Pam Ryan, Mrs. Patterson, and I'd love a cup of coffee. Have you got cream?" Bill's mother kept peeking over her shoulder at Bill as Pam kept her walking toward the house. The concern was written strongly on her face, but Pam kept a hand on her elbow.

Bill sniffed several times and fished the rag from his pocket. He blew his nose in it and wiped away his tears, smearing grease across his face in the process. Bill sobbed. "Oh Lord, help her. Then help us all."

Floyd put a hand on Bill's shoulder to steady him. "Do you remember who she left with, Bill?"

The question finally got through. "Ah, Jamie. But he wouldn't hurt her. He loved her, too." Bill froze. His biggest secret had leaked out. He'd never admitted to anyone that he loved Terri Berg.

Floyd let it slip by. "You're sure she left with Jamie Arvidson?"

"Yeah. They were kissing in the parking lot when I left," said Bill, with just a hint of resentment in his voice. "I didn't actually see them go. But I'm pretty sure that he went home with her. He has a roommate and they try not to bring girls to their place." Bill took a deep breath and blew it out. "What'd she die of?"

Floyd shook his head. "The medical examiner hasn't done an autopsy yet."

"So, it was like too much alcohol, or a car accident, or something? She didn't do drugs. She told me that."

Floyd shook his head. He had assessed Bill Patterson. "Worse than that, Bill. Someone shot and killed her last night."

"Shot her?" he gasped. "Someone shot Terry? "Oh God, Floyd. Who'd do a thing like that. Terri was...great. To everyone."

"I know, Bill. I know." Floyd threw his arm around the big man's shoulders and could feel them shaking as he shuddered with sobs.

As they drove from the Patterson's, Pam seemed uneasy. "Do you always question people like that?"

"Like what?"

She adjusted the shoulder harness on her seatbelt. "So easy. It was like you were friends."

A smile creased Floyd's weathered face. "Bill *is* a friend."

"So that's not how you do all of them?"

"I don't see any point in terrorizing quiet people. I talk to them quietly. If I get a jerk that's full of venom, I spit it right back in his face as fast as he can dish it out." He paused and thought about the right words. "The whole secret of being a good investigator is being flexible. Fit yourself to the surroundings and the situation. Try to read the person that you're questioning and go fast or slow, depending. Push hard or back off. Give them lots of time to think about answers and if they don't have an answer, wait. Quiet makes people uncomfortable and a long dose of quiet makes some people blurt out something that they don't want to say. Listen carefully and ask the same question a couple of times. If you get different answers, get suspicious."

Pam stared out the window as they passed field after field of oats and corn. "So, you think Bill Patterson would have clammed up if you'd pushed him?"

"Maybe. I can bet that he wouldn't have told me that he loved her if I'd pushed."

Pam turned and stared. "He told you that he loved her? But he's..."

"Hey Pam, middle-aged people fall in love too."

Pam opened her mouth to recant her comment, then stopped. Instead, she asked, "Do you think that he had anything to do with the murders?"

Floyd hesitated for a second. "Not a chance. He loved her, but he isn't capable of a crime of passion. It just about killed him when he heard that she was dead."

Jamie Arvidson shared a newer house on a few wooded acres near Mora. There was a man splitting wood in the yard as Floyd and Pam pulled into the driveway. The sweat glistened on his muscular torso.

"What a hunk." Pam unbuckled her seatbelt and eased out the door. "I'll question him." She gave Floyd a grin that formed dimples in her cheeks. The dimples disappeared when she heard Floyd.

"He's an idiot."

Floyd's comment froze her. "You know him?"

"Don't have to. Anybody that splits wood in the summer heat is stupid."

Pam rolled her eyes, then got out and walked across the yard to where the man was leaning on the axe. "Hi! Are you Jamie?"

The man gave her a smile that exposed a dozen crooked teeth. "He's not around right now."

When do you expect himn back?

The man swung the ax, burying the head into the chopping block. He picked up a blue checked shirt off the pile of wood and wiped his face with it. "We're pretty loose. I don't keep tabs on him. I haven't seen him this weekend at all."

"Have you been around the house?"

"His truck wasn't here when I got home about two. It wasn't here when I got up about noon."

Pam pulled out a notebook and started to make notes. "No idea where he is?"

"Like I said, we each go our own way. He hangs out at the Pine Brook Inn, sometimes. Is he in some kind of trouble?"

Pam stole a glance at the "six-pack" muscles that rippled the man's abdomen. "Terri Berg was murdered last night, and he was the last person seen with her."

A look of surprise crossed the man's face. "Wow! That's bad." The man wiped his face with the shirt again.

"Have Jamie give the sheriff's department a call when he gets back, okay." Pam pulled a business card from her pocket and handed it to the man.

The man nodded. "Ah, sure."

Floyd had been standing behind Pam. When she turned, she almost ran into him. They walked back to the car in silence.

"How'd I do?" she asked as she buckled up in the passenger's seat.

"You gave him too much. Remember, you are asking the questions. There's no rule that says you have to tell the person you're questioning anything. Stay in control. Ignore their questions and forge ahead. By giving them answers you're giving them hints. You want their undirected input, not what they think you want to hear."

Pam shrunk in the seat. "I screwed up that badly?"

Floyd cracked a smile. "It wasn't bad. It just wasn't...polished. What was that guy's name?"

"Oh shit. I didn't even get it." She reached for the door handle, then stopped. "Say, what if the dead man in Terri's house was Jamie? Shouldn't we find that out first?"

"It'll get sorted out. Remember, no preconceived notions. Open mind all the time. Let the evidence lead you to conclusions. The worst mistake you can make is to form conclusions and search for evidence to support them."

Dan Williams pulled up next to Russ Lemke's farmhouse behind a new Oldsmobile Aurora in the driveway. The sleek automobile sat in stark contrast to the hundred year old house with clapboard siding. But the house was freshly painted and the lawn was neatly groomed. Dan knocked on the door and heard a chair scraping on a wooden floor inside.

Russ Lemke opened the door and looked at Dan through the storm-door screen. Russ was dressed in an outfit that could only be described as urban cowboy, a crisp plaid shirt, with mother-of-pearl snaps, Lee jeans, and a pair of Ostrich-skin boots. The silver buckle on his belt, which was covered with turquoise, was the size of an abalone. All this was hung on a frame that was less than five-two and weighed less than one hundred ten pounds. The lines in his face indicated that Russ was probably close to forty, although the outfit made him seem much younger. Dan noted that the required ten-gallon hat was hanging on a peg behind the door. Dan's immediate thought was that Russ was too small to have created the carnage at Terri Berg's house.

"Are you Russ Lemke?" Dan asked.

"Sure am," Russ answered. "What can I do for you, sheriff?"

"Russ, I'm Dan Williams, from the Pine County sheriff's department. I'd like to ask you a few questions." Dan held his gold badge up to the screen.

Russ's face lit up with recognition at the mention of Dan's name. "Sure, I know you. I voted for you in the last election." He swung the screen door wide and gestured for Dan to enter.

"Well, I'm afraid you're mistaken," said Dan "I didn't run in the election."

Lemke pulled the door shut and led Dan down the hall past an oak staircase that had been recently refinished and coated in a glossy urethane that gave it the appearance of being wet.

"Oh, I cast my vote for Sepanen. But it was you that I voted for," Lemke said over his shoulder as he led Dan to the kitchen.

They walked into a big farm kitchen that was bright and decorated like something from Better Homes and Gardens. All the woodwork had been refinished, matching the staircase finish. The floor was white ceramic tile and a huge maple butcher block graced the center of the room. While Dan sat at the table Russ walked to the cupboard and pulled down a coffee grinder and a bag of coffee beans. He dumped a handful of beans into the grinder. It made a horrendous grinding noise.

The countertops were lined with electric appliances—Kenmore blender, Cuisinart food processor, Krup's coffee maker, a toaster oven and a Cuisinart mixer. A set of porcelain canisters sat in the corner. There wasn't a sign of dirty dishes or clutter anywhere. Dan wondered if Russ had a wife or a maid that kept things so tidy. In his experience, most men didn't bother keeping things quite this clean.

"What can I do for you, Dan? You didn't come out for coffee and conversation." Russ took down a box of coffee filters and slipped one out of the box and into the machine. He measured the coffee grounds into the filter and flipped the switch. The smell of freshly ground coffee permeated the kitchen with a lovely aroma.

"I understand that you were with Terri Berg at the Pine Brook Inn last night."

Russ poured water into the coffee machine, then sat in the Scandinavian-inspired chair across from Dan.

"It was a wild night." The smile that crossed his face, quickly turned to a frown. "Something wrong?"

"What time did you leave the Pine Brook Inn, Russ?"

The color left Russ's face and he twisted in his chair nervously. "Oh, I don't know. Maybe one. Why do you ask?"

"Did you leave alone."

"Yes, I...um." He hesitated, then spoke confidently. "Yes."

Dan stared at him a few seconds, waiting for a change in the story. "Then you came right home?"

Russ nodded. The coffee pot sputtered, announcing that the coffee was ready. Russ slid out of the chair and went to the cupboard. He pulled down two matching mugs and poured the hot black liquid into them. Dan noted that every dish in the cupboard matched. In a county where the average annual income was a hair's breadth over the poverty level, Russ Lemke's was evidently a cut above. Lemke set the mugs on a tray and opened another cupboard. He took down a sugar bowl and a creamer. He took the creamer to the refrigerator and poured Half-and-Half into it. He dropped two teaspoons onto the tray and delivered it to the table. He did all of this rather slowly, as if trying to gain enough time to collect his thoughts.

Russ stirred some cream into his coffee. He stared into the cup, deliberately not looking Dan in the eye. "Yeah, I came right home. Went to bed...alone."

Dan drank the coffee black. It was deliciously thick and rich with a hint of chocolate and almond. "Who'd Terri leave with?"

Russ looked up nervously. "Jamie. Jamie Arvidson. Why? What happened?"

Dan ignored the question. "You came directly home alone? Anyone to corroborate that?"

Russ stared at him intensely. "You say that like I need an alibi."

"You say that like you have a guilty conscience." Dan took another drink of coffee and watched Russ over the rim of the cup. Russ's body language said that there was something else that wasn't being said.

Russ stared down into the coffee cup. "No, my conscience is clear."

Dan sat quietly, letting the silence work for him. Russ nervously stirred some sugar into his coffee. "Umm...I don't want to say anymore. I think that you'd better leave now."

Dan didn't move. "You didn't leave alone, did you?"

Russ pushed back from the table. "I don't have to talk to you. I haven't broken any laws."

Dan drained his coffee and set the cup down. "But you're not being entirely honest with me, either, are you?"

Russ scowled. "Maybe if you told me what you were fishing for, I'd be able to help."

"Terri Berg died last night."

Lemke's face froze in surprise and shock. His mouth fell open and he stared in disbelief. "Terri's dead?" he croaked, visibly shuddering as he struggled to get his cup back to the table without spilling.

Dan nodded.

"How?...Why?"

Dan shook his head. "We don't know a lot right now."

"Have you talked to Jamie? I s'pose he'd be most likely to know something."

"You were with someone last night. After you left the bar. Who?"

Russ rubbed the tip of his nose. "Ah...I can't say."

"Why not? "

Russ scratched his head, leaving his thinning hair ruffled. "I...she...can't let it get out."

"Someone married?"

Russ bobbed his head. "I can't be responsible for breaking the news to her husband." His voice cracked under the stress.

"I won't even need to talk to her if everything checks out. But if this drags on, I may need to see if she knows something that hasn't come out. Who is it?"

"Ester Mujawski. She's married to Ed. He's the owner of the welding shop where I work. If this gets out I lose my job"

Dan nodded and got up from the chair, pushing it back against the table.

"Did you meet her at the Pine Brook Inn, or did she come here?"

Lemke got up and followed Dan into the living room. "She drove over after Ed fell asleep. Ed snores so they sleep in separate bedrooms. She went home about four."

Russ struggled to maintain his composure. "What happened to Terri?" he asked in a subdued voice.

"We're not sure of the cause of death." Dan stopped at the front door.

Russ stumbled along behind. "What are we talking here? Car accident? We'd all been drinking pretty heavy."

Dan opened the inner door and the heat rushed into the air conditioned entryway. "Terri was murdered. Probably beaten to death."

Russ froze. "Murdered? My God! who...," then, his eyes welled with tears. "Oh, God. It was Joey, wasn't it. That son-of-a-bitch. Not her pretty face." He turned and walked away, disappearing into his bedroom, closing the door behind him.

Dan stood for a moment, looking at the door. He should ask Lemke about Jamie, but Russ and Ester had probably left before the others anyway. He decided to leave it for the time being. Dan left the house, got into the squad and headed back to his office. It was getting late.

At 5:30 p.m. Dan was sitting in his office writing notes about his interview with Russ Lemke. Sandy Maki popped in, wearing a fresh uniform shirt. A small bandage covered the scrape on his nose.

"I rousted a couple of the usual suspects," he stated as he eased down in one of the two chairs in Dan's office and pulled out a small notebook. "Todd Brockman was working the midnight shift at the paper mill in Cloquet. I checked with his boss and he's clean. Jack Popham was home with his girlfriend. She agrees, but if we keep coming up empty, we may want to go back to him again. Bill Anderson wasn't home. His mother says that he's an over-the-road trucker with a load heading for Winnipeg. He left the Twin Cities Friday morning. I checked with the carrier and Anderson called in from Winnipeg to get a return load yesterday afternoon."

Dan nodded. "We may want to check Bill again, too. There are phones everywhere, and it's easy to say that you're in Winnipeg. Let's wait until we see what the ME has to say."

Floyd Swenson cruised into Dan's small office, with Pam Ryan in tow. Floyd settled into the other guest chair, leaving Pam leaning against the door frame.

"No chivalry in this department." Her tone of voice made them wonder if she might actually be serious.

Floyd pulled out his Swiss Army knife and cleaned a fingernail. "I thought you just wanted to be one of the guys?"

"I do. Unless I get some advantage being a girl," she said, showing her dimples.

Dan rolled his eyes. "Before you two generate a harassment lawsuit, what'd you find out?"

Sandy glanced at Floyd who nodded slightly. "The gun on Terri Berg's bed wasn't the murder weapon," she said. "There has to be another gun somewhere that killed John Doe."

Dan instantly thought about Joey's rifle. "Whoa! What makes you think that?" he asked.

Floyd interjected. "I was packing the gun up after we took the fingerprints. I looked at the barrel stamping and it's a .308 Winchester. The shell casings are all 30-06."

The news sank in quickly. Dan shook his head. "We know now that Joey isn't the cadaver. I just pulled Joey in for questioning and got a 30-06 Remington automatic out of his trailer. It still had a live shell in the chamber and it smelled like it had been fired recently. I'm having the ballistics tested against any bullets that we recovered from Terri Berg's house. I've already questioned Joey and let him go, but we may have to pick him up again, now."

The news that Joey Berg wasn't the dead man set their thoughts to churning. "If the male victim wasn't Joey, then who was it?" asked Pam, then she answered herself. "Jamie Arvidson is unaccounted for. You suppose he's John Doe?"

Dan nodded. "Sounds like he was the last one with her last night. I expect the ME will nail that down, though. In the meantime, I don't think Joey Berg did this, even if his gun turns out to be the murder weapon. I've sweated his alibi and he's either the best actor I've ever seen or he's innocent."

The deputies all glanced at one another. Sandy quickly said, "Dan and I have talked about this earlier. Terri left with Jamie in his truck, according to one of the waitresses. Terri's car was still at the Inn when I checked. Joey's truck had a flat tire. Arvidson's truck is missing. It's possible that someone took Joey's truck and gun and used them to commit the murders. We think the killer drove Arvidson's truck back to Joey's place and planted his gun."

"But where is Arvidson's truck?" asked Pam. "The

killer would have to have hidden it somewhere."

"You're right, Pam," said Dan. He looked at Sandy. "We need to do a wider search of Joey's place tomorrow. We need to find Arvidson's truck, if it's there."

Sandy nodded. "I'm on it."

"Anything else to report before we go home?" asked Dan.

Pam pulled out a notebook. "Looks like Bill Patterson was home all night with his mother after he left the Inn, and we couldn't locate Jamie Arvidson, probably for a good reason."

"Did you get the prints from the house sent to the NCIC?"

"Yeah. We put them on the wire, and sent the hair and fibers to the state lab for analysis. We got a couple of nice prints off the gun and the shells. But according to the M.E., there's one more bullet wound than spent cartridges. Maybe Oresek didn't get the count right before autopsy, or maybe the killer carried one off and thought we wouldn't count."

"Or, maybe there's one under something." Dan said, leaning forward.

Floyd finished cleaning his last fingernail. "We looked under the bed and all the furniture." He closed the knife and put it back in his pocket.

"Tomorrow, go back and check the couch cushions and chairs," Dan said. Turning to Pam, he went on, "The gun was a Remington automatic, and the spent cartridges fly a long way sometimes."

Floyd nodded agreement. "We dug one of the bullets out of the floor, under the female body. We'll send it on to the state lab tomorrow."

Dan leaned back in his chair and laced his fingers, staring at them. "Looks like what we need to do now is wait. We need to know for sure who John Doe is, but let's assume that it is Jamie Arvidson, for now. We need the results from the NCIC on the prints. Floyd and Pam, you'll go back and look for the

other casing tomorrow and catch the postmortem. I'll find out
what type of vehicle Jamie Arvidson drives and we'll put out a
statewide bulletin. Anything else?"

"How about the Bureau of Criminal Apprehension?"
Floyd asked as he leaned forward in his chair. "We should have
them run their database of known sex offenders, see if anyone
has a similar M.O."

Dan said, "Done. I called the BCA this morning.
They're checking, but they suggested rousting the local sex
offenders...which Sandy has done. Nothing promising on the
locals. Right, Sandy?"

Sandy nodded. "Doesn't look promising. But don't forget the waitress's boyfriend.

Pam gave Sandy an inquisitive look. "What's with the
boyfriend?"

Sandy turned so she could see the bandage on his nose.
"He didn't want me to interview his girlfriend. We had to wres-
tle over it...he lost. I booked him on assaulting an officer and
domestic assault."

Dan pointed a pencil at Sandy. "Any word on his identity yet?"

Sandy shook his head. "We're running his prints. No
response yet. We still don't have a name on him, either. "

"Right. I want a written report from everyone tomorrow
morning. Let's meet again tomorrow afternoon at 4:30." Dan
stood up, signaling the end to the meeting.

When Dan pulled into his driveway Sunday evening he
could see Sally moving around the kitchen. He popped two
Tums into his mouth to counteract the effects of the acid that
was drizzling into his stomach from the stress of the day. He
trudged heavily across the lawn like he had been beaten.
Between the murders and the confrontation with Doc Peterson,
the day had literally sucked him dry.

Sally met him at the door with a Michelob. "Bad day?" She pecked him on the cheek and handed him the beer.

Dan took off his shoes and set them on the mat next to the door. "Not the worst ever, but darned close to it." He took a long draw on the beer and settled into a chair at the kitchen table.

Sally had already set places with plates and silverware. She returned from the stove with a kettle that gave off a heavenly smell. She set it on a metal trivet and pushed a serving spoon into the chicken stew.

"I heard that there was a murder down by Henriette." Sally dished up a scoop of stew for herself and held the spoon out for Dan.

"Where did you hear that?" Dan poured three scoops of stew onto his plate and took a slice of bread from the bag.

Sally stirred her stew around without eating any. "I stopped by the hospital. I heard that Doctor Peterson was called out as the coroner and that you threatened him."

Dan stopped with a fork halfway to his mouth. "Word travels fast in this town. What else did the gossips have to say?"

"They said that the murder scene was so grisly that Sandy threw up on the steps." Sally watched Dan's face for a sign that he had been affected by the carnage. After twenty-three years of marriage she had become adept at reading his face.

Dan made a slight grimace and tried not to show how deeply the sights had moved him. "Sandy throws up when he cuts a finger."

"Uh huh. And you're never affected because you're such a macho tough guy."

Dan took another draw on the beer bottle. "You know that you can be a real pain in the ass?"

Sally smiled. "I'm your conscience. Now talk about it before you have nightmares and keep me awake all night." She pushed the plate aside and waited.

"Terri Berg was beaten and shot. It looked like her male companion had committed suicide. At least that was the conclusion that Doc Peterson came to. Tony Oresek took the time to actually check the body temperatures and found out that the guy had died before Terri."

Sally nodded. "So it couldn't have been a suicide. Who was the guy? Her ex-husband? I heard that they sometimes had some real knock-down-drag-outs when Joey had been drinking."

Dan shrugged. "No, Joey Berg is very much alive. That was the other grisly part. Let's say that we couldn't recognize him by his face."

"Yuck!" Sally scrunched up her face.

Dan tipped the beer bottle to her. "Wish I didn't have to see it, either. It isn't a topic for polite company."

Sally got up and moved to Dan's side, pushed his chair back from the table, and sat on his lap. She pulled the hair back from his forehead and kissed it gently. "I'm sorry. No one should have to see the things that you do."

Dan stared straight ahead. "No one should do that kind of thing to another human being. It makes us no better than animals." He turned and kissed Sally gently. "I don't think that there are any animals that do that to each other. The person that did that is worse than an animal. Whoever did this is a monster. The devil himself."

DAY

TWO

MONDAY

Chapter 11

The Monday Morning editions of the *Minneapolis Star Tribune* and the *St. Paul Pioneer Press* had front page articles about the grisly murder/suicide in rural Pine County. They had quotes from the Pine County Coroner about the severity of the attack and hints at police incompetence. Reading carefully, he found no mention of a double murder, murder suspects, or evidence left at the crime scene.

He had been very careful to remove all traces of his presence. He had wiped the spent cartridges clean. After removing his own fingerprints, he had pressed the man's fingers to the gun he had found at Terri's house so that it appeared the victim had been the murderer. He had intended the scene to look like a murder/suicide, and even the coroner had agreed with him!

He reflected on how it had been a stroke of pure genius that had inspired him to follow Joey Berg to his trailer. He had checked on Joey to make sure that he had passed out. Through the open door to Joey's closet he'd spotted the gun and took that as extra insurance. Then he swapped his own vehicle for Joey's truck. Finding the other gun behind Terri's bedroom door was an extra bonus. That way he could mislead the police even further. It would take them time to find out that the gun wasn't the murder weapon. If the murder-suicide story ever collapsed the cops would come looking for Joey first and even they wouldn't be stupid enough to miss a rifle sitting in the corner without checking it out.

The flat tire on Joey's truck had been unfortunate. He couldn't chance being seen changing the tire in Terri's yard so he had been forced to take Jamie's pickup. He'd decided to ditch it in the woods a mile or two from Joey's before walking back to get his own car. It would be just another diversion. They would have to search for the truck. With any luck, no one would find the orange pickup until fall and by then the deaths would be history. He'd checked Joey again, to make sure he'd passed out. If Joey had been awake then he would have killed him, too. He thought about it anyway, as he'd stood over the prostrate form on the bed. But he'd decided he needed to get out of there, fast.

He sat quietly with the newspapers in his lap, replaying the scene at Terri Berg's house in his mind. He watched himself unlock the door and slip silently through the house, past the clothing discarded randomly in lust. He raised the gun to Jamie's head and his heart raced as he pulled the trigger.

But the trigger wouldn't pull! He didn't know much about guns and hadn't taken the time to test this one. He had figured out how to load the shells and work the bolt to feed them into the breach. But the trigger not pulling freaked him out. He had looked around the gun until he found the button by the trigger and pushed the safety off. Again, he'd held the gun to Jamie's head. This time the trigger pulled. The gun roared. The muzzle flash in the dark room had been blinding.

Remembering Terri's screams and the surprise and terror in her face made his heart race again. He had threatened her with the gun and she'd gotten quiet. It was the gun. He was in charge. He remembered how she had felt. After she died he had to shoot her. He finally had a way to make her pay for the snubs and rejection. With the gun, he was in control now, not her.

He shook his head. The one slip up was the condom wrapper. He had handled it with gloves so it didn't have his fingerprints, but he couldn't find it later. He'd panicked. He knew he'd been there too long so he'd given up on the search.

Besides, it was unnecessary. They couldn't trace the condom wrapper to him anyway. No one had seen him buy it. He smiled. Maybe the condom wrapper could be his secret trademark. The cops were so stupid they might not even catch it. But *he* would know.

He left the gas station, where he'd bought the newspapers, and drove around. The bait shop had a sign in the window that said, "Guns Bought and Sold." He pulled in and sat in the car for five minutes. He could feel the adrenaline rise as he opened the car door. It was like being a kid and going into the drugstore to buy a Playboy magazine or condoms. Buying them was legal, but people looked at you differently when you bought them. Guns were the same.

He walked into the store and stopped in front of the showcase. Behind the counter was a rack with twenty long guns. In the locked counter were another twenty five or thirty handguns. He ran his hand over the glass and felt the heat.

"Can I help you?" The voice surprised him and he physically jumped.

"Uh huh. I...think I need a gun." He could feel the sweat forming on his forehead. He tried to gain control of himself again, not looking directly at the man, concentrating on the guncase .

The man behind the counter was slightly older than he was, but taller and in good shape. He'd probably been one of the jocks in high school that got all the cute girls. "What are you looking for?" asked the man, waving his hand over the counter.

"I...don't know. I just need a gun."

"For protection?" The man opened the doors on the back of the counter and took out a large black gun with black plastic handles. The clerk pulled the slide on the top. It opened and clacked shut. "This is a Colt .45ACP. It has a thirteen-round clip and weighs three and a half pounds. It's a great stopper. Blow a guy's shoulder right off."

He took it from the clerk. The gun was heavy and the

blue metal was cold. He turned it in his hands. He couldn't figure it out. Where did it load and what did all the little buttons
do? "It's too big. You got something smaller...and simpler?"

The clerk wrinkled his nose at the "simpler" comment.
He took the Colt automatic back and put it on the shelf. He
knelt down and looked at the shelves before pulling out a shiny
silver revolver. He recognized it as a revolver. He'd seen a
movie where they opened the side and the cylinder fell open.
The shells went in the cylinder. To shoot it, all you had to do
was pull the hammer back and pull the trigger.

The clerk was talking. "This is a Taurus .357 magnum.
It's simpler and still packs a good punch. If you can't handle the
recoil of the magnum, it can fire a .38 special shell, too. The
two-inch barrel isn't much for accuracy, but at close range it
does the job. It's double action so you can pull the hammer back
and pull the trigger, or you can pull the trigger and it will pull
the hammer back for you." The clerk handed the gun to him.

This one was it. He could feel it. The shiny chrome
reflected the sunlight and it was light enough that he could put
it in a pocket. The metal felt cool in his hand and sucked the terror from him. "I'll take it...and some bullets."

The clerk reached out his hand and took the gun back.
"We can fill out the forms." The clerk put the gun back in the
case. "And in five days you can have it."

"Five days?" He was confused.

The clerk pulled out a stack of papers and a pen. "It's
the law. Five-day waiting period on handgun purchases. We fill
out the forms, send it to the sheriff, who ignores it for five days,
and I hand you the gun after the time expires without them
doing anything. Can I see your driver's license?"

He froze. Wait...it was okay. No one would suspect this
I.D. He handed it to the clerk who entered information onto the
federal form.

The clerk pushed the forms across the counter. "Check
all the boxes 'no,' and sign the bottom."

Chapter 12

It didn't take long for Sandy to find Jamie Arvidson's truck. It was parked about a hundred yards or so in the woods about a quarter of a mile from Joey's house. There apparently hadn't even been any effort to conceal it.

Dan stood with Sandy, watching as the impound crew hauled the truck out of the woods and onto the back of a truck.

"Find anything obvious in the truck? asked Dan.

"Nothing. No keys, nothing. Still think Joey couldn't have done this?" asked Sandy.

Dan shook his head, stroking his chin. "Why would Joey go to the trouble to hide the truck out here, walk to his trailer, leave the murder weapon right out in the living room for us to find, then pass out in the bed for us to just pick him up. It just doesn't add up, and I still don't buy it."

"Joey was drunk," Sandy offered.

Dan shook his head again. "Too pat. Someone's setting Joey up."

Pam and Floyd were back at Terri Berg's house searching for the missing shell case. They dug under the cushions and into the stuffing of the couch and chair. There was no spent casing anywhere.

"I give up," Pam said, throwing up her hands. "We've looked everywhere and it's not here."

Floyd stood near the windows, staring at the blood stains on the floor. "If he was standing like this..." Floyd used his arms to simulate the position of a rifle, "...the spent casings would fly towards the wall. Some would bounce off and fly toward the bedroom."

They got on their knees and shined flashlights under the bed, nightstand, dresser, and chest of drawers. No shell casings, only the 'dust kittens' that they'd seen before and the back from an earring that they had missed behind the leg of the nightstand. They got up and went to the living room where Floyd repeated the exercise.

Pam was frustrated. "C'mon Floyd. Give it up. He took it with him."

Floyd shook his head in exasperation. "Why would he take one casing and not the others? Especially these. I could understand the one in the bedroom, where he hadn't had time to deal with it. But not these."

Floyd lifted his imaginary rifle again and turned from side to side, looking to see where the spent casings might fly. Suddenly, he snapped his finger and pulled back the drapes, inspecting the window ledge. It was bare. He let the drapes fall and heard a clunk. He grabbed the drapes and let them fall against the wall again. He heard the sound again. He pulled them up and swung the hem against the wall and it hit with a clunk. He pulled the hem through his fingers until he found a lump. He pulled down the open seam in the hem and the brass shell casing fell to the floor.

"Voila!" He bent down and slipped a pen into the neck of the casing and lifted it for inspection. Several fingerprints were clearly evident on the shiny brass.

Sandy Maki stopped off in the jailer's office to follow up on Butch's prints. Archie Miller, one of the jailers, was shuffling through paperwork at his desk.

"Hey Archie, did we get an I.D. on my assailant?"

Archie looked up from his piles of papers and recognized Sandy. "Great timing. The report came in this morning." He shuffled through the pile again, in search of the report.

"Here it is. You got a real gem in that one," he said, handing the report to Sandy. It took several pages to enumerate all the activities of the man's criminal career. At the top of the page was the name, "Brian Allen Mattson a.k.a. Butch Mattson, Butch Madson, Brian Madsen." The file listed outstanding warrants for skipping bail on an assault charge in Eden Prairie, a suburb of Minneapolis, and various parole violations. He had over twenty arrests for felony, charges ranging from assault and attempted murder to armed robbery. The record indicated that he'd spent fourteen of his thirty-three years behind bars. His first arrest was for battery on his mother.

Sandy let out a whistle. "Whew! A real sweetheart. Have you notified the agencies with the outstanding warrants yet?"

"Oh yeah. I talked to Hennepin County early this morning. They were real familiar with this guy. The clerk told me that he'd beaten a county jailer and escaped while they were transporting him for a doctor's visit. The jailer had to be put on medical retirement. They were sorry that the arresting officer here hadn't shot him."

"How about the county attorney?"

"I called and left a message on his voice mail. Nobody's been over yet. You'll love this. Mattson snarled at me when I brought him breakfast. I mean, like a damned lion, he snarled."

Sandy smiled. "And what did you do?"

Archie straightened the papers. "I can tell you that I didn't go back to pick up the tray after he finished."

Sandy chuckled. "Take a Taser with you when you go back. Maybe ten thousand volts will get his attention. If nothin' else, you'll be able to pick up the tray while he's quivering like Jello on the cell floor."

Archie smiled. "Ohhh. I'd like to do that."

Sandy took the file and walked toward Dan's office. When he got there, he could hear John Sepanen's deep voice behind the closed door.

"Dan, Ron Augustine has confirmed that there's a special meeting of the county board set up for next week, Thursday. Doc Peterson lobbied with all the board members yesterday, and he thinks that he has enough votes lined up to demand your resignation."

Dan leaned back in his chair and popped two Tums into his mouth. "Do you want me to resign?"

Sepanen leaned on his knees and looked at Dan through his bushy, dark eyebrows. "Hell, no. You're worth a hundred Doc Petersons to this department. He's a screwed up old reprobate with his own agenda and an ego too large for his own good. I talked to the county attorney last night and he says that we can probably argue that this has been decided in closed door meetings, in violation of state law. But he suggests that we get it settled before it ever gets to the board."

"How does he suggest that we do that? You know as well as I do that Doc Peterson isn't going to back down. To resolve without him backing down would mean that I would back down." Dan hesitated, considering that thought. "I won't back down. I was right."

Sepanen sat up and crossed the legs of his neatly creased uniform pants. The pleats in his military-pressed white uniform shirt were so sharp that they looked like they could cut a two dollar steak. The seven pointed gold star, with a Cloisonné center, was pinned directly on the crease through his left pocket. Dan smiled inwardly. Sepanen was a good sheriff but he sometimes seemed to be playing his role a little too much.

"We'll put Peterson in a corner," Sepanen said. "I'll call

him and tell him that the county attorney is going to bring him up on charges over botching the investigation at Berg's. We do that, then offer to drop the charges if he calls off the dog-and-pony-show before the board."

Dan put his elbows on the papers piled on his desk. "The problem is, that puts him in a corner. If he reacts like a cornered raccoon, we all end up bloody and everyone loses."

The sheriff threw up his hands. "Exactly. If he's reasonable, he capitulates. If he decides that he's right and everyone else be damned, we end up with the pissing match of the century."

Dan turned in his chair to look out the window. "John, I've never known Doc Peterson to be reasonable about anything."

"Yeah, I know. That scares me a little, too." Sepanen stood up. "Give me Tony Oresek's phone number. I want to get the story straight from him. Then I'm going to talk to the county attorney again and then to Doc. We'll see what breaks. Wish me luck."

When Sepanen exited Dan's office, Sandy Maki had already discreetly moved down the hallway, heading toward his own desk in the ready room.

Chapter 13

Pam Ryan and Floyd Swenson rushed from Terri Berg's house to arrive at Miller-Dwan hospital, in Duluth. Floyd had been to the morgue enough to be able to lead Pam through the labyrinth of hospital corridors. As they walked toward the door that said "authorized employees only," he turned to Pam and asked, "Are you ready for this?"

Pam gave Floyd her most scornful look. "I'm ready, big shot. Are you ready?" Floyd smiled and led her through the door.

Eddie Paulson, the medical examiner's assistant, dressed in blue surgical scrubs, sat at a desk in the entry room to the morgue. He was leaning over the desk, making notes on a file.

Pam looked around quickly and realized that Eddie's blue scrubs were the only color in the room. The walls were painted entirely in white. The floor was covered with white tile. Two empty metal chairs sat against a wall, awaiting some poor departed soul's family members.

Floyd said, "Hi, Eddie," offering his hand. Eddie looked up and set the pen down to shake Floyd's hand. "You met Pam Ryan at the murder scene yesterday." Eddie shook Pam's hand and gestured to a door behind the desk.

"We're all set to go. C'mon in." Eddie got up from his desk, and walked to another door at the rear of the room. They walked down a narrow hallway that smelled of disinfectant.

"By the way, we checked the man's fingerprints. We didn't get a match off the NCIC. So our John Doe remains anonymous."

"So what do you do now?" Pam asked.

"Usually, we'd do a check on dental records. But seeing the condition of the head, we don't have too much hope there. We may be able to pull a match from some of the teeth that we found. But if you have a likely victim, we could try to match his prints against some personal items from his house."

Pam frowned. "But we suspect that it's a guy with a roommate. Wouldn't the house be contaminated with both sets of prints?"

"Well, yes, but you would at least narrow your search to the roommates, and you could bring me his bottle of after-shave. There's a 99% chance that the prints will only be his."

He pushed another door that opened to a room that looked like a surgical suite, with a big light mounted over a stainless steel surgical table. There was a white sheet over what appeared to be a body resting on the table. Nearby was a gurney with a sheet draped over what Pam believed to be another body, apparently with its knees up. Tony Oresek, dressed in scrubs and wearing a face shield, was pulling on latex gloves. He looked up and gave them a perfunctory wave.

Pam looked nervously around the room. "Are we supposed to put on scrubs too?"

Eddie answered, "the scrubs and protective garb are different here than in a surgery. In surgery they wear this stuff to protect the patients. Here, we wear it to protect us from anything in the victims. You should be safe as long as you stay back,"

Floyd grinned at Pam. "Yeah, try not to get too close, Deputy Ryan."

Pam just gave him a malevolent stare.

Eddie pulled on a gown and donned gloves and face shield, while Oresek pulled out a cart covered with a green drape. He pulled off the drape, exposing an array of stainless steel knives, saws, and devices that looked like they belonged in a torture chamber. Eddie pulled the sheet off the body on the table, exposing John Doe. A paper tag was tied to one toe with a piece of string.

Floyd and Pam watched as Oresek looked over the surface of the naked body with a magnifying lamp. The skin was waxy white except for the dark underside. He noted every mole, crevice and dimple as he spoke into a microphone that hung over the table. He removed a few fibers and pieces of detritus, placing them into evidence envelopes that Eddie held at ready. Eddie marked comments on each envelope before sealing it and setting it aside.

Pam whispered to Floyd, "Why is his back dark like that?"

Oresek heard the question and answered, to Pam's embarrassment, "It's called postmortem lividity. We use it as an indicator of how long a body has been dead, along with the temperature and the onset of rigor mortis. It occurs as the blood drains from the tissues and pools on the side of the body that's down. It can also tell us if the body has been moved from where it died. If the lividity isn't against the floor we know that the body has been reoriented."

When they finished the surface exam, Oresek pulled over the cart and selected a large scalpel. He deftly made an incision from each armpit to the solar plexus, then from the apex of the other incisions to the pubis. He selected a larger knife, slid it under the ribs on the left side and lifted firmly, each rib popping as the knife broke through it.

Floyd felt Pam's hand on his arm and turned in time to see her eyes drift upward as her knees buckled. He tried to catch her, but only succeeded in slowing the rate of her fall and gently guiding her head to the floor.

"At least she didn't vomit all over the place. I hate mopping up after the spectators," Eddie said. Oresek looked up as Eddie ripped off the latex gloves and moved to help Floyd lay her on the floor. "Let's move her to the cot in Tony's office."

Pam woke up with a start. The room was unfamiliar and her first response was panic. She looked to the side and saw Floyd standing at the office door looking into the hallway.

Floyd heard her stir and turned, "Sleeping beauty awakes."

Her face went from paste white to red. "Oh God! Don't tell me I passed out."

"You can't remember?"

Pam sat up on the edge of the cot. "All I remember is the room getting dim and popping noises."

Floyd smiled. "Eddie was relieved that you didn't throw up. Most of the visitors he loses, vomit. At least he didn't have to mop up after you."

Pam ran her hand through her hair to straighten it. "Have I been out long?"

Floyd looked at his watch. "Nah, just a few minutes." He headed out of the door.

"Are you going back in there?" Pam's voice was tinged with anxiety.

He stopped at the door. "Yeah. You can stay here. Tony's got a bunch of morbid magazines over there." He nodded toward a table next to a guest chair. "I'll cover the autopsy."

Pam hesitated a second then got up. Her legs were a little wobbly, but she got them under control quickly. "I gotta do it. I'm the only female deputy, and I won't be able to take the shit I'd get if I chickened out."

"Do what you want," Floyd said. "But if you're in there and you start feeling light-headed, promise that you'll sit down or turn away before the lights go out."

Pam nodded. "Deal."

They walked down the hall and stopped just outside the door to the autopsy suite. Floyd said, "Don't feel too bad. I think that nearly every new deputy has either passed out or thrown up at his first PM. You are not a member of an exclusive club."

Pam nodded with a quick smile and took a deep breath. They walked in to see Oresek turning a piece of some pink internal organ in his hand. He handed it to Eddie, who put it on a scale and weighed it before placing it in a large plastic bag at his side.

Oresek looked up at Pam and Floyd for a second. "Our guy died instantly from massive head trauma. There are a couple of hints here on his identity. He's had surgery a couple of times; There's a really old scar from a pilonodal cyst, and a more recent vasectomy. There are also a couple of small strawberry birthmarks on his chest."

"What's a poly-something cyst?" Floyd pulled out a notebook.

"It's a common complaint in young men. Basically, it's the body trying to grow a primitive tail. You end up with a pocket of hair and skin tissue at the tip of the coccyx...the tailbone. It usually ends up forming pockets of inflamed tissue that get infected and weep. A good surgeon can cut it out and just leave a deep dimple in the crack between your cheeks."

Oresek turned back to Eddie and held up his hands. He looked at the clock on the wall. They had been at their task for over two hours. "That's it for John Doe. Let's start the woman."

Eddie hefted the bag of the man's organs off a low cart and dropped it back into the abdomen as Oresek changed gloves and flexed his hands.

Oresek caught Pam watching him exercise his joints. "Occupational hazards. Arthritis in your hands from having them buried in a cold cadaver all day, and carpal tunnel from holding the tools." He smiled, "But those are minor compared to the risk of hepatitis, and other communicable diseases that we can get through a cut."

"AIDS?" she asked.

Tony shook his head. "The virus isn't viable at the temperatures we maintain, and usually isn't viable outside of a live body for more than a very short time. But we haven't known that until recently, so there were a few tense years early on."

"I saw your name on your door. It said "M.E.," not "M.D." What's the difference?"

Oresek pulled on two pairs of latex gloves as Eddie slid the male body from the autopsy table onto a gurney and pulled the sheet over it. "Well, I'm an M.D., too. I did the college thing, the medical school thing, and then did a residency in pathology after medical school. I worked as a pathologist for a few years before I went back to school and studied forensic medicine. After that, I had a forensic medicine residency in New York. I took all of that I could stand before I decided that I wanted to move back to God's country and took a hundred-thousand-dollar a year cut in pay to move back to Duluth."

"Wow. How's that education compare to Doc Peterson's training?"

Oresek smiled. "Doc Peterson was trained as a surgeon about 1950. He was appointed as the coroner by the county board about 1960, so he could pronounce bodies dead at car accidents and drownings. I'm not aware that he's ever had any formal training in either pathology, which is the study of diseased or injured tissue, or in forensic medicine, which is the study of victims of criminal activity."

"Doc Peterson said this was a murder and suicide. What basis did you use to determine that wasn't true?" Behind Oresek, a camera flashed as Eddie took pictures of the female corpse from all angles.

Oresek walked to the table where Terri Berg was now exposed in her grotesque mask of death. The electric cord had been removed from her hands and ankles. He started working his way around the body, poking at bruises and marks on the skin. "Well, first, Eddie determined that the man's body was cooler than the woman's. There was about a two-degree difference in temperature, if memory serves me. Second, the woman had less lividity, and thirdly, she was looser...less rigor mortis. I'd have to say that she lived nearly two hours longer than he did. Judging from the bruises on her body, it was a very unpleasant two hours."

Oresek paused in his examination of the left breast. "Eddie, get the camera. Here's the bite mark you noticed at the house." He looked up at the deputies. "If you get me a suspect, we can compare his dentition with these marks. It's as good as a fingerprint." Both Floyd and Pam were taking notes.

Eddie brought a 35 millimeter camera out and focused on the spot that Oresek indicated. He took two pictures from slightly different angles.

"Looks like she put up a struggle." Oresek used a small instrument to remove a small sample from under the fingernails of the woman's right hand. Eddie carefully placed each scraping into an envelope and labeled it. Oresek fished a hair from the last sample and took it to a microscope.

After several seconds of focusing and adjusting a ring under the microscope he leaned back. "Your killer has very dark hair," he said. "Black or dark brown. It looks like the part nearest the root is lighter. I'd say it's been dyed." He looked directly at Pam. "Another strike against the murder/suicide theory. John Doe's hair was blonde, from the roots to the tips."

Oresek finished his surface exam by taking several vaginal smears. When he took out the scalpel to open the abdomen, Pam mumbled something about nature calling and quietly left the room.

When she came back, the three men were grouped around the microscope. "What's up?" Pam asked.

They parted, moving away from the scope. "We're looking at lung tissue. Couldn't find any obvious cause of death." Oresek pointed to the eyepiece of the scope and she stepped up to look through it. Underneath was a slice of pink tissue.

"So, what is it that I'm looking at?"

"Lung tissue. It should be light pink and full of air holes."

As she looked through the microscope, Pam commented, "But this is almost red. No holes."

"You win the sixty-four-thousand-dollar prize. She suffocated," Oresek said.

"You mean like a pillow over the face?" Pam quickly tried to visualize the room and didn't recall a pillow or anything like it.

Oresek shook his head. "No, more like a boa constrictor. Her trachea indicates no air restriction from strangulation and her hyoid bone was intact. A crushed hyoid is a sure sign of strangulation, but a couple of the ribs were broken. My guess is that somebody sat on her chest until she died of suffocation."

Pam's face turned ashen. "Or, the killer was really big and she couldn't breathe while he raped her." She looked at Floyd. "Bill Patterson?"

Floyd shook his head. "Nah. I just don't think so."

Oresek looked at Pam thoughtfully. "That would be consistent with the cracked ribs. They were crushed, rather than broken by a blunt instrument."

Pam's face had turned beet red. "I mean, I wasn't speaking from experience....I was just...."

Floyd rescued her. "So, we're looking for a big, or heavy, man, with dark hair that may be dyed. What's the chance that we'll get a match on the semen or tissue under the fingernails from the DNA sex offender database?"

Oresek wiggled his nose as if it itched, but he couldn't scratch it with the bloody gloves on his hands. "Last I heard, they had about fifteen thousand profiles. If your murderer is a recent offender, he may be on the system. If not..."

Chapter 14

The town of Beroun consisted of a general store, a bar, and their shared parking lot. The bar was empty except for him and the bartender. The bartender sat at the other end of the bar doing the books from the previous week, looking up every few minutes to see if the lone customer needed a refill on a lazy Monday afternoon.

After his fourth beer, he asked the bartender to put a frozen pizza into the toaster oven. While he waited for the pizza he decided to try a pickled turkey gizzard. He'd never eaten one. The bartender popped the pizza into a little oven behind the bar, then fished out a gizzard with a long fondue fork, dropping it into a paper cup.

Neither of them had been paying attention to the Twin's baseball game on the the bar's television until a reporter came on the screen, announcing late-breaking news. They both watched the screen as the bartender set the gizzard in front of him.

The reporter was standing in front of the Pine County Courthouse. In the background was a crowd, surrounding a man in the uniform of a police officer. "Sheriff Sepanen has just concluded his news conference," she announced. "According to the sheriff, the St. Louis County Medical Examiner has determined that the apparent murder/suicide in Henriette should be ruled a double murder. The investigation is continuing, and there are no suspects in custody at this time. We'll have the full details on the sheriff's news conference at six."

He casually took a bite of the gizzard as the bartender went back to his books. The vinegar bit into his tongue, but the firm meat reminded him of Terri's breasts. He'd bitten them, and beaten them until they were bruised and hard. He had to teach her a lesson for ignoring him. Terri had more than ignored him; she had rejected him. She had despised him just like every other woman in his life had. He had shown her compassion and she had recoiled from him. They had all humiliated him. Terri had paid. And so would some of the others.

Taking another bite of gizzard, he thought of Miss Binger. The female gym teacher had been a real pain. When they had coed classes she'd bring the girls over for volleyball. She and Mr. Ferguson, the boy's teacher, had stood by the side while the two best athletes had chosen sides. He and Gary Johnson had always been the last two. Even the girls were picked over Gary and him.

Their rejection had bonded he and Gary through three years of junior highschool, bonded them through Miss Binger calling them "whales" because they were too fat to do one pull up. Through taunting because they couldn't make it across the horizontal ladder. Through the laughter of the other students over their ineptitude at any sport that required coordination or strength.

He thought of Miss Binger's muscular body and how she would look when he tied her hands behind her back and pushed between her legs. He jammed the rest of the turkey gizzard into his mouth and bit down on it, like it was one of Miss Binger's tiny breasts.

The vinegar tickled his throat and he started to cough. The bartender looked up, but he signaled that he was okay. That was stupid! He shouldn't bring attention to himself. His thoughts drifted back to Terri's firm breasts and short shorts. What a piece she had been. But why had she hated him so? She never noticed his kindness and attention, never saw how nice he was to her. She always gave him a laugh, when he wanted a hug. But he'd finally had her. Yes, he'd had her. And she would never have another.

Her eyes bothered him. When he had pointed the gun at her the terror in her eyes had scared him...at first. But then he'd felt the power. She had to do what he wanted. They all had yielded to him. When Terri died she had given him everything.

The buzzer on the pizza oven jarred him back. He watched as the bartender pulled it out and cut it into four quarters with a knife. What a backwater town. They didn't even have a pizza cutter. Ha!

He ran through the scene once more as he munched on the slightly burned crust. Terri awakening in terror when the gun went off, holding her down, the fighting, her nails digging into his neck, once, twice, three times, her whimpering when he finally subdued her.

And the look she gave him when he got the wire and tied her hands! He rolled her over and then she saw Jamie and had gone nuts, kicking, fighting all over again. But he had her. He threw her to the floor and watched her face as he opened the condom. Then the surprise on her face when he pulled open his pants. The fear when she knew what he was going to do. It was almost better than actually having her.

He'd been gorging himself on the pizza while the fantasy played in his mind. He had to stop for a second to swallow. He slid his hand off the bar and rubbed the hard lump in his pants. He realized that the bartender was staring at him. He must have been making noises. Shit! Stupid! Stupid! Stupid! Stupid is how you get caught, and he wasn't stupid. He'd been too smart for them before and he was too smart for them now. They'd never catch him again. They hadn't for years. He hadn't left any fingerprints behind. It was a stroke of genius to wipe all the shell casings and the rifle, and then to press Jamie's fingers to them. He'd even taken the condom away so they couldn't do a DNA match. He was smarter than the stupid sheriff that he'd seen on television. He was smarter than all of them. And now he would have a gun of his own.

Chapter 15

Dan ran from the ready room to answer the phone in his office. He and Sandy Maki had been discussing Brian Mattson's case with the Pine County Attorney at Sandy's desk. The voice on the other end of the phone was his former partner, Laurie Lone Eagle, an investigator for the Minnesota Bureau of Criminal Apprehension. Laurie worked from the central office in the Twin Cities. "Dan, I hear you've got a pervert murderer up there. Glad I moved to The Cities where it's safe."

Laurie and Dan had been far less than close friends when they had been partnered, but over the years Laurie had proven herself to be a dedicated investigator and a close ally when things got tough. Being a single female Native American had exposed Laurie to every form of discrimination and harassment known to the legal system. She had endured and even prospered, earning a law degree to go with her license as a law enforcement officer.

Dan chuckled. The murder rate in Pine County was about one percent of the rate in Minneapolis, where Laurie's apartment was located. "Don't you worry. I'm sure the murderer is somebody that moved up from the Cities. We just have to screen all the recent refugees to find him."

Laurie's voice became all business. "In all seriousness, the director asked me to relay some information and offer assistance, if necessary. We ran the files and found two sex offenders, with multiple arrests, that routinely used condoms in their assaults. One's a guest of the state prison in Oak Park Heights. The other one's living on a farm down near Windom. He's been clean for about five years. We're trying to locate him, but last report said that he was still there."

Dan let out a sigh. "Doesn't sound too promising."

"Not from that angle. We checked on assaults with murder. One hit there, but that guy's in the southwest somewhere. Arizona, I think. We tried sexual assaults with increasing violence and got about twenty hits. So far, we've got seven of them in prison or the state hospital system, a couple in halfway houses, and a bunch on parole. We've got a couple of investigators following up on the parolees."

Dan tapped a pencil on his desktop. "We rattled the usual perverts up here, too, and came up blank. There's one thing that may be an interesting footnote. Sandy Maki got assaulted by the boyfriend of a person he went to question. The guy's name is Brian Mattson and he has a five page rap sheet. No sexual involvement, unless you count beating the crap out of his mother and girlfriend."

"Mattson...Mattson. The name is familiar."

"He had two outstanding warrants, one for assault and one for jumping bail. We were just having a discussion about charges here. The county attorney says we can take him down for assaulting an officer. We're also considering a domestic assault charge. His live-in showed Sandy where he'd burned her with a cigarette."

"I assume you sweated him on the murder?"

"Yeah. He swears he was with the girlfriend all night and she corroborates."

Laurie paused for a second. "You know that abused domestic partners often go along with their abuser's alibi. It's part of the pattern of abuse."

Dan sighed. "Yeah. Sandy says he thinks she's straight on the alibi. He's going to follow up and go over it one more time with her to see if he gets the same story."

"Hmmm. Too bad. He seems like a natural. You identify the John Doe yet?"

Dan was tapping his pencil on the desktop. "We're still checking. It's likely that it's a local guy named Jamie Arvidson. Problem is that the murderer blew away his face, and Jamie doesn't have any prints on file."

"I'll work on these parolees, and see if anything boils to the surface. Anything else I can do for you?" Laurie's chair creaked as she leaned forward to hang up the phone.

Dan gave a chuckle. "Sure. You can get Doc Peterson off my back."

The chair creaked back as Laurie's interest was piqued. "What's his problem? I mean, besides being too senile to do his job and having an ego so big it doesn't fit in the operating room with him."

Dan got up from his chair and pushed the office door closed. "Doc showed up at this double murder and declared it a murder-suicide. He wanted to bag the bodies before we collected evidence. I told him to pack his camel and ride it home. Now he's lobbying the county board to get me fired." Dan threw the pencil at the wastebasket and missed. It rolled across the tile floor.

"You've got to be kidding! They aren't listening to him, are they?" Laurie tried to make it sound like a joke, sensing Dan's concern.

Dan rubbed a hand over his face. "Most of the board members are his cronies. Sepanen's trying to run interference, but I really don't know what's going to boil up when they have the board meeting next Thursday."

Dan could hear paper shuffling and knew that Laurie was scribbling a note. Her constant notetaking had sometimes irritated him in the past, but he soon learned how they could come in handy.

"Let me make a couple of phone calls," she said. "No

guarantees."

"Don't spend too much time on it. Tony Oresek will back me, and so will Sepanen." Dan said the words, but his voice couldn't hide his stress.

"Okay. I'll get back to you when I know something."

Dan and Sandy were talking about damage control in his office. "Drew Nelson has been assigned as a public defender for Mattson" said Dan. "Mattson wants him to argue that the county should bring you up on brutality charges. Luckily, Drew is a local lawyer that doesn't like smartass thugs from the Twin Cities. He's discussing a plea bargain with Mattson, involving dropping the officer assault charges in return for a guilty plea on the domestic assault."

Sandy shook his head. "Bob Rogers said if Pine County let Mattson go back on the outstanding warrants from Hennepin County he might not have to discuss the stairway incident in front of a judge. Chances are that it won't matter what charges get filed here, the stairway fall will come up."

Dan stared into space for a moment. "Is there any chance that this guy is the Berg murderer? His background sure sounds like he's got all the right qualifications: He's been in and out of the legal system, starting as a juvenile, and he just continues to get more violent. He has an explosive temper and isn't afraid to assault someone without much provocation."

Sandy slid down in the chair. "As much as I'd like to believe he's the one, we don't have any motive that ties him to Berg's, and a gun just doesn't seem to be his style. Butch is more of a fists and knives kind of guy."

They were interrupted by Pam Ryan flying into Dan's office. She stumbled to a stop when she saw Sandy. "Oh, sorry."

Dan waved her in. "C'mon in Pam. What's up?" Floyd Swenson showed up in the doorway behind her.

"We got results on some of the prints from the Berg

house. Can I show you now?"

"Sure," Dan said.

She set some reports on top of the other papers on Dan's desk and pointed as she spoke. "All the prints on the gun and the shells were the same. NCIC came up blank, but we matched them with John Doe's prints from the morgue. And..." She paused, apparently for dramatic effect. "The prints from the gun and shells match with the prints on Jamie Arvidson's after-shave bottle. Doctor Oresek says that makes it about 99% sure that Jamie is John Doe. They've got one tooth, with a filling, and they're going to find Jamie's dentist to see if it matches, too. That'll make it 99.99% sure." She stood beaming in front of Dan's desk.

Dan looked up from the reports. "Did you find the other spent 30-06 case?"

Pam smiled. "Floyd found it...in the hem of the curtains."

"Prints?" Dan asked, expectantly.

Pam looked back at Floyd, who answered, "One was complete. And, no, it doesn't match the others. Maybe we've got one of the killer's prints after all. I sent it to the BCA and NCIC to see if they could get a match on their computers."

Pam looked at Sandy. "It doesn't match Butch Mattson," she said.

"Any surprises from the post-mortem?" asked Dan.

Floyd read back his notes without emotion. "The female victim had a bite mark on one breast that we may be able to match if we get dentals on a suspect. We also got tissue residue from under her fingernails. She got a piece of the guy. We also found foreign hair...the guy has dark brown or black hair, probably dyed from a lighter shade."

Pam jumped in. "She died from suffocation. The guy was so big, so heavy, that she suffocated under his weight during the rape."

Dan looked up at Floyd and got a subtle nod of agreement. Dan asked, "Did Oresek also reconfirm that the man died first?"

Pam fielded the question. "Yes. Roughly two hours before the woman. He said that the woman would have been lucky to have died at the same time as John Doe. The last two hours of her life were hell."

Dan raised his eyebrows. "Anything else?" There was no response. "Well, folks, here's the way it stands, then. We've got Terri Berg and Jamie Arvidson dead at the scene. Joey Berg's truck is parked out front with a flat tire. We've found Arvidson's truck hidden some distance from Joey's trailer. We know that it was Joey's gun that did the killing. And Joey's the only one, so far, that has a clear motive. We also have the print on the shell casing, and if that turns out to match Joey's prints, or if tissue under the fingernails match Joey Berg, then he'll be our guy. On the other hand, Joey is not a big man, and judging from his condition when I talked to him, he would probably have been too drunk Saturday night to carry this thing out. And even if he could have, there's the question of why he would leave his gun out for us to find it. And Joey doesn't have brown or black hair and his hair is not died. My gut feeling is that he's telling the truth " Dan pointed at his deputies with a pencil. "I want you all to be out tomorrow talking to Terri Berg's neighbors to see if any of them saw the murderer shuttling Joey's truck to her house, or if they heard the gunshots, or anything else we might be able to pick up."

Pam made a note but shook her head. "I bet a lot of them work in town someplace. They may be hard to catch."

Dan smiled. "That's why you're going to spend the whole day tracking them down and talking to them."

The room was silent. "Okay. We're going to be busy tomorrow. Let's plan on meeting here again tomorrow evening, too, same time."

For quite sometime after the three deputies had left, Dan sat mulling over the latest information in Oresek's report. Terri

Berg, dead from suffocation, ribs broken from the man's weight. Jamie Arvidson, his head blown practically off, probably by Joey Berg's rifle.

He thought of the other factors in the case, Joey's truck left parked in Terri's driveway, Jamie's truck found at Joey's place. Joey's gun was the murder weapon, and he had little doubt that John Doe would turn out to be Arvidson. All clues pointed to Joey except that Joey was not a large man, his hair was blonde, and Dan felt that he had assessed Joey's character pretty well when they had talked. The theory about the murderer's size and weight being the first cause of Terry's death could be wrong, but he doubted it. Joey as a murderer just didn't fit. Of course, if Joey's print was on the shell casing, and his tissue turned up underneath Terri Berg's fingernails, or if other evidence was taken from Arvidson's truck, then that would clinch it. But he doubted such evidence would turn up, and so he knew, somewhere, another man, the real killer, was still out there, and they would just have to keep digging to find him.

Chapter 16

Dan was about to lock up his office when the phone rang. Laurie Lone Eagle greeted him. "Hi, Dan. Close the door and grab your pencil."

She heard the door latch, then waited for Dan's reply. "Got it. What do I write?"

"Doc Peterson's license is under restrictions from the state medical board. He's had a number of malpractice cases that were settled out of court by his insurance carrier. The insurance company dropped him and then cooperated with the medical board to restrict his practice. It looks like about the only surgery he can perform is the removal of warts and bunions."

"I'll be damned! You've got to be kidding?"

Laurie laughed. "I'm embellishing. Basically, he can't do anything that involves general anesthesia. The only exception might be something considered life threatening in the absence of any other medical personnel. Is there anything else I can do for you?"

"Laurie, You're great! Hang on just a minute. I do have something else" Dan reached for the notes from the meeting with the deputies. "We picked up a print that doesn't match any others. It's from a spent shell case at the murder scene. Can you expedite a check on it? We sent it to the BCA and NCIC."

"Sure. I'll pull it and have it run first thing tomorrow." She hesitated. "When is the meeting with the county board? I wrote it down but I've misplaced it somewhere."

The enthusiasm faded from Dan's voice. "Next Thursday afternoon at two."

"Would you mind if I stopped in?"

Dan pinched his eyes shut. "I don't know that it would be worth your time."

"I'll see if I'm in the neighborhood." Laurie paused. "You never know, I might be of help." She hung up before Dan could reply.

Dan looked up the phone number for the hospital. After going through several people he finally found someone who had the surgery schedule. "Can you tell me if Doctor Peterson has any surgery scheduled for tomorrow?"

There was a pause while sheets of paper were flipped. "He's only got two tomorrow. He blocked the afternoon for a staff meeting."

"What procedures is he doing?"

"A hysterectomy and a tubal ligation."

Dan scribbled notes frantically. This was too good to be true. "Did he do any surgery today?"

Again the papers shuffled. "Four. Hemorrhoids, a gall bladder, a vein stripping and a hernia. Oh, I almost forgot, and an emergency appendectomy."

Dan scribbled notes, trying to guess at the spelling of the medical terms. "Thanks."

He scurried to John Sepanen's office. The sheriff was just taking his jacket off the hangar behind his door when Dan flew in. "John, I've got some information, and I'm not really sure how to best use it."

Sally's car wasn't in their driveway when Dan got home. The kitchen door was locked, and when he opened the door the dog raced past him to relieve herself in the yard. He found a note on the kitchen table. "Back about six. Will bring supper." Dan slipped off his shoes and headed for the bedroom.

As he changed into jeans and a T-shirt, he heard the dog bark and the crunch of tires on the gravel driveway.

He met Sally at the door and took the grocery bag from her as the dog scurried around their legs, begging for attention. The smell of fried chicken filled the kitchen. Dan pulled the greasy box from the bag and set it on the table before starting to empty the rest of the groceries into the cupboards.

Sally slipped off her shoes and patted the dog on the head before she grabbed two plates from the cupboard. "Forget the rest of the groceries. Let's eat before the chicken gets cold."

They sat at the table and divided the potato wedges and fried chicken. "What happened today?" Sally asked.

Dan answered through a mouthful of potato. "Looks like Jamie Arvidson was the unlucky guy at Terri Berg's house. Still not much of a trail to the murderer, but we do have a fingerprint that doesn't match anyone at the house."

Sally wiped her chin on a paper napkin. "How about Doc Peterson. Anything new there?"

Dan nodded. "Still meeting with the county board next week. We may have an ace up our sleeves, though. Laurie Lone Eagle called with some information this afternoon and I passed it to Sepanen. He thinks that he may be able to head off the meeting and get some sort of resolution without airing a lot of dirty laundry in front of an open board meeting."

Sally stopped eating. "Anything that you might be willing to share?"

Dan waved his arm. "It's public knowledge, but somehow it never got out around here. Doc Peterson's license has been restricted by the state medical board. I can't say much more until the sheriff shares the information with the county attorney, but there will be some mighty upset people if its true."

DAY

THREE

TUESDAY

Chapter 17

A t about 4:30 p.m. Tuesday evening, three tired deputies straggled into Dan's office for their wrap-up meeting. Sandy shared that he'd found nothing and that the Arvidson truck had yielded no further clues as yet. Pam and Floyd had much the same results in their trip through the rural area around Terri's house. No one had seen or heard a thing the night of Terri Berg's murder. The pace and strain of the last three days was plain on their faces.

"OK," said Dan. "We're all obviously tired, so let's call it quits for the day. We'll see you all bright and early tomorrow.

They had just started to rise when Pam asked the question. "Anyone else up for a beer?"

Floyd shook his head. "I'm too old for that anymore. I can't take the hangovers."

Dan said, "Can't. Got some things to clear up here and Sally's expecting me home for dinner."

Pam looked at Sandy.

Sandy looked at his watch. "Sure," he said. "Give me some time to clear up some things on my desk and change clothing."

Pam nodded. "I have to pick up some things and change, too. Where do you want to meet?"

"Jim's Bar is usually quiet, and they serve food there. Know where it is?"

Pam said, "I've never been there but I know where it is.

I'll find it."

They both left, leaving Dan and Floyd exchanging amused glances.

"Oh to be young again," said Floyd, as he headed for the doorway.

Jim's bar was dark and surprisingly noisy for a Tuesday evening. A group of men in their late teens and twenties shot pool at two tables in the back providing the background of cracking balls and laughter. The air conditioned bar was chilly compared to the eighty-degree temperature outside. It gave Pam Ryan a chill while she waited for her eyes to adjust to the interior darkness. The inside of the bar seemed like midnight compared to the blazing late afternoon sun. She finally found Sandy Maki sitting in a booth.

"You found the place, no problem?"

Pam slid in across the table from him and gave the bartender a wave. "No problem," she said.

The bartender sent a waitress to their booth that looked like she was about fifteen years old. "I'm Christy. What can I get for you?"

Sandy drained his beer and held up the Pilsner glass. "Michelob light, tap."

Pam asked for a Boodles and tonic.

The young waitress frowned. " What's a Boodles?"

Pam put up a hand. "Trust me. The bartender will know."

Christy toddled off in her cut off denim shorts and tennis shoes. Sandy took a sip of beer and watched as the waitress walked away.

"You could go to jail for what you're thinking," Pam said.

Sandy turned back and grinned. "Oops. Didn't know it was that obvious," he said, taking another sip of his beer. Pam had changed into a pair of light blue jeans and a red blouse that contrasted nicely with her honey-blond hair.

"I'll bet you get your share of looks," Sandy said, looking at Pam's blue eyes. He realized that Pam's eyebrows were the same color as her hair. That was a sure sign she was a natural blonde. He found himself to be pleased when she smiled again, flashing the dimples at him. It hadn't taken him or the guys on the force long to notice that Pam was pretty. Now, they were just waiting to see if she could hold up her end of the job.

"I used to get looks, but I stopped wearing makeup and cut my hair short. Being cute is kind of a curse for a woman in police work. People don't take you seriously, or they think you're just in it for the short term."

Christy brought Pam's drink to the table. "Do you want to run a tab?" she asked.

"Sure," said Sandy. Christy jotted something down on her order pad and toddled off again.

"*Are* you in it for the short term?" asked Sandy, turning back to Pam.

"Am I in it for the short term?" she said, repeating his question. Pam's face got serious and she shook her head. "No. I plan to make a career out of law enforcement."

"Well," said Sandy, "you can learn a lot here. Floy'd's senior deputy and he's been through it all. And Dan's the greatest."

"For sure," said Pam. "How about you, Sandy. You in it for the long term?"

Sandy swirled his beer. "Oh yeah," he said. "long term." Sandy paused and changed topics. "What'd you think of the autopsy?"

Pam's face grew somber and her eyes narrowed. "Floyd told you." It was half question and half comment.

Sandy grinned. "He mentioned it."

Pam laughed. "He told me that you chucked your cookies at every murder."

Sandy set his beer down solidly. "Why that S.O.B. He told you I ralphed?"

"I was queasy and he told me I wasn't alone." She shrugged and sipped on the drink. "It helped. Don't you ever feel...inadequate?"

"I've been around long enough to have made every mistake that can be made," Sandy said. "Experience is a tough teacher; You don't get the lessons until after the tests."

Pam raised her eyebrows. "Wow, that's sobering, no pun intended," she said, laughing, and took another drink.

"Like I say. You can learn a lot here. "1998, when I was a rookie, after I ran into a bar during a fight, Floyd told me 'Never run to a fight.' It'll still be there when you walk there and the fighters will be more tired.' That's the kind of stuff you pick up from Floyd and the other senior officers around here."

Pam sat up straight. "Say," she said, "isn't Dan younger than Floyd? Why is Dan undersheriff and not Floyd?" Pam cradled her drink in both hands and slid down a little.

"The undersheriff is appointed by the sheriff. It's usually a political crony or someone with a high profile that can bring in votes. Dan had the profile. Dan could've been elected himself, but word was he didn't want the politics of the sheriff's job and only took the undersheriff appointment with the understanding that he didn't have to do any administrative stuff. Sepanen got re-elected, Sergeant Tom Thompson does all the admin, and Dan does the investigations—and he's damned good at it."

"Is Dan really that good?"

Sandy nodded. "I can't even explain it. He has a sixth sense. I remember one investigation we had where a couple hunters found a child's mutilated body. Everyone else knew it was unsolvable, but Dan worked it through and found the murdererers When they went for the arrest the guys grabbed a neighbor's kid from a stroller and jumped in a car and took off. They cornered them just outside town and one guy put a knife to the baby's throat. Dan shot him and saved the kid's life. Later, the other guy's lawyer got him off, but he was shot on the steps, just outside the courthouse."

Pam's eyes lit up. "Hey, I remember that. It was on the news for a couple of days. Wasn't he some guy from down south that was abused as a kid? There was some deal about him getting off on an insanity plea or something."

"Yeah, that was him. He was a real sicko."

"Did they ever catch the guy that shot him?"

Sandy shook his head. "Never. Dan was so pissed that the county attorney had plea bargained away the charges that some people thought Dan had been the gunman."

"Was he? Sounds like he runs pretty deep."

"He was eating at Nicoll's, across from the courthouse, when it happened."

"So, there was one crime in the county that he didn't solve?"

Sandy smiled. "I have a feeling that no one tried very hard. The jerk had murdered around a dozen women, and left them dumped in ditches and rest stops around the country. He wasn't exactly mourned."

"My criminology prof used that case to discuss the question of whether the background of a person should be taken into consideration in punishing a person for his crimes." Pam studied Sandy's face. "So you think that it was okay to kill the guy considering his background?"

"Naw. Cops can't take the law into their own hands. But I can sympathize with whoever did kill that guy. Both of them were real slimeballs and this one was about to walk. Too many of them are getting by with that kind of crap these days."

Sandy finished his beer and signaled Christy for another round. Pam swirled her drink and finished off the last of the clear liquid as the next round arrived.

"How about our murderer? The guy is obviously out of his gourd, somehow, to do what he did to Terri Berg. I can remember from college that these guys have usually been abused and can't feel any empathy for their victims. Seeing as how Minnesota doesn't have a death penalty, what do you think? When we catch him, should he be sent to a mental institution or put in prison for the rest of his life?"

Sandy leaned forward and tipped his glass toward Pam. "So you've got this guy who's daddy used to beat him with a rubber hose when he's a kid. He's caught raping and murdering a woman. Does his history of abuse mean that he shouldn't be prosecuted and punished? In my opinion he should get the death penalty if we had it."

Pam shifted nervously. She'd obviously hit a sore point with Sandy. "Well, no. I mean it doesn't excuse him. It just maybe explains why he did it. Shouldn't that be taken into account?"

Sandy shook his head. "The defense lawyers want that explanation as an excuse. They try to convince every jury that something that happened in their client's past is an acceptable reason for their client's behavior." Sandy slid down in his chair. "I think it stinks. Society has standards. The legislature makes the laws. We're here to enforce those laws based on *how* people act, not *why* they act."

Pam thought there was more to it than that, considered briefly whether it was wise to pursue the question further, then decided to risk it. "How can you separate the two? It seems to me that good people act good, bad people act bad, but the question is how they got that way. This guy we're looking for wasn't a monster to begin with. He was made into a monster, now society holds him responsible and will probably incarcerate him for life when he's caught...right? Where's the justice in that?"

A look of exasperation crossed Maki's face, but when he saw Pam's rookie earnestness he suddenly smiled. "Hey," he said, "looks like we have another philosopher in the department! You and Floyd should get together and work all this out and then let the rest of us know."

Knowing she was skating on thin ice, Pam decided to take another tack. "What about shooting a guy, like Dan did with the kidnapper?"

Sandy shook his head. "Like I said, cops can't take the law into their own hands. Each case is different and I can't say how I would react without being there."

Pam pointed a finger at Sandy. "Let's say your girlfriend is being raped..."

Sandy waved her off. "It's ludicrous to sit here speculating on what I might do in some made up situation. Every time the opportunity comes up it'll be a split second decision that'll be replayed in slow motion a thousand times."

Pam nodded. "You mean in the review boards and court?"

Sandy tapped his temple. His voice got very soft. "Mostly in your head."

Chapter 18

He was reading in his room with the television playing in the background. The book had a thin plot and he looked up to see the credits rolling from some trashy movie that he had been ignoring. The "Showtime" logo came on the screen, followed by previews of coming attractions. He was fumbling through his pile of reading material when the background music started to come up. He was vaguely aware that the announcer said that the movie was rated MA, for mature audiences only. He settled into his chair to see what was coming on next. The opening banner for *Basic Instinct*, starring Michael Douglas and Sharon Stone, ran across the screen.

The opening scene played out as the camera swept across the ceiling of a room where a woman and man were having sex. The woman reached up and playfully tied the man's hands to the head of the bed as she rocked her hips back and forth on top of his groin.

The killer gasped and reached for the remote control. In his rush, he knocked it off the table and it clattered to the floor. As he scrambled to his knees, the woman on the television screen reached into the folds of the bedding and pulled out an ice pick. The killer let out a whimper as he desperately punched at the buttons of the remote, trying to shut off the bloody image of the woman plunging the ice pick into the man's neck.

The screen went blank and he fell to the floor, gasping

for air. A terrible scene was playing out in his mind, worse than the scene on the television. It was his own mother tying him to the bed. She was talking to him.

"I can't understand why you aren't better behaved. Why do you constantly embarrass me? WHY?"

He struggled against the cords that were permanently tied to the steel headboard. "No momma. I'll be good."

His mother finished tying the bonds and stood back. "You are such an ugly little brat. I don't know why I let you live."

She turned to leave and he cried out. "Don't leave me! I want to go to the zoo. Please don't leave me behind!"

His mother never hesitated as she walked away. He could hear his mother and sister talking outside as they walked to the car for the drive to the Twin Cities. They had been planning the trip to the Como Zoo, in St. Paul, for a week. For once, the little boy thought that he would be included in a family activity. That dream had been shattered when school report cards came out. He'd had three "D's" and an "F." The principal had included a note requesting that a parent visit the school to talk about his poor performance. The meeting had made his mother a nervous wreck, and the trip home from the meeting had been a long dissertation on behavior and punishment, and comparisons to his sister.

"Take me along to the zoo!," he cried. He struggled against the bonds, but the cords were too strong for his eight-year-old arms to break. His sister had said they would always be too strong for his fat little arms. The sound of the car engine quickly drifted away as he cried and struggled to escape.

Decades later, the hurt was still there, but there were no tears now. There hadn't been tears for over twenty years.

Suddenly, he was once again standing on the edge of the Sauk river. The little boy watched as the firemen rowed back and forth. They were pulling a rope with a grappling hook. Tears never spilled from his eyes, although he felt immense emptiness inside as they pulled his one and only friend, Gary Johnson, out of the Sauk River. He'd never seen the body, but he knew it was inside the bag they carried from the boat.

He and Gary had skipped Physical Education class. Rather than going through the humiliation of waiting for girls to choose them for ballroom dance partners, he and Gary decided to go down to the river and skip rocks. They'd been throwing rocks at a log that was sticking up in the current, pretending that it was Miss Binger.

When Gary had slipped into the water, he'd thought his friend was just playing around. He laughed at the flailing arms. Then, the current caught Gary and he went under. His head didn't come up again. Miss Binger had been wrong. He and Gary weren't so fat they couldn't sink.

He climbed back onto the chair and set the remote on the table. He sat with his fists clenched and his eyes closed until the pain subsided. He got up and turned off the lights. The red numerals on the clock said 4 a.m.

DAY

FOUR

WEDNESDAY

Chapter 19

Dan Williams was back at the sheriff's office before five Wednesday morning. He stopped off in the ready room to pour a cup of coffee that looked like it had been on the warmer since the previous day. There was a pink message slip on top of the pile of papers nearest the telephone when he got into his office. The message said that Laurie Lone Eagle had called at eleven Tuesday night. He dialed her office number, expecting to leave a voice message for her.

Laurie's voice came on the line after one ring. "BCA, Agent Lone Eagle speaking."

Dan nearly choked on his coffee. He looked at his watch. "Do you realize that it's only five in the morning? Didn't you go home last night?"

"Hi, Dan. I caught a couple of hours of sleep after I left you a message last night. The lab got right on your print. They got a match."

Dan set his coffee aside and grabbed a pencil from the desk drawer. "Already? That's got to be a record." He flipped a report over to use it as note paper. "Fire away."

"The print belongs to a guy named Timothy Ross Cooper. He goes by his middle name, Ross. He has a couple of arrests for assault, but apparently has some mental problems that have kept him out of jail. I'll fax you his file, but it's pretty thin. You may want to follow up with Stearns County, where he was arrested, to see if they can give you more detail than is on the computer database."

Dan scribbled notes furiously, then held them up to study them. "So this guy has some assaults, but never a rape or murder?"

"That's what is on the rap sheet. Like I said, maybe Stearns County has some more. There is one interesting note. He didn't show up for his last trial so there is an outstanding warrant for his arrest. That should make life easier. If you find him you can hold him on the open warrant while you interrogate."

Dan shook his head. "Wow. First you come up with information on Doc Peterson, and then you put a name on our murder suspect. Thanks. Terrific work."

"I just hope that you can nail the guy. Has Doc Peterson backed off yet?"

Dan threw his pencil at the wastebasket. "Not that I've heard. I think that we're still on for a board meeting next Thursday."

Laurie let out a sigh. "Keep me posted."

By six, Dan had contacted two investigators that had arrested Ross Cooper in Stearns County. They agreed to fax him a full history of Cooper's arrests and court proceedings.

Pam Ryan gave up after punching the snooze button for the third time. Her head was pounding and it felt like several small animals had camped in her mouth overnight. The glowing red numerals on the clock said 6:40 am.

"Oh, God. Floyd will be here in twenty minutes." She threw off the sheet and ran to the kitchen in her silk Teddy. She spilled coffee grounds on the floor and water on the kitchen counter as she quickly emptied yesterday's coffee and made a fresh pot. When the water started flowing in Mr. Coffee, she grabbed panties and a bra from the top dresser drawer and headed to the shower.

The pounding hot water brought circulation to her pained head and made it worse. She had to open her eyes and lean on the wall. She was toweling off when she heard the door knocker. "He's early! Damn!"

She grabbed her robe and ran for the door. She looked through the peephole, then pulled the door open for Floyd. As she walked back to the bedroom she spoke over her shoulder. "Coffee should be ready. Grab a cup while I get dressed."

Floyd was sipping coffee and watching Good Morning America on Pam's kitchen television set. He looked up as she came in. "Good Morning."

Pam was still tucking the tail of her uniform shirt into her slacks as she walked into the kitchen. The sun streamed through the window almost making the yellows and whites of her kitchen glow. A wrought iron rack next to the window held an array of green plants, with a spider plant drooping its babies almost to the floor.

Pam took a cracked cup from the counter and poured coffee into the mug, trying to hide her shaking hands. "Morning. You ready to go?" The spilled coffee grounds had been cleaned up. Floyd was just finishing buttering some toast.

"Any time you're ready. But I thought that you'd want to eat some toast first," he said, handing her the warm toast. Floyd downed the last of his coffee and rinsed the cup in the sink as Pam wolfed down a bite of toast and washed it with coffee. Floyd watched her patiently as he dried the cup on a towel that had been hanging on the oven handle and put the cup back into the cupboard.

"Glad I didn't go along with you and Sandy last night. You look like hell" He neatly folded the towel and hung it back in place as Pam finished off one piece of toast and threw the other into the garbage bin under the sink.

"Remind me of that before I go drinking with Sandy

again." She switched the coffee machine to off and wiped the crumbs from her mouth with a tissue.

As they got into the car, Floyd picked up the microphone and called them into service. The dispatcher acknowledged and said, "Meet 608 at the courthouse."

"Ten-four."

Chapter 20

The dispatcher, entombed behind bullet-proof glass, buzzed the security door for Pam and Floyd. The hallway smelled of disinfectant. It often did after someone either bled or puked on the carpet. They passed a damp spot on the carpeting and stopped at the door to Dan's office. Floyd peered around the corner.

"C'mon in." Dan folded up some papers and put them in a pile as Pam and Floyd stepped in and closed the door. They heard footsteps in the hall and Sandy Maki opened the door and stepped in behind them. He had a bedraggled look. He looked at Pam and they exchanged sympathetic grins.

"I heard from the BCA." said Dan. "They expedited the evaluation of prints from the last cartridge case. They belong to a guy named Timothy Ross Cooper. Joey's not our murderer."

Dan pulled some papers from a pile and handed one to Floyd. Staring back from a page of print was a poor booking picture of an immature Timothy Ross Cooper. His face was round and babyish. The hair, which appeared light in the black-and-white photo, was thick and heavy. The booking-sheet described him as five two, weighing two hundred five pounds with brown eyes and light brown hair.

Pam was looking over Floyd's shoulder. "The date on this photo is 1986," she said, more or less to herself. "This picture is fourteen years old."

"His birthdate was 1968," said Floyd. "That makes him

about...thirty two, now."

Sandy shook his head. "The kid looks as homely as a mud fence."

Dan said, "I talked to Sauk Center and Stearns County. Cooper had arrests both places. Cooper apparently assaulted the homecoming queen while she was changing in the girl's locker room. Some of the princesses heard a scream, came in, and caught them struggling. Cooper made a run for it, but the Sauk Center police arrested him outside the building. He was hiding in the bushes behind the football stadium."

"Great guy." Floyd flipped the page over, looking for more information.

Dan opened a desk drawer, pulled out a jar of Tums and popped two in his mouth. Pam listened with an unasked question on her face. "What's the matter, Pam?" asked Dan.

"Cooper must have been a minor, then. How'd you get that file?"

Dan looked at the file. "Ahh, two days past his eighteenth birthday." Dan slipped the Tums jar back into the desk. "Anyway, his lawyer argued that he had a mental problem. The court ordered him to the state mental hospital, in St. Peter, for an evaluation, and the Psych people agreed. He spent a year in an outpatient treatment program. No in-patient commitment to the hospital. No jail time."

Floyd had been studying the file. "You said Stearns County arrested him too?"

Dan nodded. "Stearns County had a couple of cases of assault on women. Not rape. No penetration. The girls all reported that the guy was fat and had light-colored hair. The Stearns County people pulled Cooper's file and it sounded right, so they brought him in for questioning and put him in a line-up. Two girls positively identifed him, and he was arrested. This was in 1987. He paid his own bail, then split. No one's seen him since."

Floyd was tapping a pencil on his knee. "The BCA didn't make any other connects with other sex crimes since then? Most perverts can't control their fantasies that long."

Dan shook his head. "They're checking. But nothing pops out. Maybe he got smarter. Anyway, the way I see it now, Joey Berg is no longer our main suspect. Even though the ballistics tests may tell us it was his gun that did the killing, I still don't think Joey did it. This print puts Cooper at the murder scene, handling the cartridge. We've got a motive, and dyed blonde hair."

Pam let out a big sigh. "So, Joey's clear, Cooper's our killer and he's been messing with us all along. What do we do next?"

A big smile broke Dan's face. "Police work. Someone has to have seen this Cooper somewhere. He has an intimate knowledge of the people in this community, he's got to be a local. We start out by showing the picture to everyone that was at the Pine Brook Inn. Then, we show it to Terri Berg's neighbors, the people at the café where Terri worked, and folks in the stores and bars in the southern part of the county."

"That's it?" Pam looked disappointed. "I thought there was some high tech thing that would tell us where he was. You know. Social security numbers. Drivers licenses."

Dan pointed a pencil at her. "Good ideas. Why don't you hit the phones and follow Cooper's paper trail while Floyd and Sandy do the rounds."

Pam looked at Dan with a frown. "And what are you going to do?"

"I think I'll go to the Sportsman's Café and have a slice of pie." He squeezed past them in the hall and walked toward the front door.

Dan Williams took I-35 north to highway 23 and drove west past the swamps and streams that threaded through the farm pastures and fields of grain. The drive gave him time to think without the distractions of the phone and people barging into his office.

Timothy Ross Cooper had disappeared from Stearns County over a decade ago. Now he shows up in Pine County. Well, his fingerprints showed up in Pine County. Pam was trying to find Cooper's trail through the "above ground" economy, but he knew there wasn't much chance that they would find him there. Somehow they needed to tap into the "underground" economy, that other world of people that never deal with credit cards, banks, the Social Security Administration, or the police. They worked for cash, payed their bills in cash, and were thus invisible to "the system." Some were more or less legit—carpenters, mechanics, musicians, but others were drug dealers, prostitutes, and bookies.

Dan drove past the town of Pine Brook which was entirely on the south side of the highway. The only two businesses that faced the highway were the Amoco station and the Pine Brook Inn. He turned into the Inn's parking lot and had his choice of parking spots so early in the morning.

He parked next to an old Caprice and walked in the front entrance as the dust he had stirred up in the parking lot drifted away in the wind. As his eyes adjusted to the interior darkness, he saw two older men sitting on bar stools at the middle of the bar. Harvey, the bartender was leaning over the bar talking to them.

Dan walked to a barstool and sat down. As Dan approached, Harvey stepped away from the bar and retrieved a cup from the back shelf. He poured a cup of coffee from the stained carafe and brought it over to Dan.

Harvey pushed the cup to Dan, and set a roll of Tums next to the cup. "I assume that you still take it black, with Tums on the side."

Dan smiled and picked up the cup. "It's been a couple of years, but you still remember."

Harvey smiled back as Dan sampled the coffee. "That's

the secret of being a good bartender. You have to remember what everyone's 'usual' is."

Dan scrunched up his face and set the cup down. "The coffee hasn't improved." He peeled the Tums package open and popped two into his mouth.

Harvey laughed as the other two patrons looked on with curiosity. "You never did like my coffee. No one else ever complains, though most folks don't come here for the coffee." Harvey noticed that the other patron's drinks were running low and waddled off to refill their glasses. Dan sipped his coffee and watched.

Harvey was back in less than a minute with his own cup of coffee. "You didn't stop by to talk about the old days when we were young. What's up? I suppose it's the Berg thing."

Dan nodded and pulled out one of the copies of the booking picture of Timothy Ross Cooper. He handed it to Harvey. "You recognize this guy?"

Harvey tipped the picture a couple of ways and then carried it to the brighter light under the back bar. He brought it back and set it on the counter. "Nah. 'fraid not. He looks kind of familiar, but I see so many faces. He got anything to do with Terri Berg's death?"

Dan shrugged. "We'd like to talk to him about it."

Harvey asked, "He looks too young to be a regular in here. What's his name? Names stick with me better than faces in grainy pictures."

"Cooper. Timothy Ross Cooper. This is a picture of him when he was younger. He grew up down by Sauk Center."

Harvey shook his head. "The name doesn't ring a bell either." He picked up the picture and tilted it again to catch the light. "He's kinda chubby. Looks a little like...Umm...I don't know." He set the picture on the bar again and shrugged.

Dan handed the picture to the other two patrons. "You guys ever see this face around?"

They passed the picture back and forth, trying to get

enough light on it to see the grainy fax image. The farthest one shook his head. The nearer one handed the picture back and said, "I don't think so, but I can't really tell."

Dan nodded and put the picture in his pocket. "Harvey, why don't you put some lights in this place?"

Harvey leaned close. "The patrons can't tell if the glasses are clean this way." He gave Dan a conspiratorial wink.

Dan chuckled and finished off the coffee. He pushed a dollar bill across the bar.

Harvey pushed it back. "I owe this bar to you. Your money is no good here."

Dan left the money on the bar. "I can't accept free Tums, and the sheriff will fire me for accepting bribes."

Harvey picked up the dollar and leaned over the bar. He jammed it in Dan's shirt pocket. "Those Tums are the ones that you left here when you broke up the fight between the bikers. They never came back again after that. Once they were gone, the locals started coming back and I've had a quiet, steady business ever since then."

Dan shook his head, then took a step toward the door. He stopped and looked back at Harvey. "Did anyone follow Terri Berg and Jamie Arvidson out of the bar Saturday night?"

Harvey shook his head. "It was too busy. I really didn't notice." Suddenly, Harvey's face paled. "Was that Jamie they found with her?"

Dan nodded in response.

Harvey shook his head. "What a shame. They were a fun-loving couple. Too bad things like that happen to nice folks."

Dan decided that while he was here he'd pursue another avenue. "What do you know about your watress's boyfriend, Brian Mattson?"

Harvey snorted. "Butch has got muscle between his ears. A real A-number-one asshole. He beats the shit out of Barb and pretends that it doesn't happen, or that it's her fault. I've tried to talk her into dumping him, but she thinks that she needs him somehow."

"Do you think that he'd be capable of killing two people?"

Harvey rubbed his bulbous nose with the palm of his hand. "I think that Butch would enjoy killing two people. A guy made a grab for Barb one night and I thought that Butch was going to rip the guy apart. I came over the bar with the baseball bat and Butch snarled at me. You know, like he was going to bite me or something. Butch is a real piece of work."

On the way to Mora, Dan mulled over Harvey's comments about Brian "Butch" Mattson. Cooper's fingerprint on the cartridge at Berg's house was strong evidence linking him to the crime scene, but Butch Mattson was a violent criminal with an explosive temper, and he could easily have had connections with Terri Berg. Dan knew he had transgressed a cardinal rule in investigative work by almost immediately eliminating Joey. He'd seen the look of skepticism on his Deputies faces. He had to be careful not to get a mind set that would cause him to overlook certain leads.

So Had Jamie Arvidson or Terri Berg done something to set Butch Mattson off? Had Jamie said or done something to Barb Dupre? Another startiling possibility occurred to him; was Mattson actually Cooper? Dan shook his head. They had identified Mattson through fingerprints when he'd refused to give his name.

Barb Dupre had told Sandy that she had spent the whole night with Mattson, but was she a reliable source? Probably, since she was willing to press domestic assault charges against Mattson. If anything, she would be more likely to leave him without an alibi so that he'd be a suspect in the Berg-Arvidson murders.

By the time Dan passed the tire store on the city limits

of Mora he had discounted Butch Mattson as a top suspect. His thoughts returned to the photograph they had received that morning, of the young Timothy Ross Cooper, heavy featured even then, a shock of thick, coarse hair hanging over his forehead, a sullen, defiant look on his face as he stared at the camera.

Chapter 21

Dan pulled into the gravel parking lot of the Sportsman's Café, in Mora, where Terri Berg had been a waitress. The late lunch crowd had cleared, but there were still a half dozen cars in the gravel lot. He parked in a spot next to the front door.

The café was about fifty years old and had the weathered look of hard use, tempered by owners that cared enough to do the maintenance necessary to make it look clean and homey. Dan grabbed a stool at the counter and picked up a menu that was jammed between the sugar jar and a ketchup bottle.

The waitress that came to take his order was no spring chicken. She pulled a pencil out of her carefully permed red hair and held it up to the pad. "What can I get you?" She was trim from working hard, but the crow's feet around her eyes said that she'd celebrated her fiftieth birthday a few years ago. She was wearing a Vikings jersey, with the number ten on the back, over her jeans. Dan smiled. She was old enough to remember when Fran Tarkenton had worn that number quarterbacking the Vikings in the Super Bowl instead of as an infomercial king.

"You got any soup left?" he asked.

She wrinkled her nose and thought for a split second. "I think that there's some hamburger sauerkraut left and there might be one bowl of navy bean."

Dan pushed the menu back to it's resting spot. "I'll take

the bowl of the navy bean and a cheeseburger and a cup of coffee when you get a second."

He watched as the waitress left with purposeful strides and hung the order on the rotating metal trolley on the pass-through between the kitchen and the dining room. Dan could see that this was a lady that had been around the business for a few years She didn't waste any words or motions. She was probably a gem of an employee, too, unlike the young teenagers that didn't understand the meaning of real work.

She was back in a minute with an empty cup and a carafe of coffee. "You take cream with that?" she asked as she poured.

Dan shook his head. "No, but I have a question for you."

She sized Dan up for a second. "About what?"

"How well did you know Terri Berg?" He took a sip of the coffee. It was a welcome change from the vile brew at the Pine Brook Inn.

At the mention of Terri's name her face got somber and a wall of defense went up. "Well enough. Who's asking?" She set the pot on the counter, looking at Dan curiously.

Dan reached into his pocket, took out his badge holder and the picture of Timothy Ross Cooper. He held the badge out for her to see.

"Pine County," she said to herself. Then, looking at him, she asked, "What are you doing over here?"

"I'm investigating Terri Berg's death."

The call, "Order up!" came from the kitchen. She put up a finger. "Hang on a minute." With that she was off delivering a pile of pancakes to a guy that looked like an over-the-road trucker. She topped off his coffee and set the carafe back on the warmer.

With that done, she came around the counter and sat on the stool next to Dan. "Poor Terri," she said. "By the way, my name is Donna Mae."

"Dan Williams." He shook her hand. "Have you ever

seen this guy hanging around?" He handed her the picture of Cooper.

Donna Mae took Ross Cooper's picture and studied it, holding it at arm's length to get it into focus. "Can't say he looks familiar to me." She handed it back. "Is that the guy that killed her?"

"At this point we don't know who killed her. We'd like to talk to this guy because we think that he may know something."

Donna Mae nodded. "I hear that Terri was pretty badly beaten up. I kind of figured that it was some sort of pervert when I read about it in the paper. You know, she was quite a flirt."

"Order up!" the voice from the kitchen said again.

Donna Mae stood up. "I think that's yours."

Dan watched her move around the end of the counter. She swept the dishes off the passthrough and was back with them in less than a minute. There wasn't a wasted motion in anything that she did. As soon as the plates were down, she was off to ring up a couple of customers at the cash register. She topped off the trucker's coffee and then slid onto the stool next to Dan's.

Dan held up the spoon. "The soup is good."

"I'll pass that along to Jo. She makes it fresh every day after she gets the pies baked. She's been doing it for twenty years."

Dan nodded in appreciation. "Did Terri talk much about her personal life?"

Donna Mae cackled. "Honey, that's all she talked about. I've heard about her asshole husband, who's now her ex-husband. I heard about her drinking buddies at the bar. Mostly I heard about Jamie the last month or two." Donna Mae froze in mid-thought. "Was it him that was with her?"

Dan nodded. "It appears so."

Donna Mae shook her head. "Too bad. It sounds like he

was a really nice guy."

"Did Terri ever talk about anyone that she didn't like, or that didn't like her?"

"Not really. I mean, not other than 'Asshole Joey.' That's what she called him all the time. I suppose that you've been talking to him."

"We've talked to Joey, and a lot of other people, too." Dan squirted ketchup from the plastic bottle onto his burger. He asked, "Did Terri ever mention someone named Butch?"

Donna looked around the café to see if she was needed while she thought. "I don't recall a Butch. Was she dating him, too?"

Dan shook his head as he chewed on the hamburger. The meat was thick and juicy, with fresh lettuce and real Cheddar cheese. He chewed slowly to see if Donna Mae would add anything else if she wasn't prompted.

Before he swallowed, Donna Mae was up and headed around the end of the counter. "I think there's only one piece of the Strawberry Rhubarb pie left. I'd better grab it now for you."

When she came back, the pie was steaming and there was a scoop of vanilla ice cream melting on top of it. Donna Mae set it next to the empty soup bowl and sat down on the stool again. "Terri talked about a guy named Bill that she thought was really handy. She had him come over whenever something around the house broke. But I don't think there was any romance between them. As a matter of fact, I think that Terri kind of used him. At least, that's my opinion. Sounded like she hung around the bar with a couple of other guys that were her age. She hasn't talked about many guys lately, other than Jamie."

Dan pushed away the last couple bites of the burger and pulled the pie closer. The hot filling was oozing from between the crusts, and half of the ice cream was in a puddle on the plate. He took a bite and the light crust dissolved in his mouth. The tangy smell of the rhubarb was offset by the mouthwatering sweetness of the homegrown strawberries.

"My God this is heavenly," Dan said with his mouth still full. "If I ate this every day I'd weigh four hundred pounds."

Donna Mae smiled. "It's the best. We only serve it when we can get fresh berries and rhubarb."

Dan wiped his mouth with a paper napkin from the dispenser. "Did Terri ever have an old boyfriend that was mad about breaking up?" He took another huge bite of pie.

Donna Mae shook her head. "Nah. She and Joey were high school sweethearts. She never had anyone else before Joey, and she's only been dating the last few months. Jamie seems to be the only one that she's been serious about since the divorce."

Dan finished the pie and left with no more answers than when he'd arrived. Everything kept pointing to Joey, and no one had ever seen or heard of Timothy Ross Cooper. Cooper the phantom. Cooper the invisible. Cooper the ghost. Cooper, who beat Terri Berg until her breasts were bruised black. Cooper, who smothered her and then shot her dead body full of holes. Cooper the devil.

Dan took highway 65 north out of Mora and wound his way through the back roads toward his home in Sturgeon Lake. His mind wandered as he drove, trying to figure out the mystery of Cooper. A white-tailed deer ran across the road and Dan slowed. There was usually a second deer behind the first.

Within seconds, a pair of spotted fawns emerged from the dense dogwood underbrush that lined the side of the road. They scampered across the road with an awkward gait, following the doe into the opposite ditch. Dan pulled over and watched them as they meandered through a hay field. Their summer coats were reddish, the color accentuated by the afternoon sun. Halfway across the field, they stopped and lay down, effectively disappearing from his sight in the uncut hay.

Dan mused. "Just like Cooper. One minute he's there and the next he just disappears." He pondered the murders and tried to find a connection point that could link Cooper to Terri Berg. How did he know her? And what about Jamie? Cooper was a sex offender, no doubt. Had he stalked Terry and found Jamie with Terri by accident and had to kill him?

No one at the Pine Brook Inn or the Sportsman's Café had ever seen Cooper. Yet Cooper would have to know about Terri and Joey to try to frame Joey as the murderer. Did he know that Jamie Arvidson would be with Terri, or was that just coincidence? Maybe Jamie was the target and Terri was an innocent victim. No, that theory didn't fit with Cooper's background and his intimate, vicious attack on her.

There were many more questions than there were answers. With that thought he removed two Tums from the package, popped two of them into his mouth and started chewing. The minty taste bit his tongue.

A semi drove past, stirring up the dust and breaking Dan's silent concentration. Regaining his thoughts, Dan reflected on past investigations. Everyone in this area knew their neighbors and their neighbor's business. There are few secrets in a small town, and even fewer places to hide. Even if Cooper was staying in an adjacent county, the law enforcement community was so closely knit that someone would find him and turn him over.

Was it possible that Cooper was a transient from the Cities? Not likely, Dan thought, Cooper had too much knowledge of the relationship between Terri and Joey. Yet it was possible that Cooper could know certain intimate details but still live and work somewhere else.

If Cooper lived in Minneapolis it would be easy for him to be invisible. The apartment houses where neighbors didn't know neighbors were as common as mosquitoes in July. An arrest warrant might be open for years before a criminal got stopped for a traffic violation or some accomplice turned a criminal in to get a reduced sentence for himself.

Pine County was different from Minneapolis. The County was a patchwork quilt of small towns and rural areas where people's existence and sanity relied on the threads that sewed them together. Everyone knew their neighbors, and their neighbor's business. They celebrated together and they mourned as a community. A person like Timothy Ross Cooper would stand out and quickly become a pariah. That's why the state didn't put halfway houses for recovering drug addicts and criminals in the rural areas. It didn't work. The residents always became the social equivalent of Biblical lepers.

Dan slipped the car into gear and pulled back onto highway 65. As he drove toward Sturgeon Lake he continued to search for a clue, a thread, a hint that someone had given him about the suspect. Cooper had managed to stay clear of law enforcement for years, but he wasn't invisible. He had left them something somewhere. There had to be other clues to where he was hidden.

Pam had been transferred among various Social Security Administration departments for two hours and still hadn't gotten an answer about any earnings credited to Timothy Ross Cooper. After brow-beating a peon in some obscure office, she was able to get to a manager that took her badge number and called back. He confirmed that Timothy Ross Cooper had no reported earnings since 1988. Pam was torn between cheering and swearing.

The sheriff walked into the ready room as she was hanging up the phone. "Have you seen Dan?"

"Last I saw was early this morning."

"Thanks, I'll have the dispatcher track him down. If he comes back, have him look me up right away." Sepanen looked at his watch as if to add emphasis. The wall clock said four fifty. Almost quitting time.

Pam went through the law enforcement data bank and searched for driver's licenses. She searched under the name Cooper, first. Over 900 names filled the computer screen. She next searched for Timothy Cooper. The list dropped to seven names. Timothy R Cooper, with an address in Sauk Center on F. Scott Fitzgerald Blvd., popped out. He had a license that had expired in 1989. She noted that he hadn't needed glasses to drive and he hadn't had a motorcycle endorsement. Since they already had Cooper's picture from 1988, it would be of no benefit to request another one from the motor vehicle department.

Every other avenue that she pursued after that came up empty. Floyd had told her that police work was like being a pilot; hours of boredom followed by seconds of terror. She was ready for a change—maybe not to terror, but certainly from the boredom.

Chapter 22

The Wednesday afternoon business at the Quamba bar was dead slow. The lighting was dim and the woodwork dark, making the lighting appear subdued. Three elderly men were playing cribbage at a table in the corner. The television behind the bar was tuned to some game show that the bartender was watching as he washed glasses. The quiet atmosphere appealed to Timothy Cooper. The subdued lighting made the makeup over the scratch marks on his neck even more effective. A radio played oldies from the 50s and 60s as the cribbage players drank hard and ignored the noise.

A mildly attractive, middle-aged woman came in and sat down on the stool next to him. She smelled of cigarettes and sweat, with an undercurrent of some cheap cologne.

"This heat is murder. I had to get outta the house to cool off for a while." She signaled the bartender and ordered a Lite beer. She took a long draw on the beer and set it down on the little square napkin. "You got air conditioning at your place, honey?

He grunted. "Sorta."

She stuck out a hand. "I'm Carol Knutson." The fingers were long and hadn't seen a manicure, but her hands weren't hard and calloused, like those of farmwives.

He took the hand and shook it, scrambling mentally for a harmless name to give her. "Everyone calls me Coop."

Carol Knutson looked at him oddly for a moment, then

cracked a smile that lit up her face. "Like pooper scooper?" she giggled. Her face was wide and full. Her smile showed off a mouth full of crooked teeth. It was obvious that she had been drinking for quite a while before she got to Quamba.

He frowned at her attempted humor and at his own anger for not coming up with a better name. "Whatever." He took a long drink from his beer. "You local?" he asked.

"A few miles north. I got a little place that I rent." She swilled half the beer. "Used to be a farmhouse. The guy that bought it lives on the next place and rents the house to me. He farms the land. It works out okay, but it's no great deal."

"Divorced?"

She gave him another funny look as she leaned back on the stool. She was apparently a little farsighted and he was sitting too close for her to focus on him. "Does it show? I mean, it's been a couple of years now. The stink hasn't worn off me yet?"

He shook his head. "Naw. Anyone as attractive as you doesn't make it to our age without getting the marriage ticket punched. Painful divorce?" He guessed that she was in her late thirties.

Carol huffed. "Aren't they all? We're from the Range. We moved down when the mines closed in the seventies. He got a job welding and I sat at home. It got tense. He wasn't making the money the union miners made and he took it out on me, by way of a bottle. I couldn't take it."

"Knutson isn't a Range name."

She cracked a smile. "Carol Mlenic. I met my ex while I was going to UMD. He came back with me to Orr about the time the taconite business was getting rolling. We had it good then."

Carol tilted her beer bottle and inspected the neck. "How about you, honey. What do you do?"

"Odd jobs, mostly I get by."

Carol swilled the last of her beer and signaled the bartender for another. "Ain't that the way it is. I been so hot I was even thinking about renting a motel room. You know, just to cool off and get some decent sleep." She leaned back again in an effort to focus. "I seen you around here before, haven't I?"

"Probably. I get here now and again." He looked at her. The hair was auburn, graying at the temples and tied back in a ponytail. She wore a thin cotton blouse and jeans. Legs looked a little hefty. That was probably why she was in jeans, not shorts.

"Can I buy you another one?" The bartender delivered Carol's beer and she pointed to Cooper's bottle.

"Sure." He drained the Grain Belt beer he'd been nursing.

Carol pushed a five-dollar bill across the bar, then poured down a slug of beer as Cooper stole a look at her chest. She wasn't buxom, but she had a definite figure that showed through the cotton.

Cooper was surprised by her next comment. "You want to share a room, honey? There's a little motel in Rock Creek that has rooms for nineteen dollars. The sign says air conditioning and cable TV." She made the offer sound entirely innocent. "I could sure use a good night's sleep. This heat is killing me."

The woman took a long draw on her new beer and sized him up. She mistook his silence for reluctance. A smile crossed her lips, making tiny wrinkles in the corners of her mouth and eyes. "You're not queer, are you?"

He was swallowing a mouthful of beer and he snorted at the question, causing beer to run out of his nostrils. He choked for several seconds. When he finally caught his breath, he answered. "No, dear, I ain't queer. Let's get outta here. You go get checked in, and I'll pick up a twelve-pack. Meet you there in a bit." He pulled his wallet from his jeans and dug out a ten-dollar bill. "Here's for my half of the room."

"Sure 'nuff," she said. "I'm driving a green Maverick.

You can't miss it."

Cooper stopped off at the Hinckley municipal liquor store and bought a 12-pack of Miller Lite. He retrieved the package of condoms from the glove compartment of the car and ripped one off. He started to put the rest away, then ripped off a second one, slipping them into his pocket.

For the entire drive to Rock Creek he kept kicking himself for revealing his real name to Carol. Why not Billy, or Jerry, or Josie—any one of these would have been better. He pounded his fist on the rim of the steering wheel. Hell, why not Jamie or Joey, even? He had to smile as he thought about taking either of those guy's names. But it was done. There'd probably be no harm in it, anyway.

The Rock Creek Motel was just off old highway 61. The parking lot was empty except for a yellow Ryder truck, parked near the office, and a green Ford Maverick, parked in front of room #9. He pulled his car beyond the Maverick, so that it was mostly obscured from the view of the motel's office. The Ryder truck effectively blocked the view of both cars from the highway.

He walked to the door marked "9" and knocked, looking around behind him to see if there was anyone else around. Cooper suddenly saw a young man going into the room just on the other side of the Ryder truck, but he didn't appear to have seen Cooper. Before he could do anything further, Carol pulled the door open.

"Get in here with that beer." Her voice was slurred, but playful as she grabbed the bag from his hands and pulled him into the coolness of the room. She had the window air conditioner's thermostat set to the coldest setting and had pulled her blouse out of her pants and unbuttoned it at the waist. She stood in front of the air conditioner and let the air blow up under the fabric as she held the tails against the top of the grille.

The inside of the room was Spartan. The ugly brown

carpeting had a trail worn into it that ran from the door to the bathroom and between the two beds. The walls were plain cement blocks that had been painted so many times they had lost all texture except for the mortar seams. The bedspreads were a dark blue plaid that had been popular in the 70s. They had seen little use and looked like they might have been in storage for three decades, or maybe the motel had seen that few guests.

Cooper stood at the closed door and watched Carol for a second. He was a little worried about the young man he'd seen going into another room. Carol had her eyes closed and seemed to be exhilarating in the rush of cold air. The cold air made her hard nipples press against her bra and show through the blouse. He decided to stay. He picked up the bag from where she'd thrown it on the bed and pulled the beer carton out. He ripped the cardboard open and pulled out a can.

Carol didn't open her eyes or leave the front of the air conditioner. "Is it cold?"

He popped the top and held it out to her. "S'posed to be. It was in the cooler." He stared at the can for a second, trying to remind himself to wipe the fingerprints off of it later.

Carol took the beer, threw back her head and poured down the cool liquid. He thought she drank like a biker. She wiped her mouth on her sleeve like a cowboy. "You owe me another buck for the room-tax. How much I owe you for the beer?" She looked at him vacantly through glazed eyes.

"Let's call it even." Cooper opened a beer for himself and took a swig while he leaned against the dresser staring at Carol's body. The dresser and a chair were the only piece of furniture other than the twin beds and a portable television that was screwed down to a swivel stand.

Carol polished off the beer in another drag and looked for a wastebasket. She disappeared around the corner and there was the sound of aluminum hitting hard plastic in the bathroom. It was followed by the sound of a zipper and then liquid running into the toilet.

Cooper must have looked surprised when Carol came out of the bathroom with her jeans in her hand. Her blouse was open in the front exposing her cleavage and a white bra. The tails of the shirt hung down over her dark blue, polka-dotted panties. Her thighs were heavy with cellulite. They slimmed to shapely calves.

"Oh, I hope you don't mind that I took off my jeans. They were kinda hot." She threw the jeans on the bed nearest the bathroom. She was very casual about her exposed flesh and took another beer from the carton, before sliding onto the bed next to the jeans. She stood a pillow on end and stuffed it behind her back.

Cooper couldn't help staring at her legs. Carol felt the stare and crossed them discreetly. "Why don't you get more comfortable, too?"

Cooper shook his head and decided to turn on the television. There was a stupid, real-life cop show on that he found offensive. He flipped the channel over to a talk show and sat down on the other bed.

Carol finished off another beer and dropped the empty can on the floor next to the bed. "Hand me another one. Would you?"

He pulled one out as he handed her the rest of the carton. They sat silently watching a string of jilted lovers spill their emotions out for Jerry Springer and the audience. Cooper looked over when he heard a can hit the floor and gurgle. She was passed out, snoring.

He used a handkerchief to carefully wipe his fingerprints from the cans that he'd handled before dropping them into the wastebasket. As he passed the television, he turned it off and made sure the door to the room was locked. He stood looking at her for a second. What a surprise she'd been. She'd made it easy. Too easy. Terri had teased him for months. He'd wanted Terri so badly, but he also knew that she'd never have anything to do with him.

When he had come to that realization, he'd had to plan his punishment for her. And when the stupid ex-husband showed up, it all came together. They'll nail that stupid jerk for the whole thing. Joey was too drunk to provide an alibi. Hell, he'd been too drunk to know someone was digging the keys out of his pocket.

Cooper stared at Carol. Her snoring bothered him. His mother had snored when she was drunk, too. It was disgusting. He walked up and rolled Carol's head to one side. She didn't wake up, but the snoring stopped.

He thought about waiting until she woke up before he had her. The fight was exhilarating. All women rejected him. All women hated him. Even his mother. She had been the worst. How could a mother hate her own child? He looked at himself in the mirror over the dresser. This one would hate him, too, if she wasn't too drunk to care.

He sat next to her on the plaid bedspread and ran his fingers over her cheek, then down her breast. She was pretty in a mature sort of way. She was a little older than Terri, but still pretty. He ran his finger down the front of her open blouse. He pulled the edges back, exposing her abdomen and chest. She was wearing a frilly bra that fastened in the front. When he released the clasp it sprang wide and fell away from her breasts as they slid to the sides of her chest. Her nipples were dark saucers against the pale skin of her chest.

She stirred slightly and he recoiled, but she quickly settled into sleep again. He stared at the large nipples, the size of half-dollars. When he touched them, they became hard despite her drunkenness. He felt his own hardness. He struggled to remove her panties, then took off his own clothes. Through it all she snored and stirred, but never became fully awake.

He was amazed at the depth of her sleep. She didn't stir through his penetration and thrusts. He slipped off of her and removed the condom, carefully tying it and dropping it into the pocket of the jeans after wiping her wetness on the panties. He stared at her lying on the bed with her legs spread wide, unaware that a man was staring at her naked body, even unaware that she'd been raped.

"Now what?" he said out loud. He put his clothes on and stared at her lying there. She was still ready for him. But it wasn't fun with her passed out. It had been like screwing a blow-up doll. Well, maybe better than a doll. She was warm and soft.

Would she even know that she'd been raped? There was no semen. Maybe if he just slipped her under the covers and left, she'd never know. Did women know? She did know his face. If she reported it as a rape she could identify him to the police. He sat on the edge of the bed and stared at her naked body. If only he'd brought the gun, he could shoot her. The thought made his heart race. No, it'd be too noisy in the motel.

Terri had died before he'd shot her. He knew it, but still didn't know why. Maybe she'd had a heart attack. No one would ever know. If they ever did figure out that it was a double murder they had Joey Berg. Joey was dead meat. All the evidence pointed to him and he had a motive.

A rush of adrenaline ran through Cooper's veins as he thought about the murders. Killing hadn't been as hard as he'd once thought. He'd gotten a rush watching Terri suffer. She deserved to suffer for ignoring him. It was really too bad that he hadn't realized she was dying. He'd thought that her lack of resistance was submission. He hadn't realized that Terri had died during the rape until after he had finished.

Jamie Arvidson's death had been a super rush. He hated these guys who seemed to have everything without even trying. They were the ones women liked. He remembered watching Jamie's chest rise and fall, then feeling the cold trigger under his finger as he watched Jamie take the last breath of his life. Cooper trembled with excitement as he played the scene back in his mind.

Looking at Carol he suddenly saw his mother's face and

his hatred boiled into rage. Cooper attacked her with savage ferocity. He forced himself upon her, placing his hands upon her throat and face, pushing up and down with all his weight, again and again, thrusting so hard that the contact against her pelvis hurt his groin even through his clothing.

Suddenly, he looked up and saw his own face again in the mirror. The image of evil and hatred that stared back startled him and he paused. His own face, at that moment, was foreign to him. He stared at it, trying to comprehend. Looking at himself, he suddenly felt overwhelming sorrow and grief. It was as though the person he thought he was, had striven to be, had died. How had he come to this? An evil stranger, even to himself. Almost always he tried to see himself differently than this image in the mirror. But there he was, really—ugly, unwanted, unlovable, rejected by everyone.

He hated them all. They felt nothing for him. They deserved nothing from him. Even his mother and sister had hated him. He was smarter than most of them, but that didn't matter. It got him nothing.

Rosemary Cooper's face was before him again on the body on the bed. His own mother. It was her fault. She had created him in both body and spirit.

"BITCH! BITCH! BITCH!" It all came out, after years and years of holding it in. He pummeled Carol's corpse until tears rolled down his face and his energy had been sapped. He fell with his face between the bruised breasts and the tears fell like rain after a long drought.

DAY

FIVE

THURSDAY

Chapter 23

On Thursday morning Dan was in Pine City, working his way through downtown. He walked from shop to shop, talking to the cashiers and customers. They looked at the Cooper picture and shook their heads. One man thought that the face looked familiar, but couldn't place it.

At noon, Dan was back at the courthouse. He collected his message slips and called his wife at the clinic. She wanted to know if he was going to be home for supper on time. The neighbors had invited them over for a steak fry. He said that he'd try to make it, but not to hold things up if he were late. Sally understood. Dan missed a lot of social engagements. Some she attended alone. Others they just skipped.

The second note was from the sheriff. It simply said, "See me." It was dated the previous day.

The sheriff wasn't in his office, so Dan walked down to the bull pen. Pam was staring at a computer screen, tapping a pencil on the desk.

"Any luck?"

At the sound of Dan's voice, she jumped. "Jesus, you scared me." She held a hand to her throat as she regained her composure.

"Sorry. Are you making any headway?" He pulled up a straight backed chair and straddled it, resting his chin on the back.

"Dead ends. No Social Security earnings. a driver's

license that expired in 1989. No marriage license. No death cer-
tificate. No military record. No real estate transactions. No
recent police record. It's like Cooper left the face of the earth."

Dan rested his chin on his hands. "Or changed his name.
Maybe he lives under an alias. Or moved out of state.
Frustrating, isn't it?"

Pam pushed her chair back from the desk. "This isn't
what we talked about in college. We talked about laws, procedures and filling out paperwork. We didn't talk about boredom
and frustration."

Dan smiled and straightened up. "Welcome to the real
world. They didn't talk about people splattered all over the
road, dragging lakes for drowned kids or bar fights, either. But
they're all a part of the job. You never know what's around the
next curve in the road."

Pam held out her arms and flexed her hands into fists.
"But all these dead ends are driving me nuts. I want to make
some progress. There's a murderer out there." She tossed the
pencil on the desk.

Dan got up and straightened the chair. "They're not
dead ends, Pam. They're possibilities that have been eliminated. That's mostly what investigations are. You knock off possibilities until there are only one or two left, then you throw
everything you've got at the last ones."

Pam leaned back in the chair and ran her fingers through
her short hair. "Are all of 'em this hard?"

"This isn't hard. We're doing great! We've got a name
and a picture. We didn't have that two days ago. Sometimes we
never get this far." He walked to the hallway. "You're doing
great. Now you can check for out-of-state driver's licenses. Try
car registrations, too, and try variations on the first name. You
know, like just an initial T, Tim or Tom. Most criminals aren't
very creative in their aliases."

Pam snapped up in her chair. "I almost forgot. The sheriff was looking for you yesterday and this morning."

"I suppose that he has some new information about Doc Peterson." Dan looked at his watch. "Maybe the dispatcher knows where Sepanen is."

"Are they going to decertify Doc Peterson or something?" Pam got up and walked to the coffee pot. She drained the old coffee into the sink and started to make a new pot.

"Naw. Doc Peterson wants my badge for chewing him out at Terri Berg's." Dan turned and went down the hall.

"He wants YOUR badge? He should have been fired!" She yelled after him.

Dan paused. "Why do you say that?"

Pam put fresh water into the pot. "Well, I was there and he wasn't using proper procedures. It's basic law enforcement 101 not to remove the corpse until evidence has been collected. He could've jeopardized the whole investigation. He even declared it to be a murder/suicide. We could've stopped there and not be looking for this Cooper guy."

Dan smiled. "Hey Pam, you're okay. Just keep remembering to do things in the right order and you'll go far in law enforcement. Of course, a little political savvy goes a long way too. Just think how far I could have gone if I didn't go around telling the coroner that he's an idiot."

Evelyn Ryberg, the co-owner of the Rock Creek motel, was fretting as only a frustrated busybody could. The Ford Maverick was still parked in front of room nine and it was nearly one o'clock in the afternoon. Her heels clicked out a steady rhythm as she paced the linoleum behind the counter. The door between the motel office and the living quarters was open, and Evelyn could see Doug, her husband, watching the Minnesota Twins playing the Chicago White Sox. Evelyn wasn't happy to be alone in her misery. Her pacing was supposed to annoy her husband, but his apparent apathy annoyed her even further.

Her anger finally surfaced. She plodded out of the office

and slapped the back of the green nylon sofa. "Doug, why don't you go down there and see what's going on?"

Doug Ryberg looked away from the game and stared at her. "I don't care what's going on." He turned back without further comment, settling into the depressions that his body had created in the sofa. In the eighteen years the Ryberg's had owned the Rock Creek Motel, he had spent half his waking hours lying on the same sofa watching sporting events on television.

"You have to care. If that woman isn't out in half an hour, she'll be past checkout time. You'll have to charge her for another day."

Doug didn't stir. The motel purchase had been Evelyn's dream. He had taken it on reluctantly, and only after she had promised that he would have to do nothing. He was retired and his dream retirement was watching the Twins and Vikings.

"Damn it, Doug. I have to make up the room. Get her out!"

This time Doug didn't even look at her to answer. "Why bother? We have eleven other rooms and I don't see any line of people waiting. Who knows, maybe she wants to stay another night."

Evelyn stomped back to the office where she could keep an eye on the Maverick. She hefted her heavy frame onto a vinyl covered chair. The metal frame sagged and groaned under her weight. "What time did her boyfriend leave last night?"

Doug didn't even look away from the television. "I didn't notice. What makes you sure it was a boyfriend? I never saw anyone. Just a car."

"What else would it have been? I almost went down there and threw them out." She tapped her long fingernails on the vinyl seat cover.

"Why? You got something against making a living? Cut folks a little slack and they may come back again. You know, it's not like every room is booked a year ahead. You keep telling me that we could use a little return business. If you make people comfortable they might come back again."

Evelyn shifted in the chair to get more comfortable. Her weight made almost any position uncomfortable after a few minutes. "Well, I don't take well to people doing illicit things here. I want to run a clean place. People like that make messes."

Doug propped himself on one elbow and looked over the back of the sofa, an incredulous look on his face. "Evelyn, as long as they pay the bill, I really don't care. I'd rather have people wear out the sheets than have the moths eat them."

Evelyn snorted. "Shows what you know. Moths don't eat cotton."

"You know what I mean. For God's sake, Evelyn, that's why we're in the business. That's what it takes to make money."

Evelyn struggled up out of the chair. "I'm going down to throw her out." Doug rolled his eyes in exasperation.

Evelyn waddled down the narrow sidewalk that separated the gravel from the rooms. Each step was an effort, her orthopedic shoes raising tiny clouds of dust. She was sweating profusely before she got halfway to room nine.

Evelyn knocked hard on the door and waited a few seconds for a response. When there was no answer, she picked through the keys on the massive ring, pulled the key stamped "9" free, slipped it into the knob, and turned. The drapes were closed and the lights were off. It took a few seconds for her eyes to adjust to the darkness before she saw the nude body on the bed. The smell of spilled beer covered the smell of Carol Knutson's death.

"Hey, it's time to check out." As Evelyn's eyes adjusted she saw the face, the vacant eyes, and the gray cast to the skin. "Oh Lord!" Evelyn whispered as she backed out of the room.

She walked as fast as her heavy body would allow back to the office, screaming her husband's name as she went. "Doug! Doug! Get out here DOUG!"

The office door slammed against the stop as Evelyn threw it back and rushed into the office. Her husband was oblivious to the commotion due to his poor hearing and the baseball crowd cheering a base hit.

"Doug, call the cops!" she yelled, between her gasps for air.

Doug pushed himself up from the sofa and gave her a frown. "What's the matter? She skip on us?"

"She's dead." Evelyn pounded 911 into the buttons of the phone as she puffed to catch her breath.

Dan flew into the ready room, looking for anyone who happened to be on duty. "C'mon, Pam. We've got a dead body at the Rock Creek Motel."

Pam Ryan jumped out of the chair and had to run down the hall to catch up with Dan as he burst through the security door. "Where's Floyd?" She asked breathlessly.

Dan took the concrete steps two at a time as he loped toward the parking lot. "Floyd and Sandy are on the way. I called the medical examiner. Oresek and Eddie are rolling, too."

They climbed into Dan's unmarked squad and were out of the county courthouse parking lot before Pam got her seatbelt fastened. The heat inside the brown squad was stifling. They raced south through Pine City with the siren wailing and soon were listening to the slap of the expansion joints on old highway 61 as they accelerated toward Rock Creek.

"What's the deal?" Pam was feeling the excitement of a new case mixed with the concern that another person had died.

Dan negotiated a curve that led under a train trestle, then slowed as they crossed the intersection with highway 70. "Don't know. The dispatcher said the Rybergs, the motel owners, called and reported a dead body in one of their rooms."

The remaining five miles to Rock Creek passed in silence. They sped past small farms and fields of corn. The empty remnants of an old farmhouse stood as a reminder of the continuing decline of the family farm in Minnesota. On the next farm, there was a small used car lot that the owner operated to supplement the meager income he generated from a small herd of white-face-mix cattle. The cows looked up at the car as it flew by. Their tails switched continuously at the annoying black flies and mosquitoes. The calves were lying down near their mothers and seemed ignorant of the squad car speeding by.

The motel sign came into view as they crested the hill and started down into the small town of Rock Creek. They passed two small houses and an abandoned service station. Dan slowed to make the turn into the long gravel motel driveway.

There were two sets of flashing lights from the other two county squads at the far south end of the motel parking lot. Dan pulled in front of room number eleven and stopped. A very agitated heavyset woman was gesturing wildly to Floyd and Sandy, while a slender, gray-haired man watched passively from the motel's office doorway. A door to one of the motel's rooms was partially open and the woman pointed to it repeatedly. Sandy was busy taking notes.

Dan judged the woman to be one of the owners, about seventy years old. She was wearing a dark dress and orthopedic shoes. Her face was bright red and her hair was matted with sweat. A white handkerchief fluttered from one hand as she spoke. She wiped the sweat from her face and looked over at Dan and Pam as they opened the car doors. Ignoring them, she went on with her story to Floyd and Sandy.

Dan nodded to Floyd as he and Pam walked behind them and stepped into room number nine. He didn't want to interrupt the story that Floyd and Sandy were getting.

The cool air rushing from the room hit them in the face as Pam pushed the door open wider. Pam expected the sickening, sweet smell of blood, like she'd smelled at the Berg murder, but the air in the motel room smelled of stale beer, urine, and feces. She started to reach for the lightswitch, but Dan laid a hand on her arm.

Pam pulled her arm back. "Oh, prints. Sure."

She pulled back from the door frame and took the long aluminum flashlight from its loop on her belt. She trained the light around the room. It fell quickly on the partially naked body. It played briefly on the vacant eyes, then to the waxy white torso. The woman's plaid blouse was still on and her bra had been unfastened in the front but never fully removed. She was naked from the waist down. A pair of polka dotted panties lay on the bed near the body and a pair of jeans was crumpled on the floor at the foot of the bed. The woman's feet were pulled up near her buttocks leaving her knees spread wide. The patch of dark pubic hair was stark against the white skin. The plaid bedspread was stained with urine and feces between the woman's legs.

As their eyes adjusted to the dark, Pam switched off the flashlight. She walked tentatively into the room. The floor between the beds was littered with beer cans. Pam disappeared into the bathroom as Dan kneeled down and pushed around the beer cans with a pen. He heard retching sounds echo off the cinder-block walls.

Pam was wiping her mouth on a tissue as she returned from the bathroom. Her face was ashen. "Do they all crap...I mean, when they die?"

Dan looked up and saw Pam standing at the foot of the bed, staring between the victim's legs. "Some release their bowels. Not all." He got up and walked next to her. "Did you notice the red blotches on her face?"

Pam shook her head. "Not really. Are they significant?"

Dan leaned close over the edge of the bed without putting his hands down on the bedspread. "They call them pettechiae. If you consider that, with the bruises on the neck, it means she was probably strangled.

"Was she raped?" Pam looked at Dan nervously when she realized that she'd been staring at the woman's crotch.

"How do you tell?"

Dan moved down the bed and leaned close to the woman's spread legs. "Sometimes there are tears...or bleeding. Did you notice anything?"

Pam turned her head away. "I can't tell." She started to gag and walked quickly into the bathroom. Dan was looking around the room for anything that a murderer might have overlooked when the sound of dry heaves finally stopped. The toilet flushed and he cringed. They wouldn't get any prints off the toilet handle. Some evidence had just possibly gone down the toilet and they may have lost some fingerprints from the toilet handle.

"Hey, Dan. Come look at this." Dan walked into the bathroom where Pam was squatting next to the wastebasket. She tipped it with her flashlight and Dan looked in. There was a black condom wrapper in the bottom.

"Same brand as the one at Terri Berg's." She let the metal basket tip back onto the linoleum.

"Lot's of men use condoms." He leaned against the painted door frame.

"Odd brand. I've never heard of them before we found one at Terri Berg's house. Black Ecstasy," Pam said. She was about to ask another question but was interrupted.

From behind Dan came Sandy Maki's' voice. "They're probably from a vending machine, not the drug stores where women usually buy condoms."

Dan nodded to Sandy. "You and Floyd get anything useful out of the woman?"

Sandy shook his head. "Naw. Mostly jawboning. She didn't see anything. She's mostly interested in getting the body out so she can fumigate and clean. Wanted us to tow the car away, too."

Dan wiped his hands on his pant legs. "Sandy, get an evidence kit and start picking up fingerprints and fibers. Make sure you get the prints off every beer can."

The three of them came out together, while Dan crawled around on the floor. Sandy and Pam opened the trunk to his squad and carried in the gear.

When Dan walked out, he spotted Floyd making notes in his squad and leaned in the passenger window. "Can you give Sandy a hand? I'll take Pam up to interview the owner's husband."

"Mr. Ryberg?" Dan addressed the gray-haired man who was standing behind the counter when he and Pam walked into the motel office. They'd had occasional calls to the motel, but had always dealt with Evie Ryberg.

"Yup." The owner was obviously a man of few words.

"You call in the murder?"

The gray-haired man shook his head. "Nope, Evelyn did. My name's Doug." He offered a handshake to both Dan and Pam.

Dan asked, "Do you know the victim's name?"

The man pulled out a recipe box. The woman's registration card was the first one in the box. He pulled it out and handed it to Dan.

Dan read it out loud. "Carol Knutson. Post Office Box 99 in Mora. That's just west of us, in Kanabec County," Dan added for Pam's benefit. He handed the card to Pam and looked back at the owner. "Was she here alone?"

The man shook his head. "Somebody else showed up about half an hour after she checked in. At least that's when I noticed that there was another car parked down there." He nodded his head toward the parking lot.

Pam asked. "You get the license number?"

Again the man shook his head. "I didn't even get a good look at the car. It was parked behind hers and it was about the same size."

Dan noticed that Pam had a spiral notebook out and was

making notes. She asked, "You get a look at the visitor?"

The man looked embarrassed. "Naw. I was watching a double-header on MSC. Evie had gone into town to run some errands, so she didn't see nothin' either. I think the car was gone by the time she got back."

Pam scribbled notes as she questioned. "What time did C check in?"

"Let me see the card." Pam handed it back to him and he flipped it over. "2:15, in the afternoon."

Pam frowned. "Isn't that awfully early?"

The man gave a sheepish grin. "Listen. This is not a busy place. She said she wanted a cool place to sleep for the night. We take our customers as they come and when they come." Unsaid was, "No questions asked."

Dan was standing at the front window of the office. Over his shoulder he asked, "Anybody else around? I mean, besides you and your wife?"

The man shook his head. "Naw. We don't have any employees. We do it all. Clean the toilets, change the sheets, fix the sinks, answer the phone."

Pam nodded and made notes. "How about other guests that might have seen a visitor?"

The man's face perked up and he snapped his fingers. "Oh yeah, there was a young couple here that was moving to Ely. They got in the night before and left later in the afternoon." He opened the box and took out the next card. "Mr. And Mrs. Ernie Ascherman. They were moving up from Iowa. Had a big yellow Ryder truck. Young couple. I didn't charge them for checking out late."

"I don't suppose you got the Ely address?" The man shook his head and handed the Ascherman registration card to Dan, who had come back from the window. The card showed an address in Ottumwa, Iowa.

Pam asked, "Did you disturb anything in the room?"

The man shook his head. "Evie unlocked the door, saw

the body, and then she ran back here and called you."

"You haven't been in the room?" Dan handed the Ascherman card to Pam, who dutifully recorded the names and the Iowa address.

Again the man shook his head. "I peeked in the door. Didn't even put a foot in."

Pam handed the registration card back. "Is the victim the same woman that checked in?"

The man froze. "I...Sure, it must be. But I didn't get a real close look at her face when she registered."

Dan watched the man closely. "I take it you know that she didn't die of natural causes?"

Doug's words stuck in his throat. They waited for him to say something. "I haven't seen any dead bodies. I mean, not outside of a funeral parlor." He hesitated. "Well, there isn't any blood, but she's naked in this terrible position and her face. Well, her face looks like...like hell. I knew she was dead without going in."

John Sepanen's unmarked squad rolled into the parking lot and pulled up to the office. Doug nodded toward the car as Sepanen stepped out. "Looks like the boss just showed up."

Dan and Pam met the sheriff on the sidewalk outside the motel office. Dan steered Sepanen toward room nine. "Another female murder victim. This one appears to have been raped and strangled."

Pam fell into step alongside the sheriff. "There's one condom wrapper in the bathroom. It's the same unusual brand as the one at the Berg murder scene."

Sepanen glanced at Dan and got a nod of affirmation. He took a cigar out of his breast pocket and rolled it between his fingers. "So, it looks like we may have a serial killer, eh? That'll make great headlines."

Sepanen stopped just inside the door, with Pam and Dan behind him on the sidewalk. He let his eyes adjust to the dim lighting and then stared at Carol Knutson's nude body briefly before turning to step back outside. He pushed past Pam, taking deep breaths. "Sonofabitch!"

After a few moments he turned and looked at Pam. She had been watching him and wondering if she had the strength to catch him if he passed out. But Sepanen appeared to have been only momentarily phased. He stuffed the cigar back into his pocket. "That's one hell of a mess."

Pam nodded, not sure how to respond. She blurted out, "At least we know who the murderer is."

Sepanen shook his head. "Then put him in jail before we have another one of these to clean up," he said, gruffly. He turned abruptly and walked to his squad car.

Pam looked to Dan for support. "What does he mean? We're trying to find the guy."

Dan watched the sheriff get into his car and pull out of the lot. "That may be the easy part. At least we don't have to stand up in front of the television cameras and explain that there are three dead people, with only a suspect that we can't even find."

The Suburban from the St. Louis County medical examiner's office rolled into the parking lot and stopped behind the county squad cars. Dan motioned Pam to follow him. "Tony's here. Let's get the show on the road."

Tony Oresek and Eddie Paulson were unloading a gurney and cases from the back of the Suburban. Oresek looked up when Dan came behind the van.

"What've we got this time, Dan?"

"Dead female. One of the motel owners discovered her body. She registered under the name Carol Knutson. Checked in at 2:15 yesterday afternoon. The owner says that she had a visitor a little while later, but that the visitor didn't stay all night."

The gurney clattered to the gravel driveway as Dan led

the way to the body. The lights were on, indicating that the switch and switchplate had been dusted for prints. Sandy and Floyd were dusting the last three beer cans for prints when the entourage came in.

"What can we touch?" Eddie set a case on the second bed, opened it and pulled out a thermometer. He held it in the air for a second and then read it.

"We've been over everything in this room. Haven't got to the bathroom, yet." Sandy finished taking the prints off the last beer can with a piece of tape. He dropped the can into the box with the others.

"The driver's license in the purse matches the name on the motel registration card," said Pam. "Carol Knutson. Same address, too. The picture is a pretty good match, but it was obviously taken several years ago."

Oresek was kneeling next to the bed, prodding the body with a latex gloved finger. "Been dead more than twelve hours." He pulled at a finger and it flopped back after he released it. He moved up near the head and touched the discolored skin around the neck.

"Strangulation?" Dan asked, moving to the other side of the bed with the respect of an amateur watching an artisan.

"Looks like it. I can't say that's the cause of death for sure until we look at the lungs and hyoid bone. But someone really choked her."

Oresek touched the mottled red spots on the woman's face, then went back to the hand and looked at each fingernail. "No signs of resistance. She was either a willing subject, or she was drugged. We'll have to test her for Rohypnol."

Eddie pulled the thermometer from a tiny incision he'd made in the abdomen and held it up. "She's down to ambient. Been dead over eighteen hours."

Oresek stood up. "Well, if she checked in at 2:15," he looked at Dan who nodded back, " and it's 1:30 now, that puts the time of death at no later than 7:30 last night. If she drank half those beers," he continued, pointing to the pile of cans on the floor, "between 2:30 and 7:30, and she weighs...what...one thirty?...her blood alcohol would have been about .05. Impaired, but conscious and still capable of resistance."

Dan could see the wheels turning in Tony's head. Dan added, "But, if her blood alcohol was elevated when she got here, and she drank three quarters of the beer and died at 4:30., her blood alcohol would be what?"

Tony shrugged. "Maybe as high as .20, assuming she wasn't legally drunk when she got here."

Dan shot a look at Sandy. "Did Evie Ryberg say if she'd been drinking?"

Sandy nodded. "Evie said something about beer on her breath. Was worried that she might throw up and leave a mess to clean up."

They all looked to Oresek. "I don't want to speculate here. We'll do a blood alcohol in the morgue. But if her alcohol was up that high, she might've just passed out."

Eddie pulled a swab from the woman's vagina and held it up. It was tinged with pink, with a dark brown blood clot on one side. "She has vaginal tears and abrasions, but no evidence of semen."

"There's a condom wrapper in the bathroom waste basket. Same brand as the Berg place." Pam sounded drained.

Oresek stood up. "Interesting." He poked at the woman's ribs, and felt along the line of the diaphragm. "She's got a cracked rib here. Maybe we've got the same guy. He seems to be into tough love."

"His name is Cooper. He's got a sheet from Stearns County." Tony and Eddie looked at Pam, surprised. She continued, "Dan got the report on the fingerprint from the spent casing found in the drapes. We've got a booking picture of Cooper back at the law enforcement center. Dan's been passing it around town this morning."

Dan spoke up. "No one had ever seen him before. I

showed the picture to Harvey at the Pine Brook Inn and to the waitress at the Sportsman's Café, where Terri Berg used to work. No one recognized the face at all."

Sandy was closing up the evidence kit when Oresek asked him, "Were there any fingerprints on the condom wrappers?"

"They were clean."

Oresek pulled at his ear. "But there were no condoms?"

Sandy shook his head no.

Dan and Oresek stared at each other. Oresek finally broke the silence. "I think that maybe this guy is playing with us. He might be thinking he's smarter than we are, getting a little bolder. Those condom wrappers may be his trademark."

Chapter 24

Sandy left the motel before the investigations had been completed. He had several interviews of the people who'd been at the Pine brook Inn remaining. He caught three people at work, and a fourth at home. His last stop of the day was at the apartment of Barb Dupre, for a follow-up, to see if her story remained the same as when she had told it to him the first time, and to show her the picture of Cooper. Barb's red Camaro was in the parking lot.

He knocked on the door and got no response. He could hear a radio playing some heavy metal song inside the apartment. He knocked harder, and when there was still no answer he tried the knob. It turned. He opened it a crack and stuck his head in. "Hello?"

Behind him, the door across the hall opened. The little old woman looked him over and apparently approved. "She's home. You just have to knock hard." The woman disappeared and closed the door.

He spoke in a loud voice again and still got no response. He stepped in, leaving, the door ajar. Inside the apartment, Sandy was amazed at how little he remembered of the décor. The living room was painted white with numerous smudges and gouges in the walls. The furniture was an eclectic mixture of garage sale items in a rainbow of colors. The same steamer truck was there, its surface covered with biker magazines. The floor was littered with women's clothing and magazines. He stepped in further and closed the door behind him. The loud music seemed to be coming from the bathroom. At first he hesitated and considered leaving. Then he became concerned for Barbara Dupre's safety.

"HELLO!"

Squeaking and thumping sounds emanated from the bathroom in response to his voice, as someone moved around in the tub. The volume of the music dropped.

"Sorry! I turned it down. Is that okay?" The female voice spoke slowly and deliberately. She sounded apologetic.

Sandy smiled, beginning to understand.

A blonde head appeared around the doorjamb. "Geez! They didn't have to call the cops!" The contrite voice changed to anger. Barb's blonde hair was plastered to her head like a helmet and her expression was irritated. Suddenly she recognized Sandy. Her anger turned to a smile. "Oh, it's you."

Sandy smiled in return. "I'm not here on a complaint about the music. I've got a picture I want to show you." Through the open bathroom door he could see the reflection of her naked backside in the mirror. There was the large starburst tattoo on her right shoulder and a smaller one on one buttock.

"Ah...sure. Just a second." Her speech was as slow as it had been the previous time. The bathroom door closed and five seconds later she was out of the bathroom, wrapped in a towel. Her legs were nicked and bleeding in three spots.

She caught him staring at her legs. "I cut myself shaving. I do it all the time." When he seemed satisfied with the explanation, she asked, "So, what's the picture of?"

Sandy snapped back and handed the picture to her. "We think this guy might have been at the bar the night that Terri Berg was murdered. Does he look familiar to you?"

Barb looked suddenly grim. "That's why you were here before, wasn't it? You thought Butch had something to do with it. I'm not going to help him out of jail, you know." She sat down on the couch and glanced at the picture. The towel pulled up showing more of her thighs. She tried to hand the picture back to him after glancing at it briefly.

Sandy tried to look at her eyes and not to steal a look at the exposed leg. "Take a good look at the picture. Is that man familiar?"

Barb glanced at it again and handed it back. "The eyes are weird. Seems like I've seen them before."

"You say you *have* seen them?" Sandy asked, with rising interest. "Can you remember who it might have been?"

"Well, I may have. But I see a lot of guys." She shrugged and handed the picture back.

"Miss Dupre," said Sandy, somewhat sternly, "Can you take a closer look at this picture please and tell me if you've seen this man around?"

Are you mad?" She asked, a pout on her lips.

Sandy sighed. "I'm sorry," he said resignedly. "I'm really tired. I just want to know if you've seen the guy, then I can go home." He took off the brown baseball cap with the star on the crown, and ran his fingers through his hair.

"Oh," she said. Then, suddenly, she asked, "You want a beer? I got Bud." She stood up and left without waiting for an answer. A moment later she returned with two cans in her right hand, her left was still clutching the towel. Her attention span seemed to be about fifteen seconds.

"Here, pop one for me. I'll be right back." She handed him the cans and disappeared down the hallway past the bath.

Sighing in resignation, Sandy looked for a place to sit and moved a pair of panties from the couch. He picked a biker magazine off the floor and set it on the scarred steamer trunk, using it as a coaster for the two beers. He had popped one of the tabs and was raising the can to his lips when he remembered that he was still on duty and in uniform. What the hell, he thought. He was in an apartment, had been on the case since early that morning.

Barb rounded the corner, pulling up the zipper on a pair

of denim shorts. A white halter top dangled over her breasts with the strings hanging over her shoulders and down her sides.

"Tie me." She turned and exposed her naked back. On her left shoulder was the blue starburst tattoo he'd seen reflected in the mirror. He took the ends as she handed them to him and tied them in bows.

Sandy felt uncomfortable with the situation. Her style was far too familiar for his taste. "You still haven't answered my question. Have you seen the guy in the picture?"

Barb picked up her beer and plopped onto the couch, too close to where he had been sitting. He picked a spot a little farther down and offered her the picture again.

She shook her head. "I don't think so. The eyes are sorta familiar. But I see a lot of guys."

She pulled her feet under her buttocks, leaned her side against the back of the couch and looked at him. "What are you doing tonight?"

Sandy stared at her. Although her face looked rough, there was an underlying beauty. With a little makeup, he thought, she could be dazzling.

"Going home. Eating supper," he answered.

She sipped the beer again. "I could use some help."

Sandy's first thought was that Butch had been released from custody and that she felt the need for protection. "What kind of help?"

"I've got a gig tonight and I need an escort." Even though Barb's words came slowly the thoughts were clear and stated with perfect English.

Sandy looked into her eyes, trying to find the agenda, but there didn't seem to be any. "Butch is gone and you need protection?"

"Yeah. I figure that you'd be pretty good. You took Butch." She sipped her beer. "And he was tough. I've seen him take lots of guys. Some were really big."

Sandy shook his head. "The Sheriff has to approve all

part-time jobs."

"Oh." She was surprised by his comment. "I won't pay you. Will that make it okay?"

Sandy looked for a smile, but she appeared to be entirely serious. "I'll pass," he said.

"You ever been to the Upper Room? I think you'd like it." Not sensing a positive response, she added, "I'll buy the beer."

Sandy had to search his memory. The place sounded familiar, but he couldn't place it. "The Upper Room?" he asked.

"In the Wolf Lodge, upstairs. They have dancers on Thursday nights. Cover charge at the door and the booze is BYOB. They sell set-ups of mix. I'm dancing with two girls from the Twin Cities. I'll get you in free and I buy the beer. What have you got to do better than that?" Again, there was no hint of humor.

"I live down in Rush City. I'd have to go home and change out of my uniform." He polished off the beer and stood up. "Thanks but no thanks. I'm really bushed."

"Butch's stuff is still in the bedroom. It'd fit." She stood up and took his hand. "C'mon, You can change. Then we'll go."

It was like she didn't hear him. She led him into the bedroom by the hand. The bedroom was much neater than the living room. The furniture was painted pink, and the bedspread matched the curtains. The clothes hamper was overflowing, but she had made an effort to get the dirty clothes into it. She pulled open a drawer filled with men's jeans and T-shirts. She pulled out a pair of stone-washed jeans and a Harley T-shirt.

"Here. Try 'em on. I gotta pack my costumes." She went to the closet and took out a canvas shopping bag. When she turned back he was still standing in front of the dresser with the clothes in his hand.

"If you're shy, change in the bathroom." She pulled out a lower drawer and started sorting through clothes, occasionally throwing something into the bag. He shrugged and walked to the bathroom.

"Time to go," she said a couple of minutes later, as she rapped on the bathroom door.

Sandy emerged in the new outfit, with the uniform rolled under his arm. "I gotta throw these in the trunk of the squad. Can we take your car?"

She picked up the keys from a table near the door and threw them to him. "Let's roll."

After locking the apartment door, she tucked her arm under his and they walked down the steps together to the parking lot. Sandy put the uniform and holster into the trunk of the squad.

They drove through downtown Pine City, past the fairgrounds without saying a word. Barb looked totally at ease, but Sandy felt uncomfortable. Just past the fairgrounds, they pulled into the parking lot of the Wolf Lodge. It was a dingy two-story building with asbestos siding and a neon sign in the parking lot. Sandy's first thought was to ask when the fire marshal had last made an inspection.

The parking lot was not paved and as they searched for an open spot in the corner of the lot, a cloud of dust followed them. There were about thirty cars already there.

Sandy put his hand on Barb's arm as she started to open the door. "You just want me to be here to protect you?"

Barb nodded. "Pretty much." She hesitated when he didn't let go of her arm. "Isn't that okay?" She looked down at his hand.

Sandy let go of her. "I just wasn't sure why I was along."

They got out and locked the doors. Barb pointed to the front door. "You go upstairs. Tell them that you're with Honey. I gotta check in and change."

"Honey?" he asked, puzzled.

"My stage name is Honey." She turned her back on him and walked quickly across the parking lot to a side door.

Sandy went through the front door and found the stairs immediately inside the door. At the top of the stairs a man stopped him and asked if he was a member.

"I'm with Honey."

The man gave him a surprised look. "Where's Butch? he asked.

"Let's just say Butch is indisposed right now," Sandy replied. The man motioned him in, eyeing him up and down curiously as he passed.

The Upper Room was a sea of male faces in a cigarette smoke haze. They were seated in a horseshoe of chairs arranged around a small stage at one end of the room. The bar was at the end of the room opposite the stage. Sandy found an empty barstool and ordered a Bud Light.

"Sorry, buddy. All you can get here is soda pop and set-ups. You got a bottle?"

Sandy shook his head. "Just Coke."

The bartender reached under the bar and pulled out a can of Coke. He slid it across the counter. "Three bucks."

Music started pounding out of speakers mounted over the stage. The talking stopped, and every eye focused on the stage. Barb slid out from behind the black curtains. She was dressed in a white bikini, and was grinding her hips to the beat of the music. Although Sandy had seen her in various degrees of nudity, this presentation was even more erotic. Her comfort with her nudity in the apartment was totally consistent with the raw sexuality that she exuded on the stage.

Barb glided across the stage to the whoops and catcalls of the crowd. Before the third song ended, her hand was stuffed with bills and her G-string bristled with money. When the music stopped, she blew a kiss to the crowd and collected the bikini top from the floor before she disappeared through the curtains.

As the next song started, a new dancer slid onto the stage. This one was a little more polished. Her dancing was more refined. Barb's dancing was more of a wiggle. The new dancer was wearing a red bikini with sequins that sparkled under the spotlights mounted over the stage and she actually had a few dance steps.

Sandy felt something against his back and turned to find Barb leaning over the bar. She stood up with a beer in each hand. "I shoulda told you to ask for my beer. They hit you pretty hard for the set-ups."

Sandy accepted the beer. "I tried to order one, but he said they only had soda pop."

Barb was wearing a white T-shirt and denim shorts. She mopped her forehead with a towel that was draped around her neck. "It's my beer. I buy it, and Walt keeps it behind the bar for me." She came around from behind the bar, wiping the towel across her forehead again, removing the fresh sheen of sweat.

"You through now?" Sandy asked.

She smiled, exposing lovely dimples. "That was just the first set. We've got two more each. The last one's the finale."

Her head jerked, and she dug an elbow into the man who had walked behind her. The man let out a yelp of pain. "Asshole! Keep your hands to yourself." The man mumbled something and then moved to a table.

Sandy watched the scene play out and thought that she was very capable of taking care of herself. "Is that why you had Butch along?"

She shook her head. "No." She leaned against his arm and ran a tattooed finger along his jaw before planting a passionate kiss on his lips. Her tongue probed his mouth briefly, then he felt her breath in his ear. "No. I need every man in this place to know that we're going home together after the show."

Accepting his cue, he ran his hand through her hair, pulled her lips to his. He whispered in her ear. "So that none of them follow you home?"

She breathed into his ear. "Uh huh."

* * *

They watched the third dancer approach the end of her set. Barb touched her lips to his. "My turn." She disappeared through a door in the corner of the smoky room.

Barb's second set was even more suggestive than the first and by the third set the tips included several fives and tens. When the last song ended, Barb made a run for the curtain with another wad of bills clutched in her hand.

Sandy sat at the bar, watching the second dancer's last set, until he felt Barb press her breasts against his back. He turned his head and pecked her cheek. "Time to go?"

She was wearing a checked cotton blouse with a pair of jeans. The canvas bag was slung over her shoulder. She seemed very anxious, her eyes searching the crowd for someone or something. Suddenly, the anxiety faded and she smiled. The dimples in her cheeks were cherubic and out of character for the venue. "Sure."

They walked to the car and Sandy unlocked the door for her. As he closed the door, he looked across the parking lot for anything that looked suspicious. She unlocked the driver's door from the inside and he climbed in. The engine roared to life and he pulled out of the parking lot going south, back into Pine City.

Sandy found the last parking spot in the apartment complex parking lot. It was on the edge of a wooded park. Barb was out of the car and headed down the sidewalk before Sandy had the doors locked. He hadn't planned to go in, but he stood there with her keys and needed to return them. By the time he took the holster and gun out of the trunk, she had disappeared into the apartment building. When he got to the building, Barb was sitting inside the entryway, obviously agitated.

"Come up. I need to know that Butch isn't there."

He held the keys out to her. "He's in the Pine County Jail."

She shook her head. "Please look."

Sandy unlocked the door. He took the Smith & Wesson pistol out of the holster and turned on the lights. He walked from room to room, checking closets, looking under the bed and in the shower. "All clear."

Barb stood near the door and looked uneasy. She clutched the canvas bag to her chest like a kid on her first day of school. Sandy could see that she was, indeed, scared. She hadn't shown fear before. He took her in his arms and Barb pressed herself against him. He gently patted her back for a few seconds.

"Let's watch the TV for a while," he said as he led her to the couch and punched the remote control. She snuggled up to him on the couch and fell asleep within a minute. He gazed at her faceas she slept. She'd obviously had a hard life. But in sleep her feaures softened and he could imagine easily what innocent beauty she had once possessed—before Butch Mattson had come along.

Chapter 25

Although Dan was very late, the lights were on in the house and Sally was sitting on the couch reading a book when he got home.

Dan slipped off his shoes as Sally closed her book and set it on the same table next to the couch. "You get any supper?"

Dan pulled his holster off and set it on the table next to the couch. "I had a burger and pie with Floyd."

Sally gave him a hug and a peck on the cheek. "Are you trying to get scurvy? There aren't many vitamins in a burger." She stared at him briefly. "Or did you really blow it and have coconut cream or something else with no nutritional value?"

Dan dropped into a chair. "It was blueberry and I had a pickle on the burger. That counts as a vegie, and even the government says ketchup counts as a vegetable."

Sally gave him a reproving look, then got up and turned off the outside light and headed down the hall to the bedroom. "What happened with Doc Peterson today? June saw him and said that he was beet red and wouldn't say a word to anyone."

Dan followed her to the bedroom and took off his clothes as Sally turned back the covers. "He's spouting off about bringing me up on age discrimination charges. He's apparently got the board about ready to put me on leave pending an investigation. Laurie Lone Eagle did some checking on Doc for me, though, and she found out he's been practicing outside his license restrictions. Doc doesn't know about this, yet, so he must just be still pissed at me."

Sally stopped and stared at Dan in disbelief. Her mouth had fallen open. "What? Doc Peterson isn't allowed to practice?"

Dan piled his clothes into the hamper. "I don't know quite how it'll be announced, but he's not allowed to do surgery involving general anesthesia. I'm sure there will be some sugar-coated version for the general public."

Sally sat hard on the edge of the bed. "But he's the only general surgeon that's on staff full-time. We'd heard that he had some problems, but is he that bad?"

Dan flipped off the lightswitch and they both slipped under the covers. "His license was restricted a couple of years ago by the state board. I checked and he's been doing several general anesthesia procedures a day in violation of the restrictions."

Sally was silent for a few minutes and Dan thought she had fallen asleep. Her voice was soft in his ear. "So you're cleared now?"

"Sepanen says it looks that way. The final resolution will be at a special county board meeting next week."

Sally leaned close and kissed him. "Doc Peterson is so arrogant and politically connected. He might find some way to punish you just to get even. You're so apolitical. You might not have a chance."

"We'll see about that," he said. Then, as if to change the subject, he asked,"Why were you sitting up? You know that sometimes I just can't get home early."

Sally stroked Dan's hair. "I know, but sometimes I just worry. I heard about the other murder on TV."

"I'm sorry I didn't call." He kissed her hair. "It's been a bad day"

Sally pulled back. "Oh no." Her voice was filled with sadness. "Is it the same guy?"

"We're pretty sure it's the same guy." Dan didn't mention the condoms being the same unique brand. That might be a key piece of evidence that shouldn't be spread around. "We have a name and an old booking picture, from 1988."

"Really? That's a lot of progress in a couple of days. Are you close to an arrest?"

"I wish. It seems like he's disappeared off the face of the earth for the last few years…other than leaving one print at the first murder scene."

"So, what do you do now?"

Dan stared into the darkness. "We've been showing his picture around and hoping that someone recognizes it." He paused. "The picture is old, when he was about eighteen. It's so damned frustrating. He has to be so close that we can almost touch him, but it's like he's invisible. This guy is something else. If word gets out about the brutality of these murders the community will go nuts. Sepanen has his hands full in handling this."

Sally laid back down. "Is he like the man on the Night Stalker television show—antisocial and only comes out after dark?"

Dan rubbed his tired eyes. "I would have guessed that yesterday, but he was at the Rock Creek Motel yesterday afternoon. It's just so crazy. How can a guy that's five-two and over two hundred pounds wander around without being noticed? Even if he grew a beard and dyed his hair, he's still short and fat."

"Maybe he blends in more easily than you think," Sally offered. "There are people that I never notice because of their jobs. Bank tellers and delivery people. Besides that, he's older now. He could have changed something else about himself to throw you off. Hair color is easy, and so is losing or gaining weight. Or maybe he's a chameleon."

Dan patted Sally's behind as he rolled to snuggle against her. "I'll tell my deputies to start looking for a lizard tomorrow."

* * *

Ross Cooper was pissed. He'd been late for work. The
sex had been bad, and the woman wasn't that pretty. She had
actually been nice to him for a while. She had invited him to the
room. That was a new twist. Maybe the problem was she passed
out. He hadn't really meant to do anything so soon after Terri.
This one had come to him. Very risky. He had to sort it all out.
Things were getting too complicated.

"Hey, watch it!" The guy's chair was halfway into the
aisle. Ross had bumped him with an elbow when he passed by.

"Fuck off," Ross growled as he walked on by with a
sneer.

"Great way to keep the customers happy!" the guy
yelled at Ross's back.

Damned customers! They want more. They want it
faster. They want the food hotter. They want their drinks cold-
er. So stupid, they don't understand. He had problems and they
weren't a part of the solution.

Ross felt a tap on his shoulder and spun around with
malice in his eyes. The boss was there.

"Hey, take it easy on the customers. They pay the bills."

Ross gave him a look of contempt and turned away.

"You don't like it here? That's fine. Give me your
notice. But if you need this job as much as I think you do, give
'em a smile and say, 'Yes sir and yes ma'am.' Got it?"

Ross grunted in response. The boss was an okay guy, a
little wimpy, but basically good. Ross stared at a red-headed girl
who was drinking a Coke with members of a softball team. She
appeared to be about eighteen. Her small breasts pressed
against the Lycra of her softball jersey. The two male softball
players she was sitting with were obviously enjoying her ath-
letic build and boyish figure. She looked like she would be a
tiger in bed.

"I bet she wouldn't pass out," he mumbled to himself.

Watching her took his mind off his troubles and he went back to work. The night was almost over anyway.

DAY

SIX

FRIDAY

Chapter 26

Friday morning was breaking when Sandy Maki's arm flopped down and he rapped his knuckles on the steamer trunk. "Damn," Sandy said, as he shook his hand in pain. He looked around and realized that he wasn't home. Scenes from the night before reeled past. He was on Barb's couch, wearing jeans and a Harley shirt. Barb wasn't there. The television was still on and the morning news was starting.

He sat up and looked at his watch. It was 5 a.m., and the sun was glowing softly through the drapes. He wandered to the door of the bedroom. Barb was face down on the sheets, wearing only a pair of panties. He decided not to disturb her. He went into the bathroom and ran cold water over his face. The dull headache reminded him of the beers. Luckily, he'd quit before he'd had enough to generate a full-blown hangover. Work was hell with a hangover.

He started running hot water into the sink and found a daisy razor on the edge of the bathtub. Hand soap wasn't very good shaving cream, but it was better than nothing. The razor felt like it had been used to cut sandpaper, tugging at every whisker and pulling the ones it didn't cut. He finished the shave and started running water for a shower.

The hot water pulsing against his body washed away the headache. He lathered with the bar of Dove soap that was on the edge of the bathtub. What a strange night. They had necked passionately at the bar for half the night, then came back to Barb's apartment where she'd fallen asleep. Barb was the most sexual creature that he'd ever met, yet he'd held her for hours, never once touching her in an intimate way.

The shower curtain shifted with the movement of air in the bathroom. Sandy peeked around the edge of the shower curtain to see what had caused the motion and saw Barb sitting on the toilet. She stared at him through droopy eyes. At the bar he hadn't noticed that her breasts were too large for her small frame. Probably silicone.

"Do you always get up this early?" She stood up and pulled up the French cut panties, apparently unembarrassed by her nakedness. Her face was creased from the wrinkles in the sheets and there were dark bags under her eyes.

"Gotta be on duty at seven. You got anything to eat for breakfast?"

Barb was already on her way out of the bathroom by the time he asked. She replied over her shoulder, "I don't do breakfast." The footsteps faded away, ending with the squeaking of the mattress.

He toweled off and put his day-old underwear back on. The refrigerator was empty except for beer and tomato juice. The cupboards had a few mismatched dishes and a couple of cans of soup. He pulled down a can of Dinty Moore beef stew and dug through the drawers for a few seconds, trying to find a can opener. He finally gave up and put the can back on the shelf. The can of tomato juice tasted salty but refreshing.

He retrieved his uniform from the squad and changed into it. It was not terribly wrinkled, but it wouldn't pass a military inspection. He would have to change into his spare uniform at the courthouse.

On his way past the bedroom, he peeked in, intending to say good-bye, but Barb was sprawled on top of the sheets, face down, obviously sound asleep again. The sheet and blanket were in a heap on the floor, on top of her clothes from the night before. He walked to the front door, released the lock and closed the door. It clicked as the lock engaged behind him.

Dan was on the phone, trying to connect with anyone that had dealt with Ross Cooper in the past. He left messages with the parole officer and the court appointed psychiatrist that had evaluated Ross after the homecoming queen assault. He called the high school and found out that both the principal and counselor that had been working when Ross' incident occurred had retired. The secretary looked up their home phone numbers and gave it to him.

The principal was out of town and Dan left a message with his wife. He tried the counselor's home next. The phone rang four times and was answered by a male voice that was apparently older, but clear and strong, "Hello?"

"Yes, hello. This is Undersheriff Williams, from the Pine County sheriff's department. I'd like to speak with Mr. Pat Glenna, please."

"I'm Pat."

"Mr. Glenna, I'm investigating a crime, and there is some evidence that Timothy Ross Cooper may be involved. I hoped that you might be able to help me out with a little background on him."

"Timothy Ross Cooper?" Pat Glenna said the name in a way that made Dan believe he was dredging up old memories. "Oh, yes. I remember him. I believe he dropped the Timothy and just went by his middle name, Ross."

Dan went on. "We have a report here that he assaulted the homecoming queen, back in the eighties. What else can you tell me about him?"

"Ummm. As I recall, he was quite an interesting case. What would you like to know?" There was the sound of a chair scraping, and what seemed to be the shuffling of papers. Glenna had apparently pulled out some of his records.

"Anything that might help us understand him," said

Dan.

The counselor paused for a moment before he finally replied. Dan could imagine him scanning his case file. "Ross seemed to be in another world much of the time, from what I gathered in my sessions with him," Glenna said. "He was a quiet boy, not very appealing physically, rather heavy. Most everyone excluded him from things. I recall him telling me that the other students ridiculed him. He told me that even the physical education teachers ridiculed him because he couldn't do pull-ups. The superintendent and I had a discussion about that with the two teachers."

Pat paused again before he went on. "Although I didn't have that many sessions with him, Ross appeared to be what psychologists sometimes call a Narcissistic personality, very wrapped up in himself. I spoke with him after the cheerleader incident and he was all over the map—agitated, angry."

"Did he ever express remorse over the assault?"

This time the counselor's reply was quicker. "Oh, no. No remorse. Narcissicism is characterized by aspects of sociopathy. These personality types tend to focus entirely upon themselves and they seem not to have gained a conscience, like most of us. They have trouble feeling empathy. It was more like he'd worshipped this girl, but she'd ignored him. She had apparently even ridiculed him for it. Kids can be so cruel to each other, you know. No, he wasn't remorseful at all. It was almost like he'd gotten even with her for rejecting him."

Dan tapped a pencil on the desktop and thought for a second before asking another question. "You said angry? He was angry while you were interviewing him?"

"Well, yes. From what I can remember, he just talked on and on. He replayed the whole assault for me. When he talked about hitting her, he even seemed to be pleased about the whole thing."

Dan asked. "He never did penetrate her. Right?"

There was a pause. "No. There's no report that he had

even attempted to have sex with the girl. Maybe he didn't have time. But it's quite clear in my mind that he was more excited about the act of revenge than he was about having run his hands under the bodice of her dress. His intentions were obviously sexual at first, but the girl rejected and humiliated him. That's apparently when he assaulted her. Did you say that you had him in custody?"

Dan pushed aside his notes. "No. We just have evidence that he may be involved in a murder. We haven't been able to locate him."

"Murder?" said Pat, incredulously. "His anger has taken him that far?" There was sadness in the man's voice.

"Did you ever get involved in any of his treatment? You said that he was all over the board during the period that you were talking to him. Do you know if he was ever diagnosed formally?"

"No. I wasn't involved with Ross except for a couple of sessions. I don't think he ever had any further sessions with anyone else. Not to my knowledge, anyway."

"Does his family still live in Sauk Center?"

"As I recall, the father had been dead for years when all this happened. There had been a step-father in the household for a time, but he was history by that time, also. It seems to me that his mother—I think her name was Rosemary—passed away shortly after all this. I understood that she was a heavy drinker."

Dan perked up. "Did you ever talk to the mother?"

The counselor let out a sigh. "When we got in touch with her she didn't even seem upset. She said that Ross had always given the family trouble and it wasn't worth her time to come down to talk to us. I heard rumors that there had been some type of abuse in the home, but I really couldn't say that I had any information to back that up. When I talked to Ross, he said nothing about it, but it was quite evident that he didn't expect his mother to come to his aid. I don't remember his words exactly, but they left me with the impression that he didn't feel any love in their relationship. He was considerably bitter and angry about that, too."

Dan pushed on with questions about the family. "Did Ross have any brothers or sisters?"

"Phew. I vaguely recall something about a sister...maybe a younger sister. I really don't remember any dealings with her. But I have 'counselor syndrome.' I remember the really good and the really bad. The other ninety eight percent passes through without leaving much of a mark in my memory."

"Well, thank you, Mr. Glenna. If you think of anything else, please give me a call." Dan recited the phone number for the dispatcher's office.

Dan dialed the number for the Stearns County Courthouse again and spoke with Kerry Trundle, the records clerk. She had asked him to call back later after she'd had some time to search for the information he had asked for.

"Sheriff Williams, I found birth certificates for Timothy Ross Cooper and Maryrose Cooper. Both were born on June 2nd, 1967, to Rosemary and Thomas Ross Cooper. Both the parents are dead. I can give you the dates of death if you'd like."

"Yes, thank you." Dan scribbled notes. "You said the brother and sister were born on the same day? They're twins then?"

"Our birth records wouldn't indicate that for sure. Only their date of birth. But that would certainly seem to be the case. We might be able to get that information from the hospital records, though."

"I'd appreciate that very much if you can do that for me. Can you tell me if the sister still lives there?"

He could hear papers being shuffled in the background. "Well, she's not listed in the phone book. But that leaves the possibilities that she's married or moved away or may not have a phone. I can check the marriage license application files, but if she's moved away..."

"I'd appreciate it if you could check further and if you find anything else from the hospital., You can call me at the Pine County Sheriff's Department. Thanks."

Dan attempted to digest the new information he'd received for a moment. Then he turned to locating the couple who'd been in the Ryder Truck at the Rock Creek motel.

Floyd and Pam drove back to Duluth for their second autopsy. As they came over the hill by Spirit Mountain ski resort, the panoramic view of St. Louis Bay was breathtaking. Pam commented, "Geez! Isn't that beautiful. I've never been here when it hasn't been foggy." Lake Superior shimmered in the sunlight, the green of the harbor shifting to tan along the shore and cobalt blue in the deeper waters."

Floyd parked at the hospital and when Pam opened the door the cool air came in a rush. Pam shivered in her short-sleeved uniform shirt. "What's the deal? It was in the eighties in Pine City. It feels like it's fifty degrees here."

Floyd smiled and locked his door. "You're in the air conditioned city. Lake Superior's surface temperature is only fifty degrees in the summer. When the wind comes around from the northeast, it chills the air." They walked to the loading door of the morgue. "Sometimes you can feel it as far south as Pine City, if there's a strong northeast wind for a couple of days."

They walked inside and Pam was rubbing her goose-pimpled arms when they met Eddie Paulson in the hall. He broke a smile. "A little cool for you today? You should be here in the winter."

"Hey, I grew up on a farm in Blue Earth. We have winter too. It actually snows."

Eddie laughed. "That's an Iowa winter. Hell, you probably don't even hit ten below zero. We get nine months of winter, followed by three months of poor sledding. The lilacs along London Road don't even bloom until late July."

Pam smiled. "Let me tell you something, Eddie. When the wind comes whipping across South Dakota into southern Minnesota, there isn't a thing wider than a blade of grass to stop it before it gets to our farm. We have snowdrifts as high as the barn some years."

Floyd held up his hand. "Enough of the winter one-upmanship. Can we get on with the autopsy?"

Eddie led them through the hallway to the autopsy room. There was a shape covered by a sheet lying on the table. Carol Knutson's knees were still in the air, as they'd last seen her in the motel room.

"Why don't you put her knees down? It looks so unladylike."

"Trust me. She doesn't care." It was apparent by the banter that Eddie was starting to get comfortable around Pam. Eddie pulled the cover off a cart of instruments and then went about gowning and gloving for the procedure. "By the way, her blood alcohol was 0.23. She may have been passed out when all this happened. At a minimum, she was seriously impaired."

Tony Oresek came in fully covered in surgical scrubs. He nodded to Floyd and Pam as he pulled the sheet from Carol Knutson's body. He immediately pulled over a lighted magnifier and started looking at the surface of the body.

Eddie used a comb to run through the corpse's pubic hair, then plucked several hairs out one-by-one and examined them under a microscope. He stepped back from the scope. "Pam, take a look."

Under high magnification the hairs looked as thick as tree trunks. Most were dark, curled and flattened. One was round and quite a bit lighter.

"Am I looking at a foreign hair that's straighter and lighter than the others?" Pam asked, as she stepped away from the scope.

Eddie smiled. "You get an 'A' today." Eddie went back to the scope and pulled the odd hair out with a forceps, placing it in a clear plastic container. "The next step is to see if it matches the one we recovered from Terri Berg," he said, and disappeared into another room.

Tony Oresek and Floyd were having a muted discussion as Tony looked at the darkened skin around the corpse's neck. Pam moved closer to hear what was being said.

"...severe bruising, apparently caused by constricture of hands around the neck of the victim. Obvious fingerprint markings and thumb marks on either side of the trachea."

Tony stepped back from the magnifier and let both Floyd and Pam look at the marks on Carol Knutson's neck.

Pam looked at Tony inquisitively. "Death by strangulation?"

Tony just nodded. "I still can't say for sure that was the cause of death until I get a look at her internal organs. But it sure looks like that's most likely the cause."

Eddie was back at the microscope. "Guess what, folks. The hair I combed out of the victim's pubic hair matches samples from the Berg murder."

Chapter 27

It took Dan a dozen phone calls to find the Ryder truck rental outlet that had received the return from the Ascherman family. The report that they had been going to Ely wasn't correct. Dan had started his calls with Ely, then spread in larger circles until he hit pay dirt in Aurora, in northern St. Louis County. Aurora was one of the small towns built along the backbone of Minnesota's Mesabi Iron Range, about forty miles from Ely.

The Ryder rental outlet was in a gas station, and the man that answered had checked in the Ascherman truck. "Yeah, a young skinny guy with a beard. Hadn't topped off the tank."

Dan perked up and grabbed a pencil to make notes. "Did he leave a local address?"

"Hmm, hang on just a minute. I'll check." Dan hung on to the phone for nearly five minutes before the man returned. "Yeah, sorry. Had a customer. He listed an address out on County Road 341. Number 3946."

Dan scribbled down the address. "Any phone number?"

"Naw. He made some comment about not getting hooked up for a while. He said that he's going to work for the Federal Bureau of Land Management office. Maybe you could get him there. It's over in Hoyt Lakes."

Dan called the headquarters of the Superior National Forest. It took three transfers to find anyone who knew Ernest Ascherman. He wasn't scheduled to start work until the following Monday.

Dan sat tapping his pencil while he considered his options. His first impulse was to drive to Aurora. He pulled out a state map and estimated that it would take three hours to get there. Even after all the driving he might find out that the Aschermans hadn't seen anything. For that matter, they might not be home. He picked up the phone and dialed the number for the St. Louis County Sheriff's Department.

Another three transfers and another call got him to Walt Boreski, a Duluth detective. Dan explained the situation.

Boreski sounded eager to assist. "We can send a deputy out to get hold of them and have them call you. If you've got a picture, fax it up and we'll send it with him. It may answer the question right away."

Dan was surprised and pleased by the help. "Thanks. Give me your fax number. We've got an old picture of a potential suspect." Dan hung up and sent the fax off to Duluth.

He considered what to do next. He wandered down to Sepanen's office and stuck his head in. The sheriff was reading one of the reports from the Knutson murder.

"What's up, Dan?" Sepanen took off his reading glasses.

"I found the Aschermans, the family that was staying in the Rock Creek Motel the night Carol Knutson died. They're up in Aurora. They don't have a phone yet." Dan sat in the straight-backed chair. "St. Louis County is going to send a deputy with a fax of Ross Cooper's picture. They're going to have Ascherman call me here."

"Any other leads?" Sepanen dropped the report on top of his desk.

Dan rolled his head like he had a stiff neck. "Nothing. Pam and Floyd are in Duluth for the autopsy. I suppose I could go back and lean on some local perverts. But I think this Cooper guy is our man. We need a different tack to find him."

"Any ideas?" Sepanen asked.

Dan shook his head. "That's why I came in here. To see

if you had any ideas."

Sepanen let out an audible laugh. "I keep you around for good ideas."

Dan cracked a smile. "Isn't that why they pay you the big bucks?"

Sepanen laughed again. "Wanna trade jobs and make the big bucks?"

Dan shook his head. He stretched the muscles that had tightened up from sitting on the phone for hours. "I've shown the picture all over the place. Nobody recognizes it. Probably too old. We need to age it. The hair at the murder scene was dark, apparently dyed. Maybe we can get an artist to work up something from the photo and color the hair darker and make it longer. I'll give the BCA a call and see if I can talk someone into sending up an artist."

"OK, Dan. Stay on top of it and keep me posted." Sepanen had already picked up the report and replaced the glasses on the bridge of his nose by the time Dan got to the door.

"John, do you realize how many times you've said that same thing to me? Don't you have any other words of wisdom?"

"Sure, arrest the bastard and get a confession out of him. I could use that kind of announcement right about now."

"No problem. What should I do after that?" Dan asked as he disappeared out the door.

Dan called Laurie Lone Eagle's number at the BCA, but got her voicemail. He left her a message to call him. It took him three more phone calls to get the name of the artist at the BCA. Helen Opheim was at her desk when he finally got through.

"Hi, my name is Dan Williams. I'm an investigator in Pine County, with a ten-year-old picture of a murder suspect. No one's been able to I.D. him from the picture and we thought that if we aged him a little we might have better luck. Oh, and the suspect in the picture is blonde. We've been finding dark hairs, so we want to do him with dark hair."

There was a sigh. "Are you sure you've got the right guy? I mean, with the hair color wrong and no one able to identify him...I'm really busy..." The woman's voice sounded tired.

"We've got a solid fingerprint from one of the murder scenes." Dan grasped for something to energize the woman. "So far we suspect him in three murders...two of the victims were raped before they were killed."

There was silence for a few seconds before she spoke up and Dan wondered if she was still there. "Where are you, Williams?" she finally asked.

"Pine City. About an hour and a half north of St. Paul on I-35."

"Yeah, yeah. I know where it is." Dan heard things rustling in the background. "Listen, it's already past noon, and Friday. I'm booked solid. There's no way that I can look at it before Monday. Why don't you drop it in an express mail envelope and it'll show up here by 10:00 Monday morning. I'll try to get to it then."

"Monday? I was hoping that we could do something today. I could drive it down and be there before three."

"Wouldn't do you any good. I'm already working on something else. It's Monday, unless you can find someone else that can do it." Her voice was just as tired and unmoved as when she'd started. Dan had a vision of a middle aged, overworked civil servant who had lost the ability to get excited about anything.

Dan tried for a trump card. "Most murders are solved in 48 hours or they go unsolved forever."

The woman retorted. "You're past 48 hours and you've already identified the murderer. Now you're just trying to find him. Give me a break. I've got other work to do."

Dan was getting desperate. "But we need to find him

before he gets to Hong Kong or Brazil."

There was a pause. "Is this the double murder that I read about near Henriette?"

Dan perked up. "Yeah, grisly affair. The murderer tried to make it look like a murder and suicide. Shot the guy in the head, then tied up the woman and raped her before he beat her senseless and shot her. The medical examiner said that she probably lived through a couple hours of torture before she died." He tried to make it sound as terrible as it was, hoping to appeal to her cop instinct.

"Deputy Williams, it's already been three days...make that four days, since the first murders. I'm swamped. It's Wednesday and I've got two days to get these other jobs out. I'm not going to jump through hoops to get something rushed before Monday."

Dan was slipping. "Look. We believe this guy is the killer of another woman here. Can't you drop what you're doing and work on this?"

"You want to call the Sherburne county sheriff and tell him that they don't need drawings of a little girl's kidnapping suspects until Monday?"

Dan knew that he'd lost her. "I heard about that this morning. Any leads?"

"We've got her best friend coming to our office in thirty minutes. She witnessed the abduction. We're going to work on it this afternoon."

"Any chance you could work on ours tonight? Or tomorrow? I can run the picture down whenever."

Helen let out an exasperated breath. "Listen, Williams. I've got a family reunion in Rochester this weekend. My mother will kill me if I miss another one. I've worked every weekend since Memorial Day. My family doesn't remember what I look like. I'm taking this one off, and I'll work on your picture Monday." By the end, she was almost yelling.

Dan was broken. "Okay, okay. I'll get the picture out by

courier this afternoon. Talk to you Monday."

There was no response and Dan was going to hang up when Helen came back on the line. "Listen...I'm sorry. I'm a little frazzled right now and I really didn't mean to take it out on you. I can't do anything before Monday. But, I'll do this. Hang onto the picture and I'll drive up Monday morning. I can be there by...say eight."

Dan let his anger down. "Yeah. That'll be okay. Sorry I pushed so hard. It's just that I want this guy."

"We'll get him. Hang tight." Her voice turned soft and reassuring. "What's the best way to get there?"

"Take the first Pine City exit right, into town. Go left at the stop lights on Main Street for about ten blocks. The courthouse is across from the water tower, and the sheriff's office is in the courthouse."

"Got it. See you Monday morning."

Sandy Maki was finishing a report when he heard the dispatcher paging his name, and he saw the flashing light on the phone. He punched the flashing button, expecting to be talking to either Dan Williams or Floyd Swenson. Instead, the voice was meek and feminine.

"Sandy...I'm sorry." The slow flow of words meant it could only be Barb Dupre. "I fell asleep on you."

Sandy looked around nervously. The room was empty. He was free to talk. "It's okay. You seemed to want to snuggle." He chuckled and was relieved to hear her laugh too.

"I work at the Pine Brook Inn tonight. Stop by and I'll buy you a beer."

Sandy took a deep breath. "You dancing?" He made a quick decision to skip it and get some sleep in his own bed.

Barb laughed. "Harvey's wife wouldn't go for that. I'm just waiting tables."

Sandy was still tired from the short night on Barb's

couch. "Thanks, but I only got about four hours of sleep. I think that I need to get about ten hours of sleep tonight."

"Oh." The disappointment was thick in her voice. "I promise to stay awake tonight."

"Well, it's tempting. But I work days again tomorrow. I have to be on duty at seven." The prospect of another sleepless night on Barb's couch was not that tempting.

"Umm. Why not take a nap when you get home for a while. Then come over late. If it's quiet, Harvey lets me go at midnight."

"I'll think about it. That's the best I can promise." Sandy twirled a pencil in his fingers.

"Sandy. Umm, You're a nice guy. I don't know how to talk to nice guys." There was a long pause. "I really want you to come...because I like you." Barb's words seemed like a line that a guy would use on a woman.

"Not just because you're scared?"

She paused a long time. "Butch...scares me. But you make me feel...safe." Again the long pause. "It's like a hot fire with Butch. Everything is hot. But you...you make me just feel warm. You're so gentle. I've never..."

Sandy looked around nervously. "I'll come over later."

Chapter 28

D an read through all the reports from the Berg murders a third time Friday afternoon. Each deputy on the scene had written a report and he read through them carefully, comparing their observations and thoughts. Something was there, but he couldn't lay a hand on it.

He got a cup of coffee from the ready room and sat down, staring at the pile of reports again. He pushed them aside and picked up the reports from the Knutson murder and started reading through them. He found it in Pam Ryan's report of the Knutson murder. He went back to her report of the Berg murder. It was there, too.

Condom wrappers and no condoms. An unusual brand, Black Ecstasy. He picked up the phone and called the pharmacy. Benny Parsons answered.

"Benny, Dan Williams here. Do you carry Black Ecstasy condoms?"

There was a pause, then Benny said,"Gee, Dan. I've never heard of that brand before. We carry a lot of the standards, but that's an odd one...uhh...I can see if I can get you a package if you want, though." Dan heard Benny laughing.

"OK, Benny. OK. You've had your fun,, now, where else would a guy go to buy condoms?"

Benny got serious. "I guess you can get them by mail order through some of the adult magazines, and I've seen dispensers in the truck stops when I've been traveling. They use a lot of names like that."

The words tripped Dan's memory. Sandy Maki had said that they were probably from vending machines, too. "Benny, do you buy condoms through a wholesaler?"

"Yeah, they supply all the over-the-counter pharmaceutical stock. They're out of the Cities. You want me to check their catalog? Hang on, they might have something that we don't order." Music played through the phone as Dan was put on hold. Pretty soon Benny returned. "Dan, nothing in that brand at all. Sorry."

"Okay, Benny. Thanks for the help, anyway." Dan pulled out the phone book and looked up the phone numbers of five local gas stations. The first three didn't stock condoms in their restrooms. He finally hit on the fourth, which was at the I-35 exit. The teenage girl who answered the phone thought that they did have condoms in the men's restroom and put one of the guys on the line.

"Yeah, what did you want?" The young male voice sounded irritated.

"Do you have a condom dispenser in the restroom?"

There was a pause. "I guess. Who wants to know?"

"This is the sheriff's department. What brands are there?"

The kid didn't sound particularly impressed. "Hey, if this is illegal somehow, I got nothing to do with it. You gotta talk to the manager."

"It's nothing illegal. I'm trying to find the name of your distributor."

"Oh." The boy went from defensive to inquisitive. "It's some guy that comes in his van once a week. He does the candy machine, too, and pays the boss a percentage."

"Okay. But I need his name."

"Umm. Hang on a second." The phone thunked on some surface and Dan could hear footsteps. It took a full three minutes before the kid was back on the line. "There's a phone num-

ber to call in case of problems. No name." He gave Dan a number. The 320 area code indicated the phone was in the St. Cloud,
Minnesota area.

Dan dialed the number and waited for three rings,
expecting an answering machine when a male voice came on
the line. "Hello?"

"This is Dan Williams from the Pine County sheriff's
department. Are you the vending machine operator for the Pine
City truck stop?"

"Ah, yeah. Is there a problem with a machine?
Somebody break into it?" The voice sounded mature, perhaps
middle aged.

"Everything's fine. I'm trying to track down where a
person would find a Black Ecstasy condom."

There was a chuckle. "Black Ecstasy. I don't stock them
in Pine City. But if you've got a special preference for them, I
suppose I could put'em in there, too."

Dan perked up. "Not my preference. We have a crime
involved and the suspect has a preference for that particular
brand." Dan paused to let the gravity of the situation sink in.
"Where *do* you stock them?"

The man sounded suspicious. "What's your name?"

"I'm Dan Williams, the undersheriff for Pine County.
By the way, what's your name? I got your number off a vending machine."

"Gene Porcini. I just wanted to check. I get a lot of damage to those machines. You know, with them sitting back in the
restroom. They take a lot more beating than the candy machines
that are out front." Dan could hear some strange scraping noises for a second. "Let me pull down my book and I can tell you
all of the places I stock Black Ecstacy. I keep a log of what I
stock where and how fast the stock gets used up."

Pages turned in the background. "You got a pencil? Let
me give'em to you. I stock Black Ecstasy in Braham, Cold
Spring, Delano..."

"Hold on a second. How many places are we talking about?" Dan scribbled down Delano.

"Well, I'm sure there's got to be at least a dozen." Again, the pages flipped. "I got regular routes and I drive around and restock a different string of vending machines every day. You've probably seen my van around one time or another. I've got the blue Econoline van with the wheelchair hoist."

The description clicked in Dan's mind. "Sure. I remember now. How far do you go?"

"I only go as far east as the Wisconsin border. I go as far west as Cold Spring, north to Mille Lacs and south to Cambridge. All together, I supply about seventy three places. But, I don't stock the same thing in all the machines. Some things sell better in some places."

"Where do you stock the Black Ecstacys close to me? You said not in Pine City. How about the Pine Brook Inn, in Pine Brook?"

"Nope, I don't have machines there. Let me look." Pages turned in the background. "Del's bait in Hinckley. The truckstop at Banning Junction. The bar in Cloverdale. The truckstop at I-35 and highway 70."

Dan couldn't keep the excitement out of his voice. "Highway 70 at Rock Creek?"

"Yeah, I guess that Rock Creek is just east of there. I don't do anything in town, though." He chuckled. "Course, there ain't much to Rock Creek."

"Is that machine one of the big volume users?"

Again the pages flipped. "Nah, I don't get a lot of volume on any of them. I put ten in last week. It was ten down in June. Before that, I hadn't put any in there since April."

"Do they have lot numbers or anything that we could use to trace them?"

The book slapped against a flat surface. "There's a number on the box, but I don't think that there's anything on the individual packages."

Dan was excited and wanted the man to move faster. "Please check."

"If it's okay, I'll call back. It'll take me a few minutes to get into the van and unstack some stuff."

"No problem. I'm going to run to the evidence locker and look at the wrappers. I'll have more information when you call back." Dan gave him the number for the dispatcher.

Dan hustled to the evidence locker and unlocked the door. He signed in on the log and worked his way through the racks of boxes until he found the box from the Knutson murder. He dug through the box until he found the plastic bag with the condom wrapper. There were tiny, embossed letters on the sealed margin of the package. It said, "Lot 59214."

By the time Dan was back at his desk, the dispatcher was paging him. He picked up the phone and punched the flashing button. "Williams."

"This is Gene Porcini. There's a lot number on the box and on the edge of each wrapper."

"What's the number of the box you have?"

"Well, it's lot 59214. I suppose that means they were the fourteenth lot made in May of 1992. The first three digits usually give the month and year of manufacture. The last two digits are the lot number. Most manufacturers use some variation of that to identify when their materials were made. Geesh, these are that old. I wonder if they have an expiration."

"Does that mean that you've been putting this same box of condoms out for some time?"

"Probably since 1992. Like I said, they're not that big a seller, and I got a deal on a whole case. Half of it's still in my van."

Dan smiled. "You ever get complaints that they're too old and break?"

Gene Porcini chuckled. "What are they going to do, sue an old paraplegic veteran for his wheelchair? Most people that buy condoms out of a vending machine don't want to be seen in a drug store. You know, kids and cheating husbands."

"Say that again." Dan sat up in his chair.

The man sounded confused. "You mean the part about the kids? They buy them and carry 'em around as status symbols."

"No. Before that. People that don't want to be seen." Dan scribbled a note to himself.

"Yeah. Why buy out of a machine at four times the price, unless you don't want to be seen buying condoms."

"Thanks." Dan's mind was racing, trying to figure out where he could go with this information. The first stop would be the truckstop at highway 70. He'd have to show the Cooper picture to every employee. He might have to track some of them down at home. "Please send me a list of all the places that have the Black Ecstacy condoms in dispensers."

"Sure thing. Can I ask what you're working on?"

"Three murders. The killer leaves a Black Ecstasy wrapper after he rapes the victims."

Porcini gave a low whistle into the phone. "No shit? A murderer is using my condoms."

Dan grabbed the picture of Ross Cooper and headed for the door. He literally ran into Pam Ryan as she walked into the ready room. "Sorry, Pam. I'm chasing a hunch."

"On the Knutson murder?" She nodded to the picture.

"Actually, it's your lead. The condoms are very unusual. They're sold only from vending machines and there are a couple of machines locally. I'm going to show the picture around a little to see if anyone recognizes our man."

Pam looked tired. "Are we still going to meet at 4:30 to review today's developments?"

"You got anything new?"

Pam shrugged. "Not really."

"I don't either. Get hold of Sandy and Floyd. Cancel the meeting for me."

* * *

Dan first stopped at the truck stop at highway 70. None of the three people working the afternoon shift recognized the picture of Ross Cooper. He got names and addresses for the other employees, and went on to check the bait store in Cloverdale. Del, of Del's bait, didn't recognize Cooper either. Del was the only employee of Del's bait.

Dan worked his way back toward home, stopping in Hinckley and at Banning junction. No one recognized Ross Cooper. He ended his workday with a list of another twenty people that he needed to talk to. It was already seven and time to knock off. The heat and lack of progress had drained him.

"Hey Sandy, Dan caught me and asked me to cancel our 4:30 meeting."

Sandy looked up at Pam in disgust. "I could've gone home. One more setback in a long day of nothing."

Floyd sauntered in and sat on the edge of the desk. "You young folks got big plans for a Friday night?"

Pam shook her head.

Sandy looked from beneath his eyebrows at Floyd. "I got invited to a bar later. That reminds me. I've got to make a call." As Pam and Floyd wandered off, he grabbed the phone and dialed the number for the Hennepin County jail where Butch Mattson had been transferred earlier in the week.

Sandy talked his way through three people at the Hennepin County jail before he got to the head jailer. "I want to know if Brian Allen Mattson is still in custody."

"You a relative?" The jailer sounded gruff, like he was being put out by the question.

"Pine County Sheriff's Department. We have a hold on him in case some judge decides to release him."

Papers rustled. "Yeah. He had a hearing Thursday. They

revoked his parole and he'll be on his way to the state prison at Oak Park Heights Monday morning. You guys won't see him for a couple of years unless you pull him out for a trial up there."

"Thanks." Sandy left for home and a nap.

Chapter 29

The crowd was thinning at the Pine Brook Inn when Sandy Maki rolled into the parking lot at midnight. He watched a car swing wide pulling out of the parking lot. It almost hit another car driving down highway 23. He made a mental note of the license number and called dispatch from the pay phone inside the front door. Another drunk driver would get his day in front of a judge.

Sandy's eyes had already adjusted to the dark of the bar when he walked in. Barb was loading a tray with drinks at the waitress station. He eased up behind her and grasped her shoulder. Instantly, her elbow plunged into Sandy's solar plexus.

"Bastard!" Barb set the tray down and turned around. When she saw it was Sandy she said, "Oh, Sandy! I'm sorry. I thought..."

Sandy struggled to draw a breath, then he nodded assurance. "Okay. I shouldn't surprise you like that." He gasped between the words and looked up to see Harvey Ostberg's round face grinning at him as he polished a beer glass.

Barb steered him to a bar stool. "Sit here while I deliver this round." She looked up at Harvey. "Don't just stand there. Give him a beer."

Sandy watched as she lifted the tray up on her shoulder, her cropped T-shirt pulling up close to the bottom of her unsecured breasts. Sandy looked at the patrons. Every male eye in the place was on Barb's midriff as she jiggled across the floor.

She leaned over to set the tray down and her breasts teased the male patrons from a different angle.

"What'll it be, Sandy." Harvey's voice jarred Sandy back to the bar.

"Whatever you got on tap is fine." Sandy gave Harvey a smile, then turned back to watch Barb collect a tip and cross the floor to the bar. She skirted the dance floor where two couples embraced as they slow-danced to the Righteous Brothers singing "Unchained Melody."

She jumped onto the stool next to Sandy. "You get your breath back yet?" The words were still slow and deliberate.

The beer slid to his elbow and Sandy acknowledged it with a nod and pushed two dollars across the bar. "I assume that's some kind of a survival reflex," he said, rubbing the spot where she'd hit him.

"You bet. I gotta let these guys know where the boundaries are. Otherwise I'd have fingerprints all over my body."

He took a long drink and nodded to her T-shirt. "I'd say that you give mixed messages."

Barb smiled and puffed out her chest. "I dress this way for the tips. That's the limit of it."

"And every guy fantasizes that he's the one taking you home."

Barb gave him a wry smile. "What's wrong with having a fantasy or two?"

A guy at the far table signaled for a round and Barb recited the required drinks to Harvey.

As she stood up, Sandy touched her arm. "How do you remember that?"

She gave him a smile. "I have a photographic memory. I had a 4.0 average at the university."

He gave her a surprised look. "Did you get a degree?"

She looked away as Harvey set the last drink on the tray. She hefted the tray onto her shoulder with a grunt. "Naw. I met a guy that showed me that there was more to life than stuffy professors and mildewed books."

As Barb left, Rose, the other waitress, moved up to the waitress station and gave Harvey an order.

Sandy leaned close to the waitress station so Rose could hear him over the music. "How's business, Rose?"

She looked embarrassed by the attention. "It's okay, I guess." Her outfit was the opposite of Barb's, a long sleeved plaid shirt with mother-of-pearl snaps, and blue jeans.

Together they watched Barb set out the round of drinks. The men paid her and she collected another hefty tip. Sandy smiled. Barb's strategy seemed to be working. "She sure gets the tips."

Rose looked at Barb with complete disdain. "She's a prostitute. She's selling her body to every guy in the place." Sandy smiled to himself as Rose turned and whisked the tray away to one of her tables at the far end of the bar.

The lights flickered briefly as Barb returned to the bar. Harvey yelled out, "Last call!" Sandy looked at his watch. It was five minutes to one o'clock. He wondered if Harvey made last call this promptly every night, or if this was a special tribute to the presence of a deputy. A dozen hands signaled for another round.

It was another 45 minutes before all the drinks were finished off and the last of the patrons were making their way to the door. One old man was pressing his sad story to Rose who was trying to clear the last of the glasses from the tables. The old guy followed Rose from table to table like a puppy. Occasionally, she gave him a push or a word of discouragement. He persisted.

A rag flew past Sandy's face as he watched Rose and the old man. "C'mon. I'm done." Barb, who had been wiping down tables, came up and looped her arm through his.

They walked across the parking lot to the red Camaro. Barb unlocked the door. "Why don't you follow me to the apartment?" Sandy's Grand Am was parked next to the Camaro.

"I should get going." Sandy looked back as the bar door slammed and Rose came out the door. The old drunk was right behind her, still pleading his case. They walked toward the last two cars in the lot.

Sandy chuckled. "Look. A classic case of 'the girls all get prettier at closing time.'"

Barb turned and watched the activities playing out. "Oooh, is he going to be sorry."

Sandy took a step to rescue Rose, but Barb put a hand on his arm. "Just watch."

The old man followed Rose to her car and talked as she unlocked the door. When she pulled the door open the man laid a hand on her arm. It was the wrong thing to do. The door flew open wide, smashing into the old man's knees. He howled in pain and collapsed onto the gravel. Within seconds, Rose was in the car, her wheels spitting gravel as she exited from the parking lot.

Barb let out a deep breath. When Sandy looked at her he saw that her face looked flushed even in the blue cast of the mercury vapor lights of the parking lot.

Barb pressed her body against him. She pressed her lips to his, grabbed his hand and pulled it under the crop top, pressing her breast hard against his palm. The nipple was already hard. Her hips pressed hard against his and she rocked sensuously. "Take me here," she whispered.

Sandy shook his head, but she tore desperately at her shorts until they were off. She pulled him on top of her on the hood of the Camaro. Their bodies were briefly lit by the headlights of the old man's pickup as he pulled out of the lot.

Sally Williams rolled over at midnight and threw her arm across the empty spot on Dan's side of the bed. She blinked the sleep from her eyes and saw the glow of lights down the hallway and the muffled sound of voices. She pulled on a robe and slipped down the hall, peeking around the corner.

Dan was sitting on the couch watching television, his face lit by the bluish projections. The table next to him was littered with beer cans and an empty can of kippered snacks. The smell of the smoked fish hung in the air, covering the smell of the stale beer.

She slipped around the corner and leaned against the wall. "Couldn't sleep?" She looked at the television screen and recognized Mia Farrow. The movie was a rerun of "Rosemary's Baby."

Dan looked up at the sound of her voice. "Too much on my mind."

She walked to the couch and tucked the robe under her legs as she sat down. They watched the movie together, with Sally's head on his shoulder. "You know, if you keep watching this creepy old movie you're not going to be able to sleep."

Dan took a deep breath and blew it out. "I don't get it. We've got a murderer, actually a triple murderer, wandering around. He's been here at least a week, and we know who he is. Hell, we've even got a picture, but no one can identify him."

Sally shivered. "Maybe he's just gone. Left the county. Maybe left the country."

Dan shook his head. "Even then, somebody would recognize him. He had to have been around. Somebody should have seen him at a grocery store or a gas station. It's like he's a vampire and is only out at night. And only his victims see him."

Sally shook her head. "The photo is old. Maybe he's just changed. How many people would recognize you from a fifteen year old photo?"

Dan stared at the television. In the movie, Rosemary seemed to accept her ugly child. From what the counselor had said, the real Rosemary Cooper's motherly instincts had failed and she had rejected her child.

"You're right," he said, resignedly. He shifted and finished off the can of beer. "We've got an artist coming up on

Monday to age the picture. The other thing is that the guy's got light hair in the picture and the hair we found at the murder scenes has been dark with light roots. Tony Oresek says that its been colored. We can change that, too. We even know how long it is." Dan paused, considering other possibilities. "I don't think he's got the money to go the plastic surgery route."

"Maybe someone's hiding him. Like a girlfriend or a relative. That way he wouldn't have to go out for groceries or gas himself."

"Hmmm." Dan considered that line of thought. "That's an interesting idea. It's hard to believe that he's got a girlfriend if he's out raping and murdering women. Maybe he's staying with a friend or unsuspecting relative. The Stearns County courthouse said that he had a sister named Maryrose, but they couldn't locate her in Stearns County. She checked on the marriage licenses and came up with nothing. She could be married and living somewhere around here under a different name. Maybe he's staying with her. Or maybe he's got an aunt or uncle locally."

Sally shivered. "How weird is this guy? I mean are we all in danger? Is he randomly breaking into houses and attacking?"

Dan raised his eyebrows. "I don't think so. He went through treatment years ago for obsessing on a high school girl. I'd guess that he chooses his victims carefully."

"But to do that he's got to be out and around town. I mean, you don't find women to attack sitting in your living room."

Dan ran a hand over his face. "We've talked to practically every person in the County. We showed them the picture. No one recognized him."

"Wait!" Sally snapped her fingers." Maybe he saw Terri in Mora. And you don't know where he met the other woman. Maybe it was somewhere else, too. Maybe you're looking too close to home. Maybe he doesn't do his deeds where he lives."

Dan shook his head. "I thought about that.I talked to the people where Terri worked in Mora. They didn't recognize the picture either. He apparently knew about Joey and Terry Berg , and also about Terri and Jamie Arvidson—enough to set up the murder/suicide as a plausible scenario. He had to be around town to catch all the connections."

"It's like a jigsaw puzzle with missing pieces." Sally got up and started to clear the beer cans from the table. They clattered into a bag under the sink. The aluminum recycling bin filled more quickly since Dan had taken the job as undersheriff, she thought.

When she finished, Sally leaned against the arch that separated the kitchen and living rooms. "Come to bed, Honey." Dan stared at the television as if he were in a trance.

He looked at her through bloodshot eyes that she recognized from his long stretches of night shifts. None of the deputies ever got enough sleep working nights. In addition to their shift they had to make court appearances. Dan seldom got more than four or five hours of sleep a day during the five-day stretch of nights.

He shook his head. "I couldn't sleep."

"You used to be able to. What's different?" She sat down on the couch again.

"When I was on the road, the days got broken up by different cases and delivering court documents. Now I get to spend all my time mulling over the evidence and replaying the same crime scenes in my mind. I second-guess every decision I make and constantly try to figure out what I've missed."

Sally cracked a smile. "You're old enough to know that we're all fallible and that we miss things. I do it all the time."

Dan's face was like stone. "But when you miss something, you correct the paperwork and it's all right. If I miss something, a killer might go free. Another woman may die unnecessarily."

Sally got off the couch and sat on his lap. "There are

how many other people working this case with you? Three? Four? And you take it all to heart." She pushed his hair back from his forehead. "Where's the sheriff? Shouldn't he be losing sleep over this too?"

Dan shook his head. "I give him a daily update. He talks to the press when they call or stop by. Mostly he's busy dealing with the politics. He doesn't have time to get involved in this. Besides, being separate gives him deniability if we don't solve the crimes."

Dan went on. "I'm the one who calls the investigative shots. I'm the one who decides what leads to follow and which to bury. I'm the one that has to let the sheriff know what he can and can't tell the media people. I have to explain why there's still a murderer out there."

"And you're the golden boy that never fails. Everyone expects you to do the impossible, just because you've done it before." She planted a kiss on his forehead. "Come to bed. I'll give you a back rub and you'll loosen up." She reached down and pulled him up from the couch.

Ross Cooper couldn't sleep, either. He turned the pages of a Penthouse magazine that he'd bought at a truck stop. The girl behind the counter had given him a look like he was a leper when she'd given him the change. The Penthouse pictures were explicit. Too explicit. He liked some mystery. He wanted to be teased. These pictures were like being rubbed with a whole chicken and he was repulsed.

He threw the magazine toward a wastebasket in the corner of the room, and shut off the light over his bed. When he closed his eyes he saw Terri Berg's face. She was a tease. Always saying leading things and wearing those erotic clothes. Suddenly, Terri's hair was blonde and it was Barb's face.

His eyes popped open. Not Barb! She was a slut. She strutted her pumped-up tits all over and shot little glimpses of them under the crop top she wore. She was as dumb as a stump. One guy had said that her age and I.Q. were probably the same. And that stupid tattoo! "Property of Butch." What a joke! He laughed out loud.

When his eyes closed, though, there was Barb again, this time lifting the crop top just enough so that he could see the bottom of her nipples. The smell of her cheap perfume filled his nostrils and he thought back to the time that he'd secretly watched her undress and saw the tattoo. He felt the hardness swelling in his crotch.

"Barb. Yeah, maybe Barb."

DAY

SEVEN

SATURDAY

Chapter 30

Sandy Maki was sleeping soundly Saturday morning when the arm hit his face. He reacted reflexively, grabbing it and rolling away at the same time. The shriek brought him to full awareness.

"OOOWWW! You're hurting me!" Barb was naked on the bed. "What the hell are you doing?" She was trying to blink her eyes open as she punched him in the ribs with her free hand.

He released his grip and fell onto the bed beside her. "Sorry, I just reacted. I was dreaming about someone following me and then you hit me with your arm."

"I rolled over," she said accusingly as she sat up, rubbing her shoulder and twisting her arm to make sure that it still worked. She seemed oblivious to the fact that she was totally naked. He'd never been with a woman as well endowed as Barb. He'd also never seen anyone so totally uninhibited about their naked body.

"I guess it still works." She punched him in the chest with a fair amount of force. "But don't do it again." She snuggled against him.

The events of the evening swirled in his mind. They'd been like two dogs in heat. First in the parking lot, then on her bed. He suddenly became alarmed. They hadn't used any protection!

"Are you on the pill, or something?" He tried to sound casual, although thoughts of AIDS and hepatitis swirled through his head.

"Naw, the pill made me sick and I forgot to take them too often. I had my tubes tied a couple of years ago." She pulled the sheets down and poked at her navel. "See, they did it through my belly button. I used to have an 'outtie.' Now I've got a cute 'innie.' Don't you like it?"

He looked closely and couldn't distinguish any sort of scarring. "Yeah, cute."

"I was tested a couple weeks ago. I don't have any social diseases. How about you?" She snuggled closer and addressed the topic as if she were asking what his favorite movie was.

"I get exposed to blood at car accidents and things like that. We get tested after every exposure. I've always been negative. I've never had the need to be tested because of sex."

"You're not a virgin," she purred, as she ran her fingers through the hair on his chest.

"Well, no. I just had one steady for a long time. We thought we'd get married...once upon a time."

"Didn't work out?"

"She couldn't deal with me being a cop."

"Her loss. You're an okay guy."

Sandy rolled over so their noses were almost touching. "Why'd you want to have sex with me?"

She ran her hand through his hair. "Because you're cute, and I enjoy sex." She pulled back a little and stared at him. "You didn't think it was love, did you?"

He was dumbfounded. "Not for me. But women..."

She rolled onto her back and let out a laugh. "Most women are prudes, afraid to admit that they could let themselves have an orgasm. Not me."

She got up, found the silky robe in a pile of clothes on the floor and put it on. The room was neat except for the clothes that they had shed. There wasn't a mirror in sight. Pretty unusual for a woman not to have a mirror, Sandy thought to himself.

"I choose my partners carefully. But I'm not above enjoying a good roll in the sack with a cute guy." She disappeared into the hall. "You gotta be on duty again at seven?"

The sun streamed through the Venetian blinds on the bedroom window. It was nearing the summer solstice when Pine City had daylight from five in the morning until after nine at night.

"Yeah, what time is it?" He pulled a pair of jeans from the floor and dug in the pocket for his watch. It said 5:30 a.m. He fell back onto the bed.

The toilet flushed. "I don't have a clock in here."

She walked back into the bedroom and threw the robe back on the floor before falling onto the bed. "I'm going back to sleep."

When Sandy got to the courthouse Saturday morning, Dan was already in his office doodling on a chalkboard. Sandy rushed past Dan's office, hoping to get a cup of coffee before Dan cornered him. The sheriff's office was still dark. John Sepanen wasn't around much on weekends. If the dispatchers needed the sheriff before noon or on a Saturday they would call his home first, then they would call Nicoll's café. He liked to have his morning coffee with his constituents.

As Sandy stirred Coffeemate into the black liquid he was thinking about last night.

"Any headway?"

Sandy was so deep in his own thoughts about Barb that he jumped at the sound of Dan's voice. "Naw, just thinking."

Dan walked to the coffeepot and poured some of the vile liquid into the cracked cup that had become his trademark. The deputies had bought it for his last birthday. Printed on the outside was the simple message, "TUMS." Dan's typical cycle was to drink a cup of coffee, then pop a Tums to counteract the effect of the caffeine.

Sandy studied Dan's face for a second. Dan's gaze was distant. "What's on your mind?"

Dan continued to stare at a spot on the ceiling as he spoke. "Something's not right with this whole investigation. We know who committed the murders, but we can't find him. No one's ever seen him. He doesn't exist. It's like he's an apparition that can appear and disappear." Dan took another sip of coffee. "Sally says that maybe he's being hidden by a friend or relative."

"And you think..."

"That he's in disguise or something."

Sandy carefully creased a message slip exactly in half, then in half again. "I hadn't thought about that aspect of it. It is kinda spooky though. A guy kills three people, we have his picture and his name, and no one has seen him. Maybe he's not local?"

Dan swirled the coffee in his cup. "Naw. He's local, 'cause he knows too much about the people in this area. This guy has to be a psycho. He seems to be into sadism as much as sex. Maybe there's something more here that fits that model."

Sandy sat down and thought. "Terri Berg was a flirt. Maybe she spurned him sometime. I don't know anything about the other woman."

Putting down the coffee cup, Dan dug a roll of tums out of his shirt pocket. He pried two off the end of the roll with his thumbnail and popped them into his mouth. "So where is he?"

"Left town?" Sandy offered.

"Maybe. But where's the trail? It's like he was never here." Dan got up and picked up the cup. "If you get any brainstorms, let me know. In the meantime, you better hit the road. You're the only road deputy until three this afternoon."

The miles on the road helped Sandy run through the case, but he found his mind drifting. Barb was using him. It was clear, but somehow he didn't care. She was like every bachelor's dream come true; a beautiful woman who wanted him for sex and didn't want a commitment. He hit himself on the forehead. "Idiot!" he said to himself. "You've got to get some condoms before you go over there again." Oh hell. Itwas too late to worry about it.

Then, there was the sex on the hood of the Camaro. What a kinky rush. He shouldn't have done it, but what the hell. It was a rush, especially when the headlights of the old man's truck had played across them.

Barb hadn't said anything when he'd left her apartment. No "Come back later." No "See you around." Nothing. What happens next? On the other hand, she didn't do mornings or breakfast. She had slept through his departure.

Dan was sitting in his desk chair staring at the chalk-board when the phone rang. He punched the intercom button. "Yeah."

"You got a call from Ernest Ascherman." The dispatch-er recited a phone number with a 218 prefix. It was from north-ern Minnesota. "The caller said that he'll be at this number for fifteen minutes."

Dan dialed the number and listened to the phone ring through the static. Someone finally picked it up on the fifth ring.

"Hello?"

"Ernest Ascherman please."

"Just a second. He's here." There was silence, a male voice came on.

"Hello?"

"Dan Williams from the Pine County sheriff's depart-ment. I need to ask you a couple of questions."

"Yeah, The cop up here told me. Something about a murder?" The word cop came out with obvious disdain.

"You stayed at the motel in Rock Creek on Wednesday night?"

"Right. We got in late in the afternoon and crashed. I think that we got going late after noon on Thursday." The voice sounded young and immature. "The cop here said that a woman was murdered that night. Was she the one with the Maverick, or did she have the Chevy?"

"You're sure you saw two cars?" Dan grabbed a pencil and scribbled 'Chevy' along the edge of a report.

"Sure. They were at the end of the parking lot. The rest of the spots were empty so they were hard to miss."

"Did you see anyone around them?"

"There was a fat woman walking in with a paper bag. Was that her?"

Dan froze. Carol Knutson wasn't fat. There had been a grocery bag in the room filled with empty beer cans. "A woman? Are you sure?"

"So that wasn't the one that got murdered?"

Dan was getting impatient as he scribbled notes about a fat woman with a bag. "Can you describe her?"

"I get it. It's one of those cop games. I get to tell you everything I know, and you don't tell me anything." Sarcasm dripped from his voice and Dan could almost envision the long haired, grubby tree hugger on the other end of the line. He had probably been busted for possession of a controlled substance that he didn't consider illegal. "Sorry," said Ascherman. "I'm not playing unless we share."

"All right," Dan relented. "The woman that was killed was sort of dishwater blonde and not fat. Maybe about five seven." He waited hoping that the fish he'd tossed would keep Ascherman on the line.

"The person I saw was short. Dark hair, and her head barely showed over the top of the cars. And, yes, I'm pretty sure that it was a woman. Although I think that I got that impression from the haircut. It was kinda long."

"Did you see her go into the room by the Maverick?"

"Naw. She got out of the other car and was walking toward the rooms when I went in my room. I didn't see her actually go into a room."

"She got out of a car. What make and color?"

"I didn't get much of a look at it. It was behind the Maverick. Maybe a GM car. I don't remember the color."

"How was she dressed?"

"I don't remember. I just remember the impression that she was fat by the way she walked. She kinda waddled as she walked." He paused as if he was done, then jumped back in. "She was in jeans. I remember dark blue jeans. Not shorts. I noticed that because it was so hot."

"Do you remember her blouse?"

"Naw. Maybe a T-shirt or something. No. Wait. It might've been buttoned. She was holding the bag in the arm closest to me so I couldn't see it very well."

"Could you describe her face?"

"She wasn't close. I don't know. She struck me as kinda fat. I like my women with a little less meat on their bones."

"Can you think of anything else? Like what state the license plates were from?"

"I didn't see the back of the car. It was gone when we left."

"Did you hear anything unusual?"

There was a long pause. "I don't think so. They were four or five rooms down. I know I didn't hear a scream or anything."

"I faxed a picture to the sheriff's department. Did it look familiar?"

"I looked at it. It was a fat young guy with a crew cut. I saw a middle-aged woman with dark hair."

Dan shook his head. A woman. Maybe an accomplice? Maybe the person that had been hiding Cooper? "Thanks. You've been a big help. If you think of anything else please call me back."

Dan hung up the phone and sat staring at it. A woman? Maybe she was totally unrelated. Someone who'd visited and left. But then, why hadn't she stepped forward when she'd read about the murder?

Dan looked up the phone number for the Rock Creek Motel and listened to the phone ring. Doug Ryberg answered the phone.

"Mr. Ryberg, this is Dan Williams, from the sheriff's department."

"Sure, I remember. What can I do for you?"

"I talked to the guy that had the Ryder rental truck. He saw a dark-haired woman carrying a bag to Carol Knutson's room. Did you rent a room to someone that matched that description?"

"Those two rooms were all that we had rented that night. We saw the car but I never saw another woman at all."

Dan was packing reports into a briefcase when Sergeant Tom Thompson came into his office.

"You want to take a look at the August schedule?" Tom set a computer-generated spreadsheet in front of Dan.

Dan scanned the sheet. "You've got three people doubling back to nights after day shifts, with only eight hours off." He handed the sheet back to Tom.

"Isn't it a great idea? It saves us a shift of overtime every time it happens. That way we won't have to hire a replacement for Roger. We save his salary, the cost of replacing his squad, payroll taxes, worker's comp insurance and benefits." Tom pulled out another sheet and handed it over. "I figure that it'll save the county seventy eight thousand next year."

Dan pushed the report back without reading it. "Tom, have you ever doubled back?" He studied the sergeant's face.

"Well, no. The sergeants never do that." Tom was wondering where this was going, but he didn't want to seem stupid. "But I know that shift workers do it all the time."

"Shift workers don't write reports past the end of their shifts. They don't arrest drunks five minutes before they are supposed to get off and have to spend two hours getting them into detox." Dan tossed the schedule across the desk. It slid off and fell on the floor before Tom could catch it. Exasperated, Dan said, "I assume this means that you haven't done anything about hiring a replacement for Roger?"

"Well, I ran an ad and got a bunch of applications." Thompson's face colored visibly. "But I haven't actually talked to any of them."

Dan shook his head. "What in hell have you been doing for the last month? I told you to make that your number one priority in June."

Tom straightened the computer printout. "Well, I knew that the board was trying to save some bucks, and..."

The explanation was interrupted by the ringing of Dan's phone. Dan held up a hand while he picked up the receiver. "Williams."

"Dan, I got a hot lead for you." Dan immediately recognized Laurie Lone Eagle's voice and an unusual level of excitement. He pushed some files aside and grabbed a yellow Post-it note pad and a pen.

"Shoot."

"A woman in Brunswick, south of Mora, reported a burglar July first. She heard someone rattling her doorknob at two in the morning and called 911. The sheriff's dispatcher didn't have a squad in the area, so it took almost fifteen minutes to respond. Before the woman finished the call to the dispatcher, the guy had slipped the lock on the door and entered the kitchen. The dispatcher heard a scream and some scuffling. When the woman came back on the phone she reported that the intruder had left."

Dan scribbled furiously. "I assume that the deputy that

responded never encountered the getaway car?"

"Right. And the woman didn't get a description of the car other than it was light colored and medium sized."

"Description of the man?"

"Short and fat, with dark hair in a pony tail. The best part is that she got a clear look at his face."

"You got a name for me? I've got a picture I want to show her."

"Emily Palmquist." Laurie followed with a phone number. "I talked to the Kanabec deputy that responded. He was not very, ah..., positive about Emily's character. She has a reputation for hanging around the local watering holes during the day and going home drunk. Sometimes she leaves with a new friend. She's reported a couple of sexual assaults by guys whose names she couldn't remember the next day. When the sheriff followed up it turned out that she may have been incapacitated during the sexual intercourse. The men they interviewed took Emily's lack of resistance as consent. The Kanabec county attorney never filed any charges."

"I take it they didn't take her burglary report too seriously?"

Laurie said, "There was no evidence of forced entry, and Emily was a little disoriented when they arrived. Maybe with a little alcohol haze. She also has three DWIs, so the deputies know her pretty well."

"Emily is single?"

"Divorced. I got the impression from the deputy that she's about forty."

Dan leaned back in his chair to ponder the new information and realized that Sergeant Thompson was still sitting in his guest chair, staring at him. "Hang on a second, Laurie."

Dan put his hand over the receiver. "Tom, schedule yourself on the road in Roger's rotation until you hire a new deputy. I don't want anyone scheduled for a midnights-to-days shift change without at least twenty four-hours off."

"But who's going to do all the administrative work?" Tom looked at the schedule sheet with obvious concern as he got up.

"I authorize you to work all the overtime you need to take care of both jobs."

"But I don't want all the overtime, I ..."

Dan lowered his voice and his eyes drilled holes in Tom. "Then do what I tell you to do without screwing around trying to save a few bucks. My job is to keep this place working efficiently. Not replacing Roger will kill the morale here...not that putting you on the road will help it."

"What do you mean by that?" Tom asked, but Dan already had the phone to his ear, dismissing Tom with a wave. Thompson stood for a moment looking at Dan. Then, he wheeled around and left.

"Laurie, I'm back. How'd you come up with this?"

There was a pause, and he could hear voices in the background.

"Sorry, what did you say?"

"How'd you find out about Emily Palmquist?"

"I've been pulling files and looking for anything that's close to your crimes in geography or M.O."

"You got authorization from the director to do that?"

"No. I've been doing it off-shift and today."

Dan shook his head. "I appreciate it, but you need to get a life."

"What time is it, Dan? Two-thirty on a Saturday, and you're out fishing and relaxing, right?"

"I've got a murder investigation, and this is the first Saturday I've been in the office for a couple of months. You're addicted to your job. I repeat, get a life."

There was a long pause as Laurie formed her answer. "There are a couple hundred lost kids out there, and no one else seems to have the resources or interest to pursue them. Besides, what other job could I take? A job with some big legal firm arguing to get guilty criminals freed? I couldn't stomach that."

"We're a deputy short. You could come back here and I'm sure we could get you a sergeant's job. I have a sergeant that you could replace easily," he said, thinking of Tom Thompson.

"Been there. Done that. I can't say that I'm interested in replaying that part of my life. The BCA is okay and finding missing kids is much more rewarding than giving out speeding tickets and serving court papers."

"Think about it. We could use you."

Laurie let out a deep sigh. "Why? You short on EOE diversity points? I can hear the discussion with the county board now, 'Let's get Laurie back, she's a two-fer. Female and Native American.' Gee, if I were a lesbian, you'd get a three-fer."

"Cut it out. We don't play those games, anymore. We hire the best talent we can get. I think that you're the best."

He remembered that Laurie had never taken compliments very well. She had always assumed that there was another agenda behind them. "Ah, I guess I should thank you," she said. "But I still don't think that I can take your offer seriously. How many female deputies have you got now?"

"One new hire that's still with Floyd. She's the only female road deputy. I've got two female jailers and four bailiffs."

Laurie let out a low whistle. "Umm. That's a big change from the old days. I was the only woman in the department for two years."

"Times change. There are lots more women taking law enforcement classes these days. People like you plowed the first furrow and opened it up for the rest."

Laurie laughed. "Yeah, Laurie, the pioneer." She paused as she shuffled papers. "Listen, I've got one more piece of information for you. The ballistics lab is going to type up a report. They'll fax it to you on Monday, but I spoke with the criminologist that does the testing last night. They test fired Joey Berg's rifle. The marks on the bullet match the bullet that you dug out of the floor at Terri Berg's house."

Dan leaned back and pondered the new information. "Umm. Well, that's kinda what I expected. I don't think it changes a thing, though. Cooper's print puts him at the scene and he has the motive. I smoked Joey pretty good and I'm convinced he didn't do it."

Laurie replied, "Well, you have Cooper's picture and now you even have a witness. Let me know how things work out with the Palmquist woman."

Dan said, "Sure thing, Laurie. Thanks for all the help," as the dial tone sounded.

He dialed Emily Palmquist's phone number in Brunswick. There was no answer after ten rings. He tucked the number into his pocket and locked his desk.

Chapter 31

Sandy Maki finished his shift at home. After a shower and changing into jeans, he called Barb's apartment, not really expecting her to answer.

"Hullo." The voice sounded like she'd been asleep. But Barb always sounded like that.

"You got any plans for supper?"

"Um, I guess not. Why?"

"Why? 'Cause I thought that maybe I'd take you out to eat. You up for that?"

Barb hesitated. "Um, not really. I'm not much of a going-out person. I see too many people that I don't want to see."

Sandy searched for a meaning, then suddenly understood. She didn't want to run into people that she knew from the Pine Brook Inn or from dancing, People she wouldn't want to socialize with, or who had less than moral memories of her.

"Tell you what. I'll pick up a couple of steaks, a bottle of wine, and some lettuce. Have you got any salad dressing?"

Barb's voice was non-committal. "I don't have salad dressing and I don't like it much, either. It's too fattening."

Sandy didn't give up. "What do you like to drink?"

"Uh, Sandy. I gotta work tonight. If I drink, I do dumb things and wake up in strange beds. It was a nice thought, but I'm really not up for it."

"Two steaks, lettuce, salad dressing and a six-pack of

Coke. What kind of dressing do you like? Italian dressing okay?"

There was a long pause. "Yeah. I like Italian. But, I like ranch better." She still sounded unsure.

"Anything else?" He thought of the sink full of dishes and the loaded dishwasher that hadn't been run. "Dish soap?"

"I don't have any."

"I'll be there in half an hour."

He waited for a response. It took a few seconds. "You don't need to do this. I like you, but you don't owe me anything for having sex. I enjoyed it, too."

"Half an hour." He hung up.

Ross Cooper pulled into a spot in front of Del's bait shop. He'd driven fifteen miles of gravel roads to get to this secluded store. He watched two kids walk out with a minnow bucket and a styrofoam container that was marked "$1.25" on the side. They climbed into a rust-ravaged car and pulled out of the lot, leaving a trail of oily smoke behind. When they were on the road he got out of the car.

The clerk was the same one that had taken his application for the gun. The moment of truth was at hand and the sweat seeped from his armpits and ran down the sides of his torso.

"Excuse me. Can I pick up my gun now?" Fear gripped him, but the narcotic call of the gun overwhelmed his fear. The keys were in the car ignition and the door was unlocked. If the gun deal went sour he'd make a run for it. Hell, if there was a delay he'd run. He'd carefully smeared mud on the license plates to obscure a couple numbers. And the eight looked like a three from a distance.

The clerk looked at him for a second before remembering the transaction. "Oh, sure. I've got everything ready for you." The clerk unlocked the counter and set the gun on the glass top. "You wanted a box of shells, too?" He reached behind the counter and selected two boxes. "You want the magnums or the specials?"

Cooper touched the cool surface of the gun, and then heard the question. He hesitated, too embarrassed to admit that he didn't remember the difference between specials and magnums. "Ah, the specials, I guess."

The clerk set one box back on the shelf and put the other box into a bag. He carried the gun and the bag to the cash register. After pushing a few buttons he looked up. "That'll be $247.93. Cash, check or charge?"

Cooper pulled a wad of bills from his pocket and peeled off thirteen twenties. He handed them to the clerk.

The clerk rang up the sale and handed Cooper the change. "Do you want me to show you how to load it?"

Cooper shook his head. "No, I can figure it out."

"There's a gun club east of town. If you go out on a weekend one of the guys can show you how to shoot," the clerk said politely.

Cooper forced a smile. "Thanks."

Cooper collapsed into the car, then hurried to start it. He wanted to get out of sight before the clerk could call the cops. Then he thought, "What cops?" The fake I.D. had worked again.

When Sandy knocked on the door, Barb opened it immediately. She was wearing a tube top that pressed her silicone breasts hard against her chest. They still protruded obscenely. She wore a pair of white short shorts and had put on green eye shadow and bright red lipstick. The makeup was overdone. Instead of making her pretty, it made her look cheap. Over her shoulder he could see that she'd made an effort to pick up and arrange the living room.

She looked nervous. "Umm, you're early."

Sandy walked past her into the kitchen. The picking-up

efforts hadn't progressed to that room yet. He pushed a few plates around and made room for the bag. She followed and was watching with interest as he pulled out a 12-pack of Coke.

Sandy handed the 12-pack to her. "Pull out a couple and put the rest in the refrigerator."

She took the cardboard carton while he unloaded the bag. He pulled out a box of dishwasher soap, opened it, and filled the container inside the dishwasher door. He closed it up and started the cycle. When he stood up, Barb handed him a can of Coke.

Barb pointed at the molding pile of dishes in the sink. "We should wash up the other stuff, too. I think that there are a couple of little knives in there that we can use for steak knives." She started to run water into the sink.

He pulled a bottle of dish-washing liquid out of the bag and squirted a little into the sink. "Don't you ever wash dishes?" He looked for a dish towel to dry the glasses that she was rinsing and setting on the counter. She pointed to a drawer.

"I wash 'em as I need 'em. Not much point in having stacks of clean stuff in the cupboard. Most of the time I just run 'em in and out of the dishwasher...until I ran out of soap."

He set out two bowls as they finished the load in the sink. He removed the plastic wrapper from a head of lettuce. He tore chunks of lettuce into two bowls while Barb wiped off the table. She pulled the dressing out of the bag and set it on the table as he carried over the bowls. She stared at him as he arranged the silverware.

"Why are you doing this?" she asked.

"I didn't want to eat alone, and I like your company." They sat down and poured salad dressing on the lettuce. After a few seconds of hesitation, she gave him a shy smile. A fork -full of lettuce stopped just short of his lips as he stared at her dimples. "I love when you smile. It makes you even prettier."

She chewed her lettuce and spoke with a mouthful. "I haven't had much to smile about for a couple of years," she said, with surprisingly little emotion.

"How long you been with Butch?"

She frowned. Her words, as always, were measured and came out slowly. "Couple of years."

"Why didn't you leave him?" Sandy looked around for a napkin as a dribble of dressing ran down his chin. She jumped up and came back with a roll of paper towels. He tore one off and handed the roll back to her.

"He protected me. You know, from all the idiots at the bars." She pushed the last piece of lettuce around her bowl, collecting globs of dressing.

"Then he beat you when you got home. Big improvement."

"He would have killed me if I'd left." She said it without emotion as she got up and collected their bowls. "Let's throw the steaks in the broiler. I think there's a pan in the broiler."

The rattles and bangs told him that there was a broiler pan, and she had pulled it out. She unwrapped the two porterhouse steaks and set them on the pan while he got out two more cans of Coke. She opened the broiler door on the bottom of the stove and pushed the steaks in.

"I haven't had a steak in years." She sidled up to him and gave him a kiss on the lips. "I can't remember the last time a man bought me one. Maybe never."

Sandy went into the living room and sat down on the couch. Barb followed and curled up next to him. "You've never asked me how I got to be a prostitute."

"You wait tables and dance. That doesn't make you a prostitute." He ran his fingers gently through her bleached hair.

"That's what I was for Butch," she said. Her voice was without emotion.

"You mean that's how you met Butch?"

"Uh uh." She shook her head. "He pimped for me. He sold drugs, pimped and protected me."

Sandy tried not to look shocked. "And you got paid?"

"Butch got paid. I got a place to live and protection." Her totally matter of fact discussion of her life always caught Sandy by surprise.

Suddenly Barb sat up. "The steaks! We've got to turn them over." She was up and rattling around with the broiler. He followed her into the kitchen and leaned against the counter while she flipped the steaks over on the broiler pan. The smell of the cooking meat filled the room. As she put them back into the broiler the dishwasher stopped.

He opened the dishwasher door and let out the steam. "Is that why you don"t want to go out? You're afraid that you'll run into customers?"

"Everywhere I go, I run into customers. I don't feel comfortable. They smile and look like they're undressing me with their eyes. If their wives are along, they pretend they don't see me."

"Why don't you leave town?"

She started pulling plates out of the dishwasher and loading them into the cupboard. "I imagine I will. But I don't have any money of my own and I don't know where I'd go. There's nothing for me anywhere else. At least I got a job here...and a nice guy that buys me steak."

He took the last two plates from the dishwasher and set them on the table with two forks and two paring knives. "You could get another job somewhere else."

"I...don't know. Who wants an ex-druggie prostitute for an employee? Besides, I'll be rich if I can keep my own money." She held up her hands and examined her fingers. "I can get a pro to touch up my tattoos. They're fading."

Sandy took her hands and kissed them. "Don't put your money into that. Put some in the bank and get enough of a bankroll to make a run out of here. Go to Las Vegas, or the West Coast. Make a clean break."

Barb put her fingers under his chin and pulled it down

so they were eye to eye. "Why do you care?" He stared into her hazel eyes and imagined that he could see all the pain that she had endured for so many years.

"You're pretty. You're smarter than you let on. You're vulnerable, even though you like to act tough." He kissed her on the tip of the nose.

Tears welled in her eyes. She quickly turned and grabbed a potholder. "Steaks must be done. I like mine rare."

He watched her pull the broiler open. "You're crying. Why?"

She kept her back to him and her voice was gruff. "I'm not crying. I ran out of tears a long time ago." She carried the broiler pan to the table and lifted a steak onto each plate as she sniffled. They ate in silence.

Barb broke the silence. "Do you really think I'm pretty?"

"You sound surprised. You don't think you're pretty?"

She smiled. "You didn't answer. You evaded my question."

"And you evaded mine." He put the last bite of steak into his mouth. "Yes, you're pretty. I've said it several times."

"I did the tattoos on my fingers so people would notice me."

He looked surprised. "You did them yourself? How?"

She picked up the plates and carried them to the kitchen. "Needle and India ink. You dip the needle into the ink and stick yourself. It's a lot easier if you're on morphine."

He took her hand and traced the blue-black lines with his finger. "How long did it take?"

"A couple of days each. They're real conversation pieces. They help a lot when you're a shy teenager that everyone ignores."

They opened two more cans of Coke and sat on the couch. "Where's home?"

Barb shrugged. "Minneapolis for a while. Before that,

Milwaukee. We lived in Eau Claire when I was a kid."

"So your parents moved a lot?"

She shook her head. "I ran away with a guy. The first guy was a biker and the first person that ever paid attention to me. I thought that was love...even though he passed me around to his friends. He told me I should be flattered."

"How long did you stay with him?"

"About two years. I was getting tired of it. He was starting to beat me whenever he drank. He got shot in a bad drug deal. I went to see him in the hospital once. It freaked me out. I went out and turned a couple tricks to get some money, then I caught a bus to Minneapolis."

"Why not home?"

"I had outgrown Eau Claire" She fidgeted with the can nervously. "I couldn't face my family. They didn't want a girl that had spent two years with a biker. Besides, I was on heroin. I had to get a supply."

"What happened, then?"

She shook her head. "I got arrested. They got me into a program at the University with an experimental drug. It worked for me. That's where I met Butch. He played along with them and took their drugs to sell on the street. He thought it was funny ripping people off with drugs from the University. They got wise and threw us both out of the program. Luckily, I was clean by then."

"When did you come here?"

"Butch was getting some heat in Minneapolis about a year ago. He decided that he had a friend up here that could line me up with some parties to dance. I started with that... What time is it?"

Sandy looked at his watch. "It's almost seven."

"I gotta go to work." She got up and went into the bedroom. Sandy followed behind. She dug through a drawer and pulled out a pair of cut-off shorts. She pulled off the white shorts and was just about to pull the others over her thong panties when she hesitated.

"You coming down to the Inn tonight? I'd like the company."

Sandy shook his head. "I've gotta get some sleep. I can't sleep away half the day like some people. I'll give you a call tomorrow. Maybe we can drive up to the zoo in Duluth or something."

At the mention of the zoo she froze. "I...don't get it."

"Get what."

"This is really weird. Guys never do anything with me two days in a row unless they've got an agenda. What's yours?" She jammed a set of keys in her pocket and opened the door for him. "I don't want to be reformed."

"I'm not trying to reform you," Sandy said. "I like you just the way you are." When they opened the apartment building door, a blast of heat hit them.

They walked to the parking lot together. She got in her car and rolled the window down. The heat came out in waves as she started the car and punched the air conditioning button. It must have been close to two hundred degrees inside the red Camaro.

Sandy leaned down and pecked her on the lips through the open window. "I've never met anyone like you," he said. "I think you're fun."

She let off a mocking squeal. "Oooh. Fun and pretty, too. I better hang onto you."

Sandy watched her pull out of the parking lot and wondered what he had gotten himself into.

Chapter 32

Cooper couldn't keep his eyes off Barb all night. Every time he got a chance, he'd turn and take a look at the tight tube-top. Barb noticed the stare a couple of times and approached him at closing time.

"What's your problem?"

"You just look really nice. That's all."

Barb gave him a look that could only be described as pity. "Thanks."

As Barb walked away, he watched the sway of her hips and the shapely legs.

At 2 a.m. Cooper drove past Barb's apartment building to make sure her Camaro was in the parking lot. No one seemed to notice him. He turned around in a church parking lot and drove back to the apartment building. This time he pulled into the lot. He sank down in his seat and sat staring at the building for what seemed like an hour. Although the evening had cooled to the upper sixties, nervous perspiration trickled down the back of his neck. He could feel the pressure of the gun in his pants pocket.

The parking lot lights seemed unusually bright, and he got paranoid about someone seeing him from the windows. Cautiously, he got out of the car and walked to the front entrance. The outside lights were too bright, so he slipped into the entryway and scanned the names on the mailboxes. When he found Dupre/Mattson he quickly went up the steps to number seven.

The hallway was a little dimmer than the entryway, but still too bright. He walked down the hall and loosened the bulb in the nearest fixture, burning his fingers and uttering a low oath. The loss of one light made it almost totally dark near the door marked seven. The peep-hole was dark. When he held his ear against the door there was no sound from inside. Conversely, the television was blaring from the door across the hall, marked "eight."

He stood for a few seconds with his ear against the door, ready to bolt for the stairs at the slightest hint of a sound. He tried the knob, but it wouldn't turn. He looked furtively down the hall while he pulled a piece of Mylar plastic from his pocket and slipped it in the door-jamb. He worked it down the strike-plate, trying to ease the bolt back. He could feel the bolt move a little each time he wiggled the plastic back and forth.

The bolt across the hall rattled and Cooper spun to face the door, his body in front of the Mylar still stuck in the jamb. The door opened against the chain and one beady eye appeared in the crack.

"I think Barb's home. Maybe if you knocked hard..." Cooper thought the single beady eye looked like it might be set in a rat's head.

Cooper was drenched in sweat. "Umm, thanks. I think she's asleep. I knocked real soft so I wouldn't wake her. I think I'll just go."

"Do you want to leave her a note? I've got paper." The head disappeared before he could protest. He quickly pulled the Mylar out of the crack in the jamb and bounded down the steps. Only when he got home did he stop shaking.

DAY

EIGHT

SUNDAY

Chapter 33

Dan called Emily Palmquist's phone number for the fifth time on Sunday morning. He let it ring eight times. He was about to hang up when a sleepy female voice answered.

"Hello."

"Is this Emily Palmquist?"

"Yeah. What time is it?"

"It's about eleven. I'm Dan Williams, from the Pine County sheriff's department. I need to talk to you about the burglary at your house last year."

The bed creaked in the background. "Yeah, sure. Hang on while I find my glasses." There was a pause. "Okay. You said Pine County?"

"Right. We think that the guy that broke into your house may be involved in some crimes here. I'd like to show you a picture to see if you could identify him."

Emily yawned into the phone. "Why the excitement all of a sudden? I mean, the cops I talked to didn't act like they wanted to hear my story."

"Like I said, we have a couple more crimes involved, and we have an old picture. If it's the same guy, you might be able to tell us how he's changed."

"What are we talking here? A few burglaries?" The voice started to sound skeptical.

"Three murders," Dan said, solemnly.

There was a long silence. Emily was suddenly awake. "I...I don't know. You think it's the same guy?"

"One look at the picture may tell us. Can I bring it over?" There was no response. "I've been trying to get in touch with you since yesterday morning."

Finally, the voice said, "I work at the bakery. I'm there until one or two in the afternoon every day except Sunday."

Dan thought about the conversation with Laurie Lone Eagle. Emily probably spent the afternoons in a bar and the evenings passed out. "Can I bring the picture over?"

"Listen, how do I know you're on the level? I mean, there are lots of kooks out there. Anyone could claim to be a cop."

"Good question. Here's the number for the Pine County sheriff's dispatcher. You call it and she'll transfer the call to me."

The phone rang less than a minute later. "Okay. Bring your picture over. How soon can you be here?"

"Where, exactly, are you?"

"You're coming from Pine City, right? So, take highway 23 to Mora. It turns south where it joins with highway 65. Stay on 65, going south about four miles to the wide spot in the road that used to be Brunswick. It's where Highway 70 goes east. I rent the bright blue house on the south end of town. As long as you don't blink you can't miss it."

"All right. I'm leaving now. I should be there in forty-five minutes."

The house was the color of a blue neon sign. Dan parked in the driveway and walked to the front door. A middle-aged woman was leaning on the front door frame, in a white T-shirt and blue jeans.

"Are all the Pine County cops as cute as you?"

Dan smiled. "Flattery will get you everywhere. Would

you call my wife and tell her what a hunk she married?"

"Damn. Why are all the good ones taken?" Emily rolled her slender frame off the doorjamb and walked into the house without issuing an invitation. Dan followed her silently into the tiny kitchen.

Emily Palmquist may have been about forty years old, but her face looked hard and weathered. Her clothes were neat and clean, and the house was uncluttered, but the patina of dust on most of the surfaces indicated that she probably didn't spend much time at home.

She sat down in one of the kitchen chairs and pointed to another. Dan sat down and set the Ross Cooper picture on the table. "Does this man look familiar?" The kitchen smelled stale, like it hadn't been used in a while. The countertops were bare and there were no pots on the stove and no dishes in the sink. Dan's impression was that Emily didn't have time to do much cooking between work and drinking.

She took up the picture and studied it. "It's really old, isn't it? I mean, the eyes are right, but the face is too young." She handed the picture back.

"Tell me what's changed about his looks."

She took the picture back and studied it as Dan got out a notebook. "Well, he's fat in the picture, but he's even fatter now. His hair was darker and a little longer. The eyes are the same, but the face droops more."

Dan scribbled notes. "How big was he, short, tall...?"

"Short. Not even as tall as me, but really heavy."

Dan folded up his notebook and picked up the picture. "We've got an artist coming up from the Bureau of Criminal Apprehension tomorrow morning. We were going to have her age the picture for us. If you could help, we'd come up with something a lot better."

Emily shifted uncomfortably in her chair. "I gotta work all this week."

"We could talk to your boss and maybe he'd let you off

for a few hours. We usually get good cooperation from employers."

Emily considered the possibility. "Well, I guess that would be OK, if the boss says so."
Dan nodded. "Could you be in Pine City by eight?"

Again the uncomfortable shifting. Emily shook her head. "I lost my license. One of the girls drives me to work for five bucks a week."

"OK," Dan said. "I'll pick you up at about a quarter to seven, Monday morning."

Barb Dupre was up early on Sunday. At noon she was taking a bag of garbage down to the dumpster in the parking lot with an unusual lightness in her step. When she came up the stairs the neighbor from across the hall met her at the top of the steps.

"I just wanted to let you know that your friend was here last night. I told him to knock harder, but he said he didn't want to wake you up."

Barb smiled. "Oh, I thought he was going to get some sleep. What time was he by?"

"It was after two. He knocked on the door and you didn't answer. I went to get him some note paper, but he left before I got back."

Barb smiled. "It's okay. He's going to take me to the zoo this afternoon. I'll see him then."

The old woman smiled. "Is he a nicer man than your other friend? I didn't think the first one was very good to you."

Barb smiled, eyes sparkling. "This one's really nice. He treats me to dinner and now the zoo. It's so weird, being around him makes me want to do domestic stuff. I'm even cleaning the bathtub."

The old woman nodded. "Just remember that the way to a man's heart is through his stomach."

Barb laughed. "He cooks for me! I'm just afraid that I don't know how to be nice in return."

At one o'clock, Barb's apartment door opened and Sandy stuck his head in. "Hello. You up yet?"

Barb came around the kitchen corner. She was in a conservative, man's dress shirt with the tails tied at her waist. She was wearing a pair of skin-tight khaki slacks that didn't show any panty lines. Her makeup was softer than usual. It brought out more of her natural beauty while hiding some of the toughness.

"You made it." Barb crossed the living room and gave Sandy a passionate kiss.

"Mmmm. Save some of that. We've got to get on the road. You had anything to eat yet today?" Sandy didn't wait for an answer. "Let's get a bite in Duluth. Have you ever been to Grandma's restaurant?"

"Heard of it. But I've never been to Duluth."

Sandy pointed out landmarks along I-35 as he drove. When they topped the Proctor hill, the morning fog had cleared. The view of Duluth and Lake Superior was spectacular.

Barb was impressed. "Wow, it's like the ocean. I mean, you can't see the other side."

Sandy smiled. "The early sailors used to call Lake Superior the great inland sea. They hoped it was connected to the Pacific Ocean."

Barb nodded. "I've read about it. I've just never seen it before."

They pulled into the parking lot at Grandma's, near the lift bridge into Duluth harbor. The interior of the restaurant was loaded with antiques and pictures reminiscent of the establishment's checkered past as a bordello. They ordered sandwiches and beer.

Amid the small talk Barb blurted out a question. "My neighbor said she saw you knocking at my door last night. I thought you were going to stay home and get some sleep?" Barb took a sip of the tap beer.

Sandy shrugged. "Your neighbor must be getting senile. I wasn't there last night."

Barb shook her head. "Rita's sharp as a tack. If she said someone was there, then someone was there."

Sandy set his beer down and wiped his lips with a napkin. "Did she say it was me? I mean, she didn't describe me, did she?"

Barb stopped to think. "No, I think she said that my boyfriend was knocking on the door. I assumed it was you. She said he left before she could get back with paper so that he could leave a note."

Sandy got very serious. "Did you have the door locked?"

Barb nodded. "Sure. I always do."

Their sandwiches came as Sandy stood up. "I'll be right back. I'm going to have someone stop over at your neighbor's apartment and get some more details."

"Aren't you overreacting?" Barb pulled her plate close and took a bite.

"Not if it's the murderer, or one of Butch's friends."

Barb's face turned white as she dropped the sandwich. "Butch?"

Sandy leaned down and tried to calm her. "He's in prison. But what about his friends?"

Barb looked around nervously. "Oh shit. I'm coming with you." She threw her napkin on the plate and followed Sandy to the pay phone in the entrance downstairs. Sandy made his call, and asked dispatch to send a car over to take a report.

Sandy hung the phone up. "Someone's checking."

Barb was breathing heavily. "Have you got a gun? I mean, on you?"

"In the trunk. Would you feel better if I got it?" Barb nodded. They walked to his car and opened the trunk. He took out a light jacket and slipped it on. He pushed the big Smith &Wesson automatic into the back waistband of his pants and covered it with the jacket.

"Let's finish lunch." He took her by the arm.

"I'm not hungry anymore." They went back into Grandma's and Sandy ate his sandwich while Barb watched. After lunch they went through the zoo, then decided to pick up some Chinese takeout and come back to Sandy's apartment.

Sandy called dispatch to get a description of the late night visitor when they got back to his apartment.

"Your neighbor gave a description that matches Cooper," he explained to Barb after the call. "I think you better stay here tonight. Do you need to go back to your apartment and get anything?"

She shook her head. "Not if I can borrow a shirt in the morning. I don't have to work again until Wednesday."

She snuggled up against him on the couch and they ate Chinese food and pretended to watch "60 Minutes," both thinking about the late night visitor and what could have happened.

DAY

NINE

MONDAY

Chapter 34

S andy had Monday off, but he was in the courthouse at six, sifting through the report taken from Barb's neighbor. Barb was still asleep at his apartment. Dan walked by on his way to the parking lot and did a double take at Sandy sitting at a desk in his civvies.

"Are you off or on today?"

Sandy smiled. "The schedule says I'm off, but I wanted to see a report," not mentioning that it was about the guy at Barb's door.

Dan nodded. "Since you're here, I'd appreciate it if you'd hang around. Laurie Lone Eagle located a woman up in Mora reporting an attempted break in. She saw the guy and gave us a description that matches Cooper. I'm going to Mora to pick her up now, and I have the BCA artist coming up this morning at eight to do an updated sketch of Cooper. I can probably make it back in time, but it would help if you could be here to meet her."

"Oh yeah. we should be able to get a really good likeness with a witness." Sandy stopped for a second and hesitated. Did he want to tell Dan about the guy at Barb's door Saturday night? "Uh, there was another development. A neighbor of Barb Dupre's, the waitress at the Pine Brook Inn, reported a man in the hall outside Barb's apartment at 2 a.m. Sunday. He apparently got scared and ran when the old lady confronted him."

"I heard that." Dan gave a knowing smile. "I also heard

that you had Barb in protective custody at your apartment."

Sandy tossed the pencil he was holding at the desk top. It bounced off and clattered to the floor. "Jesus Christ! This is a damned Peyton Place. Is nothing secret?"

Dan waved him down. "Floyd figured it out. I'm sure he hasn't spread it any further than me." He looked at his watch. "I gotta run. If we can, we should get Barb Dupre's neighbor over here, too. Can you give her a call? I'll check with you on my way back and I can pick her up then, if she agrees."

"Sure, I'll try," Sandy said, beginning to realize that his whole day off was now in jeopardy.

"OK, then. Get the artist started, but make sure she doesn't leave before I get back."

Sandy called his apartment to ask Barb for her neighbor's name. He was surprised when her slow voice answered the phone.

"Hi. Sorry to get you up. Got something important."

"It'd better be," she said. "Where are you? I didn't even know you'd left."

" You were sound asleep. I left you a note. I'm at the courthouse. I Wanted to check up on your neighbor's report. I'm trying to call her to ask if she'd come down and help us with a sketch of Cooper. You told me before but I can't remember her name."

"Rita. Rita Berry."

"OK, great. You go back to sleep. I'm going to be here for awhile. If you wanted, I can pick you up later. We can get some brunch."

"Maybe," she said, her voice even slower and heavier with sleep.

Barb's neighbor, Mrs. Berry, was apparently already up when Sandy called. She had readily agreed to come over and help out. About twenty minutes later, Dan called in from the squad, telling him about the picture of Ross Cooper he'd left on his desk for the BCA artist.

Sandy studyied the blown-up grainey picture of Cooper while he waited for the BCA artist. Cooper's face reminded him of the Neanderthal men and women he'd seen in TV shows. Even at a young age, the face was dark and brooding, untrimmed hair falling over a protruding forehead and his ears, eyes set back in deep sockets, peering out mysteriously. Sandy could well imagine how this young boy could have been the object of abuse and, as a result, his innocence turned into evil. Sandy shook his head as if to clear it. The man was a criminal. He'd raped and murdered. It was law-enforcement's job to apprehend him. That should be all there was to it.

Sandy was drawing his third cup of coffee when the dispatcher paged him to the entrance. The woman in the waiting area looked like an artist type. Her auburn hair was full but pulled tightly in a bun. She wore a yellow, short sleeved blouse with a silk scarf inside the collar. The khaki slacks were understated, hanging over bare feet, in sandals.

Sandy opened the security door. "Miss Opheim, Dan Williams asked me to see you in. I'm Sandy Maki."

She looked at him without a smile and gathered a large leather portfolio from the floor next to her chair. When she stood up, Sandy was surprised to see she was over six feet tall.

"Where can I set up?"

"Come on back. I'll clear off a desk. Sheriff Williams has a blown-up picture for you."

He directed her toward the ready room. Helen Opheim was virtually without make-up, but had a classic beauty that reminded him of a model. As she passed, Sandy judged her to be close to fifty. He led her back to the room filled with desks and pointed toward the desk he shared. As she opened the portfolio, he pushed everything into a pile, shoved it into a drawer, and layed the picture in the bare spot. She set the picture of Ross Cooper next to her easel, gazing at it intently for a moment.

"Would you like a cup of coffee, Ms. Opheim?"

She pulled out a huge artist's pad and a small box of colored chalk. "Sure. I take it black."

When Sandy got back with the coffee, she had the pad open and there was a pencil sketch of the Cooper picture on the top sheet. "I took your picture and roughed out the outline of the face. The shape of the face and the eyes don't change much, due to the underlying bone and muscle structure. The hair and some facial features change."

She took the cup and sipped from it. "My God! Are you trying to poison me?"

Sandy shrugged. "Sorry. I guess I'm just used to it."

She shook her head like a dog that had picked up a toad, then pushed the coffee cup to the farthest corner of the desk. She picked up a piece of dark chalk and started working the sketch and talking.

"What happens with aging is that the face fills out and things start to droop. How old is the picture?"

"Uh, I think it's about fifteen years old."

Strokes of the chalk added some flesh to the jowls and widened the whole face. Lines appeared at the corners of the eyes and on the forehead. Sandy watched in amazement.

"The hair is the unknown. You said that it was dark. So here, try this."

She pulled off a sheet of semi-transparent paper and taped it to the drawing. With a few strokes of the chalk there was a business-like haircut on Ross Cooper.

"That's option one." She stepped back and pulled a Polaroid camera from her bag and snapped a picture that fed out of the bottom of the camera. She threw the print and camera on the desk and untaped the cover sheet, putting another in its place.

"The problem is that most of these types of criminals don't wear business haircuts, so let's try one that's a little more in profile." With a few strokes of the chalk, dark shoulder-length hair appeared. It was straight and looked greasy. She added a shaggy moustache to the face.

"That's number two." She took another picture and set the camera down.

"Let's see. Maybe something a little more...." She sketched tight permed curls on the paper. "Did you recover any hairs from the crime scenes?"

"Yeah, a couple."

"Were they straight or curly?" She pointed at the options.

"Ahh, straight, I think."

"And how long?"

Sandy gauged the length with his fingers. Maybe six or eight inches long. Dark at the ends, but lighter at the roots."

"Hmm." She took off the cover sheet and put on a new one. A new, short page-boy hairdo appeared. "Like this, maybe?"

Before he could respond, she was up and took another Polaroid. When she was done, she picked up her coffee cup and lifted it to her lips before remembering the taste and setting it back down again. She stood next to him, looking at the snapshots. She was at least two inches taller than Sandy.

"What do you think?"

"I think it's amazing. They don't look familiar, but it's sure fun to watch you work."

Dan walked in with Emily Palmquist and Rita Berry in tow.

"Dan," said Sandy, "This is Helen Opheim, the artist from the BCA."

They shook hands and Dan introduced Emily Palmquist and Rita around. "Emily and Rita may have seen our perpetrator. We hope that they can help us improve your drawing with a recent sighting." Sandy handed the Polaroid pictures to Emily and Rita.

"They're kinda like him, but the eyes aren't right." said Emily, looking at Rita. Rita shook her head. "I don't recognize these, either" she said. "I'm not sure I'd be able to identify him. I really didn't get that good a look at his face from my doorway, and the hall light was dim."

Helen sat down on the chair and pulled the entire drawing off. She spoke to Emily. "Tell me how to make the eyes right."

"Well, they're harder, and I don't remember any crows-feet."

The crows-feet disappeared and the eyes became mean. "Like this?"

"Yes! Exactly. And the face is wider."

Helen worked the chalk on the sheet and the face got fleshier. "Like this?"

"I guess. It's hard to tell without hair."

Helen removed one of the blank, thin sheets and taped it to the top. "Tell me about the hair."

"It was short and dark, real thick."

"Yes, the man I saw had dark, thick hair," said Rita.

The voice of the dispatcher crackled over the intercom. "Sandy Maki. You have a visitor." Sandy excused himself as the hair started to form around the face on the paper.

In the waiting area outside the dispatcher's cube he found Barb sitting with hands in her lap. He looked at his watch and realized that it had been over three hours since he's left her a note in his apartment.

"Hey, I didn't expect to see you here." Sandy took her hand and motioned with his head toward the door. "Come on back and take a look."

Barb stood up, a worried expression on her face. "The phone rang. When I answered it there was this heavy breathing. Then the creep hung up. I couldn't get back to sleep."

"Did the caller say anything at all?" Sandy asked, concerned.

Barb shook her head. "No. All I I heard was breathing and then he hung up. I got scared and decided to drive here to meet you."

Sandy led her down the hall toward the ready room where Helen Opheim was sketching a face with a page boy hairdo on the poster board. Rita looked up when they walked in.

"Barb! Come see the picture we're making of the man that visited your apartment." Rita's voice was cheery and she seemed to be enjoying the outing and attention.

Barb peered at the picture, then, almost instantly she said, "That's Rose." She said it without emotion. The faces all turned to her in amazement. "I mean, the face is a little too fleshy, but it sure looks like her."

Dan put a hand on Barb's shoulder to reassure her. "Rose who?"

"You know, Rose Mahoney. The other waitress at the Pine Brook Inn."

Sandy stepped back to take a broader look at the picture. "You know, it really does look like Rose," he said, in dawning recognition.

Dan had noticed Rose at the Pine brook Inn before and saw the resemblance, too. He seemed puzzled for a moment. "Does Rose have a brother?"

Barb shrugged and her voice became defensive. "I don't know. We don't talk much about personal stuff."

Dan looked at Sandy. "Didn't you interview Rose?"

"The first day. But, I was asking about the customers. It never occurred to me that..."

Helen Opheim cleared her throat. "Excuse me. Does that mean I'm done here?"

Dan glanced at her as if he had just suddenly discovered her presence. "Oh, sorry, Miss Opheim. Yes, yes certainly. You've just been a great help. I really appreciate your coming up here. We might really be onto something here because of your help."

Helen smiled wanly as she started packing her supplies. "The Polaroid pictures are yours. I'll hang onto the drawings in my files, in case you ever need them."

When she had left, Dan said "Ladies, please excuse Sandy and me for a minute. The coffee's in the pot. Help yourself." Dan herded Sandy away from the ready room and into his office.

"Is it possible that Rose Mahoney has a brother?" Dan asked Sandy.

Sandy collapsed into a chair. "That might explain the resemblance."

Dan snapped his fingers. "I talked to Stearns County. Seems to me I remember them saying that Cooper had a twin sister named Maryrose."

"Rose is Maryrose?" asked Sandy. "Maybe Cooper's holed up in Rose's hotel room?"

Dan perked up his ears. "What hotel is she in?"

Sandy slid farther down in the hardwood chair and stared out the window. "The Frank House, in Rush City. She rents a room by the month. According to the desk clerk, she's been there a long time. Six months or more."

Dan scribbled a note. "You're off today?" he asked, forgetting that he'd asked before.

Sandy sat up in mock protest. "Oh, sure. Doesn't it look like I'm off?

Dan grinned. "When are you scheduled on again?"

Sandy sighed. "Nights, tomorrow. Why?"

Dan looked up a number in his Rolodex and dialed. "You're on overtime, as of this morning. Drive Emily back to Mora and drop her wherever she wants to go. You can take Rita back, too, and keep Barb with you and away from Rose or the bar. I want you on days tomorrow. I'll tell Tom to change the schedule...and tell him that Floyd's on nights. We're going to put 'round the clock surveillance on Rose."

One minute later, Dan was on the phone briefing the sheriff on the latest development. Sepanen, in turn, called the Chisago County sheriff and explained the situation to him. Sepanen asked permission to set up surveillance in Rush City, across the Pine County line. He was given permission and got an offer of support.

Chapter 35

By the time Dan got to the Frank House late Monday morning, an unmarked Chisago County squad had been parked in front of the laundromat for forty five minutes. The car had a full view of the front of the hotel and the side that housed the restaurant. Dan drove his personal Chevy pickup rather than saturating the area with unmarked cars. He pulled up next to the squad and recognized Roy Gordon, one of the sergeants from Chisago County. Dan stepped into the squad with Roy.

"Dan, I've been watching, but I haven't seen anyone like the description of the person you gave us."

Dan handed him a copy of the artist's drawings. Roy looked at it. "Nope. Haven't seen him. Can I keep this and pass it around."

"Keep it, but don't pass it around outside the department. We want to keep a lid on this. He's probably nearby and we don't want to spook him."

"You don't think he's already spooked and run?"

Dan shook his head. "He tried to break into an apartment in Pine City Saturday night."

Roy clipped the picture to the dash of the squad. "What do you need from us?"

"I've got people coming in from a couple of shifts. We're going to talk to the hotel and set one person up on staff. I'm going to put people on in pairs for two twelve-hour shifts.

We could use someone nearby for backup in case something goes down. Other than that, I think we've got it covered."

Roy nodded. "I checked. Rose Mahoney's room is on the back, and she's in it. None of the hallway windows look this direction. They face east and west. The main entrance here, faces north," pointing to a door under a sign. "The rear exit is on the ground floor to the loading dock, facing west. There's another way out through the West window at the end of the hall on the second floor, not for everyday use. You can go down a wrought iron fire escape that drops down next to the restaurant. There's no fire escape from the windows in the rooms, so it's really hard for someone to get out without being seen if you watch the three exits. As a matter of fact, if you have someone sit in the dining room, near the kitchen, they can watch both the ground-floor exits at the same time."

Dan grinned. "I've got a sergeant that can drink coffee all night and not have to use the rest rooms. Sounds like a job made in heaven."

"As long as your perp doesn't get nervous about seeing the same face too often. That sergeant wouldn't be Floyd Swenson, would it?"

"You know Floyd?"

Roy smiled and nodded. "The gray eagle that you use for training new deputies. He has more stories than Carter has little pills."

"You do know Floyd." Dan pulled a roll of Tums from his pocket and pried two off the end.

Roy laughed. "I s'pose that's one way of weeding out the intolerant."

Dan's cellular phone rang. "Williams."

"Deputy Williams, this is Kerry Trundle, from Stearns County records. I checked the hospital records like you asked. Timothy Cooper had a twin sister named Maryrose. They were born about forty five minutes apart. They were fraternal twins, not identical twins. Does that help."

A frown broke across Dan's face. "You said they were fraternal twins? Does that mean they look different?"

"It can go either way," said Trundle. "Fraternal twins can look very different or they can look very much alike, just as any siblings from the same parents can look alike."

"Ok, Mrs. Trundle. "Thanks for your help."

Dan punched the 'end' button and turned to Roy. "Rose Mahoney has a twin brother. He's the one we want."

Two tones rang out on the Chisago County radio and Roy leaned close and listened. "Got a fire down on Rush Lake," he said to Dan. "But we're here to help you." He started the engine of the squad as Dan got out and closed the door. "There are two local cops here in town, too, but they work only nights. They're dispatched through the county dispatcher and are on our frequency."

Roy rolled away, stopped at the corner, then accelerated hard toward I-35. Dan sat watching the front of the building from his pickup for nearly an hour before Pam Ryan's Geo Metro pulled into the parking lot beside him. She got out and climbed into the pickup.

Dan looked at her. "You look like hell." Her hair was pulled back in a ponytail and there were dark rings under her eyes.

"I'm supposed to be going on nights at eleven. I stayed up half of last night with plans to sleep all day today. Do I really look that bad?" she asked as she pulled down the visor on the passenger side and flipped the mirror open. She looked in the mirror and grimaced before folding it back up.

"So, I do look that bad. What's up? The dispatcher just told me to drive my private vehicle and to meet you here."

Dan pulled a picture off the dash and handed it to her. "The artist came up with this drawing of Cooper. Seems he has a twin sister that works at the Pine Brook Inn, named Maryrose. She has apparently dropped the Mary and goes by Rose Mahoney. She rents a room in the Frank House by the month.

We're going to set up surveillance and see if the brother shows up to visit."

Pam took the picture and looked at it with limited interest. "Any special reason to believe that he'll show up here?" She handed the picture back.

"Someone's been helping him stay out of sight. His history says that he's pretty much a loner. So my guess is that his sister is abetting him somehow."

Pam digested the information and nodded. "So what's the plan?"

"You ever wait tables?"

Pam turned and stared at him. "Say what?"

He continued to stare out the front window. "Have you ever been a waitress?"

Not seeing any hint of kidding in his question, she answered. "I put in a few months at the Hardee's in Blue Earth. But I never really waited on tables. Why?"

"My Chisago County source says that a person can watch both hotel entrances from the kitchen. I thought we might set you up as a waitress for a couple of days. If he comes around, you'll see him. I'll have Sandy Maki sit out front and watch this side from his car. He'd be ready if Cooper makes a run for it."

Pam rubbed her eyes. "We gonna do this twenty-four-hours a day?"

Dan nodded. "Floyd and I will take nights for a while."

"Are we going to follow the sister, too?"

"We may have to. For now, we'll just wait around here assuming that Cooper will show up. Let's go in and talk to the manager."

Marge Case, the hotel manager, was doing the books behind the counter when Dan and Pam walked into the lobby of the Frank House. She was in her sixties and had the hardboiled

look of a veteran newspaper reporter. An unfiltered cigarette
dangled from her lip. She looked up inquisitively at the two
Pine County officers in their civilian clothes when they
approached the counter.

"May I help you?"

"Are you the manager?" Dan proffered his badge.

Marge looked at it briefly. "Pine County? We had one of
your deputies here last week looking for Rose Mahoney, and a
Chisago county cop asked again this morning. What's going
on?"

Dan nodded toward a door behind the front desk. "I
wonder if we could talk to you in the back for a moment."

"Sure." She nodded to them and stubbed out the cigarette in an old brass ashtray. She got up, led them into the room
and closed the door. "So, what's up?"

Dan said, "This needs to be completely discreet. Not a
word outside this room." Marge nodded.

"Have you ever seen this man?" Dan handed a Polaroid
of the Ross Cooper drawing to Marge who peered at it through
the bottom of her bifocals.

"It looks like Rose."

"We think it's her twin brother." Dan watched for a
reaction.

Marge shook her head. "Hmmm. I don't think I've seen
him."

"Does Rose live alone?"

Marge handed the picture back to Dan. "I don't think
she's ever even had a visitor. She's just a nice quiet boarder that
pays her rent in cash and on time. Everything that I like in a
renter."

"We'd like to set up a surveillance to watch for the
brother. We believe that Rose may be helping him." Dan looked
at the skeptical expression on Marge's face. "We'll be out of the
way. We shouldn't disturb your guests at all."

Marge peeked through a window in the door, looking

for anyone in the lobby. "I guess it's okay with me. As long as you don't disrupt things."

Dan smiled. "This is supposed to be covert. If we're disrupting things, we've got a problem. We'd like to keep one person in an unmarked car in the laundromat parking lot, and one person inside the hotel. How late do you keep the restaurant open?"

"We close up after supper. Usually about eight. I leave a thermal coffee pot and plastic cups out all night on the table in the lobby. We open the restaurant up again at seven or so. Depending on when the cook gets here."

Dan nodded towards Pam. "How'd you like to have an unpaid waitress for a few days?"

Marge looked Pam over. "You ever wait tables, honey?" Her voice was without judgment.

Pam shook her head. "Hardees is as close as I've ever come."

"You're cute. You might bring some business." Marge looked back to Dan. "Sure. What the hell. You did say unpaid?"

"She's getting overtime pay from Pine County. Maybe you could let her keep the tips."

Marge smiled. "Honey, if you wear the right outfit, you could make some pretty good tips. Make sure you find yourself some comfortable shoes."

Dan nodded toward the stairs. "Do you know if Rose is in her room?"

Marge looked through the window again. "I'll keep your project quiet, but I ain't letting you into her room without a search warrant."

Dan smiled. "Fair enough. I'd like to have my sergeant sit around the lobby after the restaurant closes. He's good at reading the paper and drinking coffee."

"It's okay by me." Marge pulled the door open, then took Pam by the arm. "C'mon, honey. I'll show you where the aprons are."

* * *

Dan sat in his truck until Sandy pulled up at a little after 2 p.m.

"What's up, Dan?"

"Pam's inside. We've got her set up as a waitress. She can watch the back. I figure that you and I will rotate days and nights out here watching from our cars. You can finish out the day and I'll take it first shift tonight."

Sandy weighed the thought. "Okay. What'll we do if Rose leaves? Do I follow or stay here?"

Dan, acting on impulse, decided to change tactics. "Yeah," he said. "Follow her and tell dispatch to let Pam know."

Sandy shrugged. "Okay. How long are the shifts?"

"Let's try twelves for a couple of days and see what happens. If it goes beyond a couple days, we'll have to call it as I see it."

Sandy shrugged. "Fair enough. What time will you be back?"

Dan looked at his watch. "Rose works at what? Seven? Call in and follow her to the Inn. I should be here by then. You relieve me at seven tomorrow morning. If Ross shows up, call for back-up. If he makes a run for it before the cavalry shows up, use your instincts."

"I can handle that. By the way, I've still got Barb at my apartment. Is that a problem?" He watched Dan's face for a reaction.

Dan rolled his eyes. "That's not where I'd stash someone under protective custody. Haven't you got anywhere else for her?"

"She's comfortable there."

"Sandy...I can't say that it's...professional. Especially if you're..."

Sandy looked blankly out the windshield. "Too late."

"Hmmm. I'll see you at seven tomorrow morning."

Chapter 36

Sandy sat in his car through the rest of the day. He sat without the air conditioning until the heat became unbearable. He finally gave up and turned it on. A few people went into the hotel during the lunch hour. Other than that, the day remained quiet until the sun started to slip toward the horizon.

At 6:40 p.m., Rose came out and got into a tan Chevrolet Beretta that was parked down the street from the hotel. Sandy called in on his portable radio, slipped his car into gear and followed discreetly to the highway 23 turn off. He eased back so that he didn't pull up immediately behind her at the top of the exit ramp. Then, he followed her west into the town of Pine Brook. She pulled into the parking lot of the Pine Brook Inn and he watched her walk in as he drove past.

Dan pulled into the laundromat lot at 7 p.m. He rolled down the windows. As the shadows were lengthening and the hot wind of the day slowed to a breeze,the evening crowd began to leave the hotel restaurant. A few minutes later, a tired-looking Pam walked out to Dan's truck with an apron draped over her arm.

She climbed into the pickup and spread out in exhaustion. "My God. I've never been on my feet that long."

"Make any tips?" Dan stared out the window.

Pam let out a snort. "Big deal. A whole eight bucks and

a handful of change."

"Did Rose come down to eat?"

"Hot roast beef sandwich and a mountain of mashed potatoes smothered in gravy. Mountain Dew, no ice. She sat by herself and read a paperback novel." Pam slid down in the seat and rolled her head to loosen her neck muscles. "I didn't wait on her but it was obvious that she noticed me. She didn't say anything, but I caught her peeking at me over the top of her book a couple of times."

"Rose didn't eat dessert? I've heard they have great pies and cakes there."

Pam glared at him. "Dan, I hate to interrupt your restaurant review, but I'm dead. What time do I have to be back in the morning?"

"Plan on being here at seven. Floyd will be inside drinking coffee." The pickup door swung open and she was gone.

Ten minutes later Floyd pulled up next to the pickup and jumped in. "Where do you want me?"

"There's coffee and newspapers on the table in the lobby."

"What? No doughnuts?" Floyd opened the door and stepped out. "See you in the morning."

Dan leaned across the seat. "Flash your badge at Marge, the manager. She knows what's up. Rose left for work half an hour ago. She'll be back when the bar closes. Keep out of sight when she comes through."

Floyd smiled. "Just call me Mr. Invisible." He walked across the street and disappeared through the front door.

Barb was sitting on the couch, watching VH-1 when Sandy unlocked the door. "Hi," she said. "I never knew what I was missing by not having cable." Madonna gyrated around in her underwear while belting out a song.

"Did you find anything to eat for lunch?" He locked the door behind him.

Barb shook her head. "I don't eat lunch."

He took the holster off his belt and set it on the shelf in the front closet. "I thought it was breakfast you didn't eat.

"That, too. You can't keep a girlish figure eating three squares a day." She ran her hands up her legs sensuously.

"You eat chili?" He disappeared into the kitchen and started rattling pots.

"Sure, if you don't make it too hot." She followed him and watched him throw hamburger into a pot, set it on the burner and turned it on.

"Really? You struck me as a hot pepper-type person." He sliced an onion in half and diced it, then he opened a can of kidney beans and a can of tomatoes.

"Hmmm. I prefer my spice in bed." She slid happily behind him and pecked him on the neck. "This is really weird. When does it stop?"

"That's up to you." He chopped and stirred the browning hamburger. "You have free will. Go where you want. Do what you want."

She plopped into a chair and watched him drain the hamburger grease into a an empty milk carton. "I don't know what I want. Everything I've done has just kinda happened to me."

"Why don't you go back to school?" Sandy asked, as he dumped the beans and tomatoes onto the hamburger and threw the cans into a wastebasket under the sink. He took a can of chili powder down from the cupboard and shook some into the pot.

Barb watched quietly, ignoring his question. "Who taught you to cook?"

He stopped shaking the chili powder and stared at her for a second. "My mom showed me a few things. I picked a few tricks up from cookbooks. The rest is just trial and error."

"My mother never wanted me in the kitchen when she was cooking. She said I made a mess."

"So you never cooked?" He opened the refrigerator, took out two beers and popped the tabs on the cans.

"I can open cans and microwave popcorn. That's about it."

"Tell me about your dad." He handed the beer to her.

"He wasn't there. He's a vice president of a paper company in Eau Claire. He traveled a lot and spent sixteen hours a day in the office when he was in town."

"Did your mom work, too?"

"No, she did volunteer work and took Valium. She had a lover when dad was gone. She used to lock us out and tell us through the door to stay with friends."

"How old were you when that happened?"

"As soon as I have memories, I remember being locked out. I started to stay over with my friends to avoid going home. After I ran out of girlfriends I started staying out with boyfriends. I expected her to yell and holler. She didn't even care enough to check up on me."

"The chili's ready. You want to grab a couple of bowls out of the cupboard?" He took a wooden spoon out of the drawer and stirred the chili. He dripped some on his tongue. Satisfied with the flavor, he threw a pot holder on the table and set the pot on top of it. He ladeled the bowls full and then fetched a box of saltines from the cupboard.

Barb took a spoon of the chili. "Mmmm. Not bad...for a cop." Her eyes sparkled and Sandy wondered how his mother would react to a girlfriend with tattoos.

Dan sat watching the front of the hotel. The late summer shadows crept up the three-story brick facade of the hotel. The sunset lingered in the clouds, with reds and pinks fading to orange. One by one, the street lights winked on and the street was soon bathed in an eerie orange light.

As the business picked up in the laundromat, cars started to come and go. None seemed to notice or pay any attention to the black pickup. A few of the windows were lit in the hotel. Most remained dark. It was ten o'clock.

At that moment a blue and white Rush City police car pulled into the parking lot and stopped behind the pickup, blocking it in. A tall skinny man, who reminded Dan of Ichabod Crane, walked slowly to the driver's side of the pickup and stopped slightly behind the edge of the door. Dan already had the window down and was hanging his badge holder out the window.

"Pine County. What'cha doing here?" The man stepped up to the window. "Oh, hi Dan."

"Hi, Frank. How's it going?"

"Quiet. Just the way I like it. "Frank Fabin looked around nervously and unwrapped a piece of gum that he crammed into his mouth. He was probably no more than one hundred and sixty pounds and stood six feet three. He had nervous energy that was constantly being vented. "What's up?"

"Surveillance on the hotel. We suspect that a guest may have a relative visiting. We want the relative."

Frank frowned and nodded. "I heard about it. Just wanted to check things out. S'pose you don't want me standing around, then. If something comes up, I'm on the Chisago County frequency." He turned and disappeared behind the pickup. The squad rolled out of the lot and down the street.

The radio crackled with the usual business of law enforcement, checks on license plates, a domestic dispute. There was a fire somewhere near North Branch. At 11:20 p.m. Dan got out of the pickup and used the bathroom in the laundromat. The owner came to lock up as Dan was exiting the bathroom. He stared at Dan but said nothing. If the owner was smart, thought Dan, he'd go home and call the police to check out the suspicious vehicle in his parking lot.

At 1:45 a.m. the radio crackled on the Pine County frequency. "608. 623. Your subject is rolling. I'll follow." Rose had left work.

It seemed like an eternity before the radio came alive again. "608. Your subject turned east on County 11 in Pine City, toward town. You want me to stay with her?" Deputy Rod Peacock had been briefed to follow Rose south on I-35 to Rush City. The turn-off at the north Pine City exit was a surprise.

"623, stay with her. Is she stopping at McDonald's?"

A few moments passed before Peacock responded. "She's past McDonald's and the gas station. She just turned south, towards town."

"Stay back, 623, and don't spook her.

Peacock followed Rose's car through the Pine City business district. The night had cooled off because of an incoming high pressure front and it was comfortable with the windows down. The stoplight turned red at the Hardee's and the car stopped. When the light turned green, the car went straight ahead, then slowed as it passed an apartment complex. The car moved even slower at the driveway, as if it was about to turn in. Just as Peacock thought the car would turn into the apartment complex, it suddenly sped up and continued on down the road.

"608. Your subject passed through town. She looked like she was going to turn in at the apartment complex south of town. But she went on by."

"Ten-four, 623. Stay with her until she gets to the outskirts of Rush City."

Dan sat pondering the information. The apartment complex was where Barb Dupre lived. Why would Rose cruise Pine City at 1:30 a.m. and almost turn off into Barb's parking lot? Sandy had indicated that they weren't close friends. Was that where Ross was staying? Did she have another friend there? He shook his head. Not likely from what they knew about Rose.

"608. She's in town. I'm clear."

Dan picked up his phone and alerted Floyd. "Rose is

coming in, Floyd."

"Ten four. Got it covered," said Floyd.

The tan Beretta cruised past the laundromat and pulled into a spot on the street across from the hotel entrance. It was nearly in front of Dan's pickup and he had to slide down to stay out of sight. Rose didn't seem interested in anything but getting into the hotel. She waddled in the front door and disappeared.

The Rush City police car cruised past eleven times and several other vehicles went by on various streets. None of them even slowed down. By the time the sun started to crack the horizon, signs of life were returning to Rush City as people went to work. The hotel staff showed up one by one, the manager, waitress, cook, housekeeper, and Pam Ryan. Pam nodded discreetly at Dan as she went in the front door.

Floyd's car pulled out of the back parking lot and passed by on his way north. It was hardly a minute later when Sandy's Grand Am pulled up beside Dan's pickup. He got out and climbed in beside Dan.

"Quiet night?"

Dan stretched. "Quiet overstates the activity. The highlight was a visit by the local constabulary. One interesting thing...Rose cruised through Pine City on her way home and slowed like she was going to pull into the parking lot for Barb Dupre's apartment building."

Sandy turned to look at him. "You're serious? She almost turned in there?"

Dan nodded. "They aren't close, right?"

Sandy shook his head. "To hear Barb tell it, they're oil and water. Different in every way."

Dan shrugged. "Something for you to ponder while I'm trying to sleep the day away. Good hunting."

DAY

TEN

TUESDAY

Chapter 37

P̲am Ryan stumbled through the Tuesday breakfast rush. By the time it was over she had mastered the menu and was getting the right food to the right people—most of the time. The local waitress had told her as much about Rose as she knew. Apparently Rose was pretty much a creature of habit. Just as the waitress predicted, it was almost eleven when Rose came down to the restaurant for breakfast, a paperback novel in her hand. Pam watched from the kitchen.

Rose ate a heavy breakfast while reading the paperback. The only time she seemed to look up was when she wanted a refill on her coffee. Pam refilled her cup of coffee with only a brief look of curiosity and without being acknowledged or thanked. Rose apparently wasn't much for interacting with the hired help. For someone that relied on tips for a part of her income herself, she wasn't much of a tipper, either. The other waitress grumbled about the seventy-five-cent tip for five minutes after Rose disappeared back up the stairs.

The lunch and dinner rushes passed without any sign of Ross Cooper or Rose. Pam watched the back stairs and peeked into the lobby occasionally. No sign of Ross. No sign of Rose. By the time the restaurant closed she had sore feet and a mild case of depression.

Pam threw her apron on the counter in the kitchen and grabbed her handbag from the shelf near the door. The bag felt heavy with the 9 millimeter Glock in it. She threw the strap over her shoulder and walked through the lobby, touching Floyd's shoulder as she passed. Instead of going to her car, she walked across the street to where Dan and Sandy were sitting in Dan's truck.

"I suppose Sandy told you. Nothing new. Rose came down for breakfast around eleven but skipped dinner. No sign of Cooper." She leaned against the door and talked through the open window. "How long we going to keep this up?"

"Can't say. Maybe another day or two. If we see Ross, we're done. Hang in there. There's some weird stuff going on and I think that something's going to break soon. When Rose leaves for work Sandy will follow her in. I'll continue to watch here with Floyd."

"OK," said Pam. "God! This is more boring than Floyd's stories!" She turned and walked to her car.

Darkness came earlier this day, with a heavy bank of clouds that masked the evening sun. Thunder rumbled in the distance and the wind chased sand down the empty streets like a Western ghost town. The radio crackled with static and the National Weather Service announced a severe weather watch for central Minnesota.

Huge splotches of rain started to dot the street as Rose ran for her car at six forty-five. Dan and Sandy watched her slam the car door just as huge drops blurred the windshield.

Sandy hopped out of the truck. "I'll make sure that she's going to the bar. Then I'll see you in the morning." He was soaked from the rain before he could duck around the back of the pickup and unlock his own car.

Rose's Berretta rolled down the street as a cool wind swirled around the buildings. The clouds opened and torrents of rain pelted the cab of Dan's truck as gusts of wind rocked it. Sandy backed out of the laundromat parking lot and followed Rose toward the interstate.

Dan watched the town slow down again. He could see a dozen businesses from where he sat and none of them were open past six in the evening. Two people huddled in the door of the hotel, waiting for a break in the torrent. A thunderbolt clapped overhead and the lights flickered in all the nearby buildings.

Like so many little towns that had been bypassed when the interstate highway was built, the downtown area of Rush City was becoming a sideshow to the economic development along the freeway. The traveling public wanted fast food, fast gas and no stopsigns as they rushed through their day. The restaurants, family-owned businesses and downtown hotels were giving way to the big chains that built on the freeway exchanges. The city's housing area was dying in favor of ten- and twenty-acre residential lots that gobbled up farmland and wildlife habitat. The Frank House was a throwback to an earlier time.

Dan continued to watch the building through the rain that sheeted over the windshield. The rivulets twisted and smeared his vision. He thought about turning on the wipers, but decided that would be like turning on a neon sign that said, "Hey, look here. We're watching the hotel."

The couple in the hotel door gave up and ran to their car. The rain was falling so hard that Dan couldn't even tell if they were men or women.

By 1:30 a.m., the lights in the few occupied guestrooms had winked out. The rain had passed, leaving cool air and fog. Dan grew restless. After pondering various options he decided to take a look in Rose's room before she got off work. Dan reached into his glove compartment and took out a small leather pouch. He slipped it into his front pants pocket and got out of the pickup.

Floyd looked up from the paper when Dan came through the front door. "You need a break, Dan?"

"No, but you do. You were busy and didn't see me go

upstairs. Okay?" Dan started up the steps.

Floyd nodded but got up and followed. Dan gave him a frown and Floyd waved him on. At the second floor landing, they hesitated. The hallway was empty and no hint of light showed through the gaps under the old doors.

They walked directly to Rose's door. Dan pulled out a leather case, as he studied the locks. He selected a long, thin piece of spring steel and inserted it into the Yale lock. He chose a second piece of steel with a single tooth protruding from the top, slipped it into the slot next to the first strip, and twisted gently on the first while working the second back and forth. Beads of sweat formed on his forehead and a drip trickled down the small of his back. The lock cylinder turned. Dan quickly removed the picks and turned the knob.

Dan felt a light pressure on his shoulder and he yielded to Floyd, who stepped to the door with his gun drawn. The slight glow of the street lights cast an eerie glow on the contents of the room. Floyd slipped into the room then turned as Dan closed the door behind them.

"I'm going back to the lobby." Said Floyd. "I'll stall if anybody shows up." Floyd slipped back out the door.

Dan found a small table lamp next to an overstuffed chair and turned it on. The room was unremarkable. It was small, furnished only with a bed and a few old pieces of living room furniture. The smell of burnt toast hung in the air. He wasn't sure what he was seeking, but if Ross and Rose were linked, there had to be something that would point to Ross Cooper here.

He looked at a couple of envelopes, a bill from L. L. Bean, and an invitation to join a record club. There was also a flyer from a local grocery store. He dropped them back on the little table next to the lamp. On the floor was a pile of magazines. The top one advertised Salem cigarettes on its back cover.

He threw back the covers on the bed and felt under the

mattress. Nothing. A dresser in the corner was covered with bottles. He turned on another lamp and inspected them. Shampoo, Nair, Right Guard, a plastic razor, and some women's shaving cream. The top dresser drawer was full of women's panties and bras. The middle drawer was full of T-shirts advertising a range of products and places. The next was jeans. The bottom drawer had men's underwear and long-sleeve shirts. Jackpot! He heard something slide against the bottom of the drawer when he pushed the men's underwear to one side. He probed until he felt the ragged edge of a thin package. In the dim light he read the logo, "Black Ecstasy," on two condom wrappers. Double jackpot!

Dan looked around the room and spied an old clothes wardrobe in the corner. Its steel surface was rusted and the door creaked loudly when he opened it. The inside was empty except for a pile of clothes

On top was a pair of women's panties. A jolt hit him. They were small, far too small for Rose. He quickly riffled through the others. Panties, bras and a camisole. None of them matched and all were too small for Rose. The camisole had a small dark stain on the hem. He held it close to the lamp. The stain was rust brown. "Blood?" he whispered.

He looked around nervously, then threw the camisole back onto the heap in the wardrobe before closing the doors. How in hell did Ross come and go without being seen? Roy had said there was no second entrance to the room, but was there? He stepped past the overstuffed chair to the window. No stairs, just a long drop to the roof of the kitchen.

As he stepped back from the window he slipped on a magazine. He picked it up and was setting it back on the pile when he caught a look at the spine of the magazine, "Penthouse."

He set it back down. "Ross has been here. But, when?"

Dan eased the door shut and slipped the deadbolt back with the picks. As he walked down the hall he realized that he was drenched with sweat. The old stairs creaked under his weight and Floyd was staring at him when he came in view. They walked into the kitchen.

"Well?"

"Ross has been around. The bottom drawer is full of his underwear, and I found a couple of his condoms."

Floyd shook his head. "No way he's been getting past us. Where do you suppose he's been the last two days?"

Dan shook his head. "I Don't know, but we gotta get a search warrant for the room. There's a pile of women's underwear that are way too small for Rose, including a camisole I think has blood on it."

Floyd's eyes narrowed and his forehead furrowed. "A judge will want probable cause. You can't say that you've broken in and found evidence."

"Hmmm. We have to think of something."

"If we catch Ross going in..." Floyd raised his eyebrows hopefully.

"Or we get Rose to invite us in.... She already talked to Sandy."

Floyd laughed. "Yeah, but he didn't ask permission to go through her underwear. I can see it now. 'Excuse me, Ms. Mahoney. Could we dig through your underwear?"

Dan snapped his fingers. "This is a hotel. The manager could let us in the room to inspect for safety reasons. It's technically not Rose's property."

"The manager was quite emphatic about needing a search warrant."

Dan stared into the coffee cup. "But I didn't know there was evidence of a murder in there then."

"You still don't. Remember, you've never been in the room. Maybe Sandy can talk to his girlfriend and come up with something..."

Dan returned to the pickup. It seemed even cooler. The wind swept down from the north bringing a taste of Lake Superior on its breath. Dan sat and pondered Ross Cooper, Rose Mahoney, a Penthouse magazine and women's underwear.

At two a.m. Dan was running the engine to keep the windshield free of condensation as the temperature dropped below the dew point. A few minutes later the radio crackled to life. "608. This is 623." Deputy Kerm Rajacich was watching the Pine Brook Inn.

Dan Picked up the hand-held radio. "Go 623."

"She's out of Pine Brook again."

Dan looked at the glowing blue numerals on the dash. It was two eighteen. Rose was running late. "Ten-four. Let me know when you get to the outskirts of town again."

Dan sat for fifteen minutes running an inventory of the contents of the apartment back through his head. The wardrobe was a key. Did Ross steal a piece of underwear from each victim? If he did, there were more victims out there than they knew about. There must have been at least seven or eight items on the floor of the wardrobe. Or maybe he was burglarizing houses and stealing lingerie, which was common among sex offenders, but only to those who hadn't graduated to sexual assaults yet.

Dan's thoughts were interrupted by the radio. "608. The subject is turning off at County 11 again."

Dan's mind raced as he fumbled with the radio. "Drop her and get down to the other exit. I want you out of sight in the back of the apartment parking lot when she goes by."

"Ten-four."

Rajacich accelerated the squad under the County Road 11 overpass and down I-35. Within seconds his speedometer read 100 and he continued to press the accelerator hard. He raced to the top of the exit ramp and flashed the light bar for a second to go through the intersection. When he got to Main

Street there was no sign of the tan Beretta. He accelerated hard around the corner and was parked behind the last garage when the Beretta turned into the lot at the apartment building.

"608. She's coming in. She parked."

"623, observe only. Do not, repeat, do not confront."

"Ten-four." Kerm watched as the dark haired woman sat in the car for five minutes before she stepped out. She stood, staring at the building for a second, then walked up the sidewalk and disappeared into the building.

After several minutes a light came on in one of the second-floor corner apartments and he could see a short, heavy figure moving around. A second light came on in what appeared to be a bedroom. Then both lights went out and within thirty seconds the subject walked briskly out of the building to her car.

"608. The subject went into the building. She was in a corner apartment for a few minutes and then turned off the lights and left. She's back on her way south again."

"Ten-four, 623."

The ringing of the phone jarred Sandy from deep sleep. He reached over Barb and picked it up, amazed that she'd never stirred. "Hello."

"Sandy, is Barb still up?"

"Dan?"

"Yeah. I've got a couple questions for Barb. Is she up?"

Sandy pulled himself into a sitting position. The red numbers on the clock said that it was 2:50 a.m. "No. We've been asleep for hours. What do you want with Barb?"

"Where's Barb's apartment located in the building?"

Sandy looked at the phone like it was speaking a foreign language. "Second floor corner. It overlooks the parking lot. Why?"

"Rose was in Barb's apartment tonight. Kerm watched her go into the building and saw the lights in Barb's apartment."

Sandy's head was reeling. "What in hell is going on? Why didn't he stop her?"

"Take it easy. Nothing happened. But I wonder why she was there, and how she got in. Does she have a key?"

"Not that I know about. What's the other question?"

"I was in Rose's room...don't ask...and it appears that there's been a man there recently. Ask Barb if Rose has changed a lot in the last few months. Like, has she become more reclusive. Does she act like she's hiding something?"

"I'll ask her in the morning. She's out cold right now and she really doesn't function when she first gets up." He was about to say good-bye when his brain kicked in. "Why do you want to know that?"

"I figure that Rose has been hiding Ross in her room at times. Maybe it stresses her out when he's around, especially if she knows he's a felon. I have to believe that she knows he's involved in these murders."

Sandy was lost in the conversation. "Why not drag her in and sweat her? You know that she broke into Barb's apartment."

"Ross isn't around right now. If we take her in he might freak out and make a run for it."

"Hmmm. I'll ask Barb in the morning."

Dan's radio crackled. "608. She's in town. I'm clear."

Dan alerted Floyd. "Rose is coming in, Floyd."

"Got it," said Floyd.

Once again Rose's tan Beretta cruised past the laundromat and pulled into a spot on the street. As Dan watched her closely, she waddled in the front door and disappeared

Dan called Chisago County and asked the dispatcher to have the sergeant on duty contact him in Rush City. As he waited, he decided to arrest Rose for breaking and entering. He'd ask for Chisago County support in the arrest. That way, Ross

would be his prisoner to return to Pine County if he had somehow slipped into the hotel unnoticed. But there still was the big-
ger question: Had Ross slipped in and out while they had the
hotel under surveillance? He didn't see how, but maybe it was
possible. There was only one entrance they hadn't covered, the
fire escape on the west end. But it would be next to impossible
for a person to reach it from the ground, and it certainly would
draw attention. He ruled this out immediately. But if he hadn't
been slipping past them somehow and wasn't in the hotel, then
where in hell was he?

It was nearly 3 a.m. when the Chisago County squad
pulled into the parking lot. Kevin Thorson got out and walked
to Dan's truck. He opened the passenger door and slipped in.
Dan had killed the dome light so it didn't come on when the
door opened.

"Hi, I heard that you guys were watching the hotel.
What's up?" Thorson reeked of tobacco smoke. He was one of
the few deputies that smoked in his squad. He nervously opened
a pack of gum and peeled the wrapper off a piece.

"We've identified the twin sister of a murder suspect.
She's a long-term renter in the Frank House hotel. We have an
informant that's said the brother's been staying in the room with
her. We want to go up in the morning and check her out. We're
planning to question her about a burglary in Pine City. Thought
we'd keep you guys apprised."

Thorson speeded up the chewing. "You going for an
arrest?"

"Not initially. I thought we'd go up and see if she'd
invite us in. If not, we'll bring up the burglary. If the brother is
around, maybe he'll make a run for it."

Thorson studied the front of the hotel. "You got a warrant?"

"No. I doubt if a judge would bite on the limited probable cause we've got. That's why we'd go with the 'nice guy asking questions' approach first. Then question her on the bur-

glary." Dan studied Thorson's face for a hint of what was going through his head.

Thorson was silent for a few seconds, then he cocked his head like a dog studying a bug on the ground. "I guess that sounds kosher. What do you need from us?"

Dan breathed a sigh of relief. "We'll go up with four people. If you could put a squad around the corner in case someone makes a run for it..."

"That's easy. Does she have a car?"

Dan pointed through the windshield. "The tan Beretta."

Thorson nodded. "How about a man behind the car, too?"

"Sure. That'd be great."

Thorson nodded. "What time you going in?"

"My other two deputies are on at seven. I figure we'll go up at 7:30. That okay with you?"

Thorson nodded. "I'll stay over and call in a guy from the day shift. You've got our frequency if something goes down, right?"

"Right."

"See you about seven." Thorson slipped out of the truck. Dan watched him light a cigarette before getting into his squad. The squad pulled away and disappeared around the corner.

Dan pulled a thermos from behind the seat and poured coffee into the lid which doubled as a cup. Something about Ross and Rose bothered him. It was too weird. Was she tied to the murders somehow? Was there a stronger family bond than he could appreciate? Did Ross have some power over Rose? He sipped the coffee and pondered. It just didn't add up.

DAY

ELEVEN

WEDNESDAY

Chapter 38

The music blared from Sandy Maki's radio alarm at 6 a.m. Wednesday morning. He stared at the red numerals a second and rolled out of bed without Barb stirring. He let the radio play, hoping that it might wake Barb enough to make her coherent. The shower stung his skin and pushed the blood to his brain. He toweled off and went back in the bedroom. This time he opened the drapes, letting the morning sun flood the room with light.

"Damn it! Turn off the light." Barb rolled away from the window and pulled a pillow over her head.

"I've got to go to work. Come have a bite of breakfast with me." He banged around in the drawers finding clothes and getting dressed. He made an effort to generate as much commotion as possible.

Barb rolled over and said something unintelligible. He finished putting on his shoes and started a pot of coffee. As the coffee dripped, he came back into the bedroom and sat on the edge of the bed.

"Barb, I need to talk to you. Come out and have a cup of coffee with me."

"Let's talk tonight. I'm tired." She held the pillow to her head even more tightly

The radio news reporter's words caught his attention and Sandy froze. "...the guard, who suffered head and neck injuries, continues his recovery. He was transferred from St.

Croix Medical Center, in Stillwater, to St Paul's Region's Hospital. His condition has been upgraded to stable. The Washington County sheriff reports that the three escapees are still at large. They have been identified as Ernesto Delgado, Brian Mattson and Paul Gibson. All are considered dangerous. Anyone having contact with them should call the Washington County sheriff's office or the U.S. Marshal's Service in Minneapolis. It has just been reported that the stolen getaway car was abandoned in the Fleet Farm parking lot in Hudson, Wisconsin, just across the border from the intersection where the van transporting the prisoners was rammed."

"Sonofabitch. Butch is loose." Sandy punched his fist against the mattress.

Barb pulled the pillows back from her head. "What about Butch?"

"The radio just reported that he escaped from a van transporting prisoners."

She sat up in the bed, the sheet falling to her hips. "Butch is loose?" The implications swept over her. "Ah...I gotta go somewhere." She crawled across the bed and sat briefly on the edge before retrieving some clothes from the floor.

He watched her pull a T-shirt over her head. "Stay here. This is as safe as anywhere." He got up and followed her to the kitchen where she wandered aimlessly from one spot to another, like a lost child.

He finally took her by the arm and directed her to a chair. She sat quietly while he poured two cups of coffee and set one in front of her. She stared at him without speaking.

"It's safe here. Butch doesn't know where you are. They've got a ton of people out looking for him, including some U.S. marshals. I'll bet they find him in a day or two. Besides, he was headed east. They found the car in Wisconsin."

She shook her head. "Hudson is just across the bridge. They could've doubled back."

Sandy looked at her eyes. Most times they were vacuous. This morning she looked like a caged animal. He searched for words that might console her, but everything that crossed his mind seemed trivial.

She looked around the room nervously. Her eyes met his and he noticed them soften. "Sandy, stay with me today. I know I'll be safe then. Okay?"

He started to smile, and then he lifted his watch in the sudden realization that time was fleeting. It was already 6:40. "Damn! I've got to be at the Frank House in twenty minutes."

He gulped some coffee as he stood, then raced around the table to crouch next to her. He took her hands in his and stared into her eyes. "Listen. There are only three people that know you're here. You're as safe here as in the jail. Stay here until I get back. Then I can take a couple of days off and sort out a plan. Will that be okay?"

She stared back at him. There had been so many lies for so many years. People had looked her in the eye and told her she'd be okay, only to renege on the promise at the first opportunity. So much hurt. So many bastards that had told her lies.

"I...I don't know." She shook her head.

He brushed the hair back from her face. The hazel of her eyes was deep and so like a child's. "Have I ever hurt you, or lied to you?"

She shook her head. "But you could start." The hurt was deep, like scars on her soul.

He hugged her close. "No. I couldn't. I don't lie to my friends."

She pushed him back and stared at him. She pulled her hand from his grasp and touched the moistness that was rolling down his cheek. She put her finger to her lips and tasted the salt. It was real.

"I'll stay today. But let's talk about it more tonight." She gave his other hand a squeeze and then released it too. "But, you're late."

He got up and pulled the Smith & Wesson from the shelf

in the closet and clipped the holster to the belt in his lower back. He pulled the tails of his shirt over it. "Oh. I almost forgot. Rose has driven past your building the last two nights on her way home from the Inn. Were you two close, so she might stop by to talk?"

Barb shook her head. "We're not close at all. She's just too weird." Her face twisted with disgust.

"She doesn't have a key to your apartment, does she?"

Barb gave a very unladylike snort. "When turds can fly."

"Has Rose ever mentioned a brother? Or, where he might be staying locally?"

Barb shook her head at each question.

Sandy absorbed it and grabbed the door knob. "So, no reason she'd stop at your apartment that you can think of." He turned the knob, then decided to give her a kiss before he left. She pressed herself against him as he tried to give her a peck. He pushed her back for a second. "Something just struck me. Rose told me about your tattoo. How'd she know?"

"Rose has seen me undress lots of times," Barb said, matter-of-factly, "when we change our clothes in the back before and after work. She might have seen it then. I've quit dressing around her now, though. She came on to me one night, just laid a big wet kiss on me before I knew what was happening. I think she's Lesbian. She makes me feel weird."

"So, Rose is a Lesbian and she made a pass at you?" He tried to make it sound non-judgmental.

Barb sensed his discomfort and stopped to think about some way to put it differently. She ran through the experience again in her mind. Her face suddenly lit up. "You know what? Sometimes Rose reminds me more of a guy than a girl! Maybe that's why I feel so weird around her."

Sandy froze. At first he couldn't believe what he was hearing. But there it was. The answer had been right in front of them all the time.

"You're a genius!" He kissed her forehead and ran for the door. He raced to his car. When he got on the road he picked up the hand held radio. "611, 608."

He waited for what seemed like minutes for Dan to answer his call. "608, go 611."

"I'll be at your location in fifteen. I have new information concerning the subject. Use extreme caution, but take either of them into custody if they try to leave your location."

Dan smiled at Sandy's attempt to convey a confidential message over the airwaves. "We're holding, pending your arrival, 611. Be advised of new location at Rush City Police Department."

"Ten four."

Sandy parked his car in the Rush City Police Department's parking lot and jogged into the building. Floyd and the others looked up at him from their chairs as he rushed to spill out his story. They had drawings of the Hotel floor plan spread all over a folding table along the back wall.

Sandy tried to talk before catching his breath. "who's watching the hotel?" he asked.

"Pam is over there and Chisago's people are helping us out," said Dan. "What's up?"

"Rose is a man. I mean there is no Rose. Rose is Ross."

They stood staring at him until his revelations hit Dan. He slapped his hand on the table. "That's it! That explains the..." he stopped short of making a revelation about his covert entry, "...explains a lot of things." He slapped Sandy on the back. "How'd you find out?"

Sandy shook his head. "Not now."

Dan looked at him skeptically. "But you're absolutely sure?"

Sandy nodded. "Absolutely."

Dan leaned over a rough drawing of the hotel floor plan, pointing to the corner of the drawing, then said "The room is here, on the third floor. It has two windows that look over the other side of the hotel. Neither of them is an emergency exit. There's a window at the end of the hall that has a fire escape and the stairs down the front is the other egress. Floyd and I will approach the door. I'll have Pam on the main stairs and Sandy by the window, at the fire escape. You two," he nodded to the Chisago County sergeant and deputy, "will be outside, one on foot next to the suspect's tan Beretta and the other in a squad at the corner. The plan is to take the suspect into custody for questioning. Our investigation indicates we have a very unstable person, capable of murder. He may be dressed as a man or a woman. Either way, he's about five two, with dark hair, and weighs about two hundred and twenty or thirty pounds."

The Chisago County deputy smiled. "That's hard to miss," he said.

The radio suddenly crackled to life with Pam Ryan's voice. "The suspect is down for breakfast early."

"Shit!" Dan picked up his portable radio. "How many people in the restaurant?"

"Ten or eleven." Pam's whisper was barely audible.

"Hang tight." Dan looked at the others. "Let's get over there but try to stay out of sight. We'll get together in the laundromat before we go in."

The police presence was a fact that Cooper hadn't missed. As he sat down at a table he thought he saw the new waitress talking into a walkie-talkie in the kitchen. When the regular waitress came to his table, her casualness seemed to be a bit overplayed. He ordered a glass of juice, then left through the lobby when the waitress went into the kitchen.

As he was about to leave the lobby and go upstairs, he caught a glimpse of two cars pulling into the laundromat parking lot. They looked suspicious, but then both cars pulled away out of sight. He began to get worried. Better to play it safe. He went upstairs to get the gun and to pack a few things. He'd need a change of clothes and a few toiletries. Should he keep the Rose Mahoney stuff, or scrap that and go back to being a man full time? He thought for a second. That was easy, Rose got him a lot of places that Ross couldn't go.

He lumbered up the stairs and quickly unlocked his room. He pulled the gun from under the pillow and felt the cold steel in his hand. It gave him a rush. He pulled the hammer back, then set it gently back down again.

He pulled a paper shopping bag out of the wardrobe and turned to fill it. He froze. "Somebody's been in here," he said out loud. The camisole was on top with the blood showing. That was wrong. It always went on the bottom. He turned to the rest of his room and stared. Barb's thong panties were still on the arm of the chair where he'd fantasized about her after he got home. The Penthouse magazine was face up. He'd left it face down. Always face down, with an ad on top, in case someone came in.

A wave of nausea swept over him. He'd been violated! His stomach knotted. He grabbed the bag and ran for the bathroom down the hall from his room as his bowels began to spasm.

Pam was on the walkie talkie. "He ordered juice and left. Someone saw him go up the stairs." Pam's voice was controlled but the urgency crept in.

Dan grabbed the radio, "We're going in now. You got that, Chisago?" His voice was emphatic.

"Ten-four. We're in position." They saw a Chisago deputy walking toward the tan Beretta. When they got to the lobby, Pam met them, with the manager in tow.

"She doesn't want us to break down the door." Pam gave the manager a look of disdain.

Dan rolled with it. "Great! Grab your keys. We're going to inspect the room for water damage."

The five people sounded like a herd of buffalo running up the carpeted wooden steps of the old structure. They stopped on the landing below the third floor and Dan put his hand out for the keys.

"I uhh...I don't think..." The woman hesitated, with the keys dangling from her fingers.

"You open it, or watch us open it. It's your choice," Dan said in a low voice.

The manager's eyes widened and she jammed the ring into his hand. "The round YALE key is a master for the whole place."

Dan nodded to Pam. "Stay here with the manager."

Pam was about to protest when Dan, Sandy, and Floyd trotted past on down the hall. Pam walked the last steps with the manager and stopped at the top of the stairs. She gripped her 9mm Glock to her side, her thumb on the safety. The manager saw it and started to say something, but Pam's look silenced her.

Sandy went past Rose's room to the end of the hall and opened the window. After taking a look outside onto the fire escape, he gave a "thumbs up" to the others. He remained on watch at the end of the hall.

Dan was inserting the key into the lock when a low volume warning came over the radio. "Pine County, you may have a problem. I've got a partial box of Federal .38 Special ammo on the floor of the suspect vehicle. Be careful."

Dan looked at Floyd, who pulled up his shirt exposing a Kevlar vest. Floyd pointed at himself, then held up one finger to indicate that he should be first through the door because he was wearing a bullet-proof vest. Floyd pulled his Heckler and Koch from its' holster and held it high as Dan eased the key silently into the lock. Dan turned the key, then the doorknob. As the latch released, Floyd put his shoulder to the door and rushed in yelling, "POLICE!" The door flew open with a crash.

* * *

Ross Cooper had been listening to the commotion in the hall from the communal bathroom. The waves of cramps had passed and now he pressed his back against the bathroom door, with the cold steel of the revolver in his hand. He listened to the announcement of the ammunition find and tensed. Now they knew he had a gun. Now they wouldn't let him live. The anticipation rose in him like the approach of an orgasm. When he heard the door crash down the hall he couldn't contain himself any longer. He burst through the bathroom door and fired at the first thing he saw.

BOOM! The sound of the gunshot in the narrow hall was deafening. The blast was followed by the scream of the hotel manager, who'd been standing closest to the door of the restroom. The bullet had plowed into the manager's abdomen and she fell against Pam. Pam watched Ross Cooper freeze in the realization that he'd actually shot someone. Cooper was less than a foot from Pam as she struggled to free her Glock from under the manager. The Glock's hammer was caught in the manager's blouse, pulling the gun from Pam's hand. There was a ripping sound as the Glock came free. But before she could bring it up for a shot, Cooper had fired again into the screaming melee that the two of them created. Pam expected to feel pain but felt only the adrenaline coursing through her veins. The manager jerked and screamed in agony as the second bullet ripped into her shoulder.

Cooper rushed past them down the stairs. Pam leveled the Glock on his back. The gun roared and jumped in her hand, but Cooper clambered wildly on down the steps. It had all happened in only a few seconds, but had played out like a slow motion movie.

Pam looked down at the manager, who was gasping for breath. The woman's eyes rolled back in her head, her hand clutching her shoulder. A bright red splotch spread under her hand and another stained the middle of her blouse. Pam quickly reviewed her options and jumped over the woman's body as footsteps pounded down the hall toward her.

When Dan and Floyd stepped into Rose's room, Sandy had stuck his head out the window to check the fire escape again. The gunshot had caused him to pull his head around and bang it against the bottom of the sash. He watched in horror as the fat woman fired point blank at Pam and the hotel manager.

He raised his gun, but the swirling bodies in the hallway made it impossible to get a clean shot at the suspect. He had started to run down the hallway when the second shot hit the manager. Pam's back blocked his view of the shooter as she started down the stairs. He saw Pam's hands jump as she fired a shot at the retreating figure.

Floyd came out of Rose's room just as Sandy was about to pass. Dan was close behind, colliding with Sandy hard enough to slow them both down. Floyd rushed on ahead of them.

"Call an ambulance!" Pam yelled over her shoulder as she raced down the steps toward the landing.

"Don't!" Pam heard Floyd's voice over her shoulder and she froze, at the corner, her knee buckling and throwing her against the wall on the far side of the landing. The stairwell roared and a bullet smashed into the plaster just over her head She scrambled to get back out of the line of fire coming from below.

Sandy's earlier warning flashed in Pam's head. "Don't run to a fucking fight, dummy," she said to herself. She pressed her back against the wall with her knee screaming in pain.

Pam peeked around the corner and immediately pulled back. Nothing happened. He wasn't there. She ran on down to the second floor, with Floyd's footsteps right behind her. No one was down in the second floor hallway.

Floyd pointed down the hallway. "I'll check the rooms." She nodded as Sandy and Dan's footsteps pounded down behind her.

She peeked down the stairs and pulled back again. As she turned to go down, there were shots from further downstairs. She raced to the stairs leading to the lobby but stopped when she realized her feet would be visible to anyone in the lobby long before she could see them. "Shit!"

Dan raced down behind her and quickly assessed the situation. Sandy stopped on the step above Dan.

Dan took the radio off his belt. "Chisago. What's up outside?"

"He's back in the lobby. Wounded, I think. We cleared the restaurant. Cavalry's on the way. He's pinned down inside. don't stick your necks out."

"Ten four. Can you see him?"

"That's a negative. He took a shot at me and ran back inside when I returned fire. Haven't seen him since."

Floyd rejoined them from his search of the hall.

"He's in the lobby somewhere," Dan said to Floyd. "I need a mirror." Floyd nodded and headed back up the stairs.

Dan leaned toward Sandy. "Check on the manager," he said, in a low voice.

Less than a minute later Floyd was back carrying a large oval mirror that had been hanging over a table in the hall. Floyd eased next to Pam and slipped the mirror onto the back edge of the step below them. He turned it until they were looking at Ross Cooper peeking out from behind the huge walnut reception counter. He appeared to be staring at the front door. Distant sirens could be heard.

Sandy's footsteps came down the steps. "Can we get an ambulance crew through?" Dan looked up at Sandy. The expression on Sandy's face told of the manager's grim condition.

Dan pointed at the mirror. "Cooper's hiding behind the counter in the lobby. Any chance that we could use the fire escape to get her out?"

Sandy took a deep breath. "Not without a hell of a lot of work. She's in shock and fading."

Dan leaned down to Floyd, who was watching Cooper through the mirror. "What do you think?"

"He's hurting bad. Looks like he's wavering and having trouble staying upright. He may be down in a couple of minutes...if we don't stir up his adrenaline. You get his heart pounding again and he'll..."

A shot rang out and the mirror shattered in Floyd's hand. Because Floyd had been leaning on it lightly, he lost his balance, tumbling down the steps as a second, then a third shot rang out from behind the lobby counter. Chunks of plaster sprayed in all directions from the wall around Floyd as he cascaded down the steps.

Pam leaped down three steps in one bound, swung the Glock toward the counter and fired until the hammer fell on an empty chamber. Thirteen spent cartridges rolled down the carpeted stairway as the echoes died out and the air filled with the smell of burned gun powder. The empty magazine flew from the butt of Pam's gun as she fumbled to pull the spare magazine from her pocket. Dan raced past her, his gun pointed toward the counter. There were faint scraping sounds, but no sign of Ross Cooper.

Dan raced down the steps and jumped the counter as Pam slammed the spare magazine home and cycled the slide to chamber another shell. Ross Cooper was in a fetal position on the floor. Dan kicked the chrome-plated Taurus revolver aside and knelt down.

Timothy Ross Cooper looked up at him. In a feminine voice he pleaded, "Don't hurt me. Please don't hurt me any more."

Chapter 39

Dan, Sandy, Floyd, and Pam sat in the sheriff's office waiting for Sepanen to show up with the county attorney. They were all required to testify before an informal board of review.

Pam, the only Pine County deputy to fire her weapon, was officially on paid leave pending the results of the review.

Floyd sat in a straight chair in the corner, his arm in a sling for a dislocated shoulder, suffered when he fell. All of Cooper's shots had missed him. Pam sat in another corner, her swollen knee covered in bandages. She draped it over the arm of a loveseat that she had commandeered.

Sandy was sitting in an overstuffed chair, quizzing Pam and taking notes, as Dan stood and watched "So, let me read this back. You took one shot at Cooper at the top of the stairs."

"Right." Pam went on. "He took two shots at point blank range as he came out of the bathroom. The first hit the manager in the abdomen. The second hit her shoulder as she fell against me."

Sandy pointed a pencil at her. "Why didn't you shoot at that point?"

"Because my gun got caught under the manager and I couldn't get it free."

Sandy nodded. "When you got the gun free, what target were you firing at when you took that single shot."

Pam made a disgusted look. "His upper torso...I think."

They all stared at her. Dan sat back on the front edge of Sepanen's massive desk. His voice was stern. "It had better be his upper torso, for sure, or some defense attorney will pick the meat from your rotting bones." Dan pulled a roll of tums out of his pocket, pried two loose with his thumbnail, and popped them into his mouth.

Sandy continued. "Why didn't you shoot on the stairs?"

"I was never presented with a clear target."

"Good answer." Floyd punctuated his comment with a nod. "And, why did you empty your gun from the steps?"

Fire flashed in Pam's eyes. "Because stupid-assed Floyd fell down the stairs and the suspect...alleged suspect... was blazing away at him. I offered covering fire until Floyd could seek a secure position." All the others cracked up with muffled laughter, including Floyd.

Sandy went on. "Did any of your covering fire hit the suspect or any innocent bystanders."

"Why yes. How nice of you to ask. Two rounds of my covering fire struck the suspect. One in the hand and one in the thigh. None of the other shots hit another person."

"Did the covering fire, in fact, provide Sergeant Swenson a chance to find a more secure position?"

"Yes...well no. Sergeant Swenson was incapacitated as a result of his fall. But the alleged suspect was struck and intimidated by the fire to a point that he subsequently surrendered to undersheriff Williams."

Sandy leaned forward with a smile. "How badly was he intimidated?"

They all cracked up again and shook their heads.

Pam sat up straighter and said, smugly "Why, he was so badly scared that he curled up in a fetal position behind the counter and pissed his pants." Sandy, Pam and Floyd shook with laughter.

As the laughter subsided, Dan gave them a stern look. "This is all cute now. But we were lucky and we can't rely on luck. What were you shooting, Pam?"

"My nine millimeter Glock."

"Cooper took, what, two of your shots? He put two rounds of .38 special into the manager." Dan pointed a pencil at Pam. "What's the lesson?"

She shrunk from the onslaught. "Take better aim?"

Dan shook his head. "That's a good start. Two hits in fourteen shots are nothing to brag about. Also, use more gun. If you're in a position that requires deadly force, have enough punch in your hand to put the bad guy down in one shot...no matter where you hit him. The situations that allow the use of deadly force are extremely limited. If you have to shoot, you don't want to leave a guy that is still capable of doing you, and anyone else in the area, grave bodily harm. If you have reason to shoot a guy, put him down without the opportunity to get a second chance. Understood?"

Pam nodded and the others sat quietly.

Pam broke the silence, asking, "Has anyone heard how the hotel manager is doing?

"She's out of intensive care,' said the sheriff as he walked in with the county attorney and Sergeant Tom Thompson. Sepanen surveyed the group and plunked his frame into the desk chair, leaving the other two men to stand awkwardly in the back of his office.

He surveyed the faces of the deputies. "You look like you all just lost your best friends instead of having brought in a serial killer.

Dan was dead tired. He had been up for twenty hours. His voice was too sharp. "We were just running through a preliminary shooting review board. I suggest, based on our experience today, that every deputy be required to carry a gun that fires a bullet with more muzzle energy than a .38 special or a nine millimeter."

The sheriff looked surprised. "I thought we did pretty well today. Arrested a triple murderer and emerged from a major gunfight with a couple of bruises. The press ate it up and I imagine that you will all look like heroes on the evening news and in tomorrow's papers." Sepanen gave them all a smile that would suffice as a pat on the back. "Dan, what did you find out about Maryrose Cooper?"

"Ross's sister apparently went to college in Indiana where she met a guy named Mahoney and married him. She died a couple of years later in a housefire." Dan went on. "It appears that after her death, Ross took her social security number, took a driver's exam under her name and did a great job of establishing an alternate identity that was rock solid. If it hadn't been for Barb Dupre, the other waitress at the Pine Brook Inn, we'd have been hard pressed to crack this."

DAY

TWELVE

THURSDAY

Chapter 40

S andy woke Thursday morning to the sounds of activity outside his bedroom. He got up and found Barb in the living room, stuffing clothing into paper shopping bags.

"Whatcha doing?" He leaned against the corner of the wall in boxer shorts and T-shirt with his arms crossed.

Barb set the two by the door. "I gotta go." She walked into the kitchen and took a bag off the table.

"Go where?" He followed her from room to room as she searched for the rest of her belongings.

"I don't know. Maybe California. Maybe Las Vegas."

"Butch is back in prison. What's the rush?" Sandy kicked around the clothes strewn on the bedroom floor and picked up a pair of panties that he held out as she went by. She took them and dropped them into the bag.

She finally stopped by the door and stared at him. "Sandy, we're just too...different." She turned and made another search of the apartment.

"Different? How? Seems to me we've gotten along pretty well."

She gave him a look of exasperation and stalked into the bathroom. When she came out she was even more agitated. "I gotta go."

Sandy put his hand on her arm as she went by. She pulled back and gave him a look that said she was in no mood for contact.

"Hey, easy. It's okay. You can go whenever you like. I just wanted to know why."

"I...I don't know why." She sat down hard on the couch. "You are really nice, and you treat me really nice. But...you and I both know we'd never make it. You're you and I'm me. "

He sat down next to her and ran his fingers through her hair. "We've had passion. Maybe someday..."

She brushed his hand away and stood up. "Sandy. I'm just not sure about this. I'm really mixed up right now. I gotta have a little time."

Sandy got up and wrapped his arms around her. "I think you could get used to me." He pecked at her neck.

"Stop it, Sandy." She pushed him to arm's length. "This is serious. We're too different and you know it, too."

He stared into her hazel eyes. "But I'm willing to stick with it. Aren't you?"

Barb shook her head. "No. I've lived on the edge too long. I can't change that. You want quiet and stability at home. There's somebody out there for you. But it isn't me."

"Hold on. I like who you are. Don't you know that?"

Barb set her jaw and turned away. "No. I mean, yes. I don't know what I know. I just don't feel right about this. I gotta go." Without turning back, she picked up the shopping bags and left.

Dan sat in his office in anticipation of an omnibus hearing on the charges against Ross Cooper. It was going to be one hell of a day, the Cooper hearing in the morning and the county board meeting with Doc Peterson in the afternoon. Dan had chosen to wear his white uniform shirt and tan uniform slacks.

Pete Hawkins, the court-appointed public defender, knocked at the door and came in. "I got Cooper's report from his stay in St. Peter State Hospital." He handed a copy to Dan.

Dan stared at the cover sheet for a second. The body of

the report felt like it was over two hundred pages long. "Can you give me the *Reader's Digest* version?" he asked, handing the report back.

Pete leaned his elbows on his thighs as he accepted the report back from Dan. "Ross is a deeply disturbed person. A sociopathic personality. He doesn't have any empathy or sympathy with other persons and when he wants something he just takes it. The sociopathic personality results from severe rejection and abuse as a young child. His mother apparently ridiculed his physical appearance and was even physically abusive, while she lavished attention on his sister, Maryrose. When the sister died it appears that Cooper took the sister's identity, not just by stealing her social security number but psychologically, too. The psychiatrist who did the evaluation said that Cooper would probably be unable to fully assimilate to society."

Dan shook his head. "Why did the mother pick out Ross to ridicule? I know they weren't identical twins but I figured they looked a lot alike—at least that was what we were going on."

"They were fraternal twins but they looked entirely different. The report says that Maryrose was every bit as pretty as Ross was ugly. His mother never let him forget it."

Dan took a deep breath. "The judge has this information?"

Hawkins nodded. "I filed a motion to have Cooper institutionalized without further court action. I anticipate that the judge will agree and Ross will spend the rest of his life as a guest of the state in a mental facility." He looked up at Dan. "You okay with that?"

Dan stared at Hawkins. The face was young. His perfect hair and perfect suit were annoying. "I want him to hang." Dan looked away. "He killed three people."

Hawkins's eyes widened. "This state stopped executing..." he realized suddenly that Dan was speaking figuratively, not literally. "So, I guess that means that you'll go along with it?"

"I learned a long time ago that it doesn't pay to argue with doctors and judges. As long as our boy Ross doesn't ever see the streets again, I don't really care how it happens."

Hawkins studied Dan's face for a while. "I take it that you don't think much of the judicial system?"

Dan shrugged and pulled a roll of Tums from his pocket, pried two loose from the end with his thumbnail and popped them into his mouth. "I have a hard time differentiating between the killers that we lock in prison and the killers that we lock in the state hospital. I can't believe there's much difference."

Hawkins smiled. "It's easy. The one's in the prison know they did something wrong. The ones in the hospital don't." He gave Dan a somewhat condescending look.

Dan, in turn, smiled at the innocence of youth. "I think all of them know that what they're doing is wrong and they go ahead and do it anyway."

Hawkins eyes sparkled. "Probably true. I agree. But your not considering one important thing. The wackos aren't evil, the normals are." He looked at Dan in mild triumph.

Dan looked back at Hawkins like *he* was now the crazy one. "And just what the hell is that supposed to mean?"

"Well, it's a long story. Maybe you'd like to come visit me sometime and I can explain it over some drinks."

Dan got up and patted Hawkin's shoulder. "Thanks for the offer, but I try to avoid lawyers."

Hawkins got up, smiled amiably and shook Dan's hand. "I like a man with a sharp tongue and a wit to match. Maybe we'll have a chance to go toe to toe some day yet."

"Hang around this county a few years," said Dan, "and I'm sure you'll get me on the witness stand some time. No doubt about it."

Chapter 41

Dan rushed into the county board room Thursday afternoon at one fifty nine. The five board members were already seated behind the mahogany table with nameplates in front of them. Doc Peterson was schmoozing with a board member at the far end of the table. The sheriff waved Dan to an empty chair in the front row. The county attorney was seated on the other side of the sheriff. Laurie Lone Eagle was leaning over the County Attorney's shoulder speaking to him. When she saw Dan she gave him a hint of a smile and finished her conversation.

As Dan slid into the chair on the other side of the sheriff, Sepanen leaned over and whispered. "Doc's been politicking and I don't have a clue what's going to happen. Hang loose and roll with the punches."

Ron Augustine, the board chairman, rapped his gavel on the table and the din gradually slowed to a whisper. There were close to twenty people in the room. Dan recognized a number of business people from town. Conspicuously absent was anyone from the medical profession.

Ron spoke with a commanding voice. "Doctor Raymond Peterson has asked the board to consider a complaint that he's lodged against Undersheriff Dan Williams. Ray says that Dan has discriminated against him because of his age, and he wants to bring formal discrimination charges against Dan and the sheriff's department."

Dan's hands tightened on the arms of the old wooden chair. He started to say something, but he felt Sepanen's hand on his arm. The sheriff gave him an almost imperceptible shake of the head.

"The purpose of this meeting is to see if there is just cause for the allegations, and then to make recommendations to the sheriff and the county attorney regarding disciplinary and legal action." Ron turned to Peterson, who was sitting in the front row. "What've you got to say, Ray?"

The doctor took full advantage of his spotlight and adjusted his tie before speaking. "Undersheriff Williams has been harassing me for several years now. I've been putting up with it, but most recently he accused me of incompetence and used derogatory language to describe his opinion of my skills. I will spare this board from the actual words. He berated me in front of a number of witnesses at a murder scene. He has no medical background to make judgments on my competence, and he has no right to make personal attacks on my character. Certainly not any based on my age."

Ron turned to Dan. "Did you call Doc a name that he would find objectionable?"

Dan couldn't hide his disgust. "I can't recall what I called Doc. So, I can't say if he might find it objectionable."

The doctor leaned forward. "He called me an old back-country jackass!" A snicker went through the room. "And I found it objectionable!"

The chairman rapped his gavel. "Is that right, Dan?"

Dan shook his head. "I was mad, and I really don't remember what I may have said to him."

"Well, fellow board members. It seems that there has been a charge that the undersheriff can't refute. I suggest that we vote to ask the county attorney to conduct an investigation. It seems appropriate that the sheriff put Dan on unpaid suspension until the matter is resolved. Do I have a motion and second?"

"Hold on a second." The sheriff was standing in front of his chair. "I think that you've got about ten percent of the story. I suggest that we discuss a couple of other aspects of this matter."

"The sheriff's out of order. Give him the gavel."

Doc Peterson was out of his chair and approaching Sepanen's table. Ron Augustine pounded his gavel

"Sit down, Doc. I'm still running this meeting. I didn't know that the sheriff had anything to say."

Sepanen stared at the doctor. Peterson backed down and returned to his chair. "Dan" said the sheriff," tell the board why you were so upset with Doc."

Dan had to count to five before responding. "We were at the Berg murders. Doc told us that we had a murder and suicide, and tried to remove the bodies. I stopped him because I didn't want the bodies disturbed until the medical examiner arrived and my deputies had a chance to collect evidence."

Doc was up again. "Calling the medical examiner every time someone dies is a damned waste of the county money. I pronounced them dead, and that was enough!"

The gavel sounded. "Sit down, Doc! You've had your say." Ron turned to Dan. "What did the medical examiner say when he examined the bodies? Did he say that they were dead, too?" There was sarcasm in the chairman's voice and a snigger ran through the board members and crowd.

Dan shook his head. "The ME said that they were both murdered."

The veins bulged in Doc Peterson's neck and a spray of spittle flew from his mouth as he lashed out. "In his opinion! His opinion only!"

"Sit down, Doc, and shut up!" The chairman's patience was gone, and he suddenly suspected that the meeting had been set up to railroad Williams. "Go on, Dan."

A door creaked in the back. Tony Oresek, Eddie Paulson, Sandy Maki, Floyd Swenson and Pam Ryan slipped in and found seats in the back row. The sheriff touched Dan's arm and nodded to the back. Dan stole a quick glance and cracked a smile.

"The medical examiner said that the body temperature of the dead man was cooler than the woman's. That meant that the man had died first. Doctor Peterson had given his opinion that the man had killed the woman and then had committed suicide. That would have meant the man's body would have been warmer than the woman's body. That discovery by the medical examiner totally eliminated it as a murder/suicide. We later found a fingerprint on a shell casing that belonged to a known criminal from Stearns County. If we'd taken Doc's opinion, we wouldn't have even looked for a suspect and he would have gotten away with a double murder."

A note was passed from the end of the table to the chairman. He unfolded it and tried to read it. After a few seconds he took out his reading glasses and read it through. He gave a knowing nod to the man who wrote it and faced Dan. "Dan, who can substantiate your comments, or are they just your opinion?"

Dan stood up and gestured to the back of the room. "I'd like to introduce Tony Oresek, M.D., the St. Louis County medical examiner." Tony gave the board members a nod.

The chairman took off his reading glasses and craned his neck to get a look at the people in the back row. "Dr. Oresek. Do you agree with what the undersheriff has said?"

Tony Oresek stood up. "Mr. Chairman and members of the board. I have been practicing forensic medicine for fifteen years and have attended over two hundred murder scenes. There are standardized methods that are used to evaluate the time and cause of death. Based on body temperatures, lividity of the bodies and the state of rigor mortis, I determined that the male victim had preceded the female victim in death by some two hours." He paused to let the gravity of the two-hour difference register with the board members. "So, yes. I totally agree with Dan Williams. My assistant, Mr. Paulson, and the three deputies at the scene can also corroborate. In my professional opinion, Doctor Peterson rendered an unprofessional and incompetent evaluation of a murder scene. Without the good judgement of Dan Williams, Doctor Peterson would have let a murderer go free."

Ron Augustine looked around at the faces of the board members. Some looked confused and others were staring blankly at Oresek. Doc Peterson watched his support wane and was jumping up to the defend himself when the county attorney stood up and cut him off.

"I'd like to have a word with Doc in the hall." The county attorney motioned Peterson toward the doors.

"Not now," Peterson growled.

"Now!" The county attorney took Peterson's elbow and turned him toward the door.

Peterson pulled his elbow free and stalked out of the room with the attorney close behind. The board members huddled close together and chattered in muffled voices as the door closed behind Doctor Peterson.

"What's up?" the board chairman asked the sheriff, who seemed too smug.

The sheriff walked to the chairman's seat and leaned close to whisper. "They're negotiating whether we prosecute Doc for violating his license restrictions, or whether we let him retire quietly."

Two other board members leaned close as the chairman stared in disbelief. "What?"

Laurie slid in behind Dan and whispered. "I think the show is over. I'm going back to the Cities."

Dan turned and shook her hand. "I can't thank you enough."

The sheriff spoke a little louder as he addressed the county board, his voice carrying throughout the room. "The state board restricted Doc Peterson's license a year or so ago because of incompetence. He isn't supposed to do any surgery that requires general anesthesia, except in a life threatening emergency."

One of the board members sputtered. "But he repaired my hernia last summer."

The sheriff nodded. "He could lose his license and go to jail for that and many others if the county attorney decides to press charges."

Laurie slipped out the back door as the county attorney walked back into the board room alone. He approached the board table and leaned close to the chairman. The other board members pressed close to hear what he was whispering. Someone gasped, then they all returned to their seats. The gavel rang out through the quiet room as the attorney went back to his chair next to the sheriff.

"The county attorney has just informed us that Doc Peterson has withdrawn the charges. He has also informed us that Doc Peterson has resigned as the county coroner, effective immediately. Meeting adjourned."

The gavel rang out signifying the end of the meeting.

Epilogue

D an sat in a booth across from his wife, Sally, at Dick's Cafe in Moose Lake. Dick's was Dan's favorite place to eat. Sally was looking at the mural of a deer jumping over a creek. It had graced the north wall of the café for over sixty years. The rest of the restaurant had been remodeled with knotty pine in the 80's. Pictures of the Moose Lake "bombers" sports teams dotted the walls along with wildlife pictures.

Dan pushed the last piece of his hot roast beef sandwich through the gravy on his plate. "It looks like they're going to lock Cooper away in a State hospital for the rest of his life."

Sally sipped on her coffee and watched him pack away the last bite. "Somehow I get the feeling that you don't think that's justice."

"I don't. Cooper kills three people and some shrink decides that he's not capable of knowing good from bad. Instead of life in prison he gets a hospital gown and sits around playing cribbage for the rest of his life."

The waitress topped off both of their coffees. "You two want pie?" Sally shook her head and Dan reluctantly agreed to forego pie. The waitress wandered off.

"What's the answer, Dan? Capital punishment? Putting him into a prison full of predators who will abuse him for the rest of his life? You said he has passed as a woman for years. He would end up as somebody's boy toy. Is that justice?"

Dan stared into the cup. "If he didn't know good from

bad, why'd he try to frame Joey Berg for the murders?"

Sally leaned over the table and spoke softly. "He was crazy, not stupid. He knew that someone would come looking for a killer, so he diverted you. Or tried to." She sat back and said, "It sounds like Cooper suffered a lot of abuse as a kid. Could he have turned out any other way as an adult? I mean, isn't it common for abused children to turn into abusive adults?"

Dan glared at her. "You're doing this just to aggravate me, aren't you? Damned bleeding heart liberal. You were probably disappointed when Hubert Humphrey wasn't reincarnated."

Sally sat up straighter. "One thing keeps bothering me. Where has Cooper been all the years between the homecoming queen attack and Terri Berg's murders?"

Dan nodded. "That was bugging Pam, too. She interviewed Harvey again. Cooper had only been working at the Inn, posing as Rose, for about six months. Pam checked on the social security number he'd given Harvey and found out that it was registered to Ross Cooper's sister, Maryrose. From there, Pam followed the trail of jobs across Anoka and Isanti counties. Mostly he had been working in nursing homes as a nurses' aide. The local police had a few incidents in each town where Cooper worked; Stalking. window peeping. There were a few break-ins with nothing valuable stolen. If there was a witness, they always reported seeing a short, fat guy. Most of the incidents were reported by women who hung around local bars. The incidents always stopped when he moved."

Dan finished off his coffee and threw his paper napkin on the tabletop. "Pam backtracked the Knutson murder and found out that Cooper met his victim when he was dressed as a woman in the bar. Pam's theory is that Cooper spent his evenings cruising the bars, dressed alternately as Ross and Rose. The Rose persona got him close to women who would have nothing to do with Ross."

The waitress cleared the table and they declined pie again. Sally pulled two dollar bills out of her wallet and left them on the table for a tip. "So you're okay with Cooper being committed?"

Dan shook his head in irritation. "Why does everyone keep asking if I'm okay with it? I'm not really okay with it. It's too bad that Pam didn't kill him when she shot him. But then *she'd* be messed up."

After a few moments, Sally asked, "How is Pam dealing with the murders and shooting? She's only been with the department for a few weeks. This has literally been a baptism of fire for her."

Dan said, "She talked to Floyd. He's pretty good at supplying positive reinforcement. Especially since it was his butt on the line. He'll get her through it."

The phone rang in Sandy Maki's apartment. "Hello."

"Sandy." It was Barb's timid voice. "I want...can you talk to me?"

He leaned against the kitchen wall and smiled. "Sure. What's up."

She hesitated. "I need to know something. Are you always nice? I mean, do you get mad and throw things?"

"I get mad." Sandy said. "But, no, I don't throw things."

"What do you do when you get mad?" Barb's question came out slowly.

"Sometimes I yell. Sometimes I get real quiet and talk softly while I burn inside. Why?"

Barb's voice was almost pleading. "I need to know that you're real. I mean, real people get mad and yell and stuff. I tried to make you mad and all you did was talk to me. I mean, it was real weird. It was like you didn't care."

He sat down in a kitchen chair. "Honey, I've had years of training. I can't let my emotions get away from me. If I did,

I could kill somebody. I count before I say anything or do anything."

There was a long pause. "Are you mad at me?" Her voice was soft and had a child-like sound to it.

"No, I miss you."

The pause was so long that Sandy was starting to wonder if she had hung up the phone. "Can I come back for a couple of weeks? I mean, just to see what happens. No guarantees?"

Sandy smiled. "No guarantees."